He put one ...
on h...

. . . as he reached inside his evening jacket and withdrew *Shadows of Dawn*, exposing the book's title to full view.

She stared at it in frustrated panic. "I cannot walk back into the ballroom with it in my hand! Where will I put it?"

"You don't mean to say you purchased something inappropriate, do you, Miss Bennet?"

"If anyone sees this, I shall swear you were trying to tempt me into debauchery with that piece of filth—not that I have any idea what it is."

"What sort of debauchery do you think I had planned?"

Joan squeezed her hands together. Under no circumstances could she slip the book under her garter in front of him. "You have to keep it."

He sighed. "Turn around."

Before she could protest, he had taken her by the shoulders and spun her around to face the wall, then crowded up against her. She could feel him behind her. His foot had slid between hers, and his chest was right at her back. And then she felt his fingers at the fastenings of her bodice, plucking loose the lacing that held it closed.

She was immobile by his wickedness. The most notorious rake in London was unlacing her gown.

"Don't worry," he murmured next to her ear. "Your virtue is safe with me tonight."

Her virtue, perhaps, but not her imagination.

By Caroline Linden

CAROLINE LINDEN

Love and Other Scandals

AVON

An Imprint of HarperCollinsPublishers

AVON BOOKS
An Imprint of HarperCollins*Publishers*
10 East 53rd Street
New York, New York 10022-5299

Copyright © 2013 by P.F. Belsley
ISBN 978-0-06-224487-1
www.avonromance.com

First Avon Books mass market printing: August 2013

Avon Trademark Reg. U.S. Pat. Off. and in Other Countries, Marca Registrada, Hecho en U.S.A.
HarperCollins® is a registered trademark of HarperCollins Publishers.

Printed in the U.S.A.

10 9 8 7 6 5 4 3 2 1

For Julie, from Hollis-home to the Jersey shore

Prologue

The first time Joan Bennet met Tristan Burke, he burst into her bedroom late at night wearing only his trousers and holding a single red rose.

She failed to see the romantic possibilities, but then, she was only eight.

"Where can I hide?" he demanded without preamble, looking frantically around her room.

Joan sat up in bed and stared at him with interest. This must be her brother's friend, the one who had come home with him on holiday from Eton. They'd been expected around dinnertime, but Joan had been sent to her room without supper for using a naughty word. She hadn't known it was naughty—she heard her own papa use it often, after all, and even her brother Douglas said it— but apparently it was very bad for young ladies to say it. Papa had sneaked her some rolls, though, which made it all right. And now someone had come bursting into her room late at night, which was very exciting, and therefore *quite* all right with Joan. "It depends," she said. "From whom are you hiding?"

"Douglas!"

She frowned. "Why are you hiding from Douglas? And why do you have a rose? Did it come from my mother's garden?"

He went still, making furious motions for her to be quiet. Joan closed her mouth and obediently waited. She wondered if Mother approved of this boy; he had long, shaggy dark hair, and was surely almost as tall as Papa, but as skinny as a stick. She could see his ribs, even in the dim moonlight coming through the windows. His hands and feet, by contrast, were too large for his body. He looked rather wild, to tell the truth, and Mother didn't like wild.

Abruptly he flung himself against the wall, right behind the door. Joan looked at the door, expecting someone else to come bursting through, but nothing happened. The boy stayed pressed to the wall, barely breathing, his eyes also fixed on the door. Joan frowned again. "Who are you?" she whispered. He ignored her. "I think you should leave my room," she said again, a little louder.

This time he faced her, his eyes fierce in the ill-lit room. Slowly he put a finger to his lips. Joan was more than a little annoyed. "Go away," she whispered loudly.

Without warning the door flew open a second time. "I caught you, you ruddy thief!" Her brother Douglas charged into the room and stopped cold. He looked around, puzzled. "Joan?" he asked cautiously.

"What do you want?" she snapped. "I was asleep."

"Uh . . ." Douglas backed up a step. "Sorry . . .

I thought I heard . . . Well, you won't tell Mother, will you—argh!" He jumped, slapping one hand to the back of his neck. His friend had moved out of the shadows, as silent as a ghost, and tickled the rose down Douglas's back. In a flash the two boys tumbled to the floor, punching each other in a furious tangle of arms and legs. They rolled back and forth, apparently trying to kill each other, until someone's foot caught the leg of a chair and sent it crashing to the floor.

"Douglas," Joan tried to say. Neither boy acknowledged her; they continued to pound away. Joan listened again. "Douglas," she said, a little bit louder. "Papa's coming!"

That, at least, finally got her brother's attention. "What?"

"Someone's coming," she repeated, leaning over the edge of her bed to see them. "Most likely Papa." At least, it was usually Papa who came when she got out of bed and into trouble at night. Joan couldn't wait to move into a proper young lady's room far from her parents'.

"Bloody hell," said her brother, looking guilty all of a sudden. He twisted to look his friend in the face, a difficult feat since the boy had his arm around Douglas's throat. "We'll be thrashed."

"Where can we hide?" asked the other boy—for the second time, Joan thought a little peevishly. He and Douglas jumped to their feet, their fight forgotten, and now looking like the panicked twelve-year-old boys they were.

"Why should I tell you?" she asked. "I don't even know who you are. You're both going to get me in awful trouble if I help you, and I already had to miss supper, which was all your fault, Douglas—"

"Bother that, Joan," Douglas interrupted. "Help us this time, and I swear we'll be in your debt forever."

"Hmph." She crossed her arms. Everyone was very busy telling her what to do today. Besides, she knew forever meant less than a day to Douglas. "Under the bed, I suppose. But you'd better be quiet!" she added as they immediately slid under her bed, pulling the dust skirt down behind them. She heard a bare moment of scuffling from the floor, and then the door latch clicked open.

"Joan?" Papa peered around the edge of the door, wearing his dressing gown and old slippers. "Are you awake, popkin?"

"Yes, Papa," she whispered. "I—I'm sorry, I didn't mean to wake you . . ."

He came into the room. "Why are you awake, child?" He saw the fallen chair, and a slight frown touched his brow.

She jumped out of bed and began tugging at it, trying to right it. "I'm sorry, Papa, I knocked it over. I couldn't sleep, and I was—wasn't being careful . . ."

Papa picked up the chair and set it on its feet. He scooped Joan into his arms and deposited her in bed again, tucking the blankets around her. "Why couldn't you sleep?"

Joan didn't have to fake the tremble of her chin. "I was a little hungry," she confessed in a very small voice. She certainly was, now that Douglas and his friend had woken her up and made her think about the missed supper.

Her father smiled, his shoulders relaxing. "No doubt. But you shouldn't have anything to eat now; a full stomach might give you bad dreams."

Joan sighed. "I know."

He kissed her forehead. "Try to go back to sleep. Tomorrow you'll have a fine big breakfast, and be right as rain again. Agreed?"

"Yes, Papa."

"Good night, child."

"Good night, Papa."

He tousled her hair gently and left, closing the door quietly behind him. She listened to his footsteps die away, then hung over the side of her bed. "You go away now, Douglas."

Her brother crawled out, a relieved smile spread wide across his face. "You're an angel, Joan," he said fervently. "This is Tristan Burke, by the by; he's a mate of mine from school."

The boy got to his feet, too. He was taller than Douglas, and looked even skinnier next to her strapping brother. He bowed awkwardly, and Joan giggled. "Tristan Burke, miss, at your service."

"Why are you hiding?" Joan asked them. "And what are you doing running about in the middle of the night?"

Douglas looked sheepish. "A wager."

"Who won?" she wanted to know.

For the first time Tristan grinned. His eyes lit up, and a deep dimple appeared in his cheek. "I did." There was no small amount of pride in the words.

Douglas scoffed. "You cheated. Must have done."

Tristan's grin turned positively cocky. "Prove it."

Douglas grumbled under his breath, but said nothing more of cheating.

"What was the wager?" Joan asked. This was interesting enough to keep her from thinking about her rumbling stomach.

Tristan held aloft the rose, now a bit squashed from the fight and the cramped quarters under the bed. "I got a rose."

Joan waited, but he said nothing more. "From where? Why? That's a silly sort of bet, to get a rose. What's it for?"

Douglas growled. "Nothing. It's not for anything. Let's go, Tris." He tiptoed over to the door and eased it open, looking up and down the corridor.

Tristan glanced at Douglas, then back at her. "It's for you," he whispered, handing her the flower. "For saving us from a thrashing."

She took it, mildly pleased but recognizing a dodge when she saw one. "Why did you make a wager?" she asked again, but Tristan had joined Douglas at the door. After a moment, they slipped out, with one last whispered thanks from Douglas. Joan put the rose beside her pillow and flopped back down with a sigh. Her stomach grumbled loudly. A flower was lovely, but if he'd really wanted to thank her, he might have brought a teacake at the least.

The second time she met Tristan Burke was several years later. True to her first impression, Tristan had turned out to be wild, too wild for her mother to countenance inviting him back. Joan would never forget the trouble he and Douglas got themselves into during that holiday; the wager over the rose, which turned out to have been over who could get a rose from the garden without opening any doors, was by far the tamest thing they did. Mother declared Tristan Burke a bad influence within three days' time, and after that she took care to keep Joan out of the boys' path. Aside from suppers, she almost never saw him.

Of course Mother's disapproval did nothing to prevent Douglas from being firm friends with Tristan, all through Eton and university. Joan heard of him in letters from Douglas, and the occasional story about some adventure that usually ended abruptly with Douglas realizing he was telling her things a girl ought not to hear of. She had a feeling Tristan Burke was even wilder than she could imagine.

The fall of Joan's sixteenth year, Lord Burke died, and the family went to pay their respects to Tristan, now the new Viscount Burke. She knew him at once, a tall, thin young man standing with his hands shoved deep into his pockets. While her parents went to condole with his aunt, Lady Burke, Joan sidled closer to Tristan, who was watching everything with a dark, moody expression.

"I'm very sorry for your loss," she said softly.

Without looking at her, he snorted. He still looked slightly unkempt, his long dark hair now bound in a queue. His clothes, though of respectable quality, hung loosely on him. Joan didn't know how to interpret his response, and hesitated.

"They hate me," he said suddenly, with quiet

malice. Joan followed his gaze; across the room Lady Burke sat regally stiff and upright on the sofa, dressed in unrelieved black and accepting fresh handkerchiefs from her similarly clad young daughters at her side. She bowed her head as Joan's parents offered their sympathies. Joan rather thought she looked as though her world had ended. "Aunt Mary. My cousins. They think I'm a heathen wastrel, unworthy of the title, ready to throw them all into the street."

"Why would they think that?" Joan could have bitten her tongue as soon as she asked the question; that was not proper, she told herself. She had been trying very hard of late to act like a proper lady, in order not to embarrass herself in her Season next year.

"Because they listen to gossip and read the scandal sheets." Finally he turned to face her. His eyes were a glittering green, and she almost recoiled from the intensity in his gaze. "Do you, Miss Bennet?"

"Of course," she said pertly, wanting to rattle him. His gloomy brooding-poet air was annoying. He obviously didn't care about his uncle's death—all he was thinking about was how much his aunt disliked him. "They're great sport, don't you think? Everyone knows they're complete fiction."

He stared at her. "Not everyone."

"Well, everyone with all their wits," she said. "No doubt they'll realize it—"she nodded toward his aunt—"once they see you do not throw them into the street."

His gaze slid back to his black-clad aunt and cousins. "It's tempting."

"Don't be ridiculous," she said. "Why throw them out? Find your own quarters." As much as she loved her parents, Joan had always wished she might do this. Douglas had had his own rooms as soon as he left university, when he was barely older than she was now. But she would never be allowed to rent her own townhouse and live a merry life on the town. Tristan Burke should appreciate the advantages he had instead of dwelling on the troubles in his life.

His mouth twisted. "You don't understand."

Joan heaved a sigh. "No, of course I don't. I could never possibly understand what it's like to be a gentleman with my own fortune, able to do as I please with no one to say me nay. Heaven preserve me from such unbearable oppression."

He looked at her, perhaps really paying attention to her for the first time. "You're quite impertinent."

She beamed at him, instead of smacking him across the face as her hand itched to do. "Thank you."

Tristan Burke stared at her, and then he laughed. His deep green eyes lit up and a wide grin creased his face, sharpening a dimple in his cheek. He looked full of joy in that moment, and Joan's smile faded away as she stared at him.

"I'll remember you, Joan Bennet," he said. "I like an impertinent girl."

"Oh." Her voice did not sound like hers, rather breathy and soft. "Really? You would be the first . . ."

He laughed again, looking devilish and tempting. He leaned closer. "I'll wager I won't be the last."

She almost forgot to breathe. He was not looking at her with amusement or even respect; there was something alive in his gaze as it wandered over her face and hair and even down her figure. Suddenly she wished she hadn't eaten that extra muffin at breakfast. Was this how gentlemen would look at ladies—at her? If so . . . Joan felt a tiny shock to realize she liked it, very much.

The third time Joan Bennet met Tristan Burke was eight years later. She had endured several infatuations, two broken hearts, and one near scandal, but no marriage proposals. She was perilously close to being a spinster on the shelf, while he was very likely the biggest rogue in all of London, grown every bit into the wild, reckless devil he'd promised to be. He had only to walk through a room for tongues to start wagging and ladies to start sighing, and Joan knew without a doubt he was a Dangerous Influence.

But this time, she fell in love with him anyway.

Chapter 1

London, 1822

As so often happens at the crucial turning points in life, it began with something very stupid.

"Lady Drummond informed me they will be attending the Malcolm ball tomorrow evening," Lady Bennet announced at breakfast.

"Indeed," murmured her husband without looking up from his newspaper.

"She will have her daughters with her, of course," continued Mother.

"Hmm." Papa was paying no more attention than Joan was. She thought it was little surprise Lady Drummond would be out, dragging her two daughters with her. Felicity was nice enough, but Helena had a vicious way with underhanded compliments. She always managed to say something that sounded as though it should have been kind, but instead made Joan feel overweight and old. She made a vague mental note to be on guard and avoid Helena at the ball.

"Douglas must attend."

This did catch Joan's attention. "Why?" she asked with a laugh. "Douglas never goes to balls."

Mother sipped her tea. "He should be there. Felicity Drummond will be expecting him."

"She will?" Joan stared. "Whatever for? Surely Felicity doesn't expect—or rather, hope—or even *dream*—"

"Joan!"

She winced. "I'm sorry, Mother. I had no idea Douglas admired her, is what I meant to say."

"It would be a fine match," said Lady Bennet with a sharp look, "and Douglas admires her as much as he admires any lady. George, are you listening to me?" she suddenly snapped at her husband.

"Every word, my love," said Papa promptly. He still hadn't looked up from the newspaper.

"Do you not agree it would be a splendid match if Douglas were to marry the Drummonds' eldest girl?"

"Superb."

"Then he must attend the Malcolm ball tomorrow night." Mother smiled as if that settled the matter. "Send word to him this morning, before he makes other plans."

Before he finds a solid excuse, Joan thought.

"Better yet, go tell him yourself, dear," added Lady Bennet, spreading jam on her toast. "He cannot ignore his own father's request."

That finally got the baronet's attention. "What, what? Of course I won't. Douglas is a grown man.

By all means send him a note about the ball, but I refuse to order him about."

Mother's face grew stern. "George, *please*."

"Marion, *no*," Papa replied in his final voice before turning his attention back to his newspaper. Mother pinched her lips together and said no more, but her face was a study in thwarted will. Joan knew that look too well. Mother would sit and ruminate on it like a kettle building up a head of steam, until eventually it grew too much to bear and she would explode—most likely at Joan, who, unlike her lucky brother, was still living at home and couldn't escape their mother's temper. There were two choices open to her, neither appealing, but she had faced this before and dutifully screwed her courage to the sticking point.

"I could call on Douglas," she said, "and ask him if he plans to attend."

"Joan, that is very sweet of you," said Mother at once. She was still glaring at her husband in frustration, and he was still impervious to it. "I would go myself, but I'm sure he will be glad to see you instead."

Because he can say no to me, Joan thought. "It's no trouble at all. You've only just got over that cold, and I do adore dropping in on Douglas unannounced."

Mother looked suddenly alarmed. "Why, dear?"

Joan shrugged. "Oh, I might find him still green and buffle-headed from the night before, and extract any number of promises from him."

Mother closed her eyes briefly, then apparently shook off her qualms. She must have her heart set upon seeing Douglas wed to Felicity Drummond. "Then get him to promise he'll attend tomorrow. Without getting foxed beforehand!"

Joan had started to rise from her seat, but now she sank back down. "Oh, that is too much. I was willing to wheedle attendance from him, but sobriety? Mother, you cannot be serious."

Papa snorted with laughter, and even Mother smiled, though with annoyance. "Go on, you saucy girl. I declare, I always thought you were the biddable child!"

"But I am," she protested with a grin. "I'm going to see Douglas, am I not? Douglas, who would otherwise continue drinking and gambling his way through London instead of dancing with Felicity Drummond at the Malcolm ball tomorrow night. Isn't that what you wanted?"

"Don't speak of such things, Joan," said her mother automatically. "And tell him to be prompt!" The last was called after her as Joan went out the door, blowing a kiss to her father, who winked at her in return.

Papa, Joan reflected as she went upstairs, was the source of Douglas's only hope; not only would Douglas someday inherit Papa's title and fortune, he would grow into Papa's easygoing ways as well. At least, everyone devoutly hoped so, since Douglas had shown no sign of their mother's iron-willed determination. According to legend, Papa had been just as unrestrained a hell-raiser as Douglas before Mother caught him and tamed him. Now he was the most wonderful man Joan knew, and if her brother could somehow outgrow his outrageous, rakish habits and become like Papa, so much the better for everyone in the world.

But until then, Joan meant to take advantage of every opening her brother's wild ways afforded her. Since he was sure to be sleeping late under the effects of brandy or port, she dressed quickly. The earlier her call, the more desperate Douglas would be to get rid of her; the more desperate Douglas was to get rid of her, the sooner he would promise anything and everything she asked; and the sooner she secured his promise—perhaps in writing, which would be a nice touch—she would be free to do what she liked before her mother missed her. Her mother wouldn't insist on a maid accompanying her just to her brother's house, which meant this was an excellent chance at a little independence. Young ladies weren't allowed nearly the same freedom as young men, and her opportunities to slip out for an hour alone were few and far between.

Although, Joan thought a little morosely as she walked the few blocks to Douglas's house, she was hardly a young lady anymore. She was twenty-four. After four Seasons without a single marriage proposal, and three more Seasons of just being in London, she also wasn't quite tied down. On the contrary, she had a surfeit of freedom, to her mother's despair. For a moment Joan had a terrifying vision of her future, running her mother's errands because, really, what else would she be doing, with no husband or children of her own? There was only so long one could justify new gowns and shoes before it became a joke. Spinsters didn't need to look beautiful, and Joan didn't look beautiful even with new shoes and gowns. If they hadn't landed her a husband by now, how likely was it that they would get her one as she grew older and even less pretty?

Unsurprisingly, her mood had grown rather sour by the time she reached her brother's town house. It was really unfair, she groused to herself as she stomped up to the door and rapped the knocker with a vengeance. Douglas was twenty-eight, and Mother had only just started to hint that he think of marrying. She had all but stopped mentioning Joan marrying, even though Joan was four years younger. *Unfair* hardly began to cover it. When the door didn't open after a minute, she lifted the knocker and banged it several more times, hoping each clang struck her feckless brother directly in the forehead.

"What?"

Her mouth dropped open as the door suddenly flew open, and the question was shouted at her. The man holding the door was not a butler, or even a footman. He was barely clothed. Although, she thought with reviving interest, that wasn't such a bad thing. She'd never seen a man's bare chest before, and now here was one, right at eye level. It looked to be a fine specimen as well, lean and rippled with muscle—nothing soft or squashy about it—and with a thin line of dark hair running right down the middle into his trousers.

"What?" the man growled again. She tore her eyes off his nipples—goodness, she'd never thought about men *having* nipples before—and looked him in the face. "Are you trying to wake the dead?"

She considered it. "Perhaps. But if he is dead, I have to kick his body personally to be sure. My mother will insist."

A variety of odd expressions flickered across his face. Shock, amusement, pain, and finally comprehension. "You're looking for Bennet."

"Indeed I am." She knew who he was by now. It had been a while since they'd met, but she'd heard plenty of him in the meantime. Tristan, Lord Burke, was infamous. There was no bigger rake in all London, no more profligate gambler, no greater womanizer . . . and no greatest object of interest to the gossipmongers. And now he was standing in her brother's doorway, wearing only a pair of half-buttoned trousers that threatened to slide down his lean hips at any moment. How very intriguing. "Do ladies come by every day, asking to kick Douglas?"

He glanced behind him into the house. "Not every day, no."

She smiled thinly. "No. I expect they come to do something else entirely." And they weren't ladies, either. If she happened to walk in on her brother in bed with a strumpet . . . she would never, *ever*, let him hear the end of it.

Tristan Burke hadn't invited her in, but she was tired of standing on the front step like a bill collector. When he leaned backward a little bit more, obviously trying to look up the stairs, she squeezed past him into the narrow hall.

It was dark within. Joan knew her brother had proper servants, but they must have learned by now not to admit visitors, light, or fresh air before three in the afternoon. She peeled off her gloves and raised one eyebrow at the man still holding the door open, now staring at her in amazement. "How do you do, Lord Burke?"

Slowly he closed the door. "Very well, Miss . . ."

She closed her eyes for a moment. Was she *that* forgettable? Or was he that dense? "Joan Bennet. I'm Douglas's sister. We've met a dozen times at least." Well, perhaps more like half a dozen, and none at all in the last couple of years, but he didn't look in any state to contradict her.

"Have we?" He folded his arms, and managed to look rather austere and forbidding, despite his state of undress, unshaven face, and the wild tangle of his hair. He still wore it long, she noticed, right down to his shoulders . . . which were far broader and more muscular than she had remembered.

"You always seem to be unclothed when we meet," she blurted out, then smiled sweetly as his jaw dropped. "But perhaps you don't remember that time you burst into my bedroom?"

His eyes narrowed, and color washed up his face, visible even in the gloomy hall. "Now I remember you," he said in a low voice. "The impertinent girl."

She beamed. "Yes, that's the one. Shall I show myself up? I assume Douglas is still abed." She turned toward the stairs and started up.

"Where are you going? Bloody—dash it all, you can't burst into a man's bedchamber at this hour!" He bounded after her.

Joan stopped and turned to face him. Three stairs down, he was shorter than she was, so she had the pleasure of looking down at him and his naked chest. "But that's what you did to me. In the middle of the night, no less."

Deeper color roared across his high cheekbones. "We were *children*."

She pointedly looked down. "Obviously not anymore." To her immense delight, he actually crossed his arms as if to cover himself. Joan bit her cheek to keep from bursting into snickers. "But my mother sent me to see Douglas, and the longer I argue with you about it, the less time I shall have for myself after doing my duty. Don't worry," she said as he opened his mouth to argue. "I know where his room is." And she turned her back on him and hurried up the rest of the stairs, listening to his footsteps thunder up behind her a moment later.

Douglas was, as expected, sleeping off a drinking binge. Joan studied the lump under the blankets for a moment. Once she decided it could only be one person, she went to the windows and threw open the drapes. The blankets didn't stir. She opened a window, letting in a gust of spring breeze and the rattle of carriages and carts in the street below. The blankets were still. Perhaps it was all blankets and even Douglas wasn't there. That would be grossly irritating, since she would either have to find her brother or go home and tell her mother he hadn't been in. There was one way to know for sure. She grabbed the end of the covers nearest her, and yanked.

Douglas raised his head and blinked at her, his eyes bloodshot and unfocused. "Bloody hell," he said in a muffled voice. "Who the devil are you?"

"Your sister," she said briskly, tossing the blanket back over most of him. A fleeting glimpse of her brother's bare arse was more than enough. "Mother sent me."

Douglas pulled the blanket over his head, and said something that sounded very vulgar. Joan filed it away for future reference—in private, of course. Her fascination with bad language would land her in so much trouble if her mother ever discovered it.

"She wants you to come to the Malcolm ball tomorrow evening." She made a great clatter shoving things off the only chair in the room and dragging it to the side of the bed. "Shall I ring for tea?"

"Go away," he said beneath the blanket.

"I'm very sorry, I can't do that until you promise to attend the Malcolm ball. Do you promise?"

"No," her brother moaned.

Joan reached for the bell cord and pulled it, hard. "I braved your half-naked friend downstairs. What is he doing here, by the way? He really should let the footman answer the door; it was quite alarming to come face-to-face with his bare chest. Also, he *shouted* at me when he opened the door. Douglas, are you listening?"

"No," he moaned again.

"Good," she told him. "I have plenty more to complain about, and might as well do it to you."

Douglas flipped the blanket away from his face. "What will it take?" he asked desperately, "to make you go away?"

"Your promise, in writing, to attend the Malcolm ball."

"In writing?"

"So I can prove to Mother that I did, in fact, secure your promise, and that it is *not* my fault when you don't show up anyway, despite having given said promise."

Her brother stared at her for a moment, finally focusing his gaze. "I despise you, Joan," he said at last. "I really do."

She seized the blanket when he tried to pull it back over his head. "It's not my idea that you go to the Malcolm ball. Even Papa doesn't care. But Mother has it set in her mind that you would make a handsome couple with Felicity Drummond, and she'll be at the ball tomorrow night."

"Felicity Drummond?" Douglas's face was comically blank. "Who?"

"I suppose you could ignore Mother's summons and stay away, but then you run the risk of finding yourself betrothed to Felicity without having ever met her. She's sweet enough," Joan added conscientiously, leaving out any mention of Felicity's snide sister and grasping mother.

At that moment a servant stumbled into the room, breathing hard and looking as if he'd just fallen out of bed. "Yes, sir, what can I do for you?" he asked in a rush, then stopped and looked at Joan in bewilderment. "And miss," he added uncertainly.

"Tea, please," she said.

"Throw this woman out, Murdoch," croaked Douglas. "She's assaulted me in my bed!"

Joan ignored him. "Very strong tea," she said to the servant, whose gaze was swinging between her and the lump in the bed that was her brother. "With muffins, if you have any." The servant hesitated, then fell back on his training and bowed to her.

"And brandy!" Douglas called after his departing servant. "Don't forget the bloody brandy!"

"Douglas, you're a sot."

"You're a nag!" he returned indignantly, shoving himself up on one arm to glare at her. "I never woke you at the break of dawn and started yammering on about balls and betrothals and Mother! God, I'm going to have a beastly headache all day now, thanks to you."

Joan went to the small writing desk, tossed a crumple of discarded cravats off it, and got out a piece of paper. She uncapped the ink and wrote a brief line, promising to attend the Malcolm ball, then carried it and the pen over to the bed. "Sign this and I shall leave."

Douglas eyed it as if it were a poisonous snake. "You can't mean it!"

She sighed. "Then I must stay. Perhaps you can help me decide which color my new dress should be. Blue, do you think? But I've got a number of blue ones. Mother thinks pink is my color, but I really don't like it. Yellow is even worse"— Douglas wrenched the blanket back over his head—"and that leaves green. But I look like a shrub in green. I suppose there's also orange . . . What do you think?"

"Gold," said a familiar voice from the doorway. "You should wear gold."

This time Joan was prepared, having expected him to return eventually. So much the better that he'd got right to it; having a quarrel with his friend could only make Douglas even more anxious to appease her. She turned in her chair, a delighted smile on her face, and then stopped cold.

Tristan Burke was quite a sight when surly, half-asleep, and barely dressed. But with his hair slicked back and a deep green dressing gown wrapped around him, he was the essence of seduction. And he was watching her with his heavy-lidded, intent gaze as if she were as fascinating to him as he was to her.

Chapter 2

By the time Tristan located his dressing gown, the invading Fury had found her quarry. Gutted and filleted him as well, to guess by the sound of Bennet's increasingly desperate voice coming from under the covers. For a moment he stood in the open doorway and let the scene amuse him. Douglas Bennet, the devilish brawler destined to inherit a fortune and an ancient baronetcy, was cowering beneath his blankets like a sniveling boy as the Fury—his sister, if she could be believed—sat calmly beside his bed and talked about dresses.

She didn't look like a Fury. She looked rather ordinary, to Tristan's eyes. She was taller than average, with a generous figure that wasn't at all suited to the current women's fashion. It made her look . . . fat, he thought unkindly. Well, not really fat, but a little more than could be called plump. Her breasts, where a woman ought to be quite plump, were all covered up by an acre of lace, and the petticoats under her pink-striped skirt gave her quite a girth. Her hair was a nice color, but she wore it in those tight ringlets he hated; they looked like a child's hair, in his opinion. Her face . . . her face was handsome, he decided, and interesting, but perhaps that last was due to the unholy glee that sparkled in her eyes as Bennet tried in vain to escape her chatter.

But when she said orange, he cringed. Never orange. Orange was a beastly color on most women, and on her it would be hideous. Tristan considered himself something of a connoisseur of women and their clothing. He loved women, especially beautiful women, and if a woman wasn't actually beautiful, she could at least look her best. "Gold," he said. "You should wear gold."

She twisted to look at him, her face bright with delight. Her expression froze a split second later, but not before Tristan registered the color of her eyes. Deep, rich brown, like fresh coffee, glinting with golden streaks. She should definitely wear gold, a rich warm shade that would play up her admittedly fine complexion. If she would change the style of her hair and wear something flattering, she might be passable, he thought before he could stop himself.

But stop himself he did. First, because she was a Fury, and he didn't need any more of those in his life. His aunt and cousins were more than enough. Second, because she was Douglas Bennet's sister, and one didn't trifle with the sisters of drinking mates unless one wanted to marry them—and even then it was a risky business. But mostly he stopped himself because she was decidedly not his kind of woman, with those fussy little ringlets and lace-shrouded bosom and the way she banged that door knocker like Hephaestus at his anvil. God almighty, no man needed a woman like that.

"I'm sorry," she said, finding her tongue. "Have you taken up residence?"

"For two months," he said. "Until my roof is repaired."

"Ah," she said. "How lovely that Douglas will have a companion in vice so conveniently at hand."

He raised his eyebrows. "Vice? How interesting you would seize on that so quickly."

"It is the first thing that comes to mind when one considers my brother." She looked him up and down. "And you, I imagine."

"Good heavens," he drawled. "It must have been the first thing to come to your mind, then, when I opened the door for you. Should I be flattered?"

The golden flecks in her eyes glinted. "Probably not," she replied. "I imagine the two of you, thoroughly foxed, unable to walk, lying in your own filth as you sleep it off—no doubt snoring viciously and twitching every few moments." She flashed him a coy smile. "Are you flattered?"

"You sound as if you know the state well." He leered at her. "Have you been with us on a bender? I can't recall seeing you drunk as a lord, but a description such as that is no mere flight of imagination."

"Oh, but it is," she assured him. "I have a vivid imagination."

His gaze dipped again, sweeping over the lace at her neckline that didn't hide the quick pulse in her throat. Was it anger—or something else?

Tristan found himself oddly taken by the Fury's sharp tongue. "So do I," he murmured.

"I don't doubt it," she said. "Especially if you believe I shall leave without securing my dear brother's promise to attend the Malcolm ball tomorrow night." She leaned forward and poked the blankets on the bed again. "Douglas, think how happy Mother will be to call on you this afternoon, and tomorrow morning, to remind you. I shall make a point of telling her you invited her specially."

Bennet lunged out from under his refuge and across the bed to seize the pen and ink pot. Spattering ink everywhere, he dashed his signature across the bottom of the paper she thrust at him. "There! Will you leave me in peace now?"

She smiled in triumph and waved the paper in the air to dry the ink. "Of course! I told you I would go as soon as you gave your promise—and now Mother will see proof that I obtained it. Thank you, Douglas, it's been a pleasure seeing you again." She folded the paper and put it in her reticule. "Don't forget: the ball is tomorrow evening. I should hate to have to come back to remind you of it."

"Just go," snarled Bennet, diving back beneath his pillows and blankets.

His sister just smiled again, wagging her head a little from side to side. Gloating. Tristan frowned. God save poor Bennet, growing up with her.

She got out of her chair and turned to leave, but paused when she saw him standing in the doorway. The pleased look faded from her face. "Pardon me, sir."

"For badgering a poor man still in his bed? No, I will not," said Tristan.

Her brown eyes narrowed. "You are blocking the door," she said, in tones that questioned his mental competence.

He grunted. "You should have thought of that before invading the house."

"Oh yes, I forgot you live here now—perhaps as the butler, questioning the guests?"

"You're utterly charming," he said.

"Is that why you don't want me to leave?" she cooed, batting her eyelashes. "I confess, I never thought my brother would witness me being *assaulted* and *insulted* by a half-*naked* man!" She raised her voice and gave each word a dramatic inflection worthy of Mrs. Siddons. "I vow, he'll have to challenge you to a duel from the *impropriety* of it!"

"Let her go," bellowed Bennet from under his pillow. "For God's sake, Burke, get her out of here!"

"Thank you, dear brother," she told him, swatting the covers. "I shall see you in two nights' time."

This time Tristan stepped away from the doorway as she approached. "Good day, Miss Bennet."

She gave him a sunny smile. "Isn't it? Goodbye, Lord Burke." She swept past him, leaving a wisp of fragrance in her wake. It was lovely—soft and warm without being insipid or sickly sweet. Tristan revised his opinion slightly: a woman who smelled good was a step prettier than someone who didn't.

He transferred his gaze to Bennet, huddled

in bed under a mound of blankets. He still felt mostly pity, for growing up with that virago in the house, but part of him also wondered why she clearly had more spirit and spine than her brother. Bennet, for all that he was a capital fellow, was easily led. Just witness how easily he signed that paper, indenturing himself to a night among the hungry lionesses of London's marriage mart. Tristan would have torn up the paper and set it on fire as Miss Bennet watched, and he would have smiled at her while he did it. He could just imagine how she would respond to that . . .

"Burke." Bennet's voice sounded dazed, with an undercurrent of panic. "Burke, I signed that bloody paper."

"Damned foolish thing to do," Tristan agreed, dropping into the vacant chair by the bed.

"I can't go to the Macmillan ball."

"Malcolm ball," Tristan corrected him.

Bennet sat up, throwing off his covers. "It's the opening night of the new opera—there's an entirely new ballet corps. From France."

"So it is."

"So you see I can't possibly go to the bloody ball!" Bennet exclaimed. "The best girls will be taken by the end of the week."

Tristan shrugged. "So don't go to the ball."

"No." Bennet looked almost fearful. "You don't understand. Now Joan's got my promise in writing—if I don't go to the ball, there will be severe consequences."

"Your sister will come back?" Tristan was appalled. "Someone needs to rein her in—"

"No, it will be much worse." Bennet shuddered.

"It will be my mother. She'll have me at tea. At balls. Cotillions. Musicales. Philosophical meetings." He might as well have been describing the circles of hell, from his expression. Although, to Tristan's ears, those *were* the circles of hell.

"You should go to the ball, then." Tristan got up and turned toward the door. This was not his problem, after all.

"God, no! I just need to get that paper back from Joan before my mother sees it."

"You'd better run," said Tristan dryly. The sound of the door closing had echoed up the stairs just a moment ago. "She's already gone."

"Christ!" Bennet leapt out of bed and scrambled for his trousers. Tristan was almost out the door when he called, "Burke, wait! You've got to help me."

"Why?" Tristan scratched his chin. "You should have put her in her place and ordered her from the house."

Bennet gave a harsh laugh as he pulled a shirt over his head. "You don't know Joan if you think that's the way to deal with her. Help me, man, or I'll be cut to pieces."

"No more than you deserve," he muttered, but he threw up his hands. "How am I supposed to help? She obviously didn't approve of me, if you didn't notice."

Bennet was yanking on his boots. "You know how to talk to women. Just . . ." He waved one hand in the air. "Talk her out of the paper."

He'd much rather talk her out of an orange dress and into a gold one. Yes, a rich gold silk, cut low across her bosom and shoulders—without a shred of lace—and swathing her hips and waist closely. He wondered how small her waist was; with a bosom like hers, a small waist would be just the thing. There could be a true Venus under those wretched ruffles.

"Burke, I'm begging," said Bennet. "Help me, this once, in my time of desperate need."

It didn't really matter how small her waist was, or what her hair would look like unbound. She was a blackmailing Fury. One couldn't abandon a fellow man to the manipulations of such a creature, even if it was his sister. Tristan gave in. "Very well. Let me dress."

By the time he was clothed, Bennet was pacing in the hall, raggedly knotting a cravat around his neck. "She'll be almost home by now," he said. He shoved his hands through his hair, not for the first time from the looks of things. "Good God, what a plague!"

"She can't be that bad," said Tristan, thinking of his aunt and cousins. They *were* a plague, with all of Miss Bennet's sharp-tongued temper and none of her wit. All of her interest in ugly dresses and none of her bosom. All of her boldness and none of her dash.

"You've never had to live with her," muttered Bennet as he threw open the door.

Sunlight blazed into the hall. Bennet squinted and cursed some more, but clattered down the steps to the edge of the street. Then he stopped, turning from side to side. "Devil take me. Which way would she go?"

"Home?" Tristan followed more slowly, pulling his hat low on his forehead. Gads, it was bright out here. "I absolutely refuse to chase her into your parents' house."

Bennet inhaled a long breath. "Right. Home. Although Joan is fond of sneaking off on her own—she thinks I don't know, but she slips out to bookstores and millinery shops every chance she gets." He paused. "You go that way"—he pointed east—"and I'll go this way. If she's made it home . . ." He shuddered. "My father will have to step in."

Tristan wondered why he'd never noticed this spineless side of Bennet before, but he just nodded. Bennet nodded back before taking off to the west, striding down the street as though he longed to burst into a run.

He turned and strolled east, toward the shops. Where would a young lady go, alone? He hadn't noticed a maid waiting on the steps, and no servant had accompanied her into the house, where chaperonage was most needed. Most likely she'd gone home to lay the spoils of victory at her mother's feet. And if Bennet was such a coward to sign that damned paper at all, Tristan privately thought he deserved whatever he reaped.

But still. Bennet had offered him a place to stay in town where he could easily and conveniently supervise the repair of his roof, allowing him to get the work done without causing a stir. His aunt would seize any opportunity to upbraid him about his management of the estate, even though in this case he was repairing a century-old roof that his uncle couldn't be bothered to replace. If Uncle Burke had properly seen to the roof, it wouldn't have leaked for the last ten years, quietly rotting the upper story of the house before collapsing under a heavy rain last month.

He turned into Bond Street, halfheartedly looking for a flash of pink-striped skirts. God knew they were wide enough, he should be able to spot them from half a mile away. How on earth was it that women didn't learn how to dress themselves well? Why must they go like sheep after the latest style, whether it flattered them or not? Gold was definitely Miss Bennet's color, and richer, darker tones that would reflect well with her dark hair and creamy skin. Not pink, for certain.

And what the devil was he supposed to do once he found her? She wouldn't surrender that paper without a battle royal, and Tristan had no intention of engaging her in the middle of a milliner's shop. He told himself he wouldn't want to face her in private, either, no matter how satisfying it would be to take her down a peg.

He paused outside a display window, and studied the bolts of silk temptingly draped there. That shade of blue would also suit her, he thought—and then swore under his breath. A virago. A she-devil. And the sister of a mate. Not a woman who would look good in any shade of blue.

He turned away from the window, striding down the street at a brisker pace. It wasn't his fault Bennet couldn't stand up to her. It wasn't his concern if Bennet found himself bundled off to the Malcolm ball or the Macmillan ball or any other ball to dance with half the girls in Britain. Judging from the way he'd cowered before his sister, Bennet would be married off within a few months anyway, likely to another Fury; females like that tended to stick together. Lady Bennet no doubt already had the girl all chosen, and would bend her son to her will the way a stiff breeze bowed a spring sapling. It would be a pity, of course, to lose so jovial a companion, but Tristan had no desire to get between a Fury and her object. Bennet would have to save himself. It was ridiculous to take orders from a woman—any woman. Really, if Tristan wanted to help his friend, he would do better to find him and tell him to be a man, and put his sister in her proper place.

And then, from the corner of his eye, he caught a glimpse of pink stripes as she vanished into a small bookshop. His steps slowed, and a slow smile spread over his face. Quite forgetting that he had just pledged to avoid her like a deadly plague, he flexed his hands and followed her.

Chapter 3

A little bell above the door tinkled as Joan stepped into the cramped bookshop. She paused on the threshold to take a deep breath in delight. It wasn't just the smell of books—that dry combination of paper and printing ink—that reminded her of the library at Helston Hall, her family's Cornish estate. The library had been the only place she was free to indulge her passion for adventure and scandal, even if only in her mind. Today it was more than that; today it was the smell of freedom. For the next hour, she was free to wander where she liked. True, Bond Street was hardly a wild and dangerous adventure, aside from the risk of being spotted by one of her mother's friends. But in the confined life of a wellborn spinster . . . any escape was intoxicating.

Especially when one had a particular errand one was quite keen to fulfill. Keeping her eyes discreetly lowered, she found the shopkeeper and quietly cleared her throat.

"Yes, madam, may I help you?" He smiled and

bowed, patting his hands together. "Are you looking for something special?"

"Yes, sir." She smiled prettily. "Is there a new issue of *50 Ways to Sin*, by chance?"

There was a reason she had come to this shop; the proprietor didn't blink an eye at her request, nor cavil at all. In fact, he might have winked at her. "I just received several copies this morning. Shall I wrap one up for you in the back room?"

"Yes, thank you." Joan resisted the urge to twirl around in glee. A new issue, just in this morning! It must be fresh from the printing press. She'd have time to read it at least once before handing it off to her friends the next night. Abigail and Penelope were expected at the Malcolm ball as well. The only thing better than reading the latest issue was discussing it in exhilarated whispers behind their fans. Balls had become quite tolerable since *50 Ways to Sin* had appeared.

The shopkeeper disappeared through the draped door behind his counter, and Joan walked further into the store, piously stationing herself in front of a shelf of thick, dull-looking books with a thin rime of dust. To wander too near the novels at the rear of the shop would be dangerous. She would only end up pining for a book she could neither buy nor sneak into the house. Thankfully, *50 Ways to Sin* was printed as a pamphlet and could be concealed under a shawl or even—as Joan had once done in desperation—inside her garter.

The bell above the door tinkled again, and she hurriedly faced the shelf, tilting her bonnet brim to hide her face. For a moment all was silent, then slow, measured footsteps sounded, heading right for her. Joan pressed her lips together and sidled a few steps to the side, keeping her eyes glued to the shelves without registering any titles in front of her. It was a man's tread, which meant she should be well nigh invisible to him, unless by some hideous mischance he was a friend of her parents. Somehow her mother was acquainted with every prying busybody in London, and word of Joan's illicit visit here would wend its way back to Lady Bennet's ears sooner or later.

The steps came nearer, pausing at the end of the aisle where she stood. Hastily she plucked a book at random from the shelf and opened it, at the same time she casually turned her back to him. Even though she told herself she had every right to visit a bookshop, her heart thudded hard and fast against her ribs. Visiting Hatchard's would not alarm her mother overmuch; visiting *this* bookshop, on the other hand, let alone in search of the contraband she wanted, would see her locked in her room for a month. She made herself breathe evenly, listening with every fiber of her being for those footsteps to turn and walk away.

Instead they came closer, one loud echoing step at a time. Joan turned a page in the book she held, as nonchalantly as possible. Where was that shopkeeper? She would be wildly irked at him if he turned out not to have *50 Ways to Sin* after all.

"If you give back the paper Bennet signed, I won't tell anyone I saw you reading prurient poetry in here," murmured a terribly familiar voice.

Joan froze. Her heart jolted into her throat for

one terrified moment. "I don't know what you're talking about," she said, turning another page. This time she forced her eyes to read a few lines; it was not, thank the Lord and all his saints in heaven, prurient poetry. "And it's rude to interrupt someone reading."

"No?" A long arm reached past her, above her head, and drew a dusty, battered book from a shelf. "Isn't it rude to accost someone in his bedchamber and blackmail him into sacrificing his freedom?"

"How dare you accuse a lady of such unspeakable crimes." She turned another page. "It would be quite slanderous of you to say such things."

Lord Burke leaned one shoulder against the bookcase in front of her and flipped open his book. "I saw it with my own eyes, not half an hour ago."

"Indeed?" She batted her eyes at him. "When you tell the tale, be sure to mention your own shocking state of undress. My brother will demand satisfaction before the end of the day."

He gave her a slow, simmering smile. As Joan had feared, the dratted man cleaned up very well. His bright green eyes glinted with deviltry, and when he smiled like this, a dimple appeared in his cheek. She'd forgotten the dimple. "He already demanded satisfaction. Why do you think I'm here? Hand over the paper and we'll go our separate ways with no one the wiser."

"Lord Burke, my actions are none of your concern. My brother is a grown man, in body if not in mind, and I daresay if he needs a keeper, you are the last man in England fit for the post. He signed the paper of his own free will." She gave him a smile of her own, rather smug and superior.

"And you shall hand it right back to me, of your own free will." He continued smiling at her in that wicked way that hinted of languid seduction. She had dreamed of a man looking at her this way, as if he meant to pursue her to the ends of the earth, only she hadn't thought it would be over a silly piece of paper.

She snapped her book closed and replaced it on the shelf. "I don't think I'd give you anything of mine, of my own free will."

He raised one eyebrow. "No?"

"Never."

"Never?"

She tipped back her head and widened her smile. "Never."

He leaned forward, lowering his face until they were mere inches apart. "I could change your mind," he whispered.

Joan heaved a sigh, even though her pulse jumped at the way he was looming over her, almost as if he meant to kiss her senseless. One part of her was strongly tempted to goad him into doing it. Shouldn't every girl be kissed senseless by a dangerous man, just once in her life? But on the other hand, it was often better not to know what one was missing, so as not to feed sinful longings. Why hadn't Tristan Burke's dissipated lifestyle ravaged his looks? This would be much easier if he were fat or pockmarked.

"Never," she repeated, telling herself it was true. Even if he did kiss her—which she doubted he could bring himself to do, no matter what he'd promised Douglas—it wouldn't change her mind, because she would know it was only to win back that paper. If Joan were to let herself fall into a swoon over a kiss, it would be a proper kiss, given in passion and meant to seduce, not to trick.

For a moment he didn't reply. His gaze narrowed and roved over her face. "You're still too impertinent for your own good."

"Why, thank you!" She batted her eyelashes at him. "I have achieved my life's ambition."

"And you're too much trouble to be let loose on the poor, unsuspecting men of London."

Her own eyes narrowed. He trod on shaky ground now. "You seem to be the only one troubled. Even Douglas will get over his fit. The paper means nothing, you know; my mother will have him at that ball one way or another, and he knows it."

"Then give it back."

"No."

"I could take it from you." Again his eyes drifted down, his long eyelashes dark against his cheeks. His gaze seemed to sweep over her figure like a cool breeze, and she fought off a shiver. "No," he murmured. "I'd much rather you give it to me."

"Not as long as you live, Lord Burke." Her dratted voice broke on his name, so it came out breathy and soft. "Besides," she quickly added to cover it, "the ball is tomorrow night. If it means so much to you, I shall send it to you the day after next, done up with a bright pink bow."

His mouth curved again. "I imagine you have quite a lot of pink ribbon. Pink isn't your color at all, though."

"That is none of your concern," she said coolly.

"Well, I must confess it made you easier to track just now. I could see those stripes from two streets away."

Joan knew she wasn't pretty. Her dress had looked so fetching in the dressmaker's sketches, and then somehow so ordinary on her, no matter what her mother said. But it was the height of indignity to have *him* point that out. Never mind her previous fascination with his bare chest, or the way he loomed over her like a lover. He was an ass. Even worse, he had spoiled all her joy at being free for a few stolen moments. The shopkeeper had vanished, and not even *50 Ways to Sin* was worth spending another moment with Lord Boor—and for costing her that, she could have smacked him. "Thank you for that unsolicited and unwanted observation," she said through her teeth. "I hope you and Douglas drive each other mad. And you may tell him I will see him at the Malcolm ball tomorrow evening." She turned on her heel and stalked out the door, pulling it shut with a slam behind her.

Tristan scowled as she marched away from him for the second time that day. Bennet had obviously gone wrong decades ago with her; his sister was clearly set in her willful ways. Worse, the way her eyes sparkled when she defied him conveyed a gleeful pride in her obstinacy. His first thought about her was absolutely correct. She was a Fury and should be avoided.

He tried not to wonder what she would have done if he'd attempted to persuade her in earnest.

His gaze fell to the book in his hand. What had

brought Miss Bennet into this shop? he wondered. It was a far cry from Hatchard's selection of dry improving works and silly Gothic novels. He decided she'd probably had no idea and wandered in by chance, and turned to replace the book of very prurient poetry on the shelf. For a moment there, he'd been dangerously tempted to read her a selection, just to see how brightly pink her fine complexion could turn.

"Here you are, madam." A short, balding man in a shopkeeper's apron came from the office behind the counter, a package in his hand. He stopped short and glanced about. "I beg your pardon, sir."

"The lady had to leave," Tristan said.

"Indeed!" The fellow looked surprised. "Well, I daresay someone else will want it." He put down the package. "May I help you, sir?"

Tristan's eyes rested on the package. So she hadn't come by chance, but for something particular. It was flat and thin, tied in string. What had she been after? "I'll take it for the lady." He held out the book he'd been about to replace. "And this."

The shopkeeper took the book with a knowing look. "Yes, sir. Very good. Shall I wrap it?"

"No need."

The man bowed his head and Tristan counted out the coins. He took both books and went back into Bond Street, wondering where Miss Bennet might have gone. He strolled the length of the street rather aimlessly, scanning each shop for a flash of pink stripes, but never saw it.

He didn't want to admit that he felt a touch of guilt for making her storm off without her purchase. No, that was largely her own fault. If she'd been a more reasonable woman, she would have handed over the blasted note her brother had so foolishly signed. Tristan would have thanked her politely and gone on his way, with no reason to speak to her again.

Instead he would have to see her again, even seek her out. First, because he never abandoned a contest in defeat, certainly not to a woman. And second, because now he had her book and wanted to see her face when he presented it to her. He wondered if her blush was bright scarlet, or a dusky rose.

By the time he returned to Bennet's town house in Halfmoon Street, Bennet was already there. He rushed into the hall at Tristan's entrance. "Did you get it?" he demanded.

"The paper? No." Tristan tossed his hat at the hook behind the door. It missed and rolled under a table.

Bennet swore and plunged his hands into his already rumpled hair. "Curse Joan! Why the devil did you let her into the house?"

"You didn't warn me not to." Tristan retrieved his hat and paced back to his original spot. He eyed the hook, and threw the hat toward it again. It missed, again.

"Did I need to?" Bennet exclaimed. "A woman calls at the break of dawn, and you let her stroll into my bedchamber?"

Tristan fetched his hat once more and retraced his steps. "If it had been a different sort of woman," he said, adjusting his stance and staring down the hook, "you would have called me out for turning her away."

"It must have been excruciatingly obvious she was *not* that sort of woman." Bennet frowned. "You're cheating; that's a full six inches nearer than before."

"It is not." Tristan took a step backward anyway. "A pound I can make it from here."

"A guinea you cannot."

A wild and exhilarated grin touched his mouth. He bent his knees a little, turned the hat around, and let it fly once more. It sailed neatly through the air and caught the hook, swinging precariously for a moment before settling into place. Tristan made a fist of triumph as Bennet uttered another halfhearted curse.

"Take it off my board." Tristan peeled off his gloves and handed them to the servant who had belatedly come into the hall. "And I advise you to give your sister a wide berth. That female is trouble."

"As if I haven't known that for twenty years." Bennet stalked back into the drawing room and sprawled in one of the few chairs. Tristan followed, waving aside Bennet's offer of a glass of brandy. "My thanks for trying to find her, Burke."

"I found her. Murdoch, bring some coffee and bacon," he shouted into the hall before taking another of the chairs. "If we're to be up at this hour, we might as well have breakfast."

"You found her? Then why don't you have the paper? I thought you could talk any woman out of anything you wanted from her!"

"Good Lord, Bennet, you make me sound like a confidence man."

"Only where ladies are concerned."

Tristan leveled a finger at him. "I am not concerned anywhere near your sister. That woman is trouble."

Bennet turned an astonished, and increasingly amused, face to him. "She refused you."

"She refused to give back that damned paper," Tristan swiftly corrected him. "You were an idiot to sign it at all."

"So much for the celebrated Burke charm." Bennet snorted with laughter. "Turned down by a spinster!"

He glared at his friend. "She bade me tell you she looks forward to seeing you at the Malcolm ball tomorrow."

That punctured Bennet's mood. His grin vanished and he took a large swig of his brandy. "Damn it. I'm sunk, then. I managed to avoid my mother, but my father warned me she's serious this time. There will be hell to pay if I don't go, once Joan shows Mother that bloody note—which she still has, no thanks to you."

"Have a pleasant evening," Tristan told him. "I'll make every effort to be out of the house before you bring your bride home."

"It's just one bloody ball."

"It's the end of your bachelor life. Once you give way to one woman, it's only a matter of time before she has you shackled to another."

A muscle twitched in Bennet's jaw and his brows lowered. "Shut it, Burke."

"In my experience, women tend to prefer other women like themselves. She must have a regular Gorgon chosen for you."

"I'm not getting married," Bennet growled.

"But soon," added Tristan, to provoke him.

"Blast it!" Bennet leapt out of his chair. "You have to come, too, then. If you'd done a proper job of coaxing Joan to be reasonable, I wouldn't be in this mess."

"If you'd shown some spine and refused to sign her extortionate note when she invaded the house, you wouldn't be in this mess."

Bennet jabbed a finger at him. "You let her into the house. You let her stroll off with that paper. You let her keep it even after I explained how dire the situation is. You owe me. I'm turning you out of my house if you don't come with me to that blasted bloody ball tomorrow night."

Tristan sighed. He'd meant to go to the ball all along, just for the thrill of confronting the Fury again. "Very well. But you owe me the guinea."

Chapter 4

Joan soon regretted her hot-tempered exit from the bookshop. Tristan Burke was a boor, but that was no reason to let him spoil her rare independent outing. She'd stormed out of the shop in high dudgeon, only to spy one of her mother's dearest friends strolling down the pavement directly toward her. All thought of soothing her temper with a visit to her favorite bonnet shop vanished. Her only hope was to head directly home and, if confronted about being seen here, claim she'd only taken a slight detour to see if Howell's had any new printed silks displayed in the window. Heart racing, she ducked her head a little and walked as briskly as she dared to the next street, where she darted around the corner toward home.

By the time she reached South Audley Street, her irritation had blossomed into full bitterness. What business was it of Lord Burke's whether Douglas went to the Malcolm ball? Her brother, no doubt, had put him up to following her, which was utterly unfair of him. She had only asked for the signed promise to tweak his nose; if he'd asked nicely, even apologized for yelling at her, she would have given it back. It had only been a small token she could hold over his head against some future favor she might ask of him, and her brother should have known that.

Now, though, she was giving that paper to her mother, and she wasted no time in doing so. "Douglas will be at the Malcolm ball tomorrow evening, just as you wished," she told Lady Bennet when she found her mother writing letters in the morning room. "In fact, he was eager to go."

"Indeed?" Her mother's eyebrows went up.

"Oh, yes." With a flourish she took his signed note from her reticule. "He even wrote it down."

Lady Bennet still looked suspicious as she read the note, but she only nodded. "Very good. Thank you, Joan. You must have a persuasive way with him."

She smiled vindictively. "Yes, I must."

"I've told Janet to press your new blue gown for the ball. Ackermann's had the most charming hairstyle in the latest issue; would you care to try it? Janet could manage your hair as well if we begin early."

Joan looked at the magazine her mother held out to her. The illustration showed a young lady, slim and demure, with her hair drawn into a smooth coronet of braids on her crown, secured by a small tiara and ornamented with a graceful ostrich plume, with clusters of curls framing her face. It looked delicate and beautiful, and she thought she would give her most valued possession to look like that. "Oh, it's *lovely.*"

Her mother beamed. "Isn't it? And it's very fashionable." Fashion was very important to Lady Bennet.

On the other hand . . . Joan studied the illustration more closely. The young lady it showed certainly was very beautiful in her net-trimmed dress and sleek coif, but she was also a great deal more petite than Joan. More than once she had enthusiastically agreed to some new fashion, only to discover with dismay that it never quite suited her. Plumes, for instance. They only seemed to emphasize her height. There were few things more lowering to a girl's pride than watching the eyes of a gentleman climb up and up and up her figure, as if he were surveying some monstrous Amazon. "Perhaps without the plume," she murmured.

"You don't like it?" Her mother frowned and looked at the illustration.

"It might make me look even taller."

Lady Bennet turned the magazine from side to side as she pondered the seriousness of that possibility. Joan's height had always been a matter of concern. Unlike her petite mother, she could look her father in the eye, and was only a few inches shorter than her brother. "Perhaps if Janet puts it in at an angle, like this one. You need something to frame your features."

"Perhaps a few more ringlets?"

"Well, there's only one way to know. You must try it and see."

"Yes." Joan cheered up a bit as she gazed at the illustration. How wonderful it would be to look so elegant. Her new blue dress was similar in style to this one; perhaps combined with the hairstyle it would render all of her elegant.

She gave the illustrated beauty a slight nod. A new hairstyle and a new gown probably wouldn't keep her from spending the evening at the side of the room with the other unmarried and unwanted ladies, but it was worth a try. It would give her something to talk about with her friends, especially since she wouldn't even have the pleasure of discussing *50 Ways to Sin* with them, thanks to Lord Boorish Burke. Her main hope for entertainment would probably be Douglas, who might well arrive thoroughly foxed and bent on being outrageous.

"Do you really think Douglas will marry Felicity Drummond?" she asked on impulse.

Her mother turned her head aside and coughed, touching her lips with her handkerchief. "What's that, dear? Oh. It would be a very good match, and it's time he took a wife. Felicity is a lovely girl with good connections and a pretty dowry. And he's shown no interest in other young ladies; there's no reason he wouldn't be happy enough with her." Her attention had already returned to her letter. "Do you disapprove?"

Joan thought of reminding her mother how dreadful Felicity's mother was. She thought of asking why Douglas ought to get married now, when he was still as wild and untamed as a bear and obviously had no inclination to marry. It wasn't as though he needed a wife's dowry or had expressed a desire to start a family or even any boredom with his current life—which, to Joan's eyes, seemed to consist mainly of drinking, gambling, and carrying on with actresses and tavern wenches. If not for his devotion to sport, he would likely be a fat, gouty fellow by now.

But then, it didn't really matter. Once Mother made up her mind, there was no changing it. At least this time it was Douglas's future in the crucible and not hers. "No," she said. "Felicity is lovely."

"Good." Lady Bennet cleared her throat and put down her pen. She touched her throat and coughed again. "Ring for Mrs. Hudson, would you, dear? I feel in need of some tea."

Joan got up and rang the bell. She slipped out the door when the housekeeper arrived, and went up to her room since there was nowhere else to go, taking the copy of Ackermann's with her. She settled onto the chaise near the window and opened the magazine. She skipped the more earnest and scholarly sections about housewifery and history, meant to improve her mind, and read the stories and poems. Idly she flipped through the description of a recent exhibition of paintings. She would have liked to attend such an exhibit, if only she could have. Her mother approved of music but not picture viewing, where any number of immodest scenes might be portrayed under the guise of mythology. Joan had never quite grasped why it was so terrible to see a man's naked chest, even an imaginary, idealized man's chest, when she would be expected to allow a husband all sorts of liberties with her own, naked person. Her cousin Mariah, married almost two years now, had told her all about a wife's duty—although in Mariah's telling it was the most pleasant duty one could imagine, with nothing dreadful about it. Joan was quite sure Mariah saw her husband's bare chest on a regular basis, and was routinely ravished in every thrilling way. She must be, since she was due to have her first child in a few weeks.

If Mariah weren't her dearest cousin and most intimate confidant, Joan would have been wild with jealousy. As it was, the only male chest, flesh or painted, she had seen was Tristan Burke's. True, she had rather enjoyed it, which lent some weight to her mother's concern that it was indecently titillating, but it had hardly led to ruin. If anything, it only showed her how dramatically separate a gentleman's person and his personality were. Lord Burke might have a very intriguing chest, but the rest of him was obnoxious.

She picked up the magazine again and paged through it to the fashion plates. Gold, he said. What did Lord Boor know about ladies' fashions? She would never have admitted it aloud, but the thought of a deep gold gown sounded rather appealing. She did like rich colors, even if her mother deemed them inappropriate for an unmarried lady. If she ever managed to get a husband, the first thing she would order would be a gown of pure scarlet, just because she loved red.

But tomorrow evening, she was going to look elegant in blue. Pale blue, true, but with a very fine fall of lace at the neckline. And her hair—her one truly beautiful feature—would be winsome and charming, just like the young lady in Ackermann's.

She almost hoped Lord Boor would be there to gape in awe.

Chapter 5

It didn't take Tristan long to remember why he rarely went to balls.

First, there was the company. He had nothing against a good crowd, especially if there happened to be a boxing match in the middle of it. What he didn't enjoy were the stares of women: some sly, some scandalized, some just rabidly curious. Lady Malcolm had gazed at him in amazement when he followed Bennet through her door, and that turned out to be the most polite reaction he got. Every now and then he would meet the eye of a particularly bold female and give her a wicked smile. The young ones blushed, the old ones turned their backs, and the ones in the middle sometimes smiled back. He didn't care. There was only one female he had come to vanquish tonight, and she was late.

"It seems a pity to serve your penance when the judge isn't even here," he remarked to Bennet, who was leaning morosely against the fireplace mantel at the far end of the room.

"If I leave, Mother is sure to turn up ten minutes later and flay me for ducking out." He flagged down a passing footman and took two glasses of wine from the servant's tray. "Might as well drink at Malcolm's expense."

The second problem with balls, Tristan thought, was the wine. Few hosts served their best wine to the hundreds of guests who came to balls. He sipped from the glass Bennet handed him and sighed. It was either very average burgundy or watered. He didn't see the point in drinking it at all.

Bennet had already gulped down most of his. "Can't imagine what maggot got into my mother's brain. Why should she want me married already? Oughtn't she be busy getting Joan wed? Lord knows that would be enough to occupy her for another decade."

"Perhaps she's given it up as hopeless."

Bennet downed the remainder of his wine. "Well, it probably is. Joan drives people to distraction."

"Indeed," Tristan muttered. He knew that all too well. He was perilously close to it right now, scanning the room for the dratted woman.

"Still, it hardly seems right for Mother to take such an interest in my marriage," Bennet went on. "I don't need funds, and I like my life the way it is now. What could I possibly gain by marrying?"

Tristan thought about it. What did marriage offer a man? "Security," he said at last. "If your fortune, or your father's, should suffer reverses, you'd have a harder time finding a wealthy bride. If you begin now, you're more likely to have your pick of the girls."

"Reverses," scoffed Bennet. "Even I'm not daft enough to wager away too much blunt. And I'd rather economize than take on a wife who would be nattering in my ear all day and night about something. No, this is all a mania of my mother's, and I won't be cozened into it."

"Right," said Tristan, hardly paying attention. "Good man." His eye had caught the arrival, at long last, of the Fury. She was tall enough to stand out in the crowd, especially with that feather in her hair. "Go tell her that."

Bennet jerked upright. "Mother's here? Thank God. The sooner I dance with the girl she favors, the sooner I can leave."

That didn't quite sound like making a stand against Lady Bennet's manipulations, but Tristan forbore to mention it. He watched Bennet charge through the crowd like a bull. His sister had already detached herself from the slim older woman who must be her mother. Tristan tracked the bobbing plume in her hair, wondering what made women want to look like half-plucked ostriches. She soon joined a group of other young ladies, barely visible to him even though he could see over most heads in the room. His mouth thinned, and he drank half the wine in his glass without tasting it. Another thing he'd forgotten: females usually roamed in packs. He wanted to confront her in private.

He watched her through several dances, one of which was a long country reel. Footmen passed him with trays of drink, and he absently exchanged his empty glass for a full one. The claret was slightly more palatable than the burgundy, though not by much. Belatedly it struck him that she wasn't dancing. Her companions were escorted into the dance a few times, but she stayed where she was, apparently from lack of partner more than lack of interest; he could see the feather swaying in time with the music. Most likely she would sharpen her tongue on any man brave enough to ask her to dance, but Tristan vaguely remembered that dancing was important to most women.

Before he had much time to wonder if he should pity her, she finally—at long last—turned and headed out of the room with another young lady. Tristan snapped to attention and set down his now empty wineglass. As if he needed further proof this woman was trouble, he'd drunk two . . . or perhaps even three . . . glasses of lackluster wine without realizing it, all because she distracted him.

He wound his way through the other guests, ignoring the hushed whispers and surreptitious glances in his wake. The room was long but relatively narrow, and by the time he reached the door, Miss Bennet had disappeared. For a moment he paused, listening, then turned in the direction of female voices. Brilliant; he could lie in wait for her outside the ladies' retiring room.

A private parlor at the end of a long corridor had been made available to the ladies, and was occupied by several of them, to judge from the sounds of conversation and laughter. Not wanting to just stand there waiting for her to emerge, Tristan tried a nearby door and found it unlocked. He stepped into a small music room, lit by two lamps on the side table behind the harp. He left the door ajar, so as not to miss her, and strolled over to the table. The lamps caught his eye; they were made of a design he'd never seen before. It was similar to an Argand lamp, but more delicate. Intrigued, Tristan bent down to study it more closely, and then went down on one knee to see the underside. How did the wick draw from that oil reservoir?

"At last," trilled a female voice behind him. "I never thought to see you down on bended knee."

"It's not for the reason you wished," he said without looking around. "What sort of lamp is this?"

"How on earth would I know?" With a tipsy hiccup she strolled into the room.

Tristan barely glanced at her. Lady Elliot had been his lover for a few impassioned weeks last fall, before she unwisely told him she wanted marriage. Since they'd been engaged in vigorous amorous activity at the time, almost at the crucial moment, he considered it a low form of coercion. You won't get it from me, he'd told her before pulling away from her clinging limbs and walking out of her bedroom without looking back, even when she screamed at him to give her a climax at the very least.

"You're right," he said absently. "I was foolish to ask you, of all people."

"Oh, don't be like that." She walked her fingers over his collar and combed them through his hair. "I do know some things, you might remember."

Carefully Tristan slid the glass chimney off the lamp, wincing as the hot glass seared his fingers. He blew out the flame and picked up the lamp, studying it from all sides. "I remember you thought very highly of your charms."

"So did you," she whispered in a playful tone. "Perhaps you've forgotten? I could show you again . . . tonight . . ."

"I have other plans." There was some sort of clockwork device in the base of the lamp, with a key protruding from the back. He gave it a gentle turn, watching how it affected the mechanism. How clever; he'd have to ask Lord Malcolm what sort of lamp this was and where he could obtain some for his own house.

"Change them. I've missed you, Burke . . . Let me apologize for my ill-considered parting."

He glanced up. She had leaned over, putting her very impressive bosom, in its very low-cut bodice, right at his eye level. "Jessica, it's no good. I won't marry you, so find another man to grace with your favors."

She pouted, still playing with his hair. He jerked his head to one side as she plucked at the leather thong that held it back out of his face. Lord save him from women who couldn't handle champagne, yet drank it to excess anyway. "But I want you. I miss you. So vigorous, so untamed, so thrilling! Come, let's have a go for old time's sake."

"No, thank you." He went back to studying the lamp, only to curse vividly as her lace-trimmed pantalets fell over his head a few minutes later.

She giggled. "Come, my love. I know how you like it." Swishing her skirt above her knees, she backed up until she collapsed onto a chaise. Now laughing out loud, she lay back and pulled up her skirt in one motion, exposing her bared legs all the way to her waist. She spread her legs wide and kicked up her feet. "I am yours to invade!"

For a moment he was transfixed. Gads, she was even bolder than he remembered. But then he shook himself. He wasn't going to avail himself of her offer, no matter how . . . adventurous it might be.

"The door is open," he said as he set the lamp back on the table. "You're making a fool of yourself, Jessica—"

The gasp seemed to echo through the room. Tristan whipped around to see his nemesis in the doorway, her eyes wide and her mouth open. For a moment the air seemed as thick as treacle, with only the drunken giggling of Lady Elliot—still wiggling her feet and holding her skirts over her face—to break the deafening silence.

"Oh my," said Miss Bennet at last, her voice trembling.

Lady Elliot lifted her head, peering over the billows of her skirt. "Alas," she cried. "We've been discovered *in flagrante delicto*, Burke!"

"Not we," he said, tossing the pantalets at her. "You." With three strides he crossed the room, seized Miss Bennet by the arm, and pulled the door closed behind him.

"I'm so sorry," she said in mock despair as he towed her down the corridor and around a corner. "I really thought even you would have more decorum than to fornicate with the door wide open for all the world to watch—"

"Listen to me," he commanded, stopping short

and squeezing her arm. "I was not fornicating with that woman, and don't you dare go telling people I was."

"Oh, no," she murmured, lowering her eyes demurely. "That would be wrong. I could only, in good conscience, repeat what I saw with my own eyes." She gave him an outrageously saucy look through her eyelashes. "I daresay Lady Elliot wouldn't mind."

Tristan tried not to curse out loud. How did this woman always manage to get him on the defensive? "I was waiting for you," he said to throw her off.

Her head came up sharply. "For me? You, sir, are completely barmy if you expect *me* to lie down on the chaise and show you my—"

"Hardly," said Tristan, trying not to think about it. He didn't want to see under the Fury's skirts, nor imagine her gleaming eyes gone soft with desire, and he really didn't want to wonder how her penchant for unpredictability would show itself in bed. "I have something of yours and wanted to return it."

She gave him a look arch with disbelief. "Indeed. What is it?"

"Can't you guess?"

"I can't think of anything you might have that I would want."

He leaned closer, relishing how her coffee-colored eyes widened, the golden striations seeming to glow. "Nothing? Are you certain, Miss Bennet?"

Some of her condescension faded. "Yes, quite certain," she said, not sounding very certain at all.

"Interesting," he murmured. Her blush was a dusky rose, not bright pink at all.

Suddenly she flinched, and the blush faded. "You must excuse me, sir," she said quickly. "I must go."

Oh, no. He wasn't letting her go that easily. "Why the hurry?" He'd only come to this damn ball to see her. "Don't you want it?"

"Not now," she whispered, looking nervous. "You may keep it." She tried to duck around him and back into the corridor that led to the ballroom.

He put his hand on the wall, blocking her escape without thinking. "Not so quickly. I have a few things to say to you—"

"My mother is coming!" she hissed. "Let me pass!"

Indeed. The only thing Tristan clearly remembered about Lady Bennet was the frigid glare she had given him ever since the one school holiday he'd been invited home with Bennet. He'd been only twelve, but clever enough to see that he wouldn't be invited back. It had struck him as a bit unfair; most of the escapades that earned her enmity had been her own son's idea, but he doubted a mother would turn her son out when there was a much easier focus of blame. More than once in the years since, Bennet had remarked in passing conversation that his mother still didn't approve of Tristan. He hardly cared, but now . . .

"Are you afraid?" he asked, not bothering to hide his amusement as Miss Bennet tried to shove past his arm.

"Yes!" And she did look it.

He ought to let her go, just raise his arm and

allow her to slip past him. Instead he turned the knob of the door beside him and pushed her through it, following hard on her heels and easing the door closed behind him just as a pair of older ladies went past the broader corridor. "Then you should hide."

He could barely see the pale shape of her arm before she slapped his shoulder. "Why did you do that?" Her whisper seethed with shock. "Are you a complete idiot?"

"I see. You are completely unafraid of defying propriety by invading your brother's bedchamber, or by slipping off to a slightly disreputable bookseller, but the approach of your own blessed mother strikes fear in your heart."

"And it would in yours as well, if you had any brains in your head," she snapped. "What *do* you want, Lord Burke? Your charm has only grown smaller since our last encounter."

"No doubt. But I have something of yours." He drew out her package, still bound in the bookseller's paper and string, and waggled it at her. "Don't you want it?"

His eyes had adjusted enough to see her jaw drop, gratifyingly. Finally, it seemed, he had rendered her speechless. "Did you open it?" she asked in a choked voice.

"No, as you can see." He picked at the string. "There's still time, of course . . ."

"Stop," she said quickly. "Please don't." Tristan smiled. "But I can't take it now," she added. "Where would I put it?"

For the first time he really looked at her gown. It was light blue, with a terrifying amount of lace bristling at her bosom. Even worse, the skirt stood out with no less than four full flounces at the hem. His gaze traveled up. The feather in her hair actually concealed a pearl tiara that surrounded a high, tight knot of braids. But most appalling of all was the profusion of ringlets curled at her temples. In the dim moonlight, it looked like she had a bunch of grapes at each temple.

"Have you something against flattering fashion?" he asked.

Her eyes all but ignited. "This is very fashionable!"

"But not flattering on you," he said bluntly. "Even a darker shade of blue would be better. You look like you're wearing a half-opened umbrella."

"You insufferable . . . !" She drew back her fist. "Let me leave, or I shall punch you."

"Really?" He couldn't help grinning at the thought. "I've never been punched by a—ow!" The last came out in a howl as her fist connected with his nose. Rather well, truth be told; Bennet must have taught her how to do it. "You struck me!"

"And don't think I won't gladly do it again." She darted by him and opened the door. "Good evening, Lord Boor—I mean, Lord Burke."

Still holding his smarting nose, Tristan could only watch her go in impotent shock. She had bested him and exited in triumph yet again. He ought not to have pushed her into this room, but he'd only meant to tease her a little and make her ask nicely for her package from the bookseller. Instead . . . instead he was going to have a swollen nose and he still hadn't put the Fury in her place.

Enough was enough. This meant war.

Chapter 6

Joan almost ran back to the ballroom, her heart galloping inside her chest and her lungs straining against her tighter-than-usual stays. Heaven help her if her mother discovered any part of that. Not only had she spoken to Tristan Burke, the Most Wicked Man in London in her mother's eyes, but she'd punched him in the face. Although, now that she thought about it, Mother might approve that last part. Yes, she might well applaud her daughter fighting off the boorish attentions of a notorious rogue . . .

Not that Joan wanted to put it to the test by telling her mother.

At the ballroom door she slowed her steps, even though her pulse still thundered along, and tried to look proper and composed as she made her way back to her friends. Abigail Weston looked at her curiously as she rejoined them. "Where were you?"

"The retiring room," said Joan.

"After that," said Abigail, her eyebrows arching

a little. "I went with you to the retiring room, but you left first and disappeared."

Joan cast a cautious glance around. They were as ignored and alone as ever, but she lowered her voice anyway. "I was waylaid."

Penelope, Abigail's younger sister, gasped. "Really? By whom?" She seemed to have taken the wrong interpretation; her eyes were bright with interest.

"An addlepated idiot." From the corner of her eye, Joan saw the idiot himself appear in the doorway. From this distance, he was almost unbearably mesmerizing, his arms folded over his broad chest and his mouth set in a faint but wicked curve. As she peered at him over her shoulder, his green gaze suddenly connected with hers, as if he'd been searching for her. Chin defiantly high, she turned her back to him. "Lord Burke, actually. But perhaps it was because I discovered him ravishing someone in the music room."

"Ravishing?" breathed Penelope hopefully. "Truly, honestly, ravishing?"

"On a chaise with her skirts around her waist." Joan knew she ought to mention that Lord Burke had been several feet away from the chaise, but held her tongue. It served him right for leaving the door wide open. Most likely he would have been ravishing Lady Elliot in another few minutes anyway.

"Oh, my." Penelope turned wide blue eyes on her sister, who was studying Joan too closely.

"If he was occupied ravishing someone else, why—and how—did he waylay you?"

"He ran after me," Joan said with a trace of indignity. "He grabbed my arm, pulled me down the corridor, and *imprisoned* me in a room. I had to box his ears to escape."

Abigail's eyebrows shot way up, then lowered suspiciously. "Really."

"Yes, truly! Why would you doubt me?"

"Because it sounds much better to say you boxed his ears than that you made such a fuss, he let you go."

"If you must know," Joan retorted, a little haughtily, "I did not box his ears, actually."

"I knew it," murmured Abigail.

"I punched him in the face." She turned around and looked directly at Lord Burke, who was—disturbingly—still watching her with those unnerving eyes. "See? His nose will be swollen like a ripe plum tomorrow."

All three turned to look. Tristan Burke gazed back from across the ballroom, brazen and bold. He was just leaning against one of the pillars at the front of the room, hands clasped behind him, but somehow Joan felt his presence all the way back into the quiet corner where they stood. In fact, as she looked at him, he almost seemed to smile at her.

That could not mean anything good. She turned around and resolved not to look his way again.

"Was he really ravishing someone else in the music room?" asked Penelope. "Because he's looking very intently at you, Joan."

"She punched him in the face," Abigail reminded her. "We shall protect you, if he approaches," she added to Joan.

Joan gave her a limp smile. Fancy that; she

needed protection from one of the biggest rakes in England, but not for the reason any other woman would. She ducked her head near Abigail's. "Tell me the truth," she whispered in her friend's ear. "Do I look like a half-opened umbrella?"

Abigail frowned. "Who said that? You look—" Her gaze swept downward, and she blinked, a betraying hesitation Joan didn't miss. "You look lovely."

"Like a lovely, half-opened umbrella." She ground her teeth and swung around to glare venomously at Lord Burke. Damn him. The man might be handsome and good at ravishing women, but otherwise he was a cad. "Why do all the ladies throw themselves at him?" she wondered crossly.

"Because of the dimple," whispered Penelope. She was still absorbed in watching Lord Boor. "Look—when he smiles—"

"Because he's fearfully rich, and a viscount," said Abigail, a true and loyal friend.

"Oh." Penelope's gaze didn't waver. "That's very attractive, too. But you must admit he's the most compelling figure in this ballroom."

"Compelling," snorted Joan, thinking of all the insults he'd hurled at her in the last two days alone. "And rude and belligerent and coarse . . ."

"He must have some charms, besides his fortune and his title and his shoulders and that wicked dimple. As if he would need more than . . . all that," Penelope finished rather breathlessly.

"Mama will never allow it," said her sister. "In fact, if she should notice you staring, you'll find yourself locked away from all disreputable gentlemen until you reach old age."

"It might be worth it." But Penelope reluctantly turned away.

"I suppose he does look rather well without his shirt on," Joan muttered, still lost in her own thoughts.

As one, the Weston sisters turned to her, eyes round and mouths open. "Joan," one of them managed to gasp. "When did you—?"

"He opened the door half naked, when I called upon my brother," she said, ignoring the traitorous warmth creeping over her cheeks. "Apparently he's taken up residence in Douglas's house."

Penelope began to smile. Abigail tried not to, and ended up sighing. "Oh, Joan."

"It could have happened to anyone!"

"But it only ever *does* happen to you," Penelope pointed out. "And I am growing terribly jealous."

"Perhaps this will dispel it. He has my copy of the latest *50 Ways to Sin*."

Their reaction was all she could have hoped for. Penelope jerked around, eyes wide, and Abigail sucked in her breath. "There's a new one? Since when?"

"And how did he get it?" demanded Penelope.

Joan lowered her voice even more. "After I visited my brother, I went to Madox Street, to that bookseller you told me about. And he said he'd only received some copies that morning! But Lord Burke," she said wrathfully, "followed me, and made me so furious I stormed out before the bookseller could bring it out. I presume he bought it instead—because tonight he *taunted* me with it!"

"Only you," said Abigail again.

"So he's got it right now?" Penelope's face screwed up in concentration. "We could lure him outside and take it from him . . ."

"Or Joan could simply ask him for it," said Abigail, who was still facing the room. "He's coming this way."

Joan froze. She had an awful inkling of what he might do. Any man who would open the door in a shocking state of undress, allow a woman to display her bare nether regions, and practically kidnap another woman wouldn't hesitate to exact the most horrible vengeance for that fist to the nose.

And he did. The dreadful man swept to a stop in front of them, that wicked little smile lurking about his lips, and bowed. Obediently all three girls curtsied back, and Joan muttered the appropriate introductions. And then he struck.

"May I have the next set, Miss Bennet?"

She kept her chin up. "Why? Do you expect rain soon?"

He blinked, then that grin curled his mouth again. "Would you let me hide beneath your skirts, if I did?"

Joan could feel the amazed, shocked glances of her friends. In truth, she was rather shocked herself. The boor! It was bad enough for him to say it to her, but to repeat it in front of her friends . . . "Not even if there were a hurricane," she replied sweetly.

He barely moved, yet seemed to be closer by the minute. "Would you dance with me if I said I wished to apologize?"

"One needn't dance for that. In fact, you might wish to concentrate on one task at a time; you seem easily distracted, sir."

"Hmm." His gaze flicked to Abigail and Penelope, still shamelessly watching and listening. Lord Burke lowered his voice and this time he most definitely leaned toward her. "Perhaps if I relinquish your illicit object from the shop in Madox Street?"

Now she was caught. Surely she, Abigail, or Penelope would think of a way to smuggle it home. There was always her garter, after all . . . A quick sideways glance showed that her friends were in full favor of her making the sacrifice. In fact, Penelope looked ready to make it for her, which tipped the scales. "You have finally said something persuasive," she told him. "I accept."

His smile was devilishly smug. "I knew you would."

In spite of that, her heart began to pound as she put her hand in his and let him lead her out to join the rest of the dancers. More than one person glanced first at him, then at her, then again at him, this time in shock. She wondered what surprised them more, that Tristan Burke was dancing, or that he was dancing with her. Both were certainly shocking to her, but as the musicians began to play, she couldn't keep a small smile from her face. Oh heaven—it was a waltz. Joan had never waltzed with anyone other than her dancing instructor or her father, and once, under extreme duress, with her brother. Lord Burke was obnoxious, but as long as he could waltz reasonably well, she would graciously forgive him. For now.

And he was even tall enough. Joan was determined to enjoy the dance, so she kept her
eyes fixed straight ahead—not, as it usually happened, on her partner's forehead, but this time
on the silver pin stuck through his cravat. It was
a crouching leopard with an emerald eye that
seemed to gleam at her in predatory promise. Joan
smiled at the leopard. Not only was she dancing,
it was with a man taller than she was, who could
waltz—glory be—so beautifully she barely felt
the floor beneath her feet. She didn't even need to
hear his apology now. She would have been content to glide around the floor like this in perfect
silence.

He, of course, didn't allow that. "Are you contemplating your future reading hours, or plotting
my demise?"

Mention of *50 Ways to Sin* made her face warm.
"Neither," she said tartly. "I was merely saying a
quiet prayer of thanks that you know the steps. I
worried, you see."

"Ah yes, it is quite challenging. One must count
one, two . . . two . . . What comes next? Dear me, I
seem to have forgotten already." For emphasis he
turned more sharply than ever, without losing his
light yet confident hold on her. It felt like flying.
Good heavens—Monsieur Berthold had never
made it feel like this.

"I could tell," she said, sounding sadly breathless once again. From the corner of her eye she
caught sight of Douglas, who was dancing with
Felicity Drummond again and staring at them
with mingled shock and anger. It made her think
of her mother, and what her mother would say

when she heard about this waltz with Lord Burke. Joan sighed softly, her delight deflated. Everything she enjoyed seemed to be inappropriate for ladies. "You had better make your apology before the music ends."

His faint smirk faded. Unfortunately, he was even more devastatingly handsome when serious. Joan was beginning to think God hated her, to keep thrusting Tristan Burke in her path. He was obnoxious and rude and yet so bloody attractive. "Yes. I am deeply, humbly sorry for saying you look like an umbrella tonight."

Joan stiffened. She would rather have never heard *that* again.

"It strikes me as foolish for women to wear fashions that don't suit them, but of course it's none of my concern how you want to dress."

"It really isn't," she muttered.

His glinting gaze ranged over her face. "How long did it take to make all those ringlets?"

"An hour. Why? Are you thinking of trying it yourself?"

He grinned. Joan tried not to look at the dimple. "Not particularly."

"Well, it probably wouldn't suit you." Although with her luck, he would try it to annoy her, and end up looking like a romantic cavalier of old, elegant and fine in brocade and lace.

"Was it your mother's idea?"

She flushed. "Why would you think that?"

"You mentioned her the other day, when listing every color unflattering to your looks."

Joan knew she never managed to look elegant, not even in the most fashionable creations to be found in London. She agreed that light blue wasn't her favorite color, no matter how appropriate it was for unmarried ladies. But she'd wear green and orange stripes through Hyde Park before she admitted it to him. "If you must know," she said airily, "it was in the latest copy of Ackermann's. I expect it will be all the rage soon, and every woman in town will be wearing it."

"That will hardly make it suit you any better."

Her eyes narrowed. "Really, sir," she trilled. "You take such an interest in my clothing and my hair! One might begin to wonder what your intentions are!"

He didn't seem concerned; if anything, her words brought a faint grin to his lips. Staring up at his mouth, so near her own, Joan felt her stomach turn itself into another twist. Why the devil had he asked her to dance? With his one hand spread over her back, holding her close, and his other hand holding hers, it was all too easy for her wretched imagination to take flight and pretend he wasn't the biggest boor in London, but someone who had once told her he liked impertinent girls.

"You're safe with me," he said. "My intentions are to apologize, return your book, and then go do something I actually enjoy."

Joan almost rolled her eyes. Safe from ravishment, obviously, but not from irritation. "I accept your apology, halfhearted and weak though it was. I think I feel a pain in my ankle, you may escort me back to my friends now." Most gentlemen usually accepted the excuse gratefully. She hoped Lord Burke would do something decent for once.

His steps didn't falter. "Oh, no. Not yet. I'm not through with you." And before she could ask what that meant, he twirled her with a little extra vigor and sent them both around a nearby pillar and into the alcove a few feet behind it that held a stand of potted palms.

"What—?" she began in a furious whisper, but he put one gloved fingertip on her lips as he reached inside his evening jacket and withdrew *50 Ways to Sin*—which, she couldn't help noticing, was now unwrapped, exposing the title to full view.

"I also apologize for reducing you to tears in the bookshop," he said, holding it out.

She stared at it in frustrated longing. So near, and yet so impossible for her to take. "I cannot walk back into the ballroom with it in my hand! Where will I put it?"

He wagged it back and forth, the evil gleam in his eyes completely undermining the solemn innocence of his expression. "You don't mean to say you purchased something inappropriate, do you, Miss Bennet?"

"If anyone sees this, I shall swear on my grandmother's grave you were trying to tempt me into debauchery with that piece of filth—not that I have any idea what it is."

Now he was beginning to grin. "Debauchery! You strike fear into my heart—and yet a small amount of curiosity as well. What sort of debauchery do you think I had planned, some ten feet from Lady Malcolm's guests? I prefer more privacy than a pair of potted palms offers."

"Lady Elliot would be astonished to hear that."

He laughed, a low, lazy sound unafflicted by any of the nerves that gripped Joan. "She's the one who left the door open—not that I was debauching her in any way. But enough teasing. I did mean to apologize and return your little story." He leaned closer, still smiling. "Here," he said softly—almost tauntingly. "Take it."

Joan squeezed her hands together. Under no circumstances could she slip it under her garter in front of him. "I can't. You have to keep it."

He sighed. "Spare me women of no imagination. Turn around."

"Why?" Before she could protest further, he had taken her by the shoulders and spun her around to face the wall, then crowded up against her until she must be quite invisible to anyone passing by. Joan braced her hands against the plaster, struggling to keep enough space to breath. Great heavens—she could feel him behind her. His foot had slid between hers, and his chest was right at her back. She shuffled her feet, trying vainly to inch closer to the wall, and felt the brush of his knee on the back of her leg. And then she felt his fingers at the fastenings of her bodice, plucking loose the lacing that held it closed.

She was as stricken as Lot's wife, immobile at the wickedness before her. Or, rather, behind her. The most notorious rake in London was unlacing her gown.

"Don't worry," he murmured next to her ear. "Your virtue is safe with me tonight."

Her virtue, perhaps, but not her imagination. She gulped for air as her bodice grew loose. Joan closed her eyes, trying not to wish he did have designs on her virtue. Not because she wanted *him*, of course, but because she had never been the object of anyone's uncontrollable desires, and had certainly never been pressed up against a wall by any halfway desirable man. And however boorish Tristan Burke might be, even Joan couldn't deny he was desirable.

"Good Lord—how tightly did you lace this corset?"

A flush of humiliation burned up her throat at his murmur. Trust him to notice that. "Never mind," she said through her teeth. "Just hurry . . ."

He stopped her wriggling with one hand on her waist, his fingers splayed over her hip. "If you're going to lace it up tightly to display your bosom, you ought to forgo all this." With his other hand he flicked the elegant fall of lace that frothed over her gown's neckline. "What good is a delectable display of bosom if no one can enjoy it?"

"My bosom is none of your concern!"

There was a pause before he replied. "Of course not." She felt his fingers sliding along the loosened back of her gown, and then a crinkle of paper. He was putting *50 Ways to Sin* down the back of her bodice. "I hope you trust your maid."

"I don't have any choice now, do I? Lace me up!" she hissed.

He laughed very quietly, his nimble fingers tugging at her laces again. Joan glared at a thin crack running down the wall in front of her, wishing she didn't feel every stroke of his fingers on her back, even through her stays, which seemed to be growing tighter with every moment. She tried to think of what fantastical story she would tell if someone burst upon them; it seemed they had been in this alcove for an hour or more.

She spun around as soon as his fingers lifted away from her. "Thank you, now let me by."

Instead of moving aside, he only propped one elbow beside her head, blocking her in. "Why are you so controlled by your mother?"

"Controlled by . . . ?" This time she did roll her eyes. "Let me see. Because I am an unmarried female with no fortune of my own, no property of my own, and no rights of my own. Unlike you, I am not at liberty to rendezvous in secluded corners, even with someone who has no interest in my virtue, because it would be improper. Ruinous, even. Not that anyone has shown the slightest interest in besmirching my virtue, but appearances, you know, are so important for a young lady." She said the last in a creditable imitation of her mother's voice, but then sighed. "I don't suppose your mother cares about your reputation, but mine cares a great deal about mine. I really don't want to spend the rest of the Season locked in my room just because you couldn't manage to apologize in a normal and genteel manner, so please let me pass."

He raised one eyebrow. "Who said I had no interest in your virtue?"

Joan gaped at him. "You—you did!"

"No, I said it was safe with me tonight." He pinched one of her ringlets. "There's a difference."

She paused, watching him warily, but he certainly gave no sign of being overcome with passion and falling upon her in a craze of lust. Not that she should wish for such things anyway, at least not from him. She snapped her mouth shut. "You'll forgive me if I don't puzzle out that subtlety at the moment."

His mouth crooked. "Still impertinent."

"You have no idea how much," she told him.

"Believe me, I don't doubt—" He broke off, lifting his head as though listening to something, then abruptly ducked and crowded her back behind the potted palms.

"What are you doing? Is someone coming?" She tried to push him aside.

"Yes," he hissed. "Shh."

Joan blanched. "My mother?" she whimpered.

"Shh!" He wasn't paying attention to her at all, but was clearly listening for something, his expression fierce yet distant.

Oh God. Even if it wasn't Mother, it might be anyone who loved a good gossip. Joan pictured a year in exile in Cornwall, away from her friends and the shopping of town, which would surely be her punishment if she was caught practically in Tristan Burke's embrace. Her only hope was to put some distance between them. She pulled against his grip. "Let me go, or I shall scream."

"Hush," he whispered. "For the love of God, woman, hold your tongue for once."

"Why? Who is coming? You must know it would give the completely wrong impression, if someone were to see you embracing me—"

He looked down at her in disbelief. "Can you never do as anyone asks? Are you totally mad?"

Joan set her jaw. She was a very reasonable person; he was the one at fault here. He had forced her into a dark room, withheld her pamphlet, and then confronted her in full view of everyone at the ball. Now he had her pinned against the wall behind the potted palms, and even though her pulse was leaping and something awfully like excitement had set her blood surging at the way he held her, she had to get out of here. Her gaze locked with his, she drew a deep, deliberate breath to cry out.

"Damn," she thought he muttered, and then before she could make a sound his mouth came down on hers. Joan made a startled *eep* and almost fell before his arms tightened around her.

She had been kissed before—or rather, she thought she'd been kissed before. But compared to this, those previous experiences were mere pecks on the cheek. Tristan Burke held her in a way that left no doubt of his intentions; she could feel every inch of his body pressed against hers, hard and unyielding. His arm curved around her waist, and his hand—shockingly—curved around her hip, holding her body against his. His other hand was around the back of her neck, keeping her from retreating. Which, of course, she would have done at once, if only he hadn't been holding her so and kissing her so and then his tongue ran along her lips and she started to protest and then . . . he made a sound like a starving man in sight of a feast . . . and she felt the same way . . .

It might have been a year later that he lifted his head. Joan would have sworn an age had passed. As it was, she had to hold on to him—actually, she was already holding on to him; when had that happened?—and struggle to breathe again.

"You—you kissed me," she managed to gasp.

Her tight stays seemed to have cut off all her air. She groped for her fan, trying desperately not to faint.

He was staring down at her, still holding her tightly, but at her words he gave a small shake of his head. His arms loosened. "I had to hear myself think for a moment."

That stung. She glared at him, even though her heart was still leaping about inside her chest. "There are other ways—"

He leaned closer, looking intent, and Joan snapped her mouth closed. Was he going to kiss her again? And if so, should she slap him now . . . or kiss him back this time?

"This way worked," he whispered. "Don't think I won't do it again."

And he turned and walked away, leaving her— for once—utterly speechless.

Chapter 7

Somehow, Joan returned to the ballroom, hoping no one would be able to tell by looking at her what had happened. She didn't even *know* what had happened; the mere facts of the story didn't begin to explain it. Tristan Burke had danced with her. She could reason that away as part of his plan to torment her at every turn. He had apologized for saying she looked like an umbrella, which was surely just some vestige of good manners, even if it was done in his usual arrogant way. But then he had called her bosom delectable and implied he would like to see it. He hinted that her virtue might not always be safe with him. And then he kissed her, the way a rake would kiss his lover. The way a man would kiss his wife after a year's absence. The way Joan had dreamed of being kissed for the last eight years.

If it had been anyone else, she would have been floating on air. Since it was Tristan Burke who had kissed her so thoroughly and so passionately . . . she wasn't sure. And she really had no idea what to tell her friends, who would have noticed that

Lord Burke whisked her around a corner and out of sight for several minutes. There was no way on earth they would believe he had simply been handing her the copy of *50 Ways to Sin* in that time.

Fortunately she was saved from Abigail's and Penelope's curiosity by her father. "Joan, we're going now," Papa asked, catching her just before she reached the Weston sisters. "Mother's unwell."

"I—really?" Over her father's shoulder, she could see Penelope almost dancing on the spot with impatience. Even Abigail was watching her with naked curiosity. A fiery inquisition awaited her. "That's—that's dreadful. Is she very ill?"

"Well, I hope not, but she needs to rest. Are you terribly disappointed to leave early? I could ask Douglas to bring you home—"

"No, no," she said quickly. Douglas had given her a dark glare when he saw her dancing with his friend. She didn't want to have a scolding from him, of all people. "I'll come now." She raised her hand in farewell to her friends, ignoring Penelope's outraged look, and followed her father from the ballroom. They found her mother resting on a sofa in a small salon off the main hall. Lady Bennet looked pale and tired, and she coughed as they came into the room.

"Mother!" Joan forgot her anxiety over Lord Burke. She wasn't used to seeing her poised, fashionable mother laid low, and certainly never in public. "What happened?"

Mother smiled. "A spasm, dear. I've got a sore throat and can't seem to stop coughing. Your father was worried, but I don't want you to miss the ball—"

"Oh, don't worry about that," she replied hastily. "But it's more than a scratchy throat. You've been coughing for days now!"

"Do you see?" Her father stepped up, his arms folded across his chest. "Joan's noticed. Marion, you must see a physician."

Mother flipped one hand. "He'll tell me to sip warm tea and rest. I shall be fine, George."

"Then *I* need to see the physician, so he can prescribe me some physick that will keep me from worrying about you," returned her husband. "I've already sent for him."

Mother sighed. "Very well. But you must stay here so Joan needn't miss the ball. She looks so lovely, George, and took such time over her hair—"

How long it did take to make these ringlets? echoed Lord Burke's wicked voice in her head. "Nonsense," cried Joan. "To tell the truth, Mother, I was a bit tired and don't mind leaving at all." She leaned forward to take her mother's hand, and felt a crinkle along her spine. Oh yes; there was also that. Funny how she hadn't thought once of reading *50 Ways to Sin* since Lord Burke kissed her.

A footman came to tell them their carriage was waiting, and Papa helped Mother to her feet and led her out to the street. Lady Malcolm came hurrying up to wish Mother a quick recovery, and Papa thanked her. Joan gave a quick curtsy and murmured her own thanks, and then they were on the way home.

For once the ride was quiet. Normally Mother would have asked her how she found the evening, if she'd seen any intriguing fashions or met any gentlemen or heard any interesting on dits. Tonight, though, she leaned on Papa's arm and closed her eyes. Papa met Joan's gaze across the dark carriage and he gave her a smile.

"Did you enjoy yourself?" he asked quietly.

She nodded. It was safer than saying anything.

"I thought I saw you dancing," he added. "Who was the gentleman?"

"Just a friend of Douglas's," she said, hoping he really hadn't seen who it was and praying he wouldn't ask more. "I saw Douglas dance twice with Felicity Drummond," she went on, trying to keep the subject off herself. "He looked halfway besotted. Mother's plan may come to fruition after all."

Eyes still closed, Mother smiled. "I knew he would like her, if he could only be made to meet her."

To Joan's intense relief, no one said anything more of dancing. They reached home and Papa all but lifted Mother down from the carriage and helped her into the house. Joan was left to herself, which suited her perfectly. She didn't wish her mother ill, but tonight of all nights she was glad for a respite from her mother's usual keen eye. She bade her parents good night and wished her mother well, then hurried up to her own room, where Janet, her mother's abigail, was waiting for her.

"Go to Lady Bennet. She is unwell," Joan told her.

Janet had been with her mother for almost thirty years. Her eyes widened in alarm. "I'll send Polly to help you, Miss Bennet," she said before whisking out the door toward Lady Bennet's rooms.

The instant she was alone, Joan reached for the lacings at her back. If Lord Burke hadn't tied them too tightly, she should be able to find the string and get the pamphlet out before Polly arrived to help her. Not even her imagination could conjure up a suitable explanation for the most infamous story in London finding its way down the back of her dress. For several minutes she twisted and squirmed, both arms bent behind her in a silent, frantic ballet. Finally she located the string—he hadn't knotted it, thank heavens—and pulled, loosening the bodice. With a heroic stretch she crossed one arm over her shoulder and groped as far down her back as she could reach. Just as Polly tapped at the door, her fingers closed on a corner of paper and she yanked it out.

"Just a moment," she called, running across the room to shove the pamphlet under her pillow. "Come."

"La, miss, I'm sorry," gasped Polly as she bustled into the room and saw Joan with her gown sagging off one shoulder. "I came as soon as Janet told me, but if I'd known you were that eager to get undressed—"

"No, it's fine," said Joan hastily. "My stays were a little tighter than usual and I thought I could untie them myself, that's all."

"Oh." Polly clucked her tongue and hurried over to finish unfastening the gown. "I see what you mean, miss, these are tight," she said a moment later. "Shall I bring a cool cloth?"

"No," said Joan, fidgeting as Polly took the

gown away to fold it. "Just unlace me. I'm sure I'll be fine once they are undone."

And she did feel better when the constricting stays came off. She took a deep breath and held it a moment, beginning to think she would escape without serious repercussions from this evening's adventure. It was only a matter of time before Mother learned she had danced with Lord Burke, but now that she was away from him and that infuriating, unsettling gleam in his eye, Joan was sure she would think of some safe story to explain everything. Casting blame onto Douglas would be a central part of it, she decided; she would say Douglas had made a wager with his friend, and that was the only reason he'd asked her to dance. Mother wouldn't believe Douglas's insistence that he'd done no such thing—Mother might not want to know how wild her son was, but she wasn't a fool—and Joan would add that she only accepted the invitation to avoid a scene. If Mother asked about Lord Burke's behavior, Joan would say he had no manners and was boring. There would be no mention whatsoever of potted palms.

"Shall I brush out your hair, miss?" Polly asked.

She looked at her ringlets, the result of over an hour of painstaking work by Janet, and sighed. Unlike the sleek curls in the Ackermann's illustration, her hair stuck out in all directions, making her look like a poodle. "Yes."

As Polly tugged the comb through her hair, undoing all that effort, Joan studied her reflection. She really wasn't beautiful, but Lord Burke had kissed her anyway. She tried to tell herself that he had only said it because he was a notorious rake and no female was safe around him, but at the same time . . . he had called her bosom delectable. She shifted in her seat a little and inhaled deeply, trying to see what he could mean by that. Like the rest of her, her bosom was full and round. Janet had laced her stays particularly tight this evening to try to minimize it, but it hadn't worked. Joan just felt trussed like a goose, and short of breath all evening. Ever since she turned sixteen, she had viewed her rounded figure with dismay. As if it weren't bad enough to be tall, she had to be plump, too. It wasn't a fashionable figure for young ladies, who were supposed to be slim and delicate so they could wear the latest fashions to advantage. Was it possible some gentlemen might like it?

Not that she cared what Tristan Burke thought. No, she reminded herself, he was a rake. A scoundrel. A rogue. No one she ought to think about. If he was the only sort of gentleman who admired her figure, she didn't want to know, let alone care.

Although if he thought her bosom delectable, perhaps some other man would as well.

When Polly had finally gone and Joan was alone, able to take out her hard-won copy of *50 Ways to Sin* at long last, she couldn't keep her mind on it. She turned the pamphlet over and over in her hands. It looked innocent enough; *50 Ways to Sin*, it read in plain letters that might have graced any theological tract. The story inside, though, was anything but sober and edifying. Every issue chronicled the flirtations of the rather wrongly named Lady Constance, a woman of the ton. Beyond the shadowy details of being a widow of some social standing, Constance told little of herself or her history, but a great deal about the gentlemen who pursued her. And instead of coy phrases that left a great deal to the imagination, Lady Constance described every intimate detail of her amorous encounters.

That alone would have sufficed to make the stories scandalous. What made them the most sought after publication in London, though, were the gentlemen Constance took to her boudoir. Statesmen, officers, men of science and men of letters, they all bore striking resemblances to actual gentlemen. If one took Lady Constance's word for it, she consorted with the crème de la crème of English society, right under its nose. Part of society was appalled at such indiscretion; the gentlemen themselves protested their innocence of such carnal activities and offered rewards for the author's identity; and everyone else seethed with delight at the challenge of unmasking each of Constance's lovers.

Joan even knew her own mother read them, from overheard snippets of conversation with other matrons. That hardly meant she would excuse her daughter reading them, of course; if anything, knowing what was in *50 Ways to Sin* only assured Lady Bennet how thoroughly inappropriate it really was. Which, naturally, only intensified Joan's desire to read it, in spite of all obstacles. It was published in a mysterious, almost covert way, with irregular distribution. One had to know which booksellers sold it, and then one had to approach at the right time. New issues appeared without warning, and were sold within hours. This was the first issue Joan had been able to locate on her own. Previously Penelope had stolen her mother's copies and shared them with her and Abigail. All three girls were avid followers of the series.

But somehow tonight . . . Joan flipped open the cover with one finger, though she kept seeing palm fronds instead of words. Tonight she had been kissed by a true rake, and reading about fictional kisses and embraces paled in comparison to the real thing.

She wondered if Lord Burke had read any of it. She wondered if he even knew what it was. It seemed unlikely that he would have resisted making some comment about it, after the way he'd teased her in the bookshop about buying prurient poetry. But then, she never would have thought he'd buy it for her, even if his only goal was to torment her.

She pressed one hand to her temple, trying to force Lord Boor physically from her mind. Of course he hadn't read it; why would he need to, when his own life was probably ten times more debauched than anything in these pages? Assuming one could possibly be more debauched. Some issues made her blush scarlet and lie awake wondering if the acts described were even plausible. Was there a man alive who could bring a woman to such heights of ecstasy that she almost fainted? It made for a thrilling story, so thrilling that it seemed incredible. But tonight, for the first time, she began to think maybe it was possible—wildly exaggerated, most likely, but slightly, remotely, possible.

With renewed interest she smoothed open the front page. The previous issue had featured a taut scene at the opera, where Constance's lover had stolen into her box and knelt on the floor behind her chair to pleasure her. They had almost been discovered when Constance's sighs reached a pinnacle at the exact moment the music suddenly stopped. The description of the scene proved the author had been there, and everyone in London was sure they had had the box next to hers. The issue had ended with Constance's vow of greater propriety, which no one believed—or wished to believe. Joan plumped up her pillow and settled in to read how wickedly that vow would be broken.

It was exceptionally shocking. Lord Everard, described as a large beast of a man, let Constance know he had overheard her passions at the opera. It seemed to have made her attractive to him; their assignation was fixed for that very night. Joan's eyes grew wide as she read the method of their pleasure: Lord Everard spanked Constance! And then he begged her to whip him with a crop as he made love to her. By the time she reached the end of the story, Joan's mouth was hanging open. She immediately flipped back to the beginning and read it again before falling back into her bed, self-consciously wriggling deeper into her pillows.

Thanks to some books of poetry she had managed to filch from her brother, Joan knew far more than most young ladies about the ways men and women coupled. It had all been wasted knowledge, of course, for a spinster, but she hadn't given up hope yet. Perhaps someday there would be a man who found her attractive enough that he would want to marry her, and then she would be free to explore all these sensual delights—and if the acts were this stirring when she read about them, how much more so would they be when experienced in the flesh?

She ran her finger down her throat as she imagined what it would be like to be the object of such desire. To know that somewhere, a man existed who admired her, who wanted her so desperately he would risk scandal to be intimate with her, to hold her in his arms and make passionate love to her until she expired from the joy of it. She spent several minutes savoring the concept, although the mystery lover in her mind somehow began to look like Lord Burke. Even when she deliberately tried to alter her mental image of a suitor entreating her, picturing him with fair hair and a slender build, his eyes seemed to gleam at her with as much deviltry as Lord Burke's always did.

Irritably she flipped over onto her stomach, paging through *50 Ways to Sin* to re-read the key scene. This time she lingered over every word, reading again how Sir Everard brought Constance to her climax. Constance confessed that though his blows stung, they also excited her, amplifying her pleasure almost to the point of senselessness. There was obviously more to lovemaking than Joan had even guessed. Again the rogue thought crossed her mind that a rake as wicked as Tristan Burke would surely know each and every way of making a woman delirious with pleasure . . .

From the hall downstairs the clock chimed the hour of two in the morning. In the quiet house, the sudden sound gave her a violent start. The only thing worse than getting caught before she read *50 Ways to Sin* would be getting caught the morning after, when Polly came in to make the bed. Reluctantly she got out of bed and went to her writing desk, where she secreted the pamphlet between the pages of a book of household management stratagems. Her mother had given her the book, but thankfully didn't quiz her on the advice within; the book's main value in Joan's eyes was as a place for hiding illicit items like *50 Ways to Sin*.

She settled back into her bed, trying to banish the wicked images from her mind. Overall it had been a successful night. She had punched Lord Burke in the face, obtained the elusive copy of *50 Ways to Sin*, and finally been kissed by a real rake. And best of all, she hadn't been caught doing any of it. If there was anything more satisfying than being naughty, it had to be being naughty without consequence.

After a long while, Joan went to sleep with a smile on her face.

Her reprieve ended at breakfast the next day.

"Good morning, dear," said her mother, looking more like herself this morning, when Joan reached the breakfast room.

"Good morning!" She went to kiss her mother's cheek. "You appear greatly revived."

Lady Bennet waved one hand. "Yes, your father had the physician here for an hour. I just overtaxed myself."

"And you won't do it again," put in Papa from the other end of the table.

"I'm fine, George."

"You won't do it again," he repeated, turning a page of his newspaper. "Out of compassion for my nerves, if nothing else."

It looked very much like his wife wanted to roll her eyes. Joan leapt to her mother's defense. "She looks very well this morning, Papa. Anyone could become overtired at a ball. It was very hot in that room last night."

Her father gave her a glance. "Overruled, am I? Then I charge you, miss, with seeing that your mother drinks that entire dose of tonic." He nodded at a small glass at Lady Bennet's elbow, which held a dark plum-colored liquid. "I shall take myself off and try to recover from the great anxiety I experienced last night." He rose and gave a brief bow. "Your servant, ladies."

"Good-bye, Papa," said Joan sweetly. "Good luck bidding on horses at Tattersall's."

"Minx," he said with a wink, and left the room.

"Are you truly well, Mother?" Joan turned back to her mother when her father was gone. Lady Bennet did look much improved, but up close Joan could see how pale she was.

"Well enough." Lady Bennet's stern look was ruined by the brief fit of coughing that took her. Wordlessly Joan nudged the dose of tonic forward. "Oh, very well," murmured her mother. She drank it with a grimace. "There; you can report to your father that I drank the horrid concoction. And now you may tell me how you came to dance with Lord Burke last night."

As an ambush, it was masterfully done. Joan had already begun to smile in agreement with the suggestion of reporting to Papa, and thus was caught completely off guard by the next words. Instead of her poised and dismissive prepared answer, she blurted out something almost guilty. "How did you know about that?"

"A note from Lady Deveres, delivered first thing this morning."

Joan picked up her spoon and poked at her poached egg. Lady Deveres was known for the quality of her gossip; if she relayed a story, it was almost certainly true, no matter how shocking. Before today, Joan had thought that a good thing, but now she wasn't so sure. "Oh. Well, I did dance with him, but only because I feared he would cause a scene otherwise."

Lady Bennet tapped her fingers on the table. "No doubt. But he's utterly unacceptable, far too wild and unmannered."

"Like Douglas," Joan dared to add. "I expect Douglas wagered him some shocking amount of money that he wouldn't dance with me, and he did it just to spite Douglas."

"Your brother knows better than to wager with the likes of Burke. He would be way out of his depth," Lady Bennet said. "And Douglas would never involve your name in wagers."

Douglas would risk anything for a wager that appealed to him, even though Mother was entirely correct that he would be in over his head with Lord Burke. Douglas was allotted a comfortable bachelor's allowance by their father, but Lord Burke was reputed to have over twenty thousand pounds a year. He could buy and sell Douglas several times over, and had probably done so more than once. She left off mutilating her egg and poured herself more tea. "I can't think of any other reason Lord Burke would ask me to dance, and Douglas gave me such a glare whilst dancing, I felt sure I had done him a harm somehow by saying yes. And you have to admit, Douglas has got himself into more than one scrape at Lord Burke's instigation."

Her mother's lips thinned. "I shall speak to him about it."

"I think you should," Joan said somberly. "Lord Burke is staying in his house, you know. Who knows what mischief he might encourage Douglas to get up to?"

Her mother frowned. Joan decided she had said enough, and reached for another muffin.

A footman came in with a note on his tray. "Just delivered, my lady," he said, presenting it to Mother.

Mother read the direction on the front before holding it out. "It's for you."

She tore it open. "It's from Penelope Weston. She's invited me to walk with her the day after tomorrow in the park." It was a mild surprise Penelope could wait that long; she and Abigail must be desperate to know what had happened last night. Joan had half expected Penelope to break down the door at the first light of dawn.

For a moment her mother's eyes closed. The Westons weren't quite the society she preferred her only daughter to keep. Mr. Weston was an attorney's son who had made a fortune in the canals, which wasn't as bad as making it from trade but also wasn't terribly refined. Still, a fortune was a fortune, and Mr. Weston had settled large dowries on both his daughters in the hopes of seeing them move up in the world. As a result, they were invited to all but the most elegant events; the hostesses of London hardly wanted to deprive their younger sons of any opportunity to catch an heiress.

And fortune or no, Joan had found kindred spirits in Abigail and Penelope. No matter how much Lady Bennet might wish they had better connections, she did acknowledge that Mrs. Weston was a woman of taste and sense, and her daughters were formed in the same mold. "I have no objection," she said. "Joan . . . did Lord Burke tell you he was acting on a wager last night?"

She paused, half risen from her seat. "No," she said carefully. "I am only supposing . . . I don't think he truly wanted to dance with me. He certainly gave no appearance of pleasure." She firmly blocked all memory of the last few minutes of their encounter from her mind. "He argued with me and then walked off without a word of farewell when the dance was done."

Lady Bennet eyed her closely. Joan kept her face innocently blank. "It seems odd," said her mother at last, suspiciously. "I hardly think you're the sort of lady to interest a man such as he." She hid another cough behind her handkerchief, and waved away Joan's instinctive move toward the teapot. "Very well, you may go. But Joan dear, in the future, you must refuse, if he should ever ask you again. I don't trust him."

She let out her breath in relief and smiled. Never mind that her own mother didn't think she was attractive to men—at least not to devilishly handsome men. She was going to escape serious repercussions, and that's what mattered. "Of course I would refuse, Mother. Although I find it highly unlikely Lord Burke will ever seek me out again."

Chapter 8

Tristan got up early the morning after the ball and went to the boxing saloon. He hadn't been there in a while, but this time he stripped to the waist and spent almost three hours in the ring, taking on anyone who wanted to hit and get hit. He would have stayed there, too, reveling in the burn of his muscles and the thrill of each landed blow, but Bennet appeared and just stood beside the ring, glaring at him.

That was precisely what Tristan had hoped to avoid by leaving the house so early. After he'd walked away from Miss Bennet the previous night, leaving her flushed and flustered behind Lady Malcolm's potted palms, he'd just kept walking: out of the ballroom, out of the Malcolm house, all the way across town into the narrow lanes behind Covent Garden where a man could lose himself in gin houses and gaming hells. Because he'd needed to be lost. Good Lord above, he'd gone and kissed the Fury—and his mouth still hungered for the taste of hers. Not even a river of spirits could quench it.

This was a serious error, and not one he was prepared to repeat. Nor was he anxious to face the inevitable questions from her brother. What the hell could he say, anyway? It would have almost been preferable to have let Jessica Elliot find him, no matter how peevish she'd sounded when she almost discovered him behind the potted plants with Miss Bennet. And he'd thought staying hidden would be the wise choice—which proved his instincts worthless, frankly.

He ignored Bennet while he finished his bout, but Bennet stalked around the ring when he ducked out and headed for the tub of water in the corner. Tristan leaned over it and poured a few ladles of water over his head and chest. A servant held out a length of towel, and he draped it over his dripping hair. "What?" he said once his face was safely hidden.

"I was about to ask you the same question," snapped Bennet. "What the devil were you thinking to dance with my sister?"

Still toweling his hair, Tristan shrugged. "I felt sorry for her. She didn't dance a single dance."

"That's hardly your fault! I daresay she doesn't like to dance anyway, being taller than most of the men in the room."

Bennet didn't know his sister well, if he thought the woman didn't like to dance. There had been a kind of excitement in her face, a delight that was both wistful and determined, as if she meant to enjoy every moment of the dance no matter who her partner was. That expression had kept him awake far too long last night, and in fact was partly behind his quest for punishment today. She wanted to dance—longed to dance, even—and he hadn't been a very charming partner. "It's not her fault she's tall. She didn't have to accept when I asked her."

"But why the devil would you ask her at all?" Bennet demanded. "You were the one who said she was trouble and ought to be avoided; now my mother wants to tear a strip off my hide for exposing her to you! She accused me of *wagering* you into dancing with Joan—horrid thought, risking money on anything involving my sister!" He grimaced. "She'd do whatever it took to make me lose, I've no doubt."

Tristan tossed aside the towel. "Are you here to defend your sister's honor, or to mock me for dancing with such a harpy? You're not making sense, Bennet."

His friend followed him into the other room. "Both, unfortunately. Mother came to my door herself this morning to give full vent to her spleen when she learned you danced with Joan—and a waltz, no less."

"Everyone waltzes. In fact, I thought I saw you with a fetching blonde in your arms during that same waltz."

Bennet flushed. "Well—yes—Mother insisted I lead out Miss Drummond again."

Tristan uncorked a jug of cool water and took a long drink. He was still avoiding facing Bennet, which was cowardly but damned if he felt like changing. "Was I not supposed to dance, while you were swanning about the room yourself? You made me go to the blasted ball."

"Not to dance with Joan," growled Bennet.

"Blast it, Burke—" He stopped, and ran his hands through his hair. "You know my mother never warmed to you," he went on more calmly.

"Not because of anything *I've* done," Tristan said pointedly, finally spearing a hard look at the other man. "You know damned well she blames me for all your vices, without pausing to wonder how you manage to carry on at them even in my absence."

Bennet flushed darker red. "Fair enough. But there's no arguing with her now; she's fixed her mind against you. So for both our sakes, leave Joan be." He gave a rueful grin. "It shouldn't be that hard. You said yourself she's trouble. I'm doing you a favor, really—should you ever encounter her, you have my permission to run the other way."

Tristan just grunted and snapped his fingers at the boy to fetch his clothes. Trouble, yes; but even more dangerous than Bennet suspected. Because Tristan didn't want to run the other way when he saw Miss Bennet, as vexing as she was. He wanted to best her, to leave her speechless; he wanted to hear her confess that she was wrong and he was right, about anything at all. And most worrisome of all, he wanted to kiss her senseless when she did so. Maybe even before. He must be cracked in the head.

"So are felicitations in order?" he asked, trying to change the subject so Bennet wouldn't keep talking about her. "Do I need to remove myself to a hotel so your bride can redecorate?"

His friend scowled. "Damn it, Burke, I'm not betrothed—"

"Two dances with the same woman? It won't be long."

"It was to appease my mother," growled Bennet.

The servant had come back with his clothing. Tristan took his shirt and pulled it over his head. "I vaguely remember your mother. She wasn't the most dreadful woman. Why, pray tell, does she inspire such terror in her children's hearts that they cannot twitch without fearing her retribution?"

"It's not terror," Bennet exclaimed. "I just— just— It's just not wise to rouse her temper, that's all. It's more peaceful." Then he frowned. "Did Joan complain of her as well?"

The servant held out the cravat, neatly pressed again. "Wasn't your sister sneaking out after she came to your home the other day? I gathered it was in defiance of your mother's wishes, yet all she did was stroll up Bond Street. And you can't refuse so much as a request that you attend a certain ball." He began knotting the cravat, keeping his eyes on the looking glass the servant held up. "I suppose one might understand an unmarried lady being kept close by her mother," he added. "But you're a grown man. Buck up, old chap. Appeasement leads to subjugation."

Bennet snorted. "As if you'd know! Free as a bird, your entire life."

Tristan pulled the loose end of the cravat through the knot and stabbed a pin through it. "Yes, free from all that parental oversight that chafes you so." Also free from any sort of loving home, but he forbore to mention it. His parents had been dead so long, he couldn't even remember them. For all he knew, his mother might have been worse than Bennet's.

"It certainly never appeared that you minded!" Bennet clapped him on the back, apparently restored to good humor. "Just trust me—it's easier to appease Mother. I danced with the girl, everyone was satisfied, and now I'm free again."

"Did you like the girl?"

Bennet blinked. "What?"

"Did you like the girl?" Tristan repeated, pulling on his jacket. "If you're going to waltz with a girl, you might as well enjoy it."

The other man stared at him, then burst out laughing. "Bloody hell! You don't have to like a girl to like waltzing with her. Miss Drummond is nothing like the females I prefer—you know that. I might as well ask you if you enjoyed dancing with my sister!"

He should have laughed. He should have agreed wholeheartedly, and let the whole question drop. Instead Tristan pictured the curve of her lips when the music began, and felt the sway of her body in his arm. Somehow he couldn't poke fun at Miss Bennet, not even to her brother. "As a matter of fact, I did," he said, and walked away before Bennet could recover from the shock.

Chapter 9

$\sim\!\infty\!\sim$

The morning Joan had agreed to walk with the Weston sisters in the park, she lay abed late, trying to construct a tale that would satisfy Abigail and Penelope without revealing too much. It was important to stick fairly near the truth, she had learned, in order to avoid tripping herself up later. Obviously she would have to tell them about the kiss. Not only was it monumental news, it was delicious enough—and the man who gave it was infuriating enough—to require extensive analysis. Should things grow uncomfortable, though, she must have a diversion at hand. With some regret, she decided *50 Ways to Sin* must be sacrificed.

But when she finally went downstairs, she forgot all about that. Servants were hurrying past her, and Smythe, the butler, looked even more somber than usual. She paused in the hall and wondered what was going on. To her astonishment, her father came down the stairs dressed for travel and escorting Dr. Samuels, the physician who had been here just the other morning to see Mother.

"What's wrong, Papa?" she asked as soon as the physician had left.

"I'm taking Mother to Cornwall," he said. "For her health."

Joan gaped at him. "Oh—Oh dear! But then, she's not well, is she?" Mother had coughed a great deal yesterday, and gone to bed earlier than usual, but no one had suggested it was this serious.

"No," he said grimly, "she isn't. She grew worse overnight and I got Samuels up before dawn."

"What did he say she's got?"

"Something is inflaming her lungs, and London air is making her sicker." Joan had never seen her father look so grave. "Janet is finishing the packing right now; we leave as soon as she's ready."

"Poor Mother," she cried. "Papa, she's going to recover, isn't she?"

"I trust so." His smile was real, though strained. "I intend to do everything possible to see that she does."

"Of course." For a few frightening moments Joan considered her mother dying. She squeezed her father's hand. "You should have woken me— I'd no idea! I'll have Polly pack my things at once. It won't take but half an hour—"

"No," he said at once. "You're not coming— you *may* not come," he added as she opened her mouth to protest. "The physician isn't sure what's made her ill, and even if you wished to come to Cornwall, neither your mother nor I will allow it. Neither of us wants you to become ill with the same disease."

"But you're going," she protested. "Papa, I can help—"

"I know you would, my darling girl." He put his arm around her. "But you aren't coming, and that is all there is to it."

"All right." Joan was silent for a moment, trying to take it in. "Am I to stay with the Westons?"

"No." Papa hesitated. "I've no idea how long we may be away from town, and don't like to impose on Mrs. Weston so abruptly. I've asked Aunt Evangeline to come stay with you."

"Aunt Evangeline!" Her mouth dropped open again. Evangeline, Countess of Courtenay, was her father's sister, twice widowed and nearing fifty. Any presumption that her age and status might make her sober and respectable, however, was sadly mistaken. Evangeline was high-spirited, unconventional, and undaunted by anything like social censure or public disapproval. In Joan's first Season, Evangeline had caused a minor scandal by carrying on with the much-younger Sir Richard Campion, the noted explorer. They had eventually left London for Chelsea, where Sir Richard managed to procure an estate that bordered Evangeline's, which caused Lady Bennet to strike them both from her guest lists. Joan had even heard her mother call Evangeline fast, which was one of the worst things Mother called any lady. Aunt Evangeline called herself the black sheep of the Bennets, and seemed to revel in it.

And now Aunt Evangeline was coming to chaperone her? "Er . . ." She cleared her throat. "That will be lovely, I'm sure. How is Aunt Evangeline?"

"In good form," said her father, with a warning look. "Don't encourage her, Joan."

She blushed a little in spite of herself. "I'm sure I don't know what you mean."

Papa snorted. "You know very well what I mean. If Evangeline offers you brandy, you must refuse."

"Yes, Papa."

"And the same applies to whiskey, port, and any other spirit stronger than a glass of wine, my sly girl. Remember your mother."

She pursed her lips. "Surely Mother wouldn't want me to be rude to Aunt Evangeline."

"No, she will expect you to decline gracefully and charmingly, as you do so well." His mouth twitched as though he was trying not to smile. "It will make Mother worry if you don't give your promise on this, and I won't have her worried."

"No, of course not." Joan grew sober again. "How long do you expect to be gone?"

"Two months, perhaps three."

That was a long time—far longer than she had been apart from both her parents in years, in fact. It hit her hard how worried her father must be for Mother's health, for him to leave London on less than a day's notice for several weeks. "You will write to us, won't you? To let me and Douglas know how Mother is?"

"Douglas won't be in London," said her father, a new line of worry appearing in his forehead. "I had planned to go to Ashwood House next month, to see to the work there. Someone needs to oversee the rebuilding after the floods. Since I can't go, I am sending Douglas."

"Douglas?" Joan goggled at him, shocked all over again. "You're sending Douglas to build something?" First Evangeline, now this. It was as if the world had toppled onto its side, upending years of expectations.

"He doesn't have to build anything. He merely has to supervise the work and keep me apprised of it." Papa paused. "It will be rather good for him. He's only got up to trouble in town this year."

"I know, but . . . goodness." Joan didn't feel even the slightest tremor of regret for falsely impugning her brother over her waltz with Lord Burke. Not only did he deserve it, she was certain he'd done much, much worse that her parents had never learned about. "How did he take the news?"

"Well enough." The butler came up and murmured a word to Papa, who nodded and turned to Joan again. "You'll get on with Evangeline, won't you? I trust you, you know."

"More than you trust her."

"I trust her, too," he said without blinking an eye. "It's the combination that worries me."

A flutter of motion on the stairs caught her eye before Joan could reply. Janet was coming down the stairs, buttoning her traveling coat with one hand and her other arm filled with cushions and throw rugs. Behind her, moving far more slowly and gingerly, came two footmen supporting Lady Bennet between them. Far from protesting, Mother looked pale and tired, and she winced with each step. She looked ill, truly ill, and fear squeezed Joan's heart. "I'll be good, Papa," she promised in a rush. "I'll mind Aunt Evangeline and make Mother proud of me."

"I knew you would." He flashed her a quick smile before striding across the hall and taking the stairs two at a time to his wife's side. Lady Bennet gave him a weak but grateful smile as he waved aside one of the footmen and put his own arm around her.

Joan felt tears prickle the back of her eyes as her father gently lifted her mother into his arms at the foot of the stairs, handling her as if she were made of glass. All her life, Mother had been the strong one, with a will of iron and an indomitable spirit. Papa was the easygoing parent, able to wink at Joan's minor sins and willing to slip her a biscuit or treat her to a new bonnet when she'd been scolded and reprimanded by her mother. She'd never thought her father was weak—not physically, not mentally—but it was shocking to see him overrule Mother's protest that she could walk without blinking an eye, dictating every last detail to the servants, walking away from all his duties and responsibilities without hesitation.

She followed him out to the waiting carriage, and hurried to help Janet arrange the cushions under her mother's feet and at her back. Twice Lady Bennet was taken with a fit of coughing, and Joan saw the blood-spotted handkerchief before Janet whisked it away and tucked a fresh one into her mistress's hand. She sent a worried glance at her father, whose grim face indicated he'd seen the blood as well. She ducked her head and smoothed the throw rug over her mother's feet. Mother looked as if she'd shrunk, and her fingers were almost as white as the handkerchief she clutched. When Joan looked up, Mother gave her a weak smile.

"Thank you, dear," she said. Her voice was soft and raspy.

Gently Joan took her hand. "Get well again, Mother. I've already told Papa he must write to me every week and tell me how you are."

Lady Bennet smiled. "I shall do my best. And you—" She glanced at Janet. "Your father spoke to you?"

She nodded. "I gave him my promise," she said quietly. "You're not to worry about me."

Her mother's fingers tightened on hers. "I won't." Joan leaned into the carriage and kissed her mother's cheek in farewell, then stepped down.

Papa was drawing on his gloves; the butler stood behind him with his hat. "I expect it will take several days for the journey," he said. "I won't jostle her more than necessary."

"No, no, of course not." Joan blinked several times, overwhelmed by the upheaval. "When should I expect Aunt Evangeline?"

His mouth thinned and he glanced down the street. "At any moment. I sent her word this morning we were leaving as soon as possible. I'm sure she'll be here within an hour." He paused. "If she doesn't arrive today, you must go to Doncaster House."

The Countess of Doncaster was her mother's sister. Joan would have happily gone to stay at Doncaster House if her cousin Mariah were in residence, but she was not. In fact, she suspected that only the earl was in residence now; Aunt Cassandra had gone to tend Mariah for the birth of her child. Joan wasn't precisely frightened of the

Earl of Doncaster, but she was mightily intimidated by him.

"Er . . . perhaps it would be best if I went to the Westons," she said, adding quickly, "just until Aunt Evangeline arrives, of course."

From within the carriage came the sound of Mother coughing again. A spasm of worry flickered over Papa's face. "Yes, the Westons, if you like," he said distractedly. "Very good. We must be going now."

Joan gave a vigorous nod. Yes, let them be off, carrying Mother to healthier air. The sound of that coughing frightened her near out of her wits. "Good-bye, Papa. Take care of her."

"The very best care I can." He pressed a quick kiss on her forehead. "Write to us. It will keep up Mother's spirits to hear of you."

"I will, Papa, every week."

He stepped into the carriage and the footman closed the door behind him. Mother herself leaned forward to raise her hand in farewell. Joan forced a bright smile and waved back, remaining on the pavement until the traveling coach had vanished around the end of the street.

Slowly she turned and went back into the house. It seemed so large and empty suddenly, as if losing Papa's booming laugh and Mother's energy had cast a funereal pall over the whole house. She shivered and tucked her shawl more closely around her. Perhaps she should go to the Westons until Aunt Evangeline arrived; she wasn't sure she wanted to stay in this empty, echoing house.

But then, she really wasn't in the mood for gossip and laughing, either. The Weston house was always filled with both. Abigail would understand and leave her in peace, but Penelope couldn't hold her tongue to save her life. Normally Joan enjoyed every minute she spent with the Weston girls, but . . . not today.

"Shall I send for some tea, Miss Bennet?" asked the butler quietly.

She rubbed her elbows and nodded. "Thank you, Smythe."

He bowed and left her standing in the hall alone. Joan couldn't recall the last time she had been completely alone in the house. She wandered into the morning room, feeling utterly adrift. What would she do, without Mother to supervise her? Would Evangeline allow her to go out, or had Papa given her strict instructions? What would Aunt Evangeline be like?

In spite of her worries, her spirits began to lift as she thought about her renegade aunt. She hadn't seen Evangeline since Mother refused to have her in the house, but she'd heard such rumors . . . not that one could trust them, of course. Joan could believe Evangeline indulged in spirits and wore more daring gowns than Mother thought proper. She'd also seen Sir Richard Campion from across the Mall once and had no trouble believing Evangeline would throw over society's approval for such a man. But surely the rest was exaggeration. Surely a countess wouldn't attend boxing matches and wager on them. Surely a lady wouldn't ride her estate in buckskin breeches and help mend fences. And of course the stories about Evangeline driving a stage on a dare must be pure fabrication.

As if summoned by those thoughts, a carriage

rattled up the street and stopped in front of the still open door. Joan went out to welcome her infamous aunt with no small amount of curiosity.

Evangeline, Lady Courtenay, stepped down from her open barouche and swept Joan into her arms. "You dear girl," she exclaimed. "Are your parents already away? I came as soon as I got your father's note but there was a problem with the carriage wheel. Are you well?" She drew back to inspect Joan's face critically. "No tears—a good sign. You're as sturdy as the rest of the Bennets, I see."

"Oh! Well . . ." Joan gazed at her aunt in wonder. "I didn't wish to upset Mother."

Lady Courtenay smiled, sliding her arm into Joan's. "Good girl! Shall we go inside? I've come with only a valise of essentials; my maid should arrive later with my trunks. I hope you've not been alone long?"

"No, not long at all," Joan replied as they went into the house. In the hall her aunt removed her bonnet and long white pelisse. Joan's interest fixed on her aunt's dress. It wasn't the fashion of the moment, not by a long shot—and yet it was striking. The bodice was shaped to her aunt's figure in clean, simple lines, with hardly a garnishment or embellishment. The neckline swooped low, though not too low, displaying a bosom as rounded as Joan's own. The skirt seemed to cling to her hips before flaring out just above the floor. Tiny gold charms sparkled around the bell-like sleeves, like the illustrations Joan had seen of a Turkish pasha's wife. And most shocking of all was the fabric: a fine glazed cotton of brightest orange, sewn with yellow thread. She had never seen the like.

"Oh my," Lady Courtenay murmured, looking around the hall. "It's been a long time since I was here." For a moment her expression grew pensive. "Is your brother Douglas well? I remember him sliding down those stairs atop an atlas he'd carried down from the schoolroom. He was so proud of himself, and it nearly killed your mother."

Joan choked on a laugh. "He's well. Papa's sent him to Norfolk to see to Ashwood House. There was a flood and it needs to be repaired, and . . . well, somehow Papa decided Douglas ought to go."

Another smile, fainter this time, lit her aunt's face. "Ah, yes. I remember my father doing something quite similar to my brother. Well, I hope it serves Douglas as well as it served your father."

"What do you mean, Aunt Courtenay?"

Lady Courtenay winked at her. "That's when he met your mother. But enough reminiscing. Come, tell me how you are. I think we're going to get on famously, don't you? You must call me Evangeline—'Aunt Courtenay' sounds like a dotty old woman, and not in a charming way. I hope you don't mind, I simply must visit my dressmaker. I didn't come to London at all last year and I can't gallivant about town in frocks two years old."

Joan started, shaking off the diverting thought of her parents' first meeting. "Oh, no, I have no objection at all!" she exclaimed. "But . . ." She cast a longing eye over Evangeline's dress again. "Which dressmaker do you patronize? I don't recognize her work at all."

"Shh," whispered Evangeline, a teasing smile lighting her eyes. "You mustn't tell your mother. My dressmaker isn't a woman at all! He's Italian, and he has such an eye for color and texture. He makes my gowns to suit me, not the latest fashions. Do you like this one?" She gestured at her dress.

It was magnificent—and everything Joan knew her mother would never let her wear, even though she suddenly wanted a gown like that more than anything. She swallowed. "Yes. Very much."

"Then we shall have Federico make a gown for you, too." She glanced down and seemed to see Joan's dress for the first time. She paused, and her eyes widened. Joan could guess why. It was a yellow morning dress bristling with knots of blue ribbon at the flounce and bodice. It looked girlish and fussy next to the exotic starkness of Evangeline's frock, even though it had been carefully copied from the latest issue of *La Belle Assemblée*. "Or—or perhaps you have your own style," Evangeline said politely.

Joan looked down at the dress. It was pale and pretty and perfectly suitable for a petite young lady of sixteen. For a tall, buxom woman of four and twenty . . . "My mother chose it," she admitted. "It's very fashionable."

"And it is lovely," said Evangeline quickly. "Only . . . I think perhaps pale yellow isn't your best color . . ."

"What about gold?" The question popped out of her mouth without thought. Joan almost cringed when she heard herself ask it.

"Gold would be lovely on you," cried Evangeline. "Yes, indeed, with your hair and eyes, it would be very flattering. I'm sure Federico can create something—perhaps a purple underskirt, with a gold crepe overdress and bodice. And— he will never suggest this, but I think it quite smashing—jet beads! They look so striking, and no one else is wearing them."

Joan blinked at the thought: wanting to wear something no one else wore? Was that not the antithesis of fashion? But then again . . . She looked at Evangeline's radiant gown. It would take a bold soul to wear that color, even though the cut was very flattering. "Or perhaps blue," she said hesitantly. "I quite like blue as well."

"Smashing!" Evangeline beamed at her. "We'll order one as soon as we can. Smythe!" The butler had come up and waited quietly. Now a rare smile crossed his austere face as Evangeline turned to him with a happy cry. "How good to see you again, Smythe."

"Welcome back, my lady," he said with a bow.

"I remember Smythe when he was a new footman," Evangeline said to Joan. "He once saved me from a terrible thrashing by letting me in through the scullery window. I'd sneaked out to see a footrace between two footmen. It was all the way across the Thames near Vauxhall, and it took an age to get home. I had been forbidden to go but— oh my, it was absolutely legendary! Goodness, my father nearly tore his hair out, trying to learn how I'd got back in the house. I'm so glad to see you're still here," she told the butler warmly.

"As am I, my lady. I've laid the tea in the drawing room, Miss Bennet."

"Lord, I could use a cup of tea. I rushed about in a panic as soon as your father's note arrived." Evangeline drew Joan's arm through hers again. "You must tell me all the things you enjoy in town."

Joan could only give the butler a dazed nod of thanks and allow herself to be pulled into the drawing room. The world had been turned completely on its head. Douglas, the most irresponsible scoundrel in Britain, was sent to supervise the rebuilding of Papa's hunting estate. Evangeline, who gave every appearance of being as wild as Lady Bennet feared, was sent to chaperone Joan. Smythe, who had been as formal and proper as a bishop as far back as Joan could remember, had once helped Evangeline slide through a scullery window to avoid disgrace.

She had a strong premonition that the next several weeks would be even stranger than she could imagine.

Chapter 10

"**B**urke! There you are. I have a favor to ask of you."

Tristan paused warily at the top of the stairs. He'd hardly seen Bennet since the confrontation in the boxing saloon, by his own design. It hadn't been terribly hard to be out of the house most of the time, although avoiding Bennet's favorite haunts in the evenings was more difficult. He braced himself to be turned out into the street—not a terrible tragedy, to be sure, but he would hate to lose a friend over a bloody waltz. He hadn't enjoyed the dance *that* much.

What came after the waltz . . . was better off not being contemplated.

He followed his host, who had already gone back into his dressing room. "What is it?" he asked from the doorway.

Bennet plowed his hands through his hair, though it was already standing on end. "Where are my bloody boots? Not the ones from Hoby, the country ones." He stooped to peer under the bed. "Murdoch!" he bellowed. "Where are my boots?"

Tristan stepped aside as a harassed Murdoch brushed past him, a boot in each hand. "Here, sir. I was just cleaning them." Indeed one boot had been brushed, while the other still had streaks and clumps of mud stuck to it. "Another few minutes—"

"Bugger the mud." Bennet grabbed the boots and tossed them into a trunk standing open behind him. The servant flinched as dried dirt scattered over the clothing already in the trunk, but Bennet paid it no heed. "And my greatcoat? And the oilskin?"

"Yes, sir." Murdoch ducked back out.

"Planning a journey?" Tristan finally asked, relaxing enough to lean one shoulder against the doorjamb. It didn't seem as though Bennet planned to draw his cork.

"Yes." Bennet tossed aside a crumpled shirt to pull open a desk drawer and start rifling through it. "I have to go to Norfolk."

Tristan raised an eyebrow. "At this time of year?"

"At once." Bennet swore and scooped the papers in the drawer out and dropped them en masse into the trunk on top of the boots. "No time to sort that out now—Murdoch, did you send for the travel chaise yet?" he shouted.

Tristan listened. "He has," he reported after hearing a muffled "Aye!" from belowstairs. "Why such haste?"

Bennet stopped again, swinging in a circle as though he couldn't decide which task to seize on next. He looked overwhelmed. "My father is sending me to Ashwood House. There was a flood a fortnight ago, and several buildings were damaged. I'm to oversee the repairs."

Tristan's other eyebrow went up. This would be the first he could ever recall of Bennet's father asking anything of him, and it didn't strike him as a good omen that merely packing for the journey seemed to have reduced Bennet to a state worthy of any fluttery female. "How inconvenient."

"No. No, it's not terribly convenient, but . . ." He inhaled a deep breath, as though summoning his nerve. "The truth is, my mother's taken very ill. My father is taking her to Cornwall for the sea air, to improve her lungs. He planned to monitor the rebuilding in Norfolk from London, and go there himself in a month when the Season ends, but now . . . Well, he's sending me instead and that's all there is to it." With a renewed burst of determination, Bennet scooped up his shaving things and dropped them into the trunk.

Ah. So that was it. Not so much trust as necessity drove Sir George. "My best wishes for your mother's recovery." Bennet flashed him a look of gratitude. "What was the favor you wanted?" Tristan added, feeling accommodating. This was possibly the best thing for him; after a few weeks in Norfolk, Bennet would have forgotten all about that dangerous waltz. And with any luck, Tristan's own house would be fully repaired before Bennet returned, obviating any further tension over living quarters. The more distance he had from anyone and everyone named Bennet, the better.

"Oh yes—dashed near forgot." Bennet swept his hair back from his forehead. "Would you look after Joan for me?"

Tristan froze. "I beg your pardon?"

"My parents left her behind in London; my father doesn't want to risk her catching my mother's illness. He's put her in the charge of our aunt, Lady Courtenay, who's a bit . . . suffice to say I ought to stay and keep an eye on them both, if it weren't for this trouble in Norfolk."

"What do you mean," asked Tristan, choosing each word carefully, "by 'look after' her?" His heart felt like a hammer, booming loud and slow against his breastbone. Look after the Fury? Risk his sanity by spending time with her? He'd just made a vow—at Bennet's instigation, damn him—to avoid her.

Bennet waved one hand. "Keep an ear out for any trouble she might get up to. See that she enjoys herself a bit. Dance with her a time or two if she's out—just to take her mind off things, you know. Most chaps run the other way, but I daresay she'd like a dance now and then. That shouldn't be too much to ask." He gave Tristan a suddenly sharp look. "I believe you said you enjoyed waltzing with her the other evening."

"I believe you told me in that same conversation that I wasn't to approach her again," Tristan shot back. "On your mother's orders, even. Now your revered parent is away from town and you set me to dancing attendance on your sister? Do I look that big a fool to you?"

Bennet's ears turned red. "Nothing foolish about it! You don't have to dance attendance on her, just . . . do as I might do for her."

Tristan's eyes narrowed. "And what the bloody blazes would you do for her, if you were in town?

Last time I saw the two of you in the same room, you were howling curses down upon her head."

"Yes, well." Bennet cleared his throat. "That was before. Things have changed. Of course I would keep watch over my sister in my father's absence. See that she goes out, and doesn't get up to trouble. Visit her for tea and listen to her chatter. That sort of thing."

"Bennet," said Tristan with perfect honesty, "that is the most idiotic idea you've ever had."

His friend grimaced. "But the thing is, there's no one else I can ask. Dunwood is an ass, Hookham is a drunkard, and Spence . . . I don't want Spence near my sister under any circumstances. You, on the other hand, already danced with her and didn't run mad from the experience. You're— you're inoculated against her, don't you see?"

Tristan squeezed his hands into fists even as his heart sped up—from apprehension, he told himself, and not from anticipation. "You've run mad if you think I want to spend the rest of the Season being scorched and flayed by her tongue."

"Try charming her." Bennet grinned suddenly. "She outmaneuvered you once on that score; surely you want to return the favor. I'll wager ten guineas you can tame that temper of hers inside a fortnight."

He scowled and made a very rude reply.

Bennet's smile turned cocky. "Twenty guineas!"

"Sod off," growled Tristan, wishing Bennet had merely wanted to go a few rounds in the boxing ring. This—*this* was much worse. Dance attendance on Miss Bennet? Waltz with her again? Subject himself to her tongue again? And all without kissing her again, because he had sworn that was never going to happen. No, indeed. Bennet must be the one cracked in the head, if he thought this was a decent or good idea. Bennet, of all people, knew how Tristan liked his women: widowed or married, adventurous and willing. Lady Bennet would have an apoplexy if she heard what her own son had proposed.

"Burke." Bennet quit laughing and grew sober. "Damn it, Tris. My father isn't here to look after her. I won't be here. Joan can be troublesome, but she's not vile, and in the end, she's my sister; I don't want her to come to any harm. There's no one I trust as much as I trust you. I'll be forever in your debt if you do this for me."

Tris. He closed his eyes at the childhood nickname. Bennet had been his friend for almost twenty years, through hardship and misadventure, never once abandoning him like the other mates who'd come and gone. It must surely be considered a mark of that friendship that Bennet didn't see this as setting a wolf to guard a sheep— not that Miss Bennet struck him as a defenseless lamb . . . more like a surly old ewe, unafraid of anything. But Tristan was very much afraid his instincts toward her tended toward the wolfish nonetheless.

"Very well." He drew another deep breath and opened his eyes. "I'm just to keep an eye out for her. If she orders me away, I will obey her wishes. Agreed?"

Bennet's face eased. "Agreed." He stuck out his hand. "Thank you."

Hoping he hadn't made an enormous mistake, Tristan clasped his hand. "Remember you begged me to do this."

"Of course I will." Bennet turned back to his packing. "I'll ask her not to be too sharp with you."

That wasn't what I meant, Tristan thought. He gave a nod, and took himself off before he fell into any more traps.

Chapter 11

⁓⸜◯◯⸝⁓

The next day Joan got a better idea of what life with Evangeline would be like.

Her aunt's trunks arrived, along with her maid, Solly. Solly turned out to be a tall, statuesque African woman. She was missing two fingers on her left hand and spoke with a melodic accent that seemed to make her words flow like honey. She smiled and laughed with Evangeline in a familiar way that would have sent Janet into fits.

But Joan was most dazzled by her aunt's wardrobe. Evangeline's dress upon arrival had been no exception: everything she owned was bright, daring, and unconventional. And she invited Joan to examine all of it, promising they would call upon her dressmaker that very day.

"Be sure to let me know if you see something you particularly like," Evangeline told her as Solly unpacked, laying out a veritable rainbow of finery. "Federico will decide what he wants to make for you—that's how he is, vexing man—but if he refuses to listen, Solly can alter any of my gowns to fit you. We're of a height."

That was true, although Joan was fairer than her aunt. She touched a luxuriant vine embroidered across the bodice of a deep red gown. Most of Evangeline's gowns were in colors and styles far too bold for an unmarried woman of Joan's age. That didn't stop her from wishing she could wear them, but if her mother heard she was wearing orange or scarlet around London . . . "How did you discover Mr. Salvatore, Aunt Evangeline? I've never heard of a man modiste before."

"He is Sir Richard's tailor. We met in passing, and a few days later he sent me a sketch of a gown. He hadn't much liked what I'd worn when we met, so he suggested a better design." Evangeline laughed. "I thought it highly amusing, so I ordered the gown—and oh my, it was so much more flattering! Sir Richard agreed, and I've patronized Federico ever since."

"Isn't it . . . immodest to discuss such things with a man?"

Her aunt made a face. "Immodest! He doesn't require you to stand in your shift. He's got a perfectly respectable and accomplished female assistant. And what is modest, anyway? Ten years ago girls your age wore sheer white dresses that would hardly be sufficient for a shift now, and more than one lady's modesty was violated by a strong breeze. And you must know gentlemen talk about ladies' garments. I daresay they think about them almost as much as ladies do."

You should wear gold, echoed Lord Burke's voice. *You look like a half-opened umbrella.* Joan flushed. "Yes, I suppose they do," she muttered. "That doesn't mean they know anything."

"Federico does." Evangeline rose. "Let me write to him now. And do ask Solly to show you anything you want to see."

Solly proved herself a willing accomplice. She shook out and displayed morning dresses and evening gowns, pelisses and shawls. There was a wonderful variety to Evangeline's clothing, quite unlike Joan's own wardrobe.

"These are just lovely," she said wistfully, stroking a walking dress of cream silk with narrow, dark blue stripes. It would have made a perfectly fashionable man's waistcoat, but was bold and unexpected as a dress.

"Lady Courtenay likes to look her best," said Solly fondly.

Joan sighed and handed over the walking dress. She also wanted to look her best. No, she wanted to look *lovely*, which might be, she feared, better than was possible. She caught sight of herself in the mirror and tried to see any potential. She was still tall, still plump, and her hair was still straight and brown, suitable only for binding up in braids or torturing into ringlets with a hot iron. But then again . . . Evangeline was almost as tall, and just as plump. So far she hadn't worn a single ringlet. And while her clothing obviously hadn't come from the latest pages of Ackermann's, it nonetheless made her look ravishing instead of umbrella-like. Perhaps there was hope.

Solly was putting away the hatboxes. "Do you wish to see, miss? You will like this one, I think." She opened one of the boxes.

Joan lifted it out. As bonnets went, it was on the plain side, and not as unconventional as she'd expected. She held it above her head, trying to get an idea of how it would look on her. The current mode in bonnets invariably made her look like a giantess.

"Try it," murmured Solly. "She will not mind."

Joan hesitated, then smiled broadly. "Just for a moment," she agreed, and rushed to sit at the dressing table. She put on the bonnet, and turned her head from side to side. The crown was softer, not as high as was fashionable; the brim was wider and not so peaked. The only plume on it curled around the crown, adding no height at all. And best of all, it didn't make her face look round. A pleased smile touched her lips. Yes, there was definitely hope.

There was a light tap at the door. "You've a caller, Miss Bennet," said Smythe.

Admiring herself in Evangeline's bonnet, Joan barely glanced at the butler. "Yes? Who is it?"

"Viscount Burke."

She nearly sent the hatpin into her scalp. "Who?"

"Lord Burke." He held out the silver tray to prove it with the plain calling card. Joan gazed at it in alarm. What the devil could he want?

"Shall I tell him you are not in?" inquired Smythe after a long moment.

"Ah . . ." She set the bonnet back in its box. "No, I'll see him."

She told herself it was just curiosity that drove her. It had been five days since The Kiss, after all. As much as she wanted to deny it, Joan had wondered, with a bit of nervous hope, if he might call on her. If perhaps he'd found the kiss just a little more than the means to silence her for a moment. If, by some rare chance, he had been as struck by it as she had been.

From his absolute absence, she had concluded he had not, the cursed libertine.

And yet, today he was here in her drawing room. In the corridor she took a quick look in a nearby mirror. Nothing on her face; her teeth were clean; and her hair lay flat, thankfully. Lifting her chin and hoping a cool composure would hide the sudden thumping of her heart, she went into the drawing room.

"Good day, Lord Burke." She made the barest curtsy.

He was standing on the other side of the room, staring out the window, and whipped around at her greeting. For a moment he seemed frozen, staring at her with an expression perilously close to a glare before bowing. "Miss Bennet." There was a long pause. "I want to offer my most sincere wishes for Lady Bennet's full recovery."

"Thank you." He'd come to say that? Joan waited, but he merely stood there looking at her, far too attractive for her peace of mind. "Have you brought a message from Douglas?" she asked at last.

His mouth tightened. "Of a sort. He didn't send you a note, then."

"No, why would he? I understood he was to leave for Norfolk—in fact, I thought he already had. I can't think what he would have needed to say to me before he left."

Lord Burke closed his eyes for a moment, as though reining in his temper.

"Is something wrong with Douglas?" she asked, perplexed beyond measure by this visit.

"I am here to offer my escort," he said shortly. "If you wish to go out."

Joan's jaw dropped. "Escort!"

"At your brother's behest," he added. "Bennet feared you'd sit at home alone in your parents' absence."

Douglas? *Douglas* had sent him to squire her about? He was only here as a favor to her brother?

Joan drew a furious breath. How dare Douglas send his reprobate friend to dog her heels around town? And how dare Lord Boor agree to it, after the way she had made clear her dislike of him and his manners? She would show them both, she would . . . she would . . . A fiendish thought hit her, and instead of lashing out at Lord Burke, she smiled. Sweetly. She would teach them both a lesson, and have a cracking good time doing it. "Did he? How very solicitous and thoughtful of him! And how very kind of you to devote so much time to my amusement."

He had obviously expected a different reply. His vivid green eyes seemed to stare right through her. "Yes, it was very benevolent of me, wasn't it?"

"And conveyed with such solicitude and enthusiasm!" She laid one hand on her bosom, still smiling brightly. "Your reputation for charm is well earned, sir."

He gave a little huff. "I should hope so. You had better keep it in mind."

Joan made herself giggle like one of the simpering girls who always seemed to snap up husbands in their first season. "How could I forget? After our last encounter, I mean."

"Oh?" He crossed his arms and looked interested. "What, particularly, about our last encounter struck you so deeply?"

"Let me see . . ." She tapped one finger against her lips, drawing out the moment. His gaze felt like a bright light shining on her. Joan knew it was very wrong of her, but she couldn't help but enjoy teasing him. She longed to pay him back for leaving her utterly nonplussed by a kiss. She longed to pay him back for walking away from her, instead of being stunned and breathless and caught, however wrongly, by the mad hope that he might kiss her again. If he could kiss a woman like that and then walk away without a care, he deserved to be tormented. She felt positively obliged to do so, on behalf of all females. "Perhaps it was the way you asked me to dance? No, that was rather gruffly done. Was it your apology for insulting me?" He made a sound in his throat that sounded contemptuous. "No, that also was poorly done," Joan went on, clicking her tongue in reproach. "It might have been the way you offered to return my own property."

"I paid for it."

"And if you'd had any cleverness at all, you would have had a servant deliver it," she replied.

His brilliant gaze drifted over her. "I found it much more satisfactory to return it in person."

For the flash of one intense moment, Joan felt again his fingers at her back, pulling loose the laces of her gown. Her cheeks warmed. "It showed poor planning. Anything that requires hiding behind potted trees usually does."

Too late she remembered what else had required hiding behind potted trees. Her face grew warmer as a faint but wicked smile crooked his mouth, proving that he, too, remembered it.

"Not *everything*," he murmured.

Joan tried to force it from her mind, truly she did, but still—the memory of his mouth on hers refused to be banished. She tried not to think how she had clung to him, how his arms had felt around her. She tried not to remember how her heart raced, how her breath grew short, and how her skin seemed to tighten at his touch—in short, how she had reacted just as Lady Constance felt with her lovers. "So," she said to quiet the instinctive tumult inside her body just at the memory of his kiss, "does that mean you plan to kiss me again?"

"No," he said before she even finished the question. Finally he looked away from her, releasing her from the almost-physical hold his eyes had exerted.

"Good," she said with all the cool poise she could muster. "I didn't much care for it."

For a moment he didn't move. A muscle twitched in his jaw. Slowly he turned and started toward her, one deliberate step at a time. Joan held her ground, sure she'd piqued him where it hurt. It was only fair. If he'd only kissed her to make her stop talking, and couldn't even be gentlemanly enough to let her think he enjoyed it a little, she had no qualms in disdaining his skill at it.

But the closer he came, the more she wished she

hadn't said it. She didn't dare retreat, but it took a great deal of will not to. Finally, barely a foot away from her, so close she could smell the faint scent of cologne he wore, he stopped.

"That sounds remarkably like a challenge," he said, his voice low and silky. "Challenges, Miss Bennet, are mother's milk to me. Take care how you issue them."

"Still a boy with something to prove?" She gave him a patronizing look. "First climbing out windows to get roses; now kissing spinsters? I suppose you'd do it again quickly enough if someone laid you a wager on it."

Now his smile grew dangerous. "I'll take that wager. A shilling says I can kiss you and you'll enjoy it."

"I thought you didn't plan to kiss me again." She opened her eyes wide in mock innocence. "Now you want to kiss me *and* take my coin?"

His shoulder shook a little, as if he was laughing at her. He leaned forward until she could see the sparks of gold in his eyes. "I said I didn't *plan* to kiss you again," he whispered. "I never said I *wouldn't* kiss you again."

Her throat had gone dry. "That's the same thing," she tried to say.

This time he did laugh. "We'll find out, won't we?" He stepped back and gave a crisp bow, never taking his eyes off her face. "Good day, Miss Bennet."

And he walked out the door before she could move, or breathe, again.

Tristan walked out of the drawing room with every sense tingling. Good Lord, she was dangerous. He felt an unwarranted sense of elation at conjuring that breathless look on her face. She'd wanted him to kiss her, right then and there; he knew it. Unfortunately, he'd felt the same thing, which meant he had already failed a key test. No matter how much he told himself he was supposed to attend her like a brother, his mind and body refused to recognize her in any way that might be deemed 'sisterly.'

He really didn't understand that. She was no beauty, although he liked her better as she was today, with her hair smooth and soft, even if she still wore a dress that hurt his eyes. She had a nice mouth, he reluctantly allowed; very lovely, soft and pink, and dangerously tempting. And the way her eyes could sparkle was rather attractive—or would be, if he didn't know they sparkled in anticipation of spiting him. Still, he had left her wide-eyed and speechless twice now, and that was a triumph no man could overlook.

Just as he reached the hall, where a footman darted for his hat and gloves at his approach, another woman appeared. For a moment, he thought it was the Fury herself, somehow springing up for one last jab, but almost immediately he realized it was a much older woman. She had the same figure as the Fury, but wore a gown that displayed it to advantage. Her dark hair, threaded with silver, was fixed in a simple way that included not a single ringlet. And her eyes—in fact, her whole face—brightened with interest when she saw him.

This must be the aunt sent to act as chaperone, the one Bennet had said needed watching as much as his sister did. Tristan stopped and bowed. "I presume I have the honor of addressing Lady Courtenay."

"You do," she replied, not bothering to hide her amusement. "And you . . . ?"

"Viscount Burke, madam, at your service."

Her smile grew. "A pleasure to make your acquaintance, sir. You must have called upon my niece."

For some reason Tristan felt his neck grow warm. He tried to quell it; he'd done nothing wrong. He hadn't touched Miss Bennet, let alone ravished her. He'd only come because Bennet tricked him into promising to do it. "At her brother's request. He bade me inquire after her health and contentment while he is out of town."

"Contentment!" Her eyebrows went up a fraction. "How very good of you. And did you find her contented?"

He cleared his throat, wondering what the Fury would say. She'd seemed well enough when he arrived. "Tolerably well, ma'am."

"Excellent." Lady Courtenay was laughing at him, he could tell. He fought back the urge to scowl. "I hope she will remain so. I've taken her under my wing in her parents' absence, as my nephew might have told you. I plan to see that she goes out often, to keep her mind diverted from worry." She paused. "Perhaps you will come to tea."

Damn it. "Perhaps," he said, already crafting an excuse. He hated tea.

"Lovely." She smiled again. "I do so look forward to becoming acquainted with my niece's and nephew's companions. You would be very welcome the day after tomorrow."

His mind blanked. "Er." He coughed. "What?"

"The day after tomorrow," she repeated. "If you intend to squire my niece about, you must come to tea first. Good day, Lord Burke; until then."

"But . . ." His voice trailed off as she bowed her head, still smiling, only now that expression looked wily and satisfied. He cleared his throat yet again, knowing when he was beaten. "Indeed. Good day, Lady Courtenay."

"Good day, Lord Burke."

Tristan beat a hasty retreat. He couldn't leave the house fast enough. God help him; now there were two Furies to contend with.

Chapter 12

Joan hardly knew what to think when Tristan Burke left after threatening to kiss her again. "Threaten" was definitely the proper word for it. The wretched man seemed to know how much the first kiss had unnerved her. What was wrong with him, wanting to kiss a woman just to fluster her? And what was wrong with her, that she allowed it to fluster her? It was because he was a rake, she decided, who probably thought he could kiss any woman in the world and she would swoon at his feet. It meant nothing to him, and should mean nothing to her—except, she consoled herself, that it was a valuable lesson from a reputed master. When she was finally kissed by a respectable man with honorable intentions, she would be glad of a little knowledge. Yes, that was the proper way to view it. It had nothing to do with her, or with him; it was about planning for future, more romantic, encounters with true gentlemen.

And Douglas, setting that man on her! He had to know his friend's reputation. Douglas, in fact, had probably been present for most of its wicked formation. She didn't know what her brother had been thinking. He knew Mother didn't approve of Lord Burke.

Of course, Mother wasn't here. And it didn't seem as though Evangeline would protest Joan spending time with him—or with any other gentleman, not that any others had come to announce their intention of escorting her about town. She wondered why he had agreed to it, and then she said a small prayer that his attentions, whatever they might be, wouldn't cause her any trouble.

She gave herself a shake and strode back toward the dressing room where she'd been happily sampling Evangeline's bonnet collection before he arrived, only to meet her aunt coming up the stairs.

"Shall we go see Federico now?" Evangeline looked rather pleased about something. "I couldn't wait—I sent off a note warning him we may call on him this very afternoon. If we order some gowns today, they should be ready within a week. I've a feeling we shall want to go out more."

"Oh, yes." Quickly Joan banished the infuriating Lord Burke from her thoughts. She was desperately curious to meet the creator of Evangeline's wardrobe. Today her aunt wore a dress whose bodice looked more like a man's shirt than a woman's dress, with a collar and loose sleeves. It was nothing like the dress Joan wore, but it looked comfortable, and even more important, it didn't make her look like an umbrella. "Let me get my bonnet."

"You mustn't be put off by Federico's manner," said Evangeline when they were in the carriage. "He routinely runs roughshod over my every suggestion, but in the end his judgment is impeccable."

"Of course." Evangeline had been fortunate enough to find someone who knew how to flatter her figure. Joan . . . well, Joan knew her mother meant well, just as she also knew that all of Mother's carefully chosen designs never quite looked as elegant on her as they did in the illustrations. She was tired of trying to conceal her figure with tight stays. She had given up hope of looking elegant in the latest fashions. She was tired of sitting for an hour while Janet curled her hair into a style that only made her look taller and plumper. If Mr. Salvatore could produce a gown, *any* gown, that made her look attractive, Joan would wear it even if it caused a minor scandal. And that would teach Lord Boor to call her an umbrella, wouldn't it?

"Does Viscount Burke call upon you frequently?"

"Er." Joan gave a guilty start at the unexpected question. "You saw him?"

"Yes." Evangeline just waited, but her keen gaze brought a blush to Joan's cheeks.

"Oh." She cleared her throat. "Yes. Well, you see, he's a friend of Douglas's, and . . . and . . . and he came to express his good wishes for Mother's recovery." For some reason, a blithely innocent story was not coming to mind. She kept hearing him saying he could kiss her and make her like it—as if he hadn't already done so.

"How kind of him. He gets on well with your mother, then?"

Joan fiddled with her glove, thinking frantically. If she were truthful, Evangeline would probably send Lord Burke on his way without further ado. No doubt Papa had extracted a vow of good behavior from Evangeline as well. Her promise to her father most likely required that she admit to her aunt how much Mother disliked and disapproved of Lord Burke.

But for reasons she didn't like to examine, she didn't want to do that.

"I don't think he's terribly well acquainted with Mother," she said, hoping lightning wouldn't strike her for that understatement. "But he's been friends with Douglas for ages, and no doubt he called merely to be polite."

"He told me Douglas asked him to look out for you. As a surrogate brother."

Joan scowled. So much for her attempts to cast it in an ordinary, uninteresting light. "Yes. He said something of that sort to me, too."

For a moment there was silence. "He looks remarkably like his father," Evangeline remarked. "Such a tragedy. Colin Burke was one of a kind."

She darted a glance at her aunt, but Evangeline had tilted her head to peer out the window at the sky. "Oh?"

"Oh, my, yes." Something like admiration lit Evangeline's face as she smiled in remembrance. "He was the sort of young man your father was forbidden to associate with, for fear it would reinforce every wicked impulse your father had. Well, no doubt my father was right! You know your papa was once as big a rascal as Douglas, don't you? But Colin Burke . . . ah, my. He had the devil's own charm, the handsomest face in England, and not a single ounce of fear. All the

young ladies were fascinated by him—so dangerous, so attractive, so charismatic! But he was no
fool, either. He wasn't the heir, so he married the
daughter of a naval man who'd made a fortune on
the sea." Evangeline's smile faded. "Such a tragedy," she murmured again.

Joan nibbled her lip. She didn't actually know
what had happened to Lord Burke's parents, but
it sounded very sad. Perhaps it wasn't entirely his
fault he'd grown up with no manners. "Tragedy?"

"Yes." Her aunt's mouth twisted sadly. "Both he
and his bride died before the age of twenty-five.
He drowned, I believe, and she . . . I can't remember. A broken heart, perhaps. I certainly would
have, if I'd been his wife."

Joan did some silent arithmetic. "Lord Burke
must have been a very small boy when they died."

"He's the same age as Douglas? Yes, he must
have been very young. I remember hearing about
Colin Burke's death the summer I was married,
and that was the year before you were born. Ah—
here we are." The carriage was coming to a halt.

Evangeline said no more about Lord Burke, and
Joan didn't ask more as she followed her aunt. He
must not even remember his parents. As much as
she chafed under her mother's strictures at times,
Joan couldn't imagine life without her parents.
If they'd died when she was a baby, she might
have been raised by—ugh—Lord and Lady Doncaster. Not even having her cousin Mariah as a
sister would have made up for that. Somehow it
seemed unlikely her parents would have left her
and Douglas to Evangeline's care. She wondered
who had raised Lord Burke, and why, in Doug-

las's tales of him, he'd always seemed to be at some schoolmate's home for school holidays.

It wasn't a reason to like him, of course, but perhaps it was a reason not to think so harshly of him.

Chapter 13

$\sim\!\infty\!\sim$

Tristan was so preoccupied by his provoking encounter with Miss Bennet that he walked into Bennet's house without suspecting more trouble.

Murdoch met him in the hall, which was unusual enough. Even worse, the servant was worried. "There's a lady waiting for you, sir," he whispered.

For a brief, blazing moment, Tristan thought Miss Bennet had somehow darted across town to continue their confrontation. She'd clearly had more to say about his offered escort, and threatened kisses, than he had allowed her to express, and in that brief, blazing moment, he felt a thrill of anticipation.

But then reason asserted itself; of course she couldn't have made it here before he did. He'd left her house, got on his horse, and ridden straight back here. And she wouldn't come to this house in any event. The one time she had come, it had been because her brother was in residence, and Tristan's presence had been completely unknown to her.

He looked at Murdoch warily. "Who is it?" There were very few women who *would* come to see him here, and none of them were women he wished to see.

"Lady Burke," was the reply.

And that was the worst possible woman, in Tristan's opinion. He wondered if he could just turn around and leave the house again, but before he could act on that scheme, his aunt ruined it by appearing in the doorway of the small sitting room.

"Lord Burke," she said in a frosty, civil voice. "I have been waiting."

He took off his hat and thrust it at Murdoch. "I'm sure I don't deserve such an inconvenience on your part, madam. I wish you had not troubled yourself so."

"I would not have, if it weren't for a pressing matter." She looked pointedly at the hovering Murdoch. "Otherwise I wouldn't have dreamt of calling upon you."

Tristan peeled off his gloves one finger at a time, racking his brain for an excuse to cut this interview short. His aunt had never liked him, from the time he was a boy. When his parents died, he'd simply been left at his grandfather's house with a nurse for a few years. This had suited him just fine, for Nurse was getting old and hard of hearing, and he was able to play at will, sneaking away from her whenever he liked. But once he reached school age, his uncle Lord Burke decided it was proper to take more of an interest in him. Uncle Burke had arranged for him to go to Eton, and to spend holidays at the Burke estate, Wildwood, in Hampshire.

Wildwood had been a wonderful place, but

Tristan soon grew to hate it. He knew he'd been a troublesome brat as a boy, and he knew his aunt was a lady of very delicate sensibilities. Shouting and running and anything dirty were utterly abhorrent to her. She was petite and proper, and raised her twin daughters in her image, two perfect china dolls who would stare at Tristan, wet and muddy from wading in the pond, as if he were the most disgusting creature alive. It hadn't taken him very long to decide he really didn't want to live under his uncle's roof if it meant he also had to live with his aunt. To the best of his ability, he'd tried to stay out of her way for both their sakes, wheedling invitations to visit any schoolmate who would have him over holidays. In turn, Mary had all but ignored his existence, which apparently pleased her as much as it pleased him. Whatever she wanted now, she must want very badly, if she'd not only come to find him here but waited for him to return.

"Let us discuss it without further delay, then." He tossed the gloves at Murdoch and all but snarled, "Bring the lady a cup of tea."

The servant nodded once and bolted for the back of the house. Gritting his teeth, Tristan followed his aunt into the sitting room.

Someone—likely Murdoch—had pulled a pair of Bennet's mismatched chairs in front of the hearth. Aunt Mary took one chair, but Tristan leaned against the mantel. "What is this pressing matter?" he asked, hoping desperately it was something trivial.

"I have come to ask when the house in Hanover Square will be restored."

His brows lowered suspiciously. "Why?"

Two spots of color appeared in Mary's cheeks, but her expression didn't warm. "Because I believe it would be better for Alice's and Catherine's prospects if I could entertain properly in their father's family home."

For a long moment he just stared at her in amazement. This was why he disliked his aunt. She only sought him out when she wanted something, and what she wanted usually involved great inconvenience to him. Barely two months ago she had described the house as intolerable, unfit for ladies, and beneath her dignity. He understood why, when the roof collapsed within a fortnight of her departure for a house across town, completely destroying the servants' quarters and attics, flooding the bedrooms, and ruining quite a bit of plasterwork. Now she wanted to come back? "I understood, from our conversation several weeks ago, that their father's family home—which is actually my family home, too, as it happens—was too old-fashioned and cramped for a decent ball."

"And it was."

"It's a complete mess now, with the builders in."

"Not for long," she said. "I saw it the other day and was told it's nearly ready."

Ah; the light dawned. She'd gone by to see what disaster he'd wrought upon the house, no doubt expecting to see it in ruins. But instead she'd seen how he was restoring it—and not just restoring, but vastly improving it—and her views had changed. Very rightly so, in Tristan's opinion. The house *had* been old-fashioned and cramped, even aside from the neglect and decay it had suffered. Since the roof had collapsed and the whole house was uninhabitable, he had taken the opportunity to enlarge the doorways, raise the ceilings of the upper floors, and rebuild the staircase. In addition, every modern advance he admired was going to be part of his new house, from an innovative steam heating system to piping for baths and water closets on all floors. Far from being outmoded, the house would soon be one of the most modern in London. The improvements must have been just as obvious to Mary. No doubt she also wanted it on the same terms as before: free of charge.

Ruffling one hand through his hair, Tristan finally took the other chair. "Forgive me if I fail to understand. When my uncle died, I bowed to your concerns that it would be cruel and unjust to drive my cousins from their home, and left possession of the house to you and them for eight years. This spring you came to tell me in no uncertain terms that it was no longer suitable, and you were quitting it for a vastly better house in Charles Street. I gave up my other quarters in expectation of taking residence in Hanover Square. Now you say you are dissatisfied with Charles Street, and wish to return to Hanover Square? What, pray, about either house has changed?"

Her posture seemed, if possible, to grow stiffer. "The house in Charles Street is too dark. I was misled about its chimneys. And the neighborhood is not as much to my liking."

"You're a widow in possession of an independent annuity," he pointed out. "Take another house."

"It's too late in the season to find another decent property!"

"Aye, so it is. After I gave up my previous quarters, I had little choice but to impose upon friends when the Hanover house became impossible to live in—as you find me here today." He waved one hand around Bennet's spartan sitting room, which had hosted more card parties and boxing matches than anything else. There might even be sword cuts in the woodwork.

"But the Hanover Square house is still free. It is entirely within your province to give it."

"Or to keep it and live in it myself."

Mary's lips were white. "I would like to retake possession of the house," she said baldly. "As soon as it may be ready."

Tristan crossed one booted foot over his knee. "The prospect of living there has grown appealing to me as well."

"We have all missed it sorely."

"Indeed? With the leaking roof and smoky chimneys and the scullery that flooded in every heavy rain?"

"The builder assured me those problems were addressed."

"At my considerable expense," he remarked. "At my instigation. And I wonder why you took such an interest in a house you quitted, of your own wish, that you went and queried my employees as if you had any right to know what they've done since you left."

Color rushed into her face. "Will you or won't you allow me to return my daughters to their home?" she all but spat.

"No," he said politely. "I'm rebuilding the house to suit my tastes. And to be precise, it's my house; it has been for the last eight years. I allowed you to stay out of deference to your daughters, but I will have nowhere to live if I give you that house again."

Her mouth puckered up in frustration. "You can afford to take any house in London. I cannot!"

He grinned. The Burke family fortune was respectable, and his uncle had managed it capably. Aunt Mary had been left a comfortable annuity as part of her dower, and Alice and Catherine, his cousins, had each been left a marriage portion of good size. By no accounting were they destitute or poor.

But Tristan's father, like a dutiful second son, had married an heiress, the only child of a decorated admiral who left his enormous fortune to her. Upon his parents' deaths, Tristan had become far, far wealthier than his titled uncle, and it had chafed Aunt Mary to no end. Not only was that loud, troublesome, dirty boy the heir to the Burke estates and title, but those were the lesser part of his inheritance. Now, to her great resentment, he had it all, while she was pensioned off on a widow's portion, which—however comfortable—was fixed and limited. No doubt her visit today was spurred by the pinch of paying her own rent for the first time.

"What do you really want, madam?" he asked, ready to be rid of her. "Do you want me to pay the Charles Street lease? Will a new carriage soothe your upset? Does one of my cousins require a new Court dress? I intend to keep the house in Hanover Square, so you can cease asking for that."

Her throat worked for a few moments. "The rent is a greater encumbrance than I had anticipated," she said through tight lips. "That would be most generous of you."

"Very good." He jumped to his feet. "Send a copy of the lease to Tompkins, and I'll direct him to pay it for the duration of this season."

"And coal is very dear," she went on.

He nodded. "I'll pay the coal man."

"And there are a few overdue bills." Her face was dull red now, and she stared fixedly at a spot beyond Tristan's shoulder. "From the modiste. And the milliner. And—and the butcher."

He cocked his head. "So many? Perhaps I should speak to your man of business; is he not managing your funds properly? Your annuity should be sufficient to keep you in good comfort, Aunt."

"It isn't," she hissed, shooting him a hateful look.

"It should be," he replied, emphasizing the second word. "I am under no obligation to support you. I'm generously offering to do so this once, out of compassion for the extra burden you are under in sponsoring your daughters' Season this year, but you should not expect it in the future."

She rose, radiating bitterness. "That is very good of you, Lord Burke."

"Good day, Lady Burke." Tristan bowed and escorted her out of the house, although she didn't look at him again.

Murdoch edged into the hall as he closed the door behind his aunt. Tristan glared at him. "How dare you let that woman into the house?

If she ever calls again, I am not in, I will not be returning soon, and under no circumstances may she wait for me!"

The servant winced. "Apologies, m'lord. Mr. Bennet left no word, and neither did you. She bowled her way past me, she did, like she was a royal princess or something."

"Well, at least you didn't bring the damn tea. She would have stayed an hour just to put me out of pocket for the leaves." He sighed. All the crackling energy of meeting Miss Bennet had dissipated into the almost resentful tension that always gripped him after Aunt Mary's visits. Even though she no longer had any authority over him, and in fact the advantage in their relationship had decidedly shifted to him, Tristan could still feel the weight of her scolds, the sting of her distaste for him, the yawning loneliness he had always endured when he was sent to his uncle's house. She made him feel filthy and unwanted, and he hated that.

He grabbed his hat off the hook again and jammed his hands into his gloves. "I'm going out," he told Murdoch. "From now until Mr. Bennet returns, your continued employment here depends on forbidding entrance to any and every woman who calls. Throw yourself in front of the door if necessary. Tell them there's plague within. Do whatever you must."

"Yes, sir." Murdoch's expression lightened with relief. "Yes, indeed, my lord."

Tristan strode out of the house and set off for Hanover Square on foot. He could use the exercise, to clear his head. He wanted to have a word with the builder about letting other people view his house. In fact, he would issue the same commandment to the builder that he'd just given Murdoch: no women were to be allowed on the premises for any reason. Perhaps he ought to move into the house now, unsettled and unfinished as it was. Whatever Aunt Mary chose to believe, the house was nowhere near done, although it would be habitable by his standards within a month or less. He wouldn't be entertaining; he could live with wet plaster and workmen underfoot. Bloody hell—even if a little rain came in through the roof, it would be a small price to pay for peace and privacy and complete freedom from female interference.

Chapter 14

The whirlwind of recent events necessitated a long chat with Abigail and Penelope. Joan had dashed off a brief note about her parents' leaving town, delaying their walk, and Abigail had replied with all due concern and felicitations for Lady Bennet's health. But that had been days ago, and between Evangeline's arrival, Lord Burke's dangerous promise, and the visit to Mr. Salvatore, Joan was bursting to talk—and her friends were desperate to hear it, judging from the quickness of their reply to her request to see them. Abigail proposed a drive in the park, and Joan agreed at once after obtaining her aunt's permission.

"At last!" was Penelope's greeting when Joan came down to meet them. "I haven't slept a wink since the Malcolm ball, worrying about you!"

"It's true she hasn't slept, but I heard far more than worry from her lips," said Abigail. "You are about to be interrogated to the point of senselessness, Joan."

Penelope made a face. "I daresay I won't have to ask twice! It's not good for a body to keep everything inside. It relieves one's spleen to vent it."

"I was astonished you waited so long to ask."

"Papa has it in his head that he needs a country estate, to lend us stature." Abigail looked amused. "He's made us all drive out first to Chelsea, then to Greenwich and even to Richmond, to view properties. Mama told him she wouldn't live further than a day's drive from London, so I suspect he drew a circle on the map and has been sending out enquiries to every property in that range."

"Bother all that," said Penelope. "I barely saw anything at either property, I was so consumed with worry about Joan! And now you simply must tell us all or I think I shall die from the anxiety."

"We've brought Olivia to chaperone, and Jamie decided to come along at the last minute, so we haven't got complete privacy." Always cooler-headed than her sister, Abigail looked at Joan. "I hope you don't mind. It's so good for Olivia to get out."

"Of course not." Joan much preferred Olivia Townsend to Mrs. Weston as a chaperone. She was only a few years older than Abigail, and had known the Westons for years. When she went out with them, she acted more like an older sister than the respectable widow she was. Joan suspected her circumstances were somewhat strained, for she almost never saw Mrs. Townsend out in society without the Westons.

James was Abigail's and Penelope's older brother. Joan wasn't as fond of him—he was far too serious and staid—but he was always kind to her. Besides, his sisters knew how to handle him. All it took was a discussion of stockings or cosmetics to send him hurrying in the other direction. And with both Mrs. Townsend and Mr. Weston accompanying them, Mrs. Weston wouldn't see the need to go herself or send a maid to dog their heels.

They rode in Mr. Weston's open barouche to the park, James Weston riding his horse alongside. Conversation was light and carefree, and Mrs. Townsend only reproved Penelope once for laughing too gaily. It was a lovely day, and Joan lifted her face to the sun. Freckles be damned; it felt good to be outside, and with her dearest friends.

Unfortunately, everyone else seemed to have had the same thought. The park was crowded, and the parade of carriages moved at a crawl. After a quarter hour, Penelope was squirming in her seat.

"If you can't sit still, you might as well get down and walk," said Mrs. Townsend, who was sharing the seat with Penelope.

"Brilliant thought, Olivia!" Penelope beamed at her. "Jamie, we want to stroll," she called to her brother, who nodded and urged his horse forward to speak to the driver. "Will you come with us, Olivia?"

Mrs. Townsend smiled wryly. "And spoil the confidences you're dying to exchange with Miss Bennet? I wouldn't dream of it. Just sitting here in the sun for a few minutes will delight me."

It took a little while to find a spot for the carriage away from the traffic, but finally the driver stopped. Mr. Weston dismounted and helped them all down, then stayed behind to talk with Mrs. Townsend.

As soon as they were ten feet from the carriage, Penelope burst out, "Tell us everything!"

"She means to ask, how have things been since your mother fell ill?" said Abigail with a sharp look at her sister. "Are you well, Joan?"

"Oh, yes, well enough." She paused. "I'm worried about my mother. She's not usually ill, but this time . . . Papa nearly had to carry her into the carriage. It was alarming."

"Have they reached Cornwall yet?"

Joan lifted one hand helplessly. "I don't know; perhaps. Papa said they would travel slowly, to avoid tiring her. We received one brief note, saying they had reached Bath but then been compelled to stop so Mother could rest. He promised to write to me when they arrived, so I hope to hear from him soon."

"I'm sure that's very wise of him."

For a moment they were all quiet. Joan bit her lip as thoughts of her mother, weak and coughing up blood, filled her mind. She was anxious to hear from her father, but she was just as concerned that he not delay their progress merely to send her a letter saying they'd reached Devonshire. Conveying Mother safely to Cornwall was the important thing, even if it left her prey to horrible fears and worries. She'd tried not to dwell on it much, and Evangeline's presence had been a marvelous distraction, but Joan thought of her mother every night.

"Are you getting on well with your aunt?" Penelope asked hesitantly. "You never spoke of her before."

Joan made herself smile. "I never really knew

her before. My mother thought her scandalous, and she hasn't been in London much. I hadn't seen her in years."

"And your father left you in her charge?" Abigail's eyes were wide.

"Yes, although only after making me solemnly swear I would behave myself."

"That sounds like a fool's bet to me," exclaimed Penelope. "Your father ought to know better than that."

"I think he was faced with dire circumstances," Joan replied. "He's sent Douglas off to Ashwood to help rebuild after the flood there."

"Douglas? Build a house?" Penelope let out a whoop.

Behind them, Mr. Weston turned their way, a slight frown on his face. Abigail waved at him with a bright smile even as she poked her sister's arm. "Hush, Pen. Jamie's watching you."

"Pooh on Jamie," said Penelope, but in a lower tone. "How diverting to think of Douglas contemplating which paper to put on the walls and what draperies to hang!"

"Quite a thought, isn't it?" Joan grinned. "I expect he'll be tearing out his hair to come back to London within a fortnight."

"But your aunt." Abigail fixed a stern gaze on Joan. "You don't seem oppressed."

"No, quite the opposite." Joan looked around, but Mr. Weston had gone back to talking with Mrs. Townsend, and neither was paying them any mind. "She's shockingly original. She drinks brandy after dinner. She greeted Smythe, our butler, like an old friend; he once helped her sneak into the house when she'd gone out to see a foot-race. And she doesn't care a fig for fashion, but her wardrobe is so striking and flattering, I can hardly breathe from envy."

The Weston girls exchanged a glance. "I can't wait to meet her," said Penelope.

"Are you happy to have her, then?" Abigail looked bewildered.

Joan thought of the new day dress Mr. Salvatore was sewing for her at that very moment. As Evangeline had warned, he had apparently decided everything about it without once seeking her approval. Beyond the fact that it would be green, he hadn't even told her what it would look like. But his words had been kind and encouraging; he declared she had it in her to be a Venus, and that he knew how to do it. With all her heart she hoped he was right and that the dress came out well, that he had somehow seen some way to flatter her tall, round figure and not make her look like a tufted umbrella. "I believe it may be a rare stroke of good fortune." She said nothing of the dress, wanting to see their unprepared reaction when she wore it.

"I am very glad of it," said Abigail.

"As am I. Now, what happened with Lord Burke at the Malcolm ball?" Penelope asked.

"He gave me *50 Ways to Sin*." Joan swung her reticule. "Do you want it?" She'd rolled it into a tight cylinder and tied it with a ribbon to keep it confined. Mother's absence, and even more important, Janet's, had made it much easier to keep it hidden.

"You may keep it; I managed to steal Mama's copy the other night. Is that why he waltzed you out of the room?" Penelope was undeterred, to Joan's disappointment. Usually they discussed each issue with rabid interest, from the plausibility of the acts described to which gentleman of the town had inspired the tale.

"That was only for a moment."

"It was several minutes, and even though he emerged—and left the ballroom!—a few minutes later, you didn't come back for much longer, and when you did, you looked thoroughly flustered. What happened?" Abigail prodded. "I hope it was something delicious, from the way you're blushing."

"You're both horrible people." Joan glared at them. "May I not have some secrets?"

Penelope snorted. "Not about this! Or next time we shall follow you when he asks you to dance, and that will make it much more difficult for him to make love to you."

"*Penelope.*" Her face was bright red, she could feel it.

"And she denies nothing," observed Abigail. For once she was as avidly curious as her sister. "So, what did he do?"

Joan pursed her lips, but part of her was wildly eager to tell. She'd been kissed—properly kissed, near to ravishment—by a true rake. And there was even a chance he would do it again. She glanced around to ensure they were alone, and lowered her voice. "You must never tell anyone."

"No, never," her friends chorused.

"He made a very halfhearted apology for calling me an umbrella"—Penelope's eyebrows went up—"and he gave me *50 Ways to Sin* by sliding it down the back of my gown"—Abigail gasped loudly—"and then he kissed me." She said the last three words in a rushed whisper that was almost drowned out by Penelope's whoop.

"Did you enjoy it?" demanded Abigail.

"Huh! Who cares?" snorted her sister. "She was kissed by the handsomest viscount in London!"

"It was very pleasant," said Joan primly, aware that her face was scarlet. "Until he said he'd only done it to make me stop talking."

The expression on her friends' faces was comical: Penelope outraged, Abigail dismayed. And then they both began trying to hide their amusement.

"Oh, Joan." Abigail sighed, her eyes brimming with laughter. "You drove a notorious rake to distraction and he *kissed* you."

"I want to be like you someday," gasped Penelope, her shoulders shaking.

"Yes, well, that's not all. He called on me the other day and said Douglas made him promise to escort me about town. Like a brother, I'm sure he meant to say, but can you imagine?"

"I'm trying desperately," murmured Penelope.

"Naturally I thought it presented a great opportunity to pay him back for his impertinence, so I didn't tell him no. But I couldn't help asking if he meant to kiss me again, to which he replied an emphatic no." Joan smiled in satisfaction. "I said I hadn't cared for it the first time—"

"Liar," said Abigail under her breath.

"To which he replied that it sounded like a challenge," Joan went on with a dark look at her friend. "He even said he'd wager a shilling he could kiss me again and make me like it . . ." Her voice trailed off as she belatedly realized she might have revealed too much.

Penelope gave a little shriek. "A wager? Did you accept it?"

"Of course not!"

"But you wanted to." Abigail was watching her closely, still grinning. "You want him to kiss you again."

Joan opened her mouth, then closed it. "I promised my father I would be on my very best behavior. I couldn't possibly engage in such unladylike pursuits as wagering."

"Just kissing." Penelope laughed.

"But Joan." Abigail sobered. "It's very thrilling to have a gentleman steal a kiss, or even two, but what do you want to come of it? You called him Lord Boor the other night and said you punched him in the face."

"Don't be so grim, Abby," scoffed Penelope. "It was just a kiss!"

"And a wager, about more kisses. I just think Joan should be wary." Abigail lifted one shoulder. "He's a notorious rake, known for his scandalous affairs. I doubt Joan wants to be caught up in one of those."

"Not particularly," she murmured, just a shade wistfully. A scandalous affair would be very bad after it ended, of course, but while it was happening . . . well, it could be very thrilling.

"Unless he falls madly in love with her and proposes marriage," suggested Penelope. "Other scandalous affairs have ended that way. Sometimes notorious rakes do fall in love, you know."

Abigail looked at Joan. "Is that what you hope?"

She said nothing, because she had no idea what to say. It was hard to deny that kissing Tristan Burke had been pleasant. More than pleasant. It had set her nerves on fire and made her skin yearn for him to touch her again. A wicked part of her even thrilled at the thought of more intimate touches, fed by the memory of his hand on her hip and his body pressed against hers. And if he wanted the same, she didn't know how she would refuse him, no matter what his motivations. To feel desired, even for just a while, was a powerful temptation.

But Lord Boor, fall in love with her? She couldn't imagine it. He seemed determined to find new ways to be rude and impertinent every time they met. Joan didn't want to marry someone who would constantly argue with her, call her unattractive, and bully her to his will. And even if he managed to improve on further acquaintance, there was her family to contend with. Her mother would sooner lock her in a convent than let her marry the likes of Lord Burke. And if she did let herself be drawn into a scandal, a convent and a securely locked door would most assuredly figure in Lady Bennet's plans.

"No," she finally said, very quietly.

"Then be careful." Abigail gave her a rueful smile. "Not the most exciting plan, I know."

"Your pardon, but are you ready to go home? Mrs. Townsend is growing overheated in the sun." Mr. Weston's voice made all three girls jump. He had dismounted and walked up behind Abigail.

"Oh! Yes, we're ready." Penelope took her

brother's arm and led him back toward the carriage, shooting a glance of compassion at Joan. "How dare you let Olivia sit in the sun, Jamie? You ought to have stopped in the shade . . ."

Abigail fell in step beside her as they followed more slowly, ignoring Penelope's chatter. "It was really lovely, wasn't it? When he kissed you. I could tell from your face."

Joan sighed, half in longing, half in regret. "Yes."

Her friend was quiet for a minute. "It appears he wants to kiss you again, if he wagered he could make you enjoy it better next time . . ."

"He only said that to tease me."

"Are you certain?"

Joan just snorted in reply. They had reached the carriage, where Mr. Weston was helping Penelope up the step.

Instead of stepping forward to climb into the carriage behind her sister, Abigail turned to Joan. "Not wanting to be caught up in a scandal is sensible," she whispered. "But holding out hope that a gentleman's feelings might grow . . . there's nothing foolish about that."

"With this gentleman, hoping for anything is foolish," Joan replied with a bittersweet sigh, and she prayed she didn't forget it.

Chapter 15

Tristan dismounted outside the Bennet house in South Audley Street and took his time tying up his horse. With any luck, this would be a brief visit, but he was beginning to wish he'd brought his own liquid refreshment. How was his visit—for tea, no less—supposed to add to the Fury's enjoyment of the Season? If he'd had to lay money one way or the other, he would have wagered she'd rather not see him again.

For the hundredth time, he wondered how he'd let himself agree to this. When Bennet returned to London, there would be a reckoning. Look after my sister, he'd said; bloody Christ, he might as well have asked Tristan to catch a wild boar and ride it to York. The boar would have appreciated his efforts just as much.

He straightened his jacket and rapped the door knocker, bracing himself. The sooner he went inside and drank some tea, the sooner he could leave. Whatever she said to him, no matter how provoking, he must not respond. He would ask after her health; after her mother's health; if she would like him to shoot her brother for subjecting them both to this farce; and then take his leave. The thought cheered him. A few polite minutes of meaningless conversation, and he would be done.

The butler admitted him and soon showed him into the drawing room. But only Lady Courtenay was waiting for him, smiling a little too broadly.

"Lord Burke! How lovely to see you. Thank you so much for calling."

Tristan bowed, resisting the urge to peer out into the corridor behind him. If he'd had the abominably bad luck to call when Miss Bennet was out, he damned sure wasn't staying. "The pleasure is mine, madam. I was most gratified to be welcome."

"Oh, yes," she said in amusement. "Won't you sit down? My niece will return in a moment. We were just about to enjoy some tea and sandwiches. Would you care to join us?"

"That's very kind, thank you." He took the seat opposite her as the countess rang for a maid and instructed the girl to have more sandwiches and some cakes sent up with tea.

"Now." Lady Courtenay smiled at him. "How is Douglas? I haven't seen him in an age, and my niece tells me you are staying with him at the moment."

"He's gone to Norfolk, but he was in excellent health and spirits when he left, ma'am."

"Very good," she said warmly. "I remember him as such a rapscallion, always in pursuit of adventure and willing to break more than a few rules . . . oh, but I mustn't say so to you—he will never forgive me! I beg you to overlook the reminiscence of a fond aunt."

"Of course," Tristan murmured, feeling an unwanted bolt of envy for Bennet. If only his aunt had ever thought so well of him and his youthful escapades. Lady Courtenay showed no approbation, and even a little admiration.

"I must confess, he was a boy after my own heart," his hostess went on. "I knew it the moment he skidded down the stairs of this very house with an atlas for a sled. Such an uproar it caused! His parents were hosting a fine dinner, and he upset it all by flying through the hall, shouting for all he was worth."

"I defy any boy not to shout whilst sledding down a staircase," said Tristan with a slight grin. "I might have done that myself a time or two." He'd done it exactly three times, before getting caught and thrashed so hard, he almost squirmed at the memory.

Lady Courtenay leaned forward and lowered her voice, still smiling broadly. "Of course! I did it myself as a girl, once my brother showed me how. We were clever enough to wait until our parents were away, however."

"Very wise," he agreed solemnly.

The door opened, and a woman came in. "Lord Burke," she said a little breathlessly, dropping a curtsy. "What a pleasant surprise."

Tristan stared. He'd shot to his feet at the sound of the latch, but if Lady Courtenay hadn't said her niece would be returning soon, he wouldn't have believed it was truly Miss Bennet. She didn't have a single flounce or shred of lace on her. In fact, she

seemed shorn of almost all trimmings. Her dress
was a muted green—damn, he'd been right that
deep colors would suit her—and decorated only
with a wide satin ribbon around the neckline. Instead of ruffles and puffs, her skirt was embroidered, and it swayed softly from side to side as
she moved. And her hair . . . all the ringlets were
gone. Her chestnut locks were pulled back into a
heavy-looking mass of soft curls that seemed to
beg for a man's hands to run through it.

"You changed your hair," he blurted out.

She blinked. "Yes. A pin came loose and I had
to repair it."

For some awful reason, all Tristan could think
about was pulling out that pin and all its brethren,
letting her hair fall loose around her shoulders.
He cleared his throat as she crossed the room and
took a seat on the sofa. "Right. Well done."

"We were speaking of Douglas," said Lady
Courtenay. "And what a scamp he was as a boy."

Miss Bennet turned her gleaming gaze on him.
"That must be a lengthy conversation! I am sure
Lord Burke knows a great deal about the topic."

"Are you asking me to tell tales on your brother,
Miss Bennet?" He was still having difficulty believing it was the same woman, but no matter
how hard he looked, he couldn't see anything that
wasn't her. He'd just never noticed that her fine
complexion went all the way down to the swells
of her bosom. In fact, now that the lace and trimmings were gone, he had an all-too-clear view of
her bosom, along with the rest of her figure. Far
from making her look fat, as that horrid pink
dress had done, this gown made her look lush

and delectable. His hands almost itched to test the span of her waist.

"Oh, my. No doubt my aunt and I would both swoon away at your exploits." She batted her lashes at him, which only drew his attention to her eyes and the sly sparkle in them.

It made him grin. She was once more undaunted and uncowed, just as she had been the day she invaded Bennet's house. He much preferred her this way, instead of the nervous, anxious creature she'd been at the Malcolm ball. He felt no shame in admitting it, either. If he had to dance attendance on a woman, it might as well be interesting.

"Goodness, no," said Lady Courtenay with a laugh. "How can we talk of Douglas when the poor boy's not here to defend himself?"

"Much more easily than if he were here," murmured Miss Bennet.

Tristan coughed to cover a laugh. "I hope Lady Bennet is recovering her health."

"We've only had a brief letter from Sir George," said Lady Courtenay. "They were obliged to stop in Bath, which I believe may be very fortunate. I've always found Bath so invigorating, but also restful. Have you ever visited Bath, Lord Burke?"

"Er." There had been one dreadful summer, when he was eleven, when he'd been unable to secure an invitation to any schoolmate's home and had been forced to spend a month in Bath with his aunt and uncle. Aunt Mary had been expecting then, and her pregnancy had made her more unbearable than ever. Not from ill humor; on the contrary, she'd been certain she would have a son, thus removing Tristan from any claim to the Burke title, and she'd been in exceptionally good spirits the whole time. He always wondered how great her disappointment had been to have two daughters instead of a son. But he would always remember Bath for the complacent smile she had given him every day of that horrid month.

He shook off the bad memory. "Not really, Lady Courtenay," he replied. "I merely passed through once."

She was watching him thoughtfully. "You must stop sometime. It's a lovely town."

He just nodded as the maid came in with the tray of tea. Lady Courtenay bid her niece pour, barely interrupting her attention to him. "But here I am, encouraging you to leave town, when London holds so many diversions, it would take a lifetime to enjoy them all! Just this morning we were discussing which invitations to accept. Does Lady Brentwood serve decent wine at her balls?"

"Ah . . ." He stared at her. "I've no idea, ma'am."

Lady Courtenay made a face and waved one hand. "Oh, we shall have to take the risk, then. At least we may count upon Lady Martin to have a fine selection at her soiree on Thursday. Joan, you may send our acceptance to Lady Brentwood this afternoon. Will we see you there, Lord Burke?"

He looked at Miss Bennet as she handed him a cup of tea. Dancing with her once or twice would satisfy his debt to Bennet, after all. "Likely so, Lady Courtenay." The lady across from him lowered her gaze, but not before he saw her roll her eyes. "Perhaps Miss Bennet will save me a dance that evening."

Her head came up in surprise, but then a faint smirk touched her lips. "I'm afraid I cannot, sir."

Tristan almost dropped the teacup. He didn't ask many ladies to dance, but when he did, he was never refused—never. Instead of being a relief, it made him want to dance with her more than anything. He wanted to know if she still smelled lovely. He wanted to feel her against him again. And damn it, he did not want to be refused. "Your brother exacted my explicit promise to dance with you."

She smiled at him in the overly bright way he had come to mistrust. "Goodness! What a dilemma. My mother exacted *my* explicit promise not to dance with you. I expect they'll have to fight it out—although I assure you, Mother will defeat Douglas every time."

"Perhaps she should have done so before he required my own oath." That wiped the smug look off her face. "However, since neither of them is here, I propose we turn to a neutral party to render a decision. Lady Courtenay," he said, without taking his eyes off Miss Bennet, "which promise must be considered the stronger: mine to Mr. Bennet, to see to his sister's well-being and contentment, or hers to her mother, to refuse an honest entreaty to dance?"

Lady Courtenay laughed. "Well! As a woman who was once a girl, hoping not to sit out a single set, I'm sure I'd grant the dance, provided . . ." She glanced at her niece. "Provided it was solicited with the best intentions, seeking only the enjoyment of both partners, and not just out of grim obligation."

"The look on his face is quite grim, Aunt," said Miss Bennet, gleeful once more. "I cannot think he anticipates any pleasure in dancing with me."

"Should I, since the mere request for a dance has caused an argument?" Tristan sipped his tea. "I shall have the satisfaction of keeping my word, of course."

"My," said Lady Courtenay admiringly. "I never could turn down a chance to prove a man wrong."

"I accept," said her niece at almost the same moment.

A fierce burst of triumph surged through Tristan. He knew he was treading on dangerous ground; she probably intended to hand him his head on a silver platter. But he didn't care. He didn't want to think about what gossip it might stir up. He didn't want to think about the dangers of spending even more time with her. Just the prospect of touching her again seemed to override all his good sense.

A footman came into the room and handed Lady Courtenay a letter. She read the direction on the front, and almost leapt out of her chair. "Oh! You must excuse me. I've been expecting this letter and may need to reply at once. Joan dear, will you pour our guest more tea?"

"Is it bad news expected?" asked Miss Bennet in alarm.

"No, no—that is, I hope not." Her aunt was already moving toward the door. "Carry on without me. I'll be back in a moment!" She vanished out the door, pulling it gently closed behind her.

Tristan, who'd jumped to his feet when she

stood, turned to Miss Bennet. She looked as non-plussed as he felt, but she gathered herself quickly, reaching for the teapot and filling her cup to the brim again. "I wonder how long she'd been wanting to sneak out."

Slowly he returned to his seat. All his words of warning to Bennet echoed in his mind, about women maneuvering men into marriage. He'd already identified Lady Courtenay as a Fury to be reckoned with . . . "You think it was planned?"

"The letter? Perhaps, but not likely. I daresay that was merely a convenient excuse."

"And why would she want to sneak out?"

Her cheeks grew pink. "It certainly wouldn't be to escape your witty chatter. If you leave now, I shan't try to stop you."

"You've said even less than I," he observed, suddenly less eager to make his own escape. "And I haven't even finished my tea." He took a long sip, heedless of the taste but exquisitely alert to the way her eyes darkened as she watched him.

"I know why you're here," she said. "As honored as I am by your attention, please don't think I expect you to inconvenience yourself merely for my amusement. My brother had no right to impose on you that way."

"No, none at all." He leaned forward and held out his cup. "May I have some sugar? I like my tea sweet."

For a moment he thought she might throw the sugar at him, but she took a deep breath and dumped a heaping spoonful of sugar into his tea. Now it would taste vile. He sipped it anyway.

"Why did Douglas choose you, of all people, to thrust into my path?"

He shrugged. "His other friends were unsuitable."

"More unsuitable than you?" she asked dryly.

"Far, far more," he agreed, picturing the reprobates Bennet usually kept company with. "You should be flattered. He feared you would go into a decline, but knew that would be impossible if you had my escort."

"Decline!" Her eyes sparked in irritation. "As if I needed your help, or his help—" She stopped, took a deep breath, and conjured up a coy smile that put him on guard. She leaned forward and lowered her voice. "Now that you mention it, there is one thing you might do that would greatly increase my enjoyment of these long, lonely days without my family near."

"Oh?" he drawled. "What would that be?"

"There is a publication that brings me some enjoyment." She was almost whispering now. "Would you get it for me?"

Ah. He leaned forward. "The same publication I had to put down your bodice?"

Her cheeks flushed but her smile grew wider. "Yes, the very same! Only you mustn't do that again."

"Very well, Miss Bennet. Shall we arrange a rendezvous at the Brentwood ball?"

"No," she said hastily. "Perhaps you could come for tea again."

"I don't drink tea," he murmured.

She looked at the teacup in his hand. "You do drink tea. Everyone drinks tea."

Tristan grinned. "I hate tea. You must stop thinking I'm like your expectations of me. If you want your pamphlet, you must allow me some license in my mode of delivery."

She pursed her lips, but nodded once. "Very well. As long as you don't cause a scene."

"The risk of a scene is greatly reduced when you cooperate." How interesting. He was growing curious about this publication. And if it gave him something to put down her bodice again, so much the better. "What is this publication called? I forget."

"*Fifty Ways to Sin*," she whispered, casting an anxious eye at the door. "It is . . . ah . . . a ladies' serial."

"Only for ladies?"

"Well—I think only ladies read it." She pursed her lips. "You'll get it for me?"

He stared at the way her lips parted in eagerness. "If you like."

"Yes!" She beamed at him. "I would like it, very much. Thank you." She tilted her head. "Just how much attendance did Douglas make you promise?"

"A reasonable amount."

"Such as dancing with me?"

She was still smiling at him. Even though Tristan knew it was misleading—even ominous—that smile was distracting. There was something very lively and mischievous about it, tempting the wildness inside him that craved adventure and danger. He had to blink a few times to keep from being dazzled by it. "He did encourage it, if dancing pleased you."

"I hope it shall. Anything else?"

He thought a moment. "Nothing specific. It was more a general urge to see that you enjoyed yourself, and not a specific list of tasks."

She pressed her lips together in a dangerous smile. "But I could only enjoy a dance with someone of good intentions."

"Of course." He absolutely intended to avoid kissing her. That was positively noble, for him.

"Then you seek only our mutual pleasure, as my aunt suggested?" Miss Bennet looked at him through her eyelashes.

Tristan had to remind himself they were talking about dancing. What the devil was wrong with him? He should give her the satisfaction of turning him down flat, he really should—for both their sakes. "What else would I seek?"

"Hm." She cast her eyes upward and tapped one finger at the side of her mouth. His gaze was drawn to it like a magnet to true north. How had he never noticed before that her mouth was made to be kissed? And made to kiss back. For one sharp moment he felt again her lips against his: hesitant, innocent, but eager and willing. The thought of teaching her how to kiss properly was tantalizing; first, it would mean kissing her again, something he'd spent far too much time thinking about today alone. And second, it would put an end to whatever vengeance she was plotting for his earlier behavior. In fact, it might even be in his own best interest to do so. He was quite certain he could kiss her thoroughly enough to distract her from whatever schemes were whirling behind her bright eyes.

"Retribution?" she suggested.

Sometimes it seemed she could read his mind, an alarming thought. "Have you committed a crime? Other than striking me in the face, that is."

A hint of color bloomed in her cheeks. "That was retribution for you imprisoning me against my will."

"It was a good blow," he told her. "Well landed, but only because you surprised me."

"You mustn't think all ladies will fall flat on their backs the moment you show them the least bit of attention," she said tartly.

He made a face even as his blood stirred at the thought. "What man would want that? The thrill is in catching a woman and persuading her that she wants to . . . well." He grinned at her narrow-eyed glare. "That reminds me of something I've longed to teach you. Stand up and learn how to throw a proper punch."

She gaped at him. "Throw a proper punch! I've only ever needed to punch you."

"If you've ordered any more gowns like that one, you might need to know. Stand up," he said again.

Slowly she put her hand in his outstretched one and let him help her up. "You like my gown?"

The question made him look down. Standing as close as she was, his gaze landed right on her bosom. He had already been struggling to ignore the view of her voluptuous flesh, but now it was impossible. Good Lord, her bosom was spectacular, even in this relatively modest day dress. Without any ribbons and lace blinding him, he was bewitched by the smooth creaminess of her skin.

Had she really looked like this before, underneath all those pink ruffles? His fascinated gaze dropped lower; the dress hugged her waist, indicating how long her legs were. He liked tall women. He liked buxom women. And a tall, buxom woman with radiant skin . . . if she'd been wearing this dress at the Malcolm ball, he didn't know what would have happened behind the potted palms.

"You think this dress is more flattering?" she asked again, interrupting his study. Tristan jerked his gaze back up to her face, unsettled. It was one thing to recognize a splendid bosom, and another thing to be caught staring like an uncouth boy.

"Yes," he admitted. "It's quite the loveliest dress I've ever seen you wear."

She smiled in pleased surprise. "No more umbrella?"

His jaw tightened for a moment in chagrin. What had possessed him to say such a thing, when he'd guessed from the first time he saw her that she might be a siren? "Not a bit. I have already confessed I was wrong to say such a thing. It was unpardonably rude."

Her merriment faded. "Then why did you?" Her tone was curious, but the question itself carried a note of reproach that pricked his conscience. He knew better than to insult a lady; the fact that there was something about Joan Bennet that tormented and provoked him beyond all reason was no excuse.

"Because I am a rude, unmannered lout," he said, trying to disguise an honest reply behind a flippant air.

She pursed her lips. "That's pissing more than you drank."

Tristan's eyebrows shot up in delight. "Such language from a lady!"

"I'm sure you've heard far worse," she retorted. "But . . . please don't tell my aunt I said it. It slipped out before I could stop myself."

"What a clanker! You enjoyed saying it. Nevertheless," he added as she glared at him, "your secret is safe with me. I like a woman with dash."

"Is that why you act like a rude, unmannered lout—to turn away anyone who hasn't got dash?"

"No. Women with dash are simply drawn to my rude behavior, and as I like their sort better than any other, I have no motive to change."

"Fast women," she scoffed, "and scapegraces like my brother."

"Your brother is quite the scapegrace," he agreed.

"My mother blames you for all his wild behavior."

His mouth flattened. "How gratifying," he said curtly. "Quite a feather in my cap, corrupting the scion of such an estimable family."

Miss Bennet regarded him thoughtfully, not put off at all. "Oh, I know Douglas would be dreadful even without your corrupting influence. Still, I think even he has better manners than to call a woman ugly to her face."

"I never called you ugly," he said at once. "I insulted your dress, not your face."

She made a noise suspiciously like a snort. "It was hard to tell the difference."

"There is a vast difference." His gaze slid over

her complexion, as fresh as new cream. Her lips were as pink and ripe as they'd been at the Malcolm ball, and he tried not to think about how they had tasted. Her eyes weren't snapping sparks at him now, but he feared the open, honest look in them even more. "I would never insult your face," he said, only half aloud. "I never could. You'd hidden everything lovely about yourself behind ridiculous hairstyles and unflattering dresses, and that was what I insulted. Not you at all."

Her lips parted and her eyes grew round. "Thank you," she said softly. "That was nearly a compliment."

It had been one. He didn't dare say anything else; his thoughts were straying down dangerous paths as it was. The frightening truth was that Joan Bennet grew more and more attractive every time he saw her. She smelled delicious. She made him laugh. She provoked him and teased him and dominated his thoughts until he would swear she was a sorceress, bent on driving him mad. Her mouth still taunted him to kiss her again. And now that she'd got a decent dress that showed off her bosom and her waist and made him imagine her long legs wrapped around his hips . . .

He cleared his throat. "Do you want to learn to throw a punch or not?"

She heaved a great sigh. "I don't think I need to."

Sighing made her bosom plump up. He curled his hands into loose fists and raised them to fighting position. "You should know how. Hands like this." She rolled her eyes but raised her hands to mirror his. "Now, hit me."

"What?" she exclaimed, lowering her hands. "No!"

"You've already done it once. Hit me again, like this." At slow speed he extended his right hand in a jab.

"I don't want to hurt you."

Tristan laughed. "You won't."

"I did before," she reminded him with a whiff of pride.

"Because you caught me off guard. You won't hurt me. Imagine it's Douglas here in my place."

Some of the fire came back into her expression. "Very well." She punched him in the arm.

"Not there, in my face," he said in exasperation. "You'll never dissuade an impertinent man that way." She scowled and tried again. Tristan turned his head away and received only a glancing blow on the jaw. "Better, but you must strike faster, to surprise him."

"I can't surprise you when you're telling me to punch you," she said through her teeth.

He grinned. "But you want to punch me, don't you? You think I deserve it, don't you? You long to crack my jaw or break my nose—" She threw another punch and he dodged, taking it on his shoulder. "Almost, almost!" he said, enjoying this. Her eyes positively glittered now, and her cheeks were flushed. He wondered if she found this as arousing as he did. "Try harder. Step into it."

"I am!" She swung again, this time directly at his nose. Instinctively he caught her fist in his hand, then he caught the rest of her as the momentum of her punch carried her forward. For a moment neither moved. He could see her pulse beating at the base of her throat. Her rapid breath was the only sound in the room. Her eyes were more golden than ever, wide and round as she stared up at him. There was an odd roaring in his ears. All he had to do was lower his head and his mouth would meet her soft, rosy lips, already parted in expectation. All he had to do was let his hand slide around her waist and she would be in his arms, her glorious bosom against his chest. All he had to do . . .

With a jerk she stepped backward. "I think that counts as a hit."

His hands fell to his sides. It did feel as though she'd landed a direct hit to some part of him. "Yes. This time."

She wet her lips. "I don't think there needs to be another time, Lord Burke."

"If you wish," he murmured. "Joan."

She started at the sound of her name. "That's very familiar!"

"You've already accused me of being uncouth and unmannered. You might as well leave off the pretense of decorum and call me by name, too."

"How very modern. I'm sure I don't deserve such an honor." She smiled and batted her lashes, though her blush gave away her true feelings. When Joan grew uncomfortable, he noticed, she acted like a fluttery female, with giggles and simpering smiles.

In spite of himself a wicked smile curved his mouth. "A shilling if you call me Tristan."

"I don't need your shilling."

"You might. I seem to recall we have a wager." The color bloomed in her cheeks again, but instead of denying it, she said, "You haven't won anything yet."

He nodded. That was right: he hadn't won *yet*. But he would, and damn the consequences. "Would you care to go driving tomorrow?"

"That is taking your obligation to my brother far too seriously," she said. Unless he missed his guess, her teeth were clenched behind her smile.

"The question had nothing to do with your brother. Would you go driving with me?" he repeated.

"Where, my lord?" She kept wetting her lips, and it was tormenting him.

His mouth quirked and he tilted his head toward her. "Where would you like to go, Joan?"

"Oh—well—" Her name seemed to disconcert her completely. He ought to use it more often. "Anywhere but the park," she blurted out.

A half-remembered saying about the road to hell floated through his mind. He'd intended to drive around the park. That was the normal way to pay a woman attention, wasn't it? Instead she surprised him yet again. "Not the park," he said thoughtfully. "A challenge. I shall have to think of some unusual, entertaining destination."

She appeared to reconsider. She gave a trill of nervous laughter, her gaze darting to the door again. "I didn't mean it to be a challenge. I just think it's so dreadfully dull and ordinary to drive around the park like horses in the ring at Astley's."

He laughed. "How right you are. We shan't be dull or ordinary, then. Perhaps tomorrow is too soon; I must have time to deliberate. To think of something . . . exciting."

"I didn't agree to go with you!"

"Oh?" He raised one brow. "You didn't refuse, either. Do I need to . . ." His gaze dipped again, first to her lips and then to her bosom. "Must I persuade you?"

For a moment she paused, as if she'd understood exactly what he meant and was considering provoking him to do it. For a moment, Tristan allowed himself to think of pulling her into his arms and kissing her until she said yes. Hell, he ought to have done it earlier, when she almost fell into his arms. As much as he told himself this was just a passing urge that would go away if he could only keep away from her, he couldn't seem to follow his own good sense for even a few minutes around her. Perhaps he just ought to kiss her and be done with it.

"How could I refuse such a courteous threat—I mean, request? I would be delighted." She curtsied. "Until tomorrow—or rather, whenever something interesting occurs to you, Lord Burke."

"Call me Tristan," he said. "Until then, Joan." He bowed and walked out of the room. It was time to make his escape before he lost his mind and whisked her into his arms to see if her skin tasted as sweet as her mouth.

Chapter 16

Joan was still standing stock-still, staring at the door when Evangeline returned.

"Oh, my, has Lord Burke gone already?" her aunt asked, her eyes alert and her tone far from disappointed.

Already? Surely he'd stayed far too long. "Yes."

"I'm sorry to have missed a chance to bid him farewell. Did you have a pleasant conversation?"

"I suppose." Joan frowned. At first it had seemed much like every time she'd spoken to him: confusing and infuriating. But then there had been that moment when he looked at her as though he found her more than simply challenging—as though he wanted to kiss her in truth, not to make her stop talking or to win a wager. He said he could never insult her, only her taste in clothing, and the expression on his face indicated he meant it. And for that moment, she had found herself thinking that she might owe Douglas a very great favor for having sent Lord Burke to look after her.

Then he turned back into himself, and provoked her into hitting him, not once but several times. Mother would be appalled at her for that—although not as much as for the fact that Joan had somehow promised to dance with him and go driving with him. Oh, help; she would be in so much trouble when her mother discovered that. Parading around Hyde Park in a carriage with Lord Burke would ensure a dozen letters to Cornwall from the gossiping hens.

Still . . . driving in the park was a perfectly ordinary thing to do. Her stomach had fluttered when he asked so persistently, even threatening to *persuade* her. If he'd tried to kiss her to persuade her . . . curse him, it would have worked. No matter how aggravating the man was, she couldn't shake the memory of that kiss at the Malcolm ball, or the way he looked when he said he could never insult her face. Abigail's advice, and Penelope's suggestions, rang in her ears; sometimes wicked rakes did fall in love and settle down. Her own father had, after all. Was it wrong of her to wonder if Lord Burke might be the same? And would it be wrong of her to encourage him to do so, if he showed any signs of reforming his wicked ways and falling in love with her? He was so attractive, so tall and strong, and he danced so well; he even smelled good, as she'd learned with some dismay when she almost fell into him and caught a whiff of his shaving soap.

Joan sighed. She wasn't likely ever to know if he reformed his wicked ways. It must have been a moment of lightheadedness that caused him to pay her so much attention. He stared at her bosom because he was a rake; to him, all bosoms were delectable. It made her angry all over again. If she had finally managed to attract the lascivious attentions of a rake, why couldn't it have been a charming rake? It was a great testament to her poise and restraint that she hadn't accepted his invitation to punch his handsome face with alacrity.

"Are we trying to bring Lord Burke up to scratch?" Evangeline asked all of a sudden. She had settled back into her chair, and must have deduced what occupied Joan's thoughts.

She blushed furiously. "No!" Her aunt's eyebrows went up at the vehemence of her outburst. She tried to calm her voice. "Pooh! What a thought. I don't believe he's the marrying sort. He'll be one of those men who grows into an old roué, leering at the maids and avoided by decent women."

"Well, that will likely make some indecent woman very happy."

Joan gaped at her. "Evangeline!"

"What?" The older woman was unrepentant. "He's a handsome devil. Such shoulders! And when he smiles, that dimple . . . yes, I daresay he's a bit wild, but wild men can settle down, my dear; the dull men remain dull their entire lives. Do you want to marry a dull man?"

"Well—no—"

"You could do much worse than Viscount Burke," Evangeline pointed out. "And you'd never worry that he married you for your dowry."

She scoffed. "He doesn't need a farthing!"

"Of course not. And he's a strong-willed fellow, I think. If he offers marriage, it will be because he wants you desperately."

All this thinking and talking of Tristan Burke was making Joan's head hurt. Worse, it was making her heart ache, and she didn't like that at all. She had suffered infatuations before; they always came to naught, and after a few days of tears and moping, she'd forgotten what had caught her eyes in the first place. She had waited hopefully for calls from the proper, respectable gentlemen her mother presented to her, only to find she couldn't wait for them to leave once they arrived. As soon as she decided a man was intriguing, he promptly fixed his affections on another girl; and as soon as a man showed any interest in her, however trifling or transient, she quickly realized how insipid he was. She didn't see how Tristan Burke could possibly turn insipid now, but she still didn't want to see him turn his wicked smile and lethal charm on any other girl.

"Aunt Evangeline," she said firmly, trying to force her thoughts into safer paths. "He doesn't want to marry me. I don't think he'll ever marry anyone. He's paying me attention because Douglas tricked him into a promise—"

Her aunt snorted. "Do you honestly believe he would fulfill it if he found you offensive?"

"Well—perhaps—he did say once that he found challenges irresistible," she said, feeling the color in her face rise again. "But that means he sees me as a challenge, not as a potential bride. There is a wide gulf between 'not offensive' and 'desperate to marry.' And I promise you, he is not going to marry me."

"Not if you keep cutting him off every time he pays you a compliment."

Joan was shocked. "He didn't pay me any compliment!" Saying she had finally worn a dress that wasn't ugly didn't count as a real compliment, even if he'd managed to make it sound like one. "If he had, I would have . . ." Fallen over in shock, she thought. Shock, and a wicked daze of delight. "I would have thanked him very politely."

Evangeline laughed softly. "My dear child. The way he *looked* at you was a compliment."

Mouth open to retort, Joan froze. She closed her mouth with a snap and sat back on the sofa. There was no argument there. But a lady could hardly thank a man for *looking* at her. Even if it made her skin tingle. In fact, she probably ought to slap him if his regard made her skin tingle.

Although . . . he might like that. His eyes had lit up when she punched him.

"And what's more, I think you like him. I never saw your face more animated than when you were talking to him."

"I can't think why we're even discussing this," Joan said, stirring her cold tea energetically. "My parents would never approve of him, so even if he crawled on bended knee to our door and begged Papa for my hand, he would leave disappointed."

Evangeline scoffed lightly. "You know that's not true. If you truly care for him—or for any other suitor—you should tell your parents. Neither of them wants you to be unhappy or alone. I cannot believe they would refuse to let you marry a man you really loved, Joan."

She swallowed. It was hard to imagine Papa refusing her in that situation, but she wasn't so sure about her mother. "It doesn't matter," she said softly. "Not now, anyway."

"Just remember what I said, dear," came Evangeline's gentle reply. "Don't let fear of your mother guide your heart."

"I don't fear my mother." She paused. She didn't, truly she didn't . . . she was just a little nervous about telling her mother certain things. "And if I had any affection for Lord Burke, let alone true love, and if he showed any such feeling in return, even to the point of wanting to marry me, you may rest assured I would ask Papa to agree if he asked for my hand. As it stands now, though, I see no reason to mention Lord Burke to either of my parents—and I hope you don't, either," she added, suddenly having a horrible vision of Evangeline writing to her father in favor of Lord Burke's as-yet-nonexistent suit, and the attendant furor such a letter would provoke.

Her aunt flinched, and Joan instantly regretted her outburst. "I am the very last person on earth who would press you to marry against your inclination," Evangeline said softly. "I'm sorry, Joan. I didn't mean to cause you discomfort. I won't trouble you about it again." She got up and left the room before Joan could think of anything to say.

With a groan, she put down her cup and dropped her face into her hands. What a disaster. What had she been thinking? More people than just Evangeline would think she was trying to bring Lord Burke up to scratch, once she was seen driving and dancing with him. She must have been mad not to say a loud and definite no when he asked. Instead—she took an unsteady breath as her pulse skipped a beat. Instead she was looking forward to both sins.

That meant there was only one thing to do, for

the good of her nerves and her spirits; there was only one sure way to distract her from her worries and settle her mood, and Joan felt a bit better just at the thought of it.

Go shopping.

Fortunately Abigail Weston could be counted upon. Penelope was great fun, but her attention was always drawn to the most shocking and titillating bit of anything. Abigail, on the other hand, was more thoughtful and mindful of proper behavior, which was probably why she was free to stroll down Bond Street and her sister was not. Penelope, as it turned out, had been careless, and her mother had discovered her reading *50 Ways to Sin*.

"It was her own fault she got caught," Abigail said as they walked arm in arm a few steps behind Mrs. Townsend. "I warned her that Mama was expected home at any moment."

"She was reading it in the drawing room?" Joan couldn't believe it.

Abigail nodded. "Bold as brass, settled in the window seat with a cup of tea and a plate of biscuits. Mama saw her from the street, of course, and when she came in and asked what Pen was reading, the silly girl tried to lie."

"Oh, dear," murmured Joan.

"So now Mama knows Pen has been stealing her copies—and you know what the last issue was about."

She remembered Lady Constance's adventure with the rutting Lord Everard all too vividly. The thought of what her own mother would say if she knew Joan had read that sent a shiver down her spine. "How long will she be punished?"

"A week. Mama has forbidden her from every sort of ball and party. She's not permitted to leave the house except to go to church, and Mama has been opening her letters."

"But how did you escape trouble?" Joan asked, perplexed. Mrs. Weston must know that anything Penelope did, Abigail was likely to know about.

A faint blush crept into her friend's cheeks. "Pen swore up and down that I wasn't part of it, that she'd hidden it from me. I didn't think that would sway Mama, but somehow she believed it, and I was only warned not to follow my sister's bad example. So Pen made me vow to repay her by smuggling any new issues into the house, since Mama will be watching her like a hawk."

"I was amazed at her selflessness, but now I begin to understand it," said Joan with a grin.

"Yes, very selfless," agreed Abigail wryly. "It was her own fault, but I'm very grateful not to be confined to my room, too. The only trouble is, she's badgering me to find a new issue when I don't know how to get them without drawing Mama's eye onto me as well. And if Mama discovers that both Pen and I lied to her . . ." She shuddered. "I should hate to die young, Joan."

She choked on a laugh. "Oh, never! Even my mother would only lock me in a convent until I was too old to care about naughty stories."

Abigail smiled. "True. But I fear Pen really will murder me just out of boredom if I don't bring her something interesting soon." She cast a wistful glance down Madox Street, which they were just passing. "But there's no way I can slip off to inquire about new issues without making Olivia suspicious."

Joan steadfastly resisted turning her head to look at the unprepossessing bookshop where Tristan Burke had followed her for the sole purpose of insulting and irritating her. "No, don't risk it. I may have a way to procure issues without any danger to either of us."

"What?" Abigail's face lit up. "How?"

She eyed Mrs. Townsend's back apprehensively. The young widow appeared to pay them no mind, and Abigail had sworn that Olivia Townsend would keep their confidences in any event, but Joan wasn't so sure. She lowered her voice. "Never mind how. It may not work, but if it does, I promise to share my copies with you and poor Pen."

"Oh!" Abigail's eyes grew wide. "Don't tell me your aunt allows you—?"

"Hush!" Joan pinched her arm frantically. "As if I would even ask! My father made her vow to behave, just as he did me, and somehow I doubt even Evangeline would think *50 Ways to Sin* is polite reading material for a young lady."

"How can you be certain? For all you know, she's the author."

"Abigail!" she gasped in horror.

Her friend ducked her head. "Sorry. Of course that was appallingly insensitive. But don't you think Lady Constance is begging to be exposed?"

"You mean to London at large, rather than just to one gentleman at a time?"

Abigail snorted with amusement. "Yes! How can she not know she's tempting fate to engage in such acts at the theater? I overheard Lady Willets talking with Lady Moulter the other night, and they both were at that performance, when the violinist broke his bow, and they both agreed they did hear moans such as a person in—in—in extremis might utter. She must have been very near them!"

"But who uttered them? Who is Constance, and who is Sir Gallant and Lord Everard?"

"I'm positive Sir Gallant is Sir Perry Cole," Abigail said. "It must be! He was overheard expressing his exceeding fondness for opera, and he's a handsome military man who lost his hand. It has to be Sir Perry."

"But he declared to all that he was not at the opera house that night. If it truly happened—as Lady Willets heard—then he had to have been there."

Her friend shook her head. "He might lie to conceal it. But I've no idea who Lord Everard is." A frown knit her brow. "I'm sure half the men in London know. I expect Jamie knows." She grabbed Joan's arm. "And Lord Burke *must* know!"

For some reason a flush burned her face. "I doubt it," she mumbled. "I don't think he reads them."

Abigail stopped dead. "Did you ask him? Oh mercy—*Joan*. He's going to get the new issues for us, isn't he?"

"Not if you tell all of Bond Street!" Joan hissed in a nearly silent whisper. "He might get them for me, if the infuriating man can be trusted to keep his word, but I am quite, quite sure he doesn't know what it is."

"Why not?" Abigail lurched forward when Mrs. Townsend looked back at them curiously. "How do you know he isn't interested in them?"

"He would have teased me mercilessly if he did," she said honestly. If Tristan Burke would threaten to kiss her just to get her to dance with him, what would he demand in return for procuring the most prurient pamphlet in London? The only reason Joan could find for his almost careless agreement to do so was that he had no idea what they were.

"Ah." Her friend tilted her head. "So you're on better terms with His Lordship, are you? No more Lord Boor?"

"He's still a boor," she said at once, "but perhaps . . . well, we might have made peace."

"And he's going to bring you wicked stories." Abigail's eyes gleamed with mirth. "After he wagered money over whether you would enjoy it if he kissed you again. Oh, that I could strike such a peace with a handsome viscount!"

"You sound like Penelope."

The other girl laughed. "Poor Pen! She would love the story." She sobered. "Do you think Lord Everard could be Lord Burke?"

"No!"

Olivia Townsend turned around at Joan's exclamation. Both girls immediately assumed cheery expressions and waved at her, but Abigail said, through her bright smile, "That was emphatic."

Joan did not want to think of Lord Burke's hands on Lady Constance. Unfortunately, the rest of the description fit him; he was big and strong and definitely untamed. Would he spank a woman, and ask her to beat him in return? It certainly seemed he had enjoyed it when Joan punched him—at his command, no less. Would he arrange a rendezvous with a woman for one night of pleasure without any thought of further attachment? He'd firmly said he wasn't consorting with Lady Elliot, but the fact remained that she took off her pantalets for him the night of the Malcolm ball. The mere thought of Tristan Burke being Lord Everard completely soured Joan's enjoyment of the scene. If he hadn't consorted with Lady Constance yet, it was probably only a matter of time before he did . . .

She scowled. "Lord Everard is much more likely to be Lord Hammond. He looks like a bear and I don't know how any woman could be intimate with him if she weren't allowed to whip him. Let's go to Madame Carter's to see if she has any new bonnets." She walked away without waiting for Abigail to reply, telling Mrs. Townsend they wanted to look at bonnets.

In the shop, she wandered away from her companions, who were drawn to the most fashionable bonnets with high crowns and plumes. As Joan knew all too well, those bonnets made her look twenty feet tall. She studied the plainer bonnets on the shelves, wishing she dared suggest they visit Mr. Salvatore's shop. She'd been so pleased with the day dress he made for her, she'd ordered several more, but they weren't ready yet. Papa could withhold her pin money for the next two years if he disapproved; Joan had finally found a dressmaker who knew how to flatter her, and she wanted more. If the one green day dress could improve Lord Burke's opinion of her looks so greatly, what might happen in a ball gown from Mr. Salvatore? She hoped she would have at least one more flattering dress by the time Lord Burke decided to take her driving.

Of course, a pretty dress would be covered by her pelisse, while her bonnet would be right in front of his face. Joan tilted her head and stared at a simple straw bonnet with a flatter brim and lower crown. Perhaps that one, with a silk ribbon and just a small flower . . .

She looked around, but the shopkeeper was assisting Abigail and Mrs. Townsend. Joan knew Abigail tried to buy small gifts for Mrs. Townsend whenever they went shopping, but it always took her some time to persuade the widow to accept them. Joan thought it might be easier this time, as Mrs. Townsend was trying on a very beautiful bonnet that suited her heart-shaped face perfectly. Abigail was effusing over it, and the shopkeeper, anticipating a sale, was nodding and smiling in agreement.

The shop assistants were all attending to an older lady with her two daughters, who seemed to be quite demanding customers. The two young ladies were as alike as Joan had ever seen two people be, slim and petite with shining blonde curls and sky-blue eyes. Their dresses, lavishly trimmed in the latest fashion, were marvels of striped pink silk and blond lace. The pair of them looked like an Ackermann's illustration come to life, and in spite of herself Joan couldn't keep back a tiny sigh of longing. As much as she loved her new green gown, and even felt somewhat attractive in it, why couldn't she have been born looking like one of those dainty angels? Then any bonnet in the room would have looked lovely on her.

One of the girls looked up and saw her watching. Joan nodded politely and turned back to the straw bonnet, but to her surprise the girl walked right up to her. "Miss Bennet, I believe," she said. "You're angling for Viscount Burke, aren't you?"

Joan blinked at the blunt accusation. "I—what? Er, no, of course not."

"You're a fool," the girl replied. Her voice was surprisingly strident for someone so delicate. "You're a fool to want him, and you'd be a far sorrier fool if you got him."

Oh dear. Had this girl set her cap for him? Joan had never been the focus of another girl's envy over a gentleman's attentions. Although it was somewhat flattering that someone thought her capable of being a rival—and over Lord Burke, no less—she didn't know what to say. She glanced around in discomfort, but Abigail was still occupied with persuading Mrs. Townsend to accept the bonnet. "I'm terribly sorry, I don't recall making your acquaintance . . ."

"I'm Alice Burke. Lord Burke is my cousin." A wash of pink stained her cheeks, making her look quite fetching even though her eyes flashed ominously. "And I hate him."

Ah yes, now she remembered. The Misses Burke were a few years younger than she was, and were considered two of the handsomest young ladies on the marriage mart this year. Rumor was that their mother had refused to allow them to marry anyone lower than an earl. They didn't generally move in the same circles the Bennets preferred, and as they were beautiful, they never languished in the corners of ballrooms, like Joan and the Weston girls did. Joan knew who they were, but she hadn't been formally introduced to them.

And nothing about this meeting was making her sorry she hadn't become acquainted with either Miss Alice Burke or her sister, Kitty. "How do you do, Miss Burke?" she said brightly. "It's a pleasure to make your acquaintance." Surely Abigail would notice and come save her—then again, perhaps not. Abigail, unlike Penelope, was not one to thrust herself into an uncomfortable moment.

"I'm sure your mother would be horrified if she could see the way you're throwing yourself at him," went on Miss Burke, as though she hadn't heard. "My mother can barely speak to him, even though she's forced to."

Joan wondered who on earth could possibly think she was throwing herself at Tristan Burke; if anything, she had tried to avoid him. Just her luck that people would form the exact opposite impression. "Oh? Who on earth would force her to speak to him?"

"Pray your father doesn't die and leave you at the mercy of reprobates." Miss Burke's mouth trembled as if she would cry. "Mama's had to face Lord Burke regularly for several years now, since my father died and that horrid man inherited everything."

"How dreadful," said Joan sympathetically. "I do pray for my father's continued good health every night, thank you." Though if Papa died, leaving Douglas as head of the family, Mother would keep Douglas even more firmly under her thumb. She wondered if Miss Burke spared any compassion for her cousin, who had lost both his parents at a far younger age. "It must be so dreadfully difficult for you, unable to go out in society for fear of meeting him."

Her brow creased in revulsion. "As if we would be cowed by him. He's the one who ought to avoid us! I'm sure no one wants him about anyway!"

"That would explain why he's invited everywhere," Joan murmured.

"He's a horrible person," Alice Burke repeated. "I only wanted to warn you."

She blinked. "Horrible?" It was one thing to dislike a man's manner, but to think him truly horrible? "How so, Miss Burke?"

"He forced us out of our home, and he won't let us return. Mama begged him—pleaded with him—and he only laughed and said no. What sort of man does that, Miss Bennet?"

"I thought the roof collapsed on that house." She frowned a little, racking her brain. She had twitted him about living in Douglas's house, and he'd said he had no choice, that his house was a ruin. "He can't even live there himself."

The other girl sniffed in scorn. "It's nearly repaired. My sister and I grew up there—all our memories of our dear papa are there—but he won't let us return. I had always dreamed of having my wedding breakfast in the dining room there, but now it shall be utterly impossible. That's the sort of man you've been dancing with, Miss Bennet."

Joan pursed her lips. It was hard to argue that Tristan Burke was a model gentleman. She could picture him laughing and refusing a request, if it annoyed him. And she dimly remembered, once upon a time, his declaration that his aunt and cousins hated him, and he hated them. But this sounded spiteful, and somehow she couldn't see him stooping to that level. Why would he? "Thank you for the warning, Miss Burke. You must excuse me, I see my friends beckoning me." She bobbed slightly and went to join Abigail and Mrs. Townsend.

To conceal the disquieting encounter, she bought the straw bonnet, but fell quiet as they left the shop. Abigail and Mrs. Townsend chattered happily about the bonnet Abigail had indeed impressed upon her friend, leaving Joan to her thoughts. Could Tristan Burke have treated his aunt and cousins as cruelly as Miss Burke described? Joan's main experience of gentlemen was her brother. She thought over all the times they had quarreled and snapped at each other, and knew there was a wide gulf between what she thought cruel and what Douglas thought cruel. Men simply thought differently from ladies. Miss Burke, with her blonde curls and big blue eyes, was probably utterly unaccustomed to being denied anything by a member of the male sex, let alone something she desperately desired. And Lord Burke seemed to be less susceptible than most men to female sensibilities.

Still, it would be very rude to laugh in the face of a mother pleading to restore her children to their home, even for him. Not that he hadn't laughed in Joan's face, more than once, and she'd thought him very rude then, even over trifling matters like the note she made Douglas sign. It only made a sharper contrast to his actions when he came to tea, when he'd been . . . admiring. Intriguing. Attentive. And the way he'd looked at her, with that heavy-lidded gaze and wicked hint of smile . . .

She said a bad word under her breath. Not even shopping for a new bonnet had succeeded in driving him from her mind. Was it always this way, dealing with gentlemen? In all her dreams of suitors, she'd never guessed that having one could be so frustrating.

It took her several minutes to realize that she had begun to think of him as a suitor.

Chapter 17

Before she reached the breakfast room the next morning, Joan could tell her aunt had a visitor. She could hear a soft rumble of conversation, a man's voice as well as her aunt's lighter tone, and then, just as she turned the knob to enter, a sharp bark.

Evangeline and a very handsome gentleman glanced up like two guilty lovers at her entrance. Her aunt looked happy, flushed pink with laughter and one hand stroking a small dog curled up on her lap. She had been leaning forward, her whole body tilted toward her guest, but now sat back in her chair. "Good morning, Joan!" She gave her companion a rueful look. "I didn't expect to see you so early. This is Sir Richard Campion. Sir Richard, my niece, Miss Joan Bennet."

Sir Richard was already on his feet, and swept a gallant bow. "A very great pleasure, Miss Bennet."

"And mine," she replied, eyeing him with interest. So this was the fearless explorer who had climbed mountains in Switzerland and traveled into the dark recesses of Africa—and who was also her aunt's reputed lover. According to rumor, he was far younger than Evangeline, but Joan wouldn't have guessed it to look at him. He was about Papa's height, and very fit, almost lean. His light brown hair was streaked with silver threads, and his face was tanned and lined, especially around his eyes. But those eyes, a startling blue, were keen and alert, and his whole manner crackled with energy. He was dressed like a country squire but moved with the grace of a London gentleman.

The ginger dog in Evangeline's lap barked again, a sharp little yip. Evangeline smiled fondly as she scratched the dog's ears. "And this is Louis. Sir Richard has been caring for him while I'm here. He brought my Louis for a visit."

"He missed you so, my dear," said Sir Richard, smiling at her. He spoke with a trace of accent, clipped but soft.

"You must meet him properly, Joan. Here; take a bit of bacon and call him." The little dog, his fur bristling, jumped to the floor as Joan got a piece of bacon from the sideboard. He trotted over to her feet and sat, his tiny tail wagging furiously and his dark eyes fixed on the bacon. "Good boy, Louis," said Evangeline. "Be polite!"

Louis sat back and raised one front paw, holding it in front of him like a cavalier begging for a lady's hand for a dance. "Oh, how darling you are, Louis," cried Joan. She stooped and held out the bacon. He delicately nipped it from her fingers and settled down to chew it. Joan looked up. "Why didn't you bring him with you, Evangeline?"

Her aunt waved one hand. "He's a demanding

little fellow. I knew he wouldn't have enough exercise here in town. He's much happier in Chelsea."

"Oh." Louis had finished the bacon and was regarding her hopefully, tail wagging once more. Joan let him sniff her hand and lick her fingers, then stroked his fur. He stretched his neck and his eyes drooped closed as she scratched under his chin with its ruff of soft fur. "I wouldn't mind if he stayed."

She looked up in time to catch the wary glance exchanged between her aunt and their visitor. "You promised me I might have him for a month at least," said Sir Richard lightly. "Who else will keep Hercule in line?"

Evangeline smiled—gratefully, Joan thought. "Poor Hercule! I imagine he cannot wait for Louis to be gone."

"Who is Hercule?" Joan came and took a seat, held out for her by Sir Richard.

"Hercule," said Sir Richard as he returned to his own seat, and there was a scratching from the far side of the room. To Joan's shock, the biggest dog she had ever seen came padding around the table. Mostly black with brown and white markings on his head and legs, he sat obediently next to Sir Richard's chair, where his head was almost level with his master's shoulder.

"He's enormous," she said faintly.

"But very amiable in temperament." Sir Richard took a sausage from his plate and offered it to the dog. Hercule sniffed it and ate the entire sausage in one bite. "I brought him back from Switzerland," Sir Richard added, leaning over to scratch the dog's throat. Hercule put his head back and gave a gusty sigh of pleasure. "He was born to climb mountains and herd goats, and all I give him is London streets."

"And a pestilential little dog to plague his every waking moment," Evangeline said wryly as Louis wormed his way between Hercule's massive paws and began sniffing for a stray bit of sausage, walking all over the bigger dog as he did so. "Louis! Come here," she scolded her pet.

Louis gave a sharp yip, but returned to her. Evangeline scooped him up and rested her cheek in his fur, only smiling as the little dog licked her chin.

"We must be on our way," said Sir Richard, taking one last sip from his coffee cup before rising from the table. "The streets should be safe from geese now, and we can make it home without peril."

"Very well." With a sigh Evangeline put her dog on the floor, and Sir Richard slipped a lead over his head.

"Good day, Lady Courtenay." Sir Richard raised Evangeline's hand to his lips. From her chair, Joan caught a glimpse of her aunt's glowing face. Whatever rumor had got wrong about them, it was very clear that Evangeline adored Sir Richard. He bowed to her as well. "Miss Bennet." He went to the door, Hercule following close behind. Louis went willingly as well, but doubled back around Hercule to plant himself in the doorway and bark sharply at Evangeline. Joan could almost hear the demand in that bark: come along!

"Louis," said Sir Richard firmly, nudging the little dog with his foot. Louis ignored him, dancing out of the way of his boot to bark again at his mistress. Sir Richard gave Evangeline an exasperated look.

"Louis," she said in reproach, and her pet's tail drooped. He gave one more bark, dispirited, and then went with Sir Richard and Hercule, his tiny feet tapping on the polished floors.

It was very quiet in the room after they left. Joan filled a plate at the sideboard, noticing how the maid came at once to clear away the complete setting from Sir Richard's place. His visit had not been a short one. It was early now; he must have arrived at least an hour ago. And Evangeline must have expected him, for her to be up so early and already dressed—and very becomingly, for a morning.

"Why didn't you bring Louis with you?" she asked as she took her seat again. "I'm sure Papa wouldn't mind."

Evangeline, still gazing at the door, started at Joan's question. "Why, my dear, it would be the height of rudeness to bring a dog when one is a guest! Louis is well settled with Sir Richard at his house in Chelsea; he can run in the garden and not be chased by geese, who frighten him to no end. Sir Richard nearly had to carry Louis in his coat pocket when they met a pack of geese on the way to market this morning." She smiled and reached for the teapot. "Can you just picture it? Louis's head peeping from Sir Richard's greatcoat pocket, yapping frantically at a marauding goose?"

Joan buttered her toast with great care. She had told enough evasive truths in her life to recognize one when she heard it. Evangeline had given

up her dog and her companion to come play at
chaperone, and there was no mystery why. It was
surely no accident that both had come very early,
before Joan was expected to rise, before the neighbors would remark a man or dogs visiting. Joan
couldn't see her father protesting the dogs, but
now that she thought about it, her mother disliked
animals in the house. And she could only imagine what Mother would say about the gentleman.

She waited until the maid had left the room
with the tray of dishes. "Are you going to marry
Sir Richard?"

Evangeline's eyes flew to meet hers, wary and
unreadable.

Joan bit her lip and forged on. "I know it's rude
to ask, but . . . well, I could see you care for him,
very much, and he must care for you to bring your
dog to visit so early in the morning. My mother
keeps assuring me that I'll find a man who cares
for me and then marry him, so I only wondered
why, when you've found a man who cares for you,
you haven't married him."

Evangeline slowly set down the teapot. She
added sugar to her tea and stirred it, then added
more sugar, all without looking at Joan. "It's not
as simple as that. Sir Richard . . . I . . ." She took
a deep breath and seemed to give herself a tiny
shake. "The truth is I don't want to marry again.
I've buried two husbands already." She smiled
ruefully. "It's bad luck to marry me! Everyone
who's done so has died within ten years of the
wedding. The poor man is better off as he is."

"Did you care for your husbands?" Joan asked
softly.

Her aunt took a long sip of tea. "No. The truth is, Joan, you are very fortunate your parents want you to find someone you care for, who cares for you in turn. Not everyone views marriage so tenderly."

"It sounds so simple when you say it that way—find someone you care for who returns your regard—but it really isn't," she said with a sigh. "My mother wants me to find a man who cares for me . . . who also has the right breeding and manners, good connections, and with some fortune of his own. While I—"

"Yes?" prodded Evangeline gently when she stopped speaking. "What do you want?"

Joan shrugged. "What every girl wants, I suppose. A man who is kind and considerate, handsome and graceful, tall and strong. There seems to be a terrible shortage of such men in London at the moment, sadly."

"And Lord Burke is none of those things . . . ?"

She nibbled at her toast, trying to pretend she had never thought of him. "Lord Burke? Well, he's tall, I'll grant him that."

"And very handsome," added her aunt. "He moves like a pugilist; so light on his feet. I daresay he's an accomplished dancer. And a man who boxes is often quite strong."

Joan threw down her toast. "He's not considerate, and he's been downright rude to me. He told me I looked like a half-opened umbrella."

Evangeline's eyebrows went up. "Indeed! When he was here for tea?"

"No," she said, aware that her face was flushing. "At a ball a fortnight ago. He asked if I had something against flattering fashion."

"I expect his opinion changed," murmured her aunt. "He seemed very struck by your appearance in that lovely green frock, my dear."

Yes, he had. The memory brought a small smile to Joan's face in spite of herself. "Perhaps a little," she allowed. "But I heard something of him the other day . . . Were you ever acquainted with his aunt, Lady Burke?"

"Oh, Lord. Her." Evangeline took a deep breath. "Very slightly. What did she tell you about him?"

"I've never met her," Joan hastened to say. "But I heard he's been rather callous to her, and I wondered if it could be true. A man who is cruel to his aunt and cousins cannot be considered kind, can he?"

"Callous!" Evangeline gave a cynical snort. "Mary Burke is a prickly woman, and always has been. She was a beauty in her day, but her manner turned off the most eligible men. She married Edward Burke, who was a handsome fellow even if the dullest man in Christendom, which was a step up for her family. You may recall what I said about the current Lord Burke's father?" Joan nodded. "He was as charming and gregarious as his older brother was reserved and staid, and Mary disapproved mightily of him. She made no secret of the fact that she thought he would come to no very good end . . ." Evangeline's eyes grew shadowed. "And I suppose she was right. But the worst thing Colin Burke did, in Mary's eyes, was wed an heiress. Most of young Burke's fortune comes from his maternal grandfather, not from his father."

"Which means he was wealthier than his uncle

even when he was a small boy," said Joan slowly. "And his aunt . . ."

"Lord Burke is very like his father, so she was bound to dislike him anyway. But yes, I'm sure the money stung her pride as well."

"So you would discount her words about him?"

Evangeline made a face. "If anything, I'd credit the exact opposite of her words about him, or anyone else."

That cast a completely different light on things. Not only had Lord Burke lost his parents when he was practically an infant, it appeared he'd been right when he said his aunt and cousins hated him. Joan fiddled with her spoon. Surely if they had treated him so coldly, a little callousness on his part could be forgiven. If Miss Burke's manner in the millinery shop was any indicator of the way they treated him, he was probably justified in hating them. Still—to turn them out of their house?

"Is Lady Burke in dire straits?" Miss Burke's costume had been exquisite, but it could have been bought on credit. If they had been left without a place to live, that would seem very hard.

"I doubt it," said Evangeline in surprise. "The Burkes have always had money, and I never saw a less likely spendthrift than the late Lord Burke."

Joan nodded. That didn't eliminate the sentimental attachment Miss Burke had claimed, but it hardly stooped to cruelty.

There was a tap on the door, and Smythe entered with two florist's boxes. He placed one box before each of them.

"My," said Evangeline in surprise as she untied the string. "I wonder who would have sent these?"

Joan ignored her aunt's rhetorical question and busied herself with opening her own box. She had received bouquets before, but none since her second Season, years ago. And these flowers were unlike those long-ago daisies in every way. Inside the box lay a sheaf of long-stemmed lilies, of such stark simplicity she could only stare.

"Arum lilies," said Evangeline. "How exotic!"

"They're beautiful." Joan lifted one out to see it better.

"Lord Burke knows his flowers, I see." Evangeline fished the card out of her box, which held a bouquet of brilliant tulips.

She dropped the lily back into the box and ripped open her own card.

I hope you will grant me the pleasure of your company on a drive two mornings hence, it read. *Be ready early. It will be worth the wait.*
—*Burke*

For a moment she had to fight back a pleased smile. He might be an enigma, but sending flowers meant something, didn't it? He certainly hadn't needed to; it wasn't as though he was courting her . . . was he? From anyone else, flowers and invitations to drive might be construed as such, but from him, it was impossible to tell.

"He asks permission to take you driving the day after next." Evangeline held her card out. "I will grant it, if you want to go. But if I've misread you, dear, and you don't want to go with him, I am perfectly willing to take the blame and refuse him."

She bit her lip. His note to Evangeline was only a little longer, but far more polite. He thanked her for tea the other day and asked very properly for permission to take Joan driving. It seemed he could be a gentleman when he wished to be one. And what did he mean, the wait would be worth it? What did he plan to do? She handed the note back. "He did mention something about driving, but I expected him to forget all about it."

Her aunt just gave her a wry look.

She pressed her lips together. "Even now he hasn't fixed a time—early! What does that mean? Is he going to turn up before dawn with some mad plan to drive to Greenwich?"

"Absolutely not," said Evangeline. "Your father would murder me."

"Well, it would be very like one of Douglas's friends to ask and then not arrive. Two days is a long time to delay."

"I expect he'll come. No one made him ask to take you driving. Don't say Douglas did," her aunt added as Joan opened her mouth. "Douglas is hundreds of miles away. Besides, Lord Burke doesn't look the type to take orders well."

That was true. "That doesn't mean he won't regret asking."

Evangeline just smiled. "Perhaps you should trim that new bonnet, just in case."

For some reason this made her shoulders tense. Two days might be enough time for Mr. Salvatore to deliver another new dress, but she didn't have a decent bonnet. And for some reason Joan was loath to wear her old, unflattering bonnet on the drive. "I don't know how to do it without it making me look tall."

"But you are tall," her aunt pointed out. "How do you plan to hide it?"

"Obviously I cannot hide it," said Joan wistfully. "But I don't have to wear a bonnet that makes me look even more enormous."

Evangeline laughed. "Enormous! Oh, really. You've been standing next to the wrong people. You are not too tall."

"Not next to you, but next to everyone else I am."

"Nor next to Lord Burke." Joan glared at her. Evangeline tried to look innocent. "It's true! He must be at least five or six inches taller. You could wear my beaded silk shoes with the lovely heel and still be shorter than he."

"Everything need not involve Lord Burke!" she growled. Although she wouldn't mind wearing shoes like those ivory silk ones, and if the only person she could conceivably dance with while wearing them was Lord Burke . . . perhaps it would be worth the sacrifice.

She got to her feet and picked up her bouquet. "I'll just go have Polly put these in some water before I consider the bonnet."

"Make sure she fetches the proper vase," said her aunt as she headed for the door. "Arum lilies are very tall." Joan glanced over her shoulder suspiciously to see Evangeline hold a pink tulip to her nose. "Lord Burke seems fond of tall things," she added almost idly.

"You're incorrigible," she declared.

Her aunt grinned. "I know. Don't tell your mother."

Joan shook her head and turned to go, but the butler came into the room again with the post. She lingered as Evangeline sorted through it.

"Several invitations," she remarked. "And—oh my—" She dropped the stack of letters and tore one open.

Joan tried not to spy, but abandoned all pretense when she recognized the writing on the front. "It's from Papa!"

"Yes, it is. Here is one for you." Her aunt handed over a smaller letter, which had been sealed inside the other. Joan seized it and unfolded it, and the room was quiet as they both read.

Papa wrote that they had remained in Bath. Mother had been very tired from the journey that far, and once she recovered enough to go on, she had asked him to reconsider going all the way to Cornwall. The weather in Bath was very fine, enabling them to venture out almost every day, and Mother's lungs seemed to be improving in the country air. They had taken a house in the Crescent and were spending the days very quietly, although Mother hoped to have some society as her health returned. Papa was insisting that she visit the hot baths every day, and the waters had done her a world of good. The tone of his letter was wry and amused, and Joan unconsciously relaxed as she read. It had been a fortnight since her parents had left, and she could tell Papa was far less worried about Mother now than he had been. Mother must be improving if she had the strength to argue with Papa over going to the baths.

"Mother is doing much better," she said, folding her letter. "I'm so relieved!"

"Yes, it is very good news!" Evangeline beamed at her. "Your father says they might return within the month."

"So soon?" Joan tried not to think what that would mean for drives in the park with Lord Burke. "The doctors must be very confident. I thought Papa would insist she remain in the country for the rest of this year."

Evangeline ducked her head and began folding her own letter. "Yes, he's always been very protective of her. And wisely so, in this case."

And when Mother and Papa returned, Evangeline would leave. Joan gazed at her aunt, whom she had barely known a fortnight ago and now felt a deep kinship with. She would miss her aunt, with her unconventional demeanor and agreeable nature. She got up again to leave, then hesitated at the door. "I do hope Louis comes again. And Sir Richard, if you would like to see him. I'm sure my mother wouldn't object." After all, Mother had allowed Evangeline to come in the first place. Joan told herself a short visit from a small dog surely wouldn't count for much, and Sir Richard had behaved as properly as anyone might wish.

Evangeline's face softened. "Thank you, dear. Thank you so much."

Chapter 18

Aside from the note with the lilies, there was no further word from Lord Burke about their drive. Joan told herself not to count on him, but when she found herself awake early on the morning he'd indicated, she got up and dressed instead of lying in. She reasoned it was just so she wouldn't be caught off guard, or that perhaps Sir Richard would bring Louis to visit again, and in any event it was healthy to get up early. She could walk in the park with Abigail, or persuade Evangeline to take a trip down Piccadilly in search of new bonnet trimmings. She certainly wasn't going to spend her day waiting on Tristan Burke, but neither was she going to allow him to find her unprepared.

And it was all a good thing, she found, when the sound of carriage wheels rattled to a stop on the street outside just as she finished her breakfast. Joan almost broke her teacup, setting it down with a crash of china. She hurried into the hall to catch Smythe before he could send Lord Burke—if indeed it was he—on his way.

The butler had just opened the door, revealing the infuriating man himself on the doorstep. "I've come to call for Miss Bennet," he said, looking far too alert for this time of day—and unspeakably attractive. It hit her anew how terribly handsome he was, especially when he wasn't bent on tormenting her. The slanting morning light seemed to magnify the span of his shoulders and render the angles and planes of his face in stark, glowing relief.

Smythe turned around, his expression stiff with disapproval. He had seen her come running and now waited for a word from her. Joan checked the urge to rush forward, and managed to glide into the hall as gracefully as Mother might have done. "Good morning, sir," she said with a proper curtsy. "You were right to specify 'early.'"

A grin lit his face. The dimple was especially noticeable today. "Grand adventures take a bit of time."

"Grand adventure?"

He just dipped his head. "Are you ready to go?"

Goodness. Grand adventure! What on earth could he mean by that? As usual, he was not behaving as she expected . . . and as usual, it made her unbearably intrigued. "Just a moment."

Joan hurried to get ready. She buttoned up her gray spencer with unsteady fingers, and had to take a deep calming breath before allowing herself to go back downstairs, this time at a stately, dignified pace that hopefully hid her quickened pulse.

Outside a very smart curricle waited, gleaming in the early light. A fresh-faced boy in livery held the horses' heads. Tristan helped her into the carriage and took the reins from his tiger. He snapped the reins and the horses started off. When she asked what grand adventure he was taking her on, he refused to say. He headed north, out of town, and for a while Joan just watched the scenery go by, enjoying a ride through the streets at an hour when she was normally still abed. It was like a different town, with maids out busily sweeping the steps and the main streets filled with carts on their way to market instead of carriages carrying ladies on calls. They rolled past the park, where a bank of mist hovered over the open grass, and crossed Oxford Road, leaving the familiar part of town behind. The fog was thicker here in the larger fields and more scattered houses, and it was like driving into a fairyland.

She had just begun to wonder where he was taking her when he pulled something from his coat pocket. "I mustn't forget to deliver the object of your desires," he said, holding out a crisp issue of *50 Ways to Sin*.

Joan gaped at it before snatching it from his hand. "Thank you."

He watched her try to conceal it under her gloves. "The shopkeeper gave me quite a look when I asked for it."

"I'm sure he did." She prayed the breeze would keep her blush at bay. Affecting disinterest, she stuffed the pamphlet into her reticule. "I told you it's a lady's serial. You're likely the first gentleman in all of London to purchase it."

"It's got a lurid title." He lowered his voice

suggestively. "Are you certain you're not reading something you should not?"

"It's a comedy of love, ironically titled," she lied. "Very romantic, with scandalous rakes pursuing fair ladies, who hold them at bay until they declare their love in poetry and song and repent of their sins to become devoted husbands. You may read it if you like." It was a bold move; if he called her bluff . . .

"No, thank you. Just knowing it's a ladies' serial is enough deterrent." He reached into his pocket again, and slapped something down on his knee. A bright shilling winked up at her. "And there's my stake," he said, "for our wager."

In the blink of an eye Joan went from being weak with relief to being keenly aware of how close he was to her. The seat seemed to have shrunk as she stared at the coin balanced on his well-muscled thigh, so near her own. "We haven't got a wager; both parties must agree before it is binding."

"Ah, you're a coward."

"Nothing of the sort."

"Then you know you would lose."

She tore her fascinated eyes off his knee. "Perhaps I just don't want to take your coin."

"I see." He pinched the shilling between two fingers and held it up, studying it. He handled the horses quite easily with one hand, the reins playing between his gloved fingers. "You drive a hard bargain, miss. The stakes are far too low for a gamester of your style, it appears. I'll make it a guinea."

"You could make it a monkey and I wouldn't play," she retorted airily.

"A monkey!" His eyes lit up. "Great God, what a contest that would be! It must be some feat of great daring and skill that will decide the matter; five hundred pounds is no trifle . . . What was it we were wagering on?"

Joan had to laugh. "Do you wager on everything?"

"It makes most things more interesting."

"A mere shilling can transform a question of no importance into something that must be accomplished at all costs?" She shook her head. "Gentlemen are the oddest creatures."

"I never said this question was of no importance." He dropped the shilling back into his pocket and turned the curricle off the road, slowing the horses as he drove over the grass. "Rather, a wager was one means of gaining the desired result."

"You never thought of asking courteously?" Joan clutched the edge of the curricle with one hand and her bonnet with the other as the vehicle lurched over the uneven ground, heading uphill.

He gave her an odd look, half amused, half alarmed. "And ruin my hard-won reputation? What on earth for?"

"Well, it's often easier," she observed. "And it costs you nothing."

"Hmm." He stopped the horses and set the brake, then turned to face her. "But if you don't win a shilling from me, how can I win a shilling from you?"

"Who says you'll ever win a shilling from me?" she asked, trying to ignore the way her heart leapt. That damned wager about kissing; now he was looking at her mouth with far more interest than a single shilling could inspire . . .

Slowly he leaned toward her. Joan held her breath. "I like contests," he murmured. "And I intend to win this one. Shall we get down and walk?" he added in his normal voice. "Kit, hold the horses." He jumped down from the carriage as his tiger went running to the horses' heads, and held out a hand to help her. "Joan?"

She realized her mouth was hanging open, and snapped it closed. She had just noticed a balloon, rising above the mist like a multicolored cloud. "Someone's going ballooning!" she exclaimed. "How exciting! I've only seen one once before, last year for the King's coronation. Do you think they're going up soon?"

"Yes." He waggled his fingers. "Will you step down now?"

She let him help her down, gazing breathlessly at the balloon all the while. It was beautiful, towering over the field in vivid stripes, like a sectioned orange in red and white. Long lines of ropes crisscrossed around it, forming a net that tapered down to a basket that looked ludicrously small beneath the balloon. Joan needed no urging to keep up with Tristan as he led the way up the rise across the damp grass. She'd never seen a balloon up close. It was enormous, but beautiful.

A man in country clothing strode out to meet them. "Lord Burke," he said genially. "Good morning, sir. Madam." He made a quick bow but hardly spared her a glance.

Tristan tipped his head back, squinting at the sky. "How are the prospects this morning?"

"Very good, very good. The mist is burning away, but the cool air is a benefit. The burner is working well today; we're nearly ready to be away."

"Excellent." Tristan glanced at Joan. "Shall we go up?"

Her mouth fell open again. "Up? In the balloon?"

"No, in the car beneath it," he said. "The balloon is filled with gas. There's no place for you in the balloon."

"I—we—you can't mean it," she protested, looking up at the balloon with trepidation. Now that she looked closely, she could see the fabric ripple, exactly like a piece of fine silk when caught by a breeze. It looked more fragile than beautiful from this near. The thought of taking flight in it was deeply alarming. She was sure Mother would faint dead away at the thought. Proper ladies surely would. And yet . . .

"I mean to go up," said Tristan, his eyes glinting with the same wild excitement she felt, although apparently undiluted by any fear. "I thought you would find it thrilling. No more circuits of the park."

She turned her dazed eyes to the balloonist, who nodded vigorously. "It's quite all right, ma'am. I've gone up dozens of times."

"This is Mr. Charles Green, who lofted the balloon from Green Park last year for the coronation," Tristan put in. The balloonist swept off his broad-brimmed hat and smiled politely, although not managing to hide his eagerness to be off. "We should be able to view all of London from five hundred feet."

"Five hundred feet!" She began shaking her head. "Oh, no, that's much too high."

"It's only a little higher than the dome of St. Paul's. Come—you may hold my hand."

"Fifty feet," she said, trying to tug free of his grip.

"Three hundred," he countered.

Joan anxiously surveyed the balloon. It swayed gently from side to side. A dozen men stood around the car beneath it, obviously waiting for it to ascend. "My father will kill you if I fall to my death."

Tristan turned his back to Mr. Green and clasped her hands between his. "If you don't want to go up, you don't have to. But it's beyond thrilling—to slip free of the earth and rise like a bird . . . I can't even describe it. We can go up a short way and you may decide if we go higher."

"What if Mr. Green wishes to go higher than I do?" she whispered.

"He'll do what I ask him to do," he said. "Where do you think he got the funds for his new burner?"

Her eyes widened. "You invested in this?"

"It's ingenious, the way he's got it arranged. It burns ordinary gas, rather than hydrogen. The burner is more efficient, and it costs far, far less—" He stopped and grinned. "But you aren't interested in all that. Will you come up with me?"

Her heart began to pound. His enthusiasm was contagious, and now that she'd got over the surprise of it, the idea grew more appealing by the minute. She pressed his hand and smiled, a little nervously. "Yes."

Tristan felt a wild exultation when she agreed.

She put back her head to study the balloon again, her eyes bright and a small smile curving her lips, and he very nearly leaned down to kiss her, right in front of Green and all his men. That was the look he'd been hoping to put on her face, pleased and excited even if a bit uncertain. Instead he squeezed her hand and followed Green, feeling like a boy on the brink of a great adventure.

The car was woven of stout wicker, with a wooden floor. It wasn't very large, and equipment took up some space. As Green and his men worked to get the balloon ready, Tristan drew Joan back against him. "We've got to stay out of their way," he explained when her coffee-colored gaze flashed at him. "Wouldn't want to upset the aeronautical preparations." His hand lingered on the curve of her hip. Thank God she'd bought some decent gowns and left off wearing a dozen petticoats. He could feel the shape of her through the crisp cotton, and it fueled a hundred wicked images he'd sworn he wouldn't let himself picture.

He took a deep breath, which only served to remind him how delicious she smelled. He was proving himself a very great idiot. A few desultory dances, a call or two, and he could have satisfied his obligation to Bennet. He was sure that's all Bennet had had in mind when he extracted Tristan's vow. There was certainly no need to wager on how well he could kiss her, because he wasn't supposed to kiss her again—even if he thought about it every time he saw her, and definitely not because she sometimes looked at him in direct challenge that all but demanded he kiss her into soft, happy silence. He ought to spend less time with her, not more.

But after tea the other day, when she looked so shockingly lovely and he couldn't think of anything but touching her, Tristan had been determined to do something to please her, as a way of making up for his past failings. Taking her ballooning seemed an excellent choice: something she'd probably never do on her own, but thrilling and exotic. He wanted her to remember this morning for the rest of her life. He knew he would.

Green cast off another bit of ballast, and the car wobbled, rising an inch or so off the ground. Joan gasped and clutched at his arm. "I forgot to ask how we shall get down again," she said with a shaky laugh.

"My assistants will pull us down," said Green. "In free flight, we would cast all the ropes off, but Lord Burke assured me he didn't wish to spend the day drifting through the skies—although it is one of the most remarkable sights man may see," he added with a hopeful glance at Tristan.

"Not today." But Lord, he wouldn't mind it. As Green cast off the rest of his ballast and the ropes creaked and the balloon rose into the steel-blue sky, Tristan wanted to shout aloud in elation. This was what he loved, a triumph of science and engineering combined with the unparalleled thrill of thwarting gravity. He spread his feet for balance, and unconsciously put his free hand on Joan's back to steady her; she still clung to his other hand where he held the wicker car's edge, but she was leaning forward to peer over the edge and didn't seem to notice.

"Oh my," she gasped. "We're so high!"

He grinned. They couldn't be more than thirty feet off the ground. "Just wait. Look at the view."

Green had chosen a spot on Parliament Hill, which already commanded a good view of London. As they rose above the mist and trees, the city spread beneath them like a land of mystery, a gauzy blanket of fog shrouding all but the tallest buildings. The Thames wound through it like a dark vein, sparkling in the east where the clouds must have cleared. The land was a patchwork of verdant fields sliced by hedges, with small towns such as Camden and Islington looking like villages of children's toy blocks.

A gust of wind set the wicker car to swaying; the balloon strained at the ropes with an audible whoosh. Joan gave a little cry, gripping his arm with renewed strength.

"Are we falling?" she gasped, craning her neck to see the balloon above them. "Is it bursting?"

"No." He slid his hand around her waist, pulling her closer. To his great surprise—and pleasure—she let him, even pressing against his chest, although her eyes remained fixed on the balloon. "It's perfectly normal." He had to put his mouth close to her ear as Green fiddled with his burner and it roared anew. "The wind is stronger up here."

She glanced at him. The wind had loosened a wisp of hair from beneath her bonnet, and it teased around her mouth. "You've done this before?"

"Three times. As you can see, I have yet to suffer any grievous harm."

"All it takes is one time," she retorted, but he felt her body ease against his.

"If we plummet to the ground, I shan't argue at all if you ring a peal over me as we fall."

She blinked, then smiled. And then she laughed, her eyes glowing. "I would blister your ears for taking me to my death!"

"No doubt," he said, grinning. "Although it's not precisely how I would like to spend my last minutes on earth."

"What would you do instead? Place wagers on the odds of surviving?"

He reached up to stroke away that tormenting wisp of hair, and let his fingertip slide over her lower lip. If Green weren't two feet away, he would kiss her right now. "No."

Her lips parted. She understood his meaning. "Well." She cleared her throat, still gazing up at him. "I suppose you wouldn't be able to collect on those wagers anyway."

"No. But I would try to settle another wager."

Her cheeks flushed dark pink. "Oh?"

He smiled and dipped his head, until his lips brushed her ear. "Surely you wouldn't deny a man's last request . . . to hear his given name."

She jerked and gave a shaky laugh. "Rest assured, you would hear it, loudly and repeatedly— mingled with a great many curses and condemnations."

He laughed. "That's the usual way I hear it. But tell me truly." He swept one hand to the side. "Surely this is worth chancing it."

Joan looked out over the mist and caught her breath. She had been so fascinated by watching

the ground recede, and then by the way he held
her, that she'd barely taken in the view. By now
they had risen so high, the men holding the ropes
beneath them were small figures blurred by the
fog. But rolling down the hill toward the river lay
a beautiful vista. London had never seemed so
small. She squinted at the tiny buildings, searching for anything to anchor the scene.

"Is that St. Paul's?" she asked excitedly, pointing at a familiar dome.

"Yes, and there is Westminster Abbey." He
turned and gestured to the east. "On a clear day
one can see the Royal Observatory in Greenwich,
and if we were to go a little higher, the crenella-
tions of the Tower of London."

"Oh, my," Joan breathed. She tried to pick out
streets and familiar places, but it was all so different from up here. London looked as quiet and
sleepy as any country village, with none of the
noise and smell and bustle she identified with it.

Just like the man behind her. With his boots
braced wide and one hand on the overhead
bracket that held the burner, Tristan Burke bore
no resemblance to the infuriating rake who
teased her at Lady Malcolm's ball or the arrogant
boor who called her an umbrella. His face was
alive in a way she'd never seen before. He threw
his head back and inhaled deeply before looking
right at her with those brilliant green eyes, and
burst out laughing as if he couldn't contain the joy
inside him. "Isn't this grand?" he shouted over
the burner.

Joan smiled back. It was. She'd never dreamed
of doing this—and she kept a firm grip on the

edge of the car, just in case the wind grew too strong—but it was exhilarating. His obvious, unfettered joy only added to it. When he was happy, Tristan was . . .

She turned her gaze away from him. He had leaned over to ask Mr. Green something, and since the car was so small, he had to press against her. She could feel the warmth of his arm around her waist right through her dress and spencer. This was by far the longest time they had spent together without arguing, and the unfortunate result was only that she found herself wishing he would be like this all the time. When he was in this mood, she couldn't help reconsidering her answer to Evangeline, about bringing him up to scratch. Not that she knew what her answer to any marriage proposal would be, but she had an alarming feeling she would like being courted by Tristan, very much. Part of her didn't want this balloon voyage to end, and for a moment she even thought of telling Mr. Green to cast off his ropes and let them drift on the wind for hours, away from London and society and everyone who would be shocked speechless to see her with him.

Not for the first time, she felt a bit annoyed by that. He wasn't so very high above her touch; she was a baronet's daughter, after all, with very respectable connections. It was true that he was wealthier than her father, but Papa was hardly destitute, and his title was far older than the Burke viscountcy. Why shouldn't she have as much of a chance at someone like Tristan as any other girl in London? Handsome men had married plain ladies before. She might be an Amazon, but, as

Evangeline had observed, he was even taller. And as much as he could infuriate her, she was becoming more and more certain that he wasn't the rude reprobate she had accused him of being. Alice Burke had called him horrid, but even Joan had never seen him behave that badly. He had only responded to her as she had treated him—which only made her wonder what would happen if she tried flirting with him . . .

They stayed aloft a while longer, taking in the view from all sides as Tristan pointed out whatever landmarks grew visible as the mist burned off. The clouds were blowing away, and the sun had come out. It made the viewing much better, but it was still considerably cooler here than on the ground, and Joan finally rubbed her arms, wishing she had worn something warmer than her gray spencer.

"Are you cold?" asked her companion. Without waiting for her reply, he ducked around the burner. "Mr. Green," he called. "We're ready to descend now."

"Oh, it's not that cold," Joan protested, but he pretended not to hear over the wind. He drew her close again and turned the front of his driving coat around her. Joan closed her eyes and let him hold her, again wishing they could stay aloft longer—especially like this. Tucked inside his coat, securely held in his arms, she had absolutely no wish at all to go back down.

But Mr. Green was already leaning over, waving his hat at the men on the ground. Within moments she felt the first pull on the ropes, reeling them back to earth. Slowly the grand view disappeared from sight, until they settled back onto the grass with a thump.

Tristan leapt from the car first and held out his arms. When she put her hands on his shoulders, he lifted her right over the side as if she were a mere slip of a girl. She stumbled a bit when her feet touched solid ground again; it was remarkably steady after the sway of the wicker car. But his hands were at her waist in an instant, steadying her, and Joan had to make herself move away, she liked the feel of it so much.

He said a few words to Mr. Green, to whom Joan curtsied and said thank you as well. They left as the men swarmed the balloon, retying the ropes that held it down and loading the car with ballast.

The world looked very flat and small from down here, after the view from on high. Joan pictured again the rolling hills and winding river, the clusters of buildings and the gleaming spires of churches, and gave a happy sigh. What an adventure! She never would have dreamed of such a sight.

"Thank you." She paused, then repeated, "Thank you, Tristan."

At the sound of his name, his head came up, and he looked at her sharply. His piercing green eyes were wary for a moment, and then a smile bent his mouth. "Ah, the lady triumphs. I owe you a shilling."

Joan rolled her eyes. "Keep the bloody shilling. I was merely trying to thank you."

His smile dimmed, and for just the flash of a moment, he looked uncertain. "I had to do something impressive."

"Why? A simple drive was all I expected."

"A simple drive!" He made a bored grimace. "Who wants that? So conventional, so ordinary, so dull—your own words, madam."

"And nothing with you must be conventional or ordinary," she said dryly. "I suppose I must be grateful you didn't hire the balloon for the middle of St. James's Park."

He grinned. "That would be a sight! Would you have come with me, if I had?"

"Most certainly not."

"Wouldn't you?" His voice dropped a register. "But you enjoyed it. What would be different, if people had *seen* you enjoying it?"

"They would have seen me with you," she said before she could stop herself.

"Right." His coaxing grin disappeared. "Heaven save you from that."

"No." She stopped in her tracks and a few paces later he did as well. "I didn't mean that," she apologized. "I did enjoy it, and it was entirely thanks to you, for having such a brilliant, unexpected idea and going to some considerable trouble to arrange it."

He just looked at her. His long hair had come partly untied by the winds aloft, and a stray strand blew near his cheek. For once there was no trace of mockery or arrogance or even humor in his expression. He simply stood there, waiting for her to explain.

And she owed him an honest explanation, not some prevarication about her mother's approval. Joan had often wished she possessed more courage, more bold willingness to blaze her own path and pursue her own interests, no matter what her mother or society said. But her rebellions were of the small sort; when faced with the thought of public censure or her mother's disappointment, she curbed her impulses. Hiding a copy of *50 Ways to Sin* was a minor transgression. Gallivanting about London with Tristan Burke would not be viewed the same way. "I'm just not accustomed to people staring at me," she went on awkwardly. "It isn't usually for the right reason, and it rarely ends well for me."

"What would be the right reason?" he asked after a moment.

"Well . . ." She quickly closed her mouth. The right reason would be that she was wearing something stunningly fashionable, or had lost two stone of weight and six inches of height and looked like a siren, or that she'd just done something amazing, such as revealed a hitherto unknown talent for singing Italian opera. Or even, perhaps, attracted the most eligible, elusive gentleman in town to her side . . .

"It just never is," she said with a sigh. "When people stare at me, it's because I've worn something frightful or suffered another ball without dancing once. Sometimes they stare at me in pity, when my brother's done something particularly dreadful. Or, lately, they stare in expectation of my aunt corrupting me into her scandalous and outrageous ways."

His jaw tightened. "And being seen with me would be scandalous and outrageous."

It would be. All of London would be shocked. Abigail would be worried. Penelope would be thrilled. Evangeline would probably be proud. But her mother . . . Her mother would be appalled. Not only did she distrust Tristan Burke, she had extracted a firm promise from Joan not to see him. Ballooning with him, anywhere, would definitely count as a violation of that promise, even if Joan invented a whopping story involving highwaymen and abduction at gunpoint to explain it.

"You must admit you have worked hard at creating that impression," she said, dodging a direct reply.

"Have I?" He rocked back on his heels. "You give me too much credit."

She scoffed. "You open doors half naked, you wager on everything, you fornicate in public—"

"Never in public," he said immediately.

"Near enough!"

He shrugged. "Not nearly enough, in Lady Elliot's opinion. She's the one who took off her pantalets and threw them at me."

Joan's cheeks burned. "I can't believe you said that! That's indecent!"

"You brought it up," he said, unrepentant.

"You really don't know how to talk to ladies, do you?" she exclaimed, but the moment she heard the words aloud, they made perfect sense. It explained a great deal about her infuriating encounters with him. He didn't follow the usual rules of gentlemanly conduct or conversation, and he refused to give ground. No topic of conversation was out of bounds—in fact, he seemed to delight in shocking and unsettling her. Telling her that women took off their pantalets for him! As if she wanted to picture Lady Elliot offering herself to him on the chaise; Joan had thought it a particularly juicy bit of gossip a few weeks ago but now it put her in a cross mood, even crosser than when Abigail suggested Tristan could be Lord Everard in *50 Ways to Sin*. Only a very loose woman would do such a thing, of course, but . . . she wished Evangeline hadn't said Tristan would make some indecent woman very happy. It wasn't right. It wasn't right that it sounded so dreadfully fascinating. Why couldn't he be just a little more proper and save her from the most terrible thoughts? Why couldn't he want to make a moderately decent woman happy?

There was only one thing to do. She must think of her mother. She must try to think *like* her mother. And above all, she must not wonder what he might do if a woman . . . such as Joan herself . . . were to tempt him to win that cursed wager right here and now . . .

He gave her his slow, heavy-lidded smile, the one that almost burned with wicked suggestion. "No? I seem able to convey my intentions well enough."

Think of Mother. What would Mother say? Joan inhaled a desperate breath. "That's exactly what I mean. You talk approvingly of loose women who pull up their skirts for you. You talk with notorious gossips because you delight in sending them off with some wild rumor you know isn't true. But the rest of womankind you avoid, because you haven't the slightest idea how to be genuinely polite or charming or considerate. You're like a child, Lord Burke, taking delight in shocking and outraging people."

He did not look reproved, or even moderately abashed. In fact, her stern rebuke appeared to amuse him, as his smile grew. "Oh?" he drawled. "You prefer dull, dry men who can't say one interesting thing all evening?"

Not in the slightest. Even Mother wouldn't agree with that statement. Joan glared at him in impotent frustration. "At least they don't drive me mad!"

"Do I really drive you mad?" His voice dropped as he asked the question, managing to make it sound seductive and—and—and interested.

Oh, help. Surely not even Mother would know what to say to a man when he looked at her this way.

"You make me want to kick you sometimes," she told him in a fury.

He stared at her a moment, then threw back his head and shouted with laughter. She pressed her lips closed and stomped past him toward the carriage. She was going to ask Sir Richard if he could have Hercule chase Lord Boor out of town. If Hercule tore a large hole in the seat of his trousers, she would applaud the dog.

Tristan ran after her. "Joan, wait!" She whirled around, seething, when he touched her elbow, and he put up both hands in a gesture of surrender. "I was wrong." She raised one eyebrow and waited. He adopted a penitent expression and placed one hand over his heart. "My dear Miss Bennet, I'd no idea my presence and demeanor were so disturbing to you. My humblest apologies."

"Very well." She glared at him. "Just don't talk to me of women removing their pantalets for you."

"Never again," he said at once. "The word shall never cross my lips."

"Nor any other unmentionables," she added. "Not stockings, or petticoats, or stays, or shifts or bodices or garters or anything a woman might wear." Douglas was a master at finding ways to circumvent promises, and Joan had learned to pin him down very closely. The last thing she wanted to hear was how another woman had let Tristan Burke unlace her stays.

His lips twitched, but he nodded somberly. "As you wish. I shan't speak of anything more indelicate than a handkerchief, ever again. May I escort you home before you are irrevocably corrupted by my polluting influence?"

She eyed him warily, but finally put her hand on his offered arm. "You may."

For the trip back into London, Tristan behaved with as much decorum as Joan could have wished; as much, even, as Mother could have wished. He apologized for driving too quickly over the cobbles. He commented upon the weather, but nothing more controversial. He called her Miss Bennet without fail. He ignored the furtive, skeptical glances she gave him from time to time. And Joan found, to her complete dismay, that she was thoroughly bored. He was behaving just as a gentleman ought to, and she didn't enjoy it at all. She tried to tell herself it was because she knew it was all a facade, but deep down she feared it was because she liked him better as a rogue. Rogues were interesting and exciting, even if sometimes infuriating, and perhaps she'd been too hasty. What if he kept up this gentlemanly act, just to torment her?

In South Audley Street he maneuvered the curricle right up to her steps and jumped down. He helped her down from the carriage and waited while she adjusted her bonnet. Then he took her hand and bowed very properly over it. "Thank you for the pleasure of your company, Miss Bennet." He clasped her hand in both of his and gave her a smile. "I enjoyed it immensely." But as he released her hand, he pushed something under the edge of her glove.

Her eyes widened at the feel of cold metal against her skin. "What—?"

"Your winnings," he murmured, giving her the sly look that never failed to make her heart skip a beat. "After all, you're going to need that shilling . . . later."

And he jumped back into his curricle and left her standing there, speechless and blushing, his shilling held tight in her fist.

Chapter 19

Evangeline was pacing the hall when Joan came into the house. "Oh, Joan!" she exclaimed, stopping short at her entrance. "There you are!"

It dawned on Joan that she'd been gone a long time—and that Evangeline had been worried. She untied her bonnet and handed it to Smythe. "Yes, at last! I've no idea how the time got away from us."

Her aunt's mouth tightened. "Indeed." Mustering a patently false smile, she held out her arm. "It must have been an exceedingly pleasant drive. Come tell me all about it. Smythe, ring for tea, please."

The butler, who wore his usual stony face, bowed. Joan chewed her lip as she followed her aunt to the drawing room. Oh, dear. She'd got used to her aunt's more permissive attitude, and gone too far. She thought of what Mother would say if she were here, and felt a little nauseated.

"Well?" Evangeline closed the drawing room door behind her.

"You'll never guess—we went ballooning!"

Joan put on a wide smile and prayed for the best. "It was such a complete surprise to me, but I shall never forget it!"

Her aunt's lips parted. "Ballooning? Up in the *air*?"

"Oh, yes, and it was brilliant!" she enthused, remembering the view. "We didn't go very high, but could still see ever so far—the city looked like a trifling little huddle of buildings along the river, visible all the way from St. Paul's to Chelsea and even further! I never dreamt of such things!"

"Nor did I!" said her aunt with no trace of delight—rather the opposite, in fact. "When you were gone so long, I feared—well, never mind. But Lord Burke asked to take you *driving*. On the ground."

"We did drive—to Parliament Hill, where the balloon was."

"Parliament Hill?" Evangeline blanched. "All the way out of town?"

"Mm-hm." Joan nodded with a bright smile, trying to maintain the illusion that the outing had been utterly normal, completely respectable, and unworthy of further comment. She hadn't really thought about her aunt's reaction when Tristan urged her to give it a go. Somehow she hadn't thought about Evangeline, or Mother or Papa, at all. "You ought to try it. I'm sure Sir Richard would accompany you, if you asked."

Her aunt's mouth closed with a snap. "Sir Richard is a grown man. If he wants to allow himself to get blown away in a balloon, that is his choice."

"We couldn't get blown away," Joan tried to say. "There were men holding the ropes."

"And if those ropes had broken, where would you be?" exclaimed her aunt. "Still drifting over England, I expect! Or worse. I remember a balloonist who fell to his death when his balloon deflated suddenly. What would I have told your parents?"

Joan bit her lip. "That I was a grown woman able to choose my own fate?"

"Your father would strangle me before I got to the end of the sentence." Evangeline pressed her fingertips to her forehead and inhaled loudly. "Joan, dearest, you must understand. I never had children of my own. Your parents paid me the greatest compliment they could have when they left you in my charge. I don't pretend that I know what it's like to leave a child to someone else's care, but I know I would throw myself in the Thames if something happened to you—and not merely to spare your father the trouble of doing it himself. Please, my dear, dear girl, please don't try to make my heart give out by going ballooning again."

"I didn't know we would," she replied in a very small voice. "Tristan didn't tell me."

"Nor did he tell me, more fool him!" said her aunt tartly. "I shall speak to him about that."

"Very well," she whispered, thoroughly cowed now.

Evangeline hesitated, then shook her head and went to the cabinet in the corner. "A year of my life, gone in one morning!" She unstopped the brandy and poured herself a generous finger. "It's a good thing I never had children; I would have made a terrible mother." She tossed back half the brandy in one gulp.

"Oh, don't say that!" Joan hurried across the room. "I'm very sorry. I shouldn't have gone. I just—I just didn't think of it that way. It seemed a daring adventure, and there were the ropes, and Tristan said it would be perfectly safe . . ."

Her aunt eyed her closely. "And you don't get enough daring adventure on your own, do you?"

It seemed disloyal to Mother, but she shook her head anyway. She didn't. Whether it meant she was a wild hoyden at heart, ungovernable and reckless, or that she was a very disappointing daughter for being unable to respect her mother's teachings, all she knew was that ballooning had been one of the most thrilling things she'd ever done in her life. When the car left the ground and Tristan gathered her into his arms to steady her, she'd felt alive and nervous and exuberant all at once, and more excited than ever before in her life.

Evangeline took another sip of her brandy, then put the glass down. "Come here." She led the way to the sofa and patted the cushion near her. When Joan took the seat, Evangeline leaned forward. "Was it exciting because you've always longed to go ballooning? Was it exciting because your mother doesn't allow you to venture off much, and it was just the chance of doing something new?" She paused. "Or was it exciting because Lord Burke took you?"

She blushed. "I'm sure it would have been the same with anyone else."

Evangeline raised one eyebrow. "Oh? It didn't have any special meaning because Tristan was there?" She drew out his name for significance, making Joan realize she had been calling him that since she returned.

"He did ask me to call him by name," she defended herself. "I've known him since we were children, and he's such firm friends with Douglas, and of course I wouldn't call him by name in public. But as for the rest . . ." She lifted one hand and let it fall. "I suppose all of those things made it exciting."

"I see. And yet you remain convinced he has no intention of marrying you."

"He didn't mention that, no." She avoided her aunt's gaze.

"And if he were to mention it . . . ?"

Joan didn't say anything.

"I thought as much," said her aunt gently. "Why do you believe your mother is so set against him?"

"She thinks he's wild—and he is," Joan added, trying to be fair to her mother. "He can be rude and arrogant and completely indiscreet. He doesn't care what people say about him, and you know how Mother prizes propriety."

"And yet?" Evangeline prodded. "What has changed your mind about him?"

She closed her eyes. "I never had such a thrill as today," she confessed. "And he arranged it just for my enjoyment. He infuriates me, but partly because he often says the things I long to say but dare not. I look forward to seeing him because there's something irresistible about him: it's like a contest I grow more and more determined to win every time he confounds me."

"He's a very handsome fellow," remarked

Evangeline. "And I must say, he hasn't been rude in my hearing."

She squirmed. "I think Mother's opinion of him was formed at an early date, when he came home with Douglas on holiday from Eton. They got up to so much trouble, even Papa raised his voice with them."

"Nonsense. It would be cruel to hold a man's childhood antics against him."

"He hasn't done much to redeem himself since then. He reinforces Douglas's dissolute inclinations and seems to thrive on being wicked." Joan sighed. "She made me swear not to dance with him again."

"Ah. And does your father share this disdain for Lord Burke?"

She blinked. "I've no idea. I can't recall ever hearing his opinion of Tris—Lord Burke. Most likely he agrees with Mother, though."

For the first time a faint smile touched Evangeline's mouth. "That would be hypocritical of him! I daresay a ballooning outing would have been just the thing to appeal to my brother when he was younger, although he wouldn't have wanted any ropes tying him to the ground. Lord Burke reminds me a great deal of your father at the same age, to be perfectly honest. And I well remember how he changed when he met your mother."

Sometimes notorious rakes fall in love . . . "How did he change? I cannot imagine Mother falling for a scoundrel."

"He was a scoundrel until he wanted to please her," said Evangeline. "And she disdained him at first—oh, yes!" She nodded at Joan's amazed expression. "She wouldn't dance with him, and when he begged to know why—he was considered a catch, you know—your mother told him exactly why. He gave up his worst friends, curtailed his gaming, and kept asking her to dance. I know gossip held that she played him like a fish on a line and tamed him to her hand, but if he hadn't wished to win her favor, it wouldn't have mattered. For her, he changed some of his habits, and she grew to understand him and accept the rest."

She nibbled her lip. "But what about you? You said you didn't love your husbands."

The light faded from Evangeline's face. "My father chose my first husband. I was very young—too young to understand how different Lord Cunningham and I were. My second marriage was less decorous; I did have more hope of loving Lord Courtenay, but . . . your parents were wiser in love than I was."

"But Sir Richard." Joan peeked at her aunt. "You love him."

A veil came down over Evangeline's expression. "We are talking about you, and whether you wish to encourage Lord Burke."

Put that way . . . yes, she did. "He makes me feel attractive," she confessed. "No one else does that."

"He finds you very handsome, judging from the way he looks at you."

"He also makes me want to hit him at times," Joan added.

Evangeline smiled. "It sounds very promising to me! I never understood why people think a marriage should be unalloyed bliss and agreement."

"So you think I should encourage him."

"He arranged a balloon expedition, just to impress you. He asked you to dance—he even argued for your acquiescence. I've heard enough gossip to know he's not regularly out in decent society, and certainly not to dance with unmarried young ladies. Even if you wish to blame all that on your brother," Evangeline said as she pursed her lips, "I'm quite certain Douglas never told him to look at you as if you were a fascinating riddle he can't stop thinking about and longs to solve."

"Well, that feeling is mutual," muttered Joan. Tristan Burke was an enigma to her, but somehow she seemed unable to stop thinking about him. The shilling, still where he had slipped it inside her glove, was like a talisman of his promise to kiss her again. "But in other respects I think we might drive each other mad."

"I recommend you let him kiss you," said Evangeline.

Joan's eyes nearly popped from her head. "What?"

"First, it will prove he wants to kiss you—that he views you as a desirable woman. Second, you can tell a great deal about a man from the way he kisses. A light peck means little; men kiss their sisters so. A devouring kiss that goes too far often means a man's interest is limited to . . ." Evangeline coughed delicately. "Improper attentions. But a kiss that coaxes and seduces and tempts, rather than demands, a response . . . that is the sort of kiss that a man bestows when he wants to win a woman's heart."

"How on earth can you tell the difference?" asked Joan when she could speak again. Her face must be scarlet. Her heart pounded in her ears. He'd already kissed her, and so far it had only confused things even more.

"By how much you want him to kiss you again." Evangeline must have misinterpreted her stunned silence. She leaned forward to take Joan's hand. "A kiss—*only* a kiss, mind you—is not ruination. I daresay your own mother allowed your father to kiss her before she agreed to wed him. A woman must be sure of her feelings before she pledges herself to one man for life."

"Thank you for the advice," Joan managed to squeak. She excused herself and hurried from the room, her hands trembling and her heart thumping. The shilling seemed to be burning a hole in her palm. She stripped off her glove and shoved the gleaming coin deep into the drawer of her writing desk. She slammed the drawer shut and sat for a moment, hands gripped tightly together, replaying the kiss in her mind with her aunt's words as guide.

It had not been a light peck, as a man might give his sister. Had it been devouring? If so, she was somewhat shaken to admit she'd wanted to be devoured, because it felt so . . . so . . . good. But he hadn't done anything but kiss her. She remembered with acute clarity how she'd ended up pressed against Tristan, but he hadn't tried to touch her bosom, even though he'd called it delectable. As she knew from *50 Ways to Sin*, when a man truly wanted a woman, kissing was merely the prelude. Not that she would dare engage in the debauchery Constance described, but . . . one couldn't help wondering . . .

Joan took a deep breath and ran her fingers lightly down her throat, over her breast, trying to imagine it was Tristan touching her. Her flesh responded by tightening, and her nipple rose into a hard knot of exquisite sensitivity. She shivered. Would Tristan touch her like Sir Everard touched Lady Constance? Would he want to make love to her and pleasure her until she nearly swooned? She stroked herself again, thrilled and startled by the sensations. Janet had scolded her many times that it was wicked even to look at one's naked self in the mirror, but Lady Constance reveled in baring herself to Sir Everard's admiring gaze.

Oh, help. Was this what it was like to be pursued by a man? To be wanted? Her skin felt too hot and too tight for her bones and blood. She squeezed her eyes shut and pressed her knees together, for the ache in her breasts had spread all the way down her body. It was one thing to be titillated by reading a story about a man touching a woman, and quite another thing to imagine a particular man touching *her*.

She opened her eyes and caught sight of her reticule, lying where she had thrown it on her bed. With a start she jumped up and went to get it, pulling out the new issue of *50 Ways to Sin*. She stared at the simple cover illustration. Despite what she had told him, there was little of love or romance about these prurient stories. They were as wicked as could be, and she wondered if he really didn't know what they were. And if he knew, would he dare to get them for her without having some hidden motive? It seemed impossible anyone could be unaware of them, but he was unlike anyone else she knew. He didn't attend most society events; Joan could count on one hand the number of times she'd seen him at balls or soirees before that fateful meeting at Douglas's house. If he kept company with Douglas, he probably spent his days at boxing matches and horseraces, and his nights at gaming clubs and taverns. Every woman in town might be talking of *50 Ways to Sin*, but as far as she could tell, Tristan avoided most women . . .

Except her.

She put the pamphlet aside, suddenly alarmed by what thoughts it might inspire. Who would have guessed that being courted could be so unsettling?

Chapter 20

When Tristan thought about the balloon voyage, he was left with two distinct impressions.

First, he would enjoy winning back his shilling. He'd spent an unpardonable amount of time watching Joan's mouth, and had come to realize it was damned near perfect, just the right shape and a very appealing shade of pink. He thought about kissing her when she exclaimed aloud in delight, as they hovered above London, and he thought about kissing her when she pursed up her mouth in affront because he said the word "pantalets." He even thought about kissing her when she declared a desire to kick him, which probably ought to be taken as a warning sign of insanity, but he never could resist a challenge.

Which all led to his second impression, that he was playing with fire by continuing to see her. Douglas Bennet had asked him to see that she didn't waste away in unhappiness. Tristan could excuse ballooning as a means of fulfilling that promise. He could not, in any way, excuse his increasingly lustful thoughts about Bennet's sister, and the more time he spent around her, the more numerous and more lustful his thoughts became. When Joan listed every undergarment a woman could wear, all he thought about was removing each item from her body, possibly while he won back his shilling.

This inspired real alarm in his breast. A few weeks earlier, he'd thought her the most intractable Fury. Now he was thinking about having her naked while he kissed her into happy oblivion. That was not only the way to madness, it could even lead to worse: marriage.

Tristan viewed marriage as something to be avoided at all costs. It was a trap, baited with a pretty face or a plump dowry, but a trap that sprang shut with alarming quickness, and had only one way out: death. Men had stepped into it willingly, of course, but how many of them regretted it later? Once the dowry was spent and the bride lost her bloom, all that was left was imprisonment, one man and one woman chained together in eternal matrimony.

People had told him his parents cared for each other. He wondered if it was true. If so, love hadn't been enough to keep his father at home with his wife and son, instead of venturing out in a fierce storm and drowning. And according to Tristan's childhood nurse, love had sent his mother to her grave soon after, her heart broken over her husband's death. None of it spoke well of love matches, and as for the other kind . . . he could remember all too well the evenings at Wildwood, when he was forced to sit quietly in the corner while his uncle drowsed by the fire and his aunt embroidered in frosty silence, the only sound the crackling of the fire. God alone knew what had drawn those two together, but it looked like the worst sort of hell to Tristan. He had sworn he would never find himself in that miserable existence, penned in by a woman's demands and disapproval.

Although, in fairness, it did seem unlikely that Joan could ever be like Aunt Mary. When he tried to picture her embroidering by the fire, the image rapidly devolved into one where she cursed her thread and threw the thing into the fire, whereupon he laughed and kissed her until they ended up making love on the hearthrug. He could just picture her, head thrown back in desire, skin bathed in golden firelight, her perfect lips sighing in passion, urging him on as he drove himself deep inside her . . .

Bloody hell. The mere thought of making love to her brought a sweat to his brow and an aching hardness to his groin. He tried to tell himself the thought of making love to any woman would do the same, but each woman he tried to picture on that imaginary hearthrug somehow looked like Joan, with coffee-colored eyes glinting with gold, long chestnut hair spread around her, and the finest bosom he'd ever dreamed of, like a feast of berries and cream.

Still, he didn't need to get married. He didn't need a wife's dowry. He could bed any number of willing women if he set his mind to it—not Joan, it was true, but there were other women with lovely bosoms and sparkling eyes. Just because he didn't feel like searching out any of them meant nothing. Besides, he had done his duty by calling on her and taking her ballooning. In fact, he probably had done more than enough and didn't need to see her again. After a few days he would forget all about removing the Fury's unmentionables, let alone kissing her to reclaim his shilling.

The next night he purposely avoided the Martin soiree, where Lady Courtenay had mentioned they would be, and went to a gambling hell instead. He invited a buxom blonde to sit on his knee, and then promptly sent her away when she giggled at everything he said. He lost over two hundred pounds at faro. He drank too much and arrived home in a hack, barely able to walk but consumed with wondering if she had looked for him that night.

The next day he tried the boxing saloon, but not even a pounding in the ring distracted him. The day after that he went to the horse auctions, and ended up bidding on a sweet bay mare he didn't need; it was a lady's mount, taller than most mares but with a smooth gait and a gentle disposition. In the nick of time someone outbid him, and then he was furious at himself for being disappointed to have lost the horse. He tried the theater, but his preference for outrageous wit played him false, and he heard every saucy line as if Joan Bennet had murmured it in his ear. He spent hours and hours at his house, overseeing the builders, and found himself wondering far too often what she would think of the glass dome over the stairs or the new conveniences he'd installed.

That was the final straw. When he found himself curious to know her thoughts on plumbing, he gave up the pretense of disinterest. The next day he went to South Audley Street.

He still planned to be as dull as possible, reasoning that his usual behavior seemed to provoke her to respond in kind. Perhaps if he acted in the complete opposite manner, so would she. Then she would seem like any other respectable young lady, ordinary and uninteresting, no longer posing any sort of challenge. It would also help if she wore one of her more unflattering dresses, with enough lace to cover her entrancing decolletage. He was not used to being so consumed by thoughts of one woman, and he didn't know what to do about it.

Lady Courtenay received him alone, to his disappointment. He bowed and took the seat she indicated, trying not to watch the door. Perhaps Joan was coiling up her shining hair, pinning it into that alluring arrangement that displayed her slender neck so well. Perhaps her garter had come untied, and she was pulling up her skirt, exposing her long legs to tie it . . .

"How kind of you to call again," said his hostess. "I've wanted a chance to have a word with you, sir."

Tristan guiltily jerked his gaze back to her. "Indeed, ma'am?"

She fixed a stern eye on him. "Ballooning?"

He brightened. "Did she tell you about it? I hope Miss Bennet enjoyed it as much as I did."

Her brow arched. "How much did you enjoy it?"

"Enormously. I've been funding Mr. Green's experiments with new burners. He strives to make it easier and safer, and he was accommodating enough to take us up for a view of the countryside."

Lady Courtenay smiled faintly. "How very daring it sounds! I'm not certain I could watch the earth recede so far away from me, with only a thin balloon of silk to hold me up."

He grinned. "Yes, Jo—Miss Bennet said much the same thing. But I never would have asked her to go up if I weren't completely satisfied it was safe."

"And you are persuaded it was safe?"

"Absolutely," he confirmed.

"In all ways?" Something about the way she said "all" caught his attention. Tristan narrowed his eyes and tried to think what she really meant. At his silence, Lady Courtenay sat forward, her expression serious. "I presume you are aware of your own reputation." He nodded warily. "Good. I have trusted that you are a gentleman, gossip notwithstanding, and will act accordingly, but I must tell you that inviting Joan to go ballooning will create the appearance of . . ." She paused delicately. "Intentions. Take care not to create any expectations you don't plan to fulfill."

"Are you warning me off?" he asked. His muscles had tensed until he felt as stiff as a board.

Lady Courtenay looked surprised. "Not at all! Rather the contrary. Merely letting you know the scope of the challenge ahead of you."

"What challenge?" he growled, but the door opened before she could reply, and Joan walked in.

The question faded from his mind, along with almost everything else. She wore a dress of brilliant turquoise that seemed deliberately wrapped around her curves, and without a shred of lace to hide anything. Tristan managed to bow, but couldn't take his eyes off her.

"What a surprise to see you again, my lord," she said.

He watched, fascinated, as she took the seat opposite him. The dress was trimmed with gold cord that snaked over her shoulders, coiled just below her bosom as if to highlight the lush bounty of her breasts, and then went around her waist. It put him in mind of a sacrificial virgin, bound and ready to be given to the god. "Surprise? How so, Miss Bennet?"

She smiled. "It seems I've lost my wager with my aunt."

"Oh?" He tried to shake off the pagan images streaming through his mind. "I thought you disapproved of wagering."

She widened her eyes innocently—as if he hadn't learned by now to be on guard when she looked like that. "By chance, I found a stray shilling, and couldn't resist risking it."

He shouldn't respond, he knew it, and yet . . . "Are you certain that was wise? One should never wager what one cannot afford to lose."

She waved one hand in careless dismissal. "I doubt I'll notice the loss."

Oh Lord; he was being drawn in again. Tristan ignored the little voice in his head warning him to sit back and nod like a dullard. "Tsk, tsk. It's never good to purposely embark on a losing streak."

She leaned forward, just enough to remind him of the absence of lace. "I remain firmly convinced

I would have won. But, as our dispute was never put to the test, that hardly matters now."

"Quite so!" exclaimed Lady Courtenay. Tristan had almost forgotten she was in the room. "Some matters simply must be put to the test; no theoretical argument will decide them, one way or another. Don't you agree, Lord Burke?"

He let his eyes slide down Joan's figure, so temptingly bound. "I do, ma'am."

Joan gave her aunt a baleful look. Lady Courtenay just smiled. Tristan barely noticed. He couldn't drag his eyes away from Joan. She looked ethereal, like some kind of sensual goddess. Intentions—expectations—challenges—the words beat at the edges of his brain, half temptation, half warning. He wasn't ready to marry . . . but if he were looking for a bride, she'd bloody well look like Joan did right now.

"My niece tells me you are rebuilding your house," Lady Courtenay said.

"With as many improvements as one house will hold, ma'am." Tristan grinned in spite of himself. Possibly the only subject that could distract him from Joan's new and vastly more flattering wardrobe was his house.

"Was it really uninhabitable?" Joan asked. "Did the roof really fall in?"

"It most certainly did, with a spectacular crash that sent the neighbors running into the street in alarm, and only through pure chance was no one hurt. It ruined all the attics and servants' quarters, and water came down through the east side of the house, buckling the plaster and ruining the woodwork."

"Goodness!"

"It must have leaked for years, given the scope of the damage. My uncle was a bit parsimonious with his housekeeping maintenance, and I doubt Aunt Mary ever gave one thought to the roof, so it wasn't discovered until earlier this year."

"But you said it collapsed."

"That was how I discovered the leak," he said dryly. "Barely a week after I took possession, too. After the collapse, my aunt claimed to have had no warning that it was in danger, but I did wonder at her sudden desire to quit the house after so many years."

"I shouldn't doubt it," murmured Lady Courtenay.

"Although . . . in a way I'm not sorry at all," Tristan continued slowly. "It provided the perfect opportunity to rebuild it. Once you've lost the roof, it's easy enough to raise the new one and add more space. Once you've pulled out an entire wall of plaster, it's little more work to enlarge the doorway. Now the house will be as I want it to be, and not cramped and dark as I remember it."

"So perhaps it's not the worst that could have happened," Joan said. "If you disliked what was ruined."

"My thought exactly." He flashed her a pleased look. "Would you like to see it?"

Tristan didn't even know why he offered. Joan blinked as though she didn't, either. But Lady Courtenay jumped into the breach. "Why, I should like it above all else! I've often contemplated improvements to my own house, but it's so difficult to picture them. Have you installed any water closets?"

"On every floor," he said with a touch of pride.

"I simply must see it." Lady Courtenay glanced at her niece and laughed. "What a strange woman you must think me, eager to see the water closets!"

"There's far more than that to see," he said, watching Joan.

"Well, then." She lifted her chin, a small smile touching her lips. "Let's go see it."

The carriage was ordered, and soon they were on their way. Tristan guided his horse alongside the carriage, partly pleased and partly anxious. The pleased part was easy to explain; he had lavished attention on his house, and felt his pride in the result was entirely justified. But as for his anxiety . . . he wondered if Joan would approve of the place, and then he wondered why he cared. It wasn't her house.

He tried to see it with fresh eyes as they went into Hanover Square. The house stood on the northeast side, built of dark brick. It had been one of the first houses built, a full century ago, and until recently it had looked every bit that old. He was having it updated inside and out, with new railings and a small portico to protect guests from the rain, but for now it was clearly a work in progress.

He helped the ladies down and led the way inside. Barely inside the door, he had to stop to move a box of tools out of the way. "Mind your step. It's a bit of a shambles," he said in understatement.

The hall was modest, with the stairs set well

back from the door. That had been the biggest change, pushing the stairs back to allow for a door into a small parlor, partitioned off the long, narrow library behind it. He fancied it for a morning room, since it faced east. To the right was the dining room, where Tristan directed his visitors.

It was clean, but the plaster was still fresh. Two walls were unpainted, and the chandelier was swathed in cloth. The floor was badly scuffed and some of the oak paneling still remained on one wall, looking very dark and out of place with the fresh walls. But the windows had been repaired, and the fireplace surround had been cleaned of a century's accumulation of soot.

"This must be a handsome room," remarked Lady Courtenay.

He took in the high ceiling and gracious proportions of the room. "I hope it will be, eventually."

"Did the water penetrate the house so thoroughly?" Joan motioned to the gaps in the woodwork.

He grinned. "No. That was simply ugly."

She laughed. "How opportunistic!"

"Yes, a great many ugly things have been removed." Tristan rubbed his toe over a burn mark on the floorboards. He could still smell tobacco in this room from the many cigars Uncle Burke used to smoke after dinner. He'd come to hate that smell because it meant he would be interrogated about his schoolwork and personal habits, when his aunt had left the room. Not until the carpet was removed did he discover that the ashes had burned down to the floor. Those scars would also be sanded away.

"I remember coming here when your uncle died, to make our condolences," Joan said quietly. "It was such a dark house. I never imagined it could be so bright. What will you put on the walls?"

"Ah . . . I've no idea." He turned on his heel, trying to picture the room without the blood-red wall papers and dark oak paneling. "What do you suggest?"

She blinked at him. Lady Courtenay had strolled to the far end of the room and vanished into the adjoining parlor, leaving them somewhat alone. "It is your house."

"It's becoming mine, at any rate." He surveyed the room again. "I always hated being here."

"Why?"

He lifted one shoulder. "It was dark, as you said. Cold. Miserable. I only came here when I had no other choice."

"Was that why you came to Helston Hall with Douglas?"

He chuckled. "I remember that house! Does the window on the servants' stair still make a terrible creak?"

"It does not," she said with a laugh. "My father nailed it shut after you and Douglas caused such mayhem. My mother insisted."

"Right." He grimaced. "I completely destroyed her good opinion of me, didn't I?"

She looked self-conscious. "Oh—well, I'm sure you and Douglas were equally responsible . . ."

"No, I know she laid the blame at my feet. And I can hardly claim innocence, can I?" He gave her a wry grin. "Still, I was sorry not to be invited

back. That was one of my favorite holidays from
school."

Her face blanked in surprise. "Why?" She
clapped one hand over her mouth. "I meant to say,
I'm glad you enjoyed your time there . . ."

"No, no." He waved aside her polite correc-
tion. "I know your mother took an instant dislike
to me, but Helston was still a warm, comforting
place. Even when your father reprimanded us,
he was patient and reasonable about it. You'd be
surprised how many schoolmates had homes as
gloomy and grim as mine."

"Did you go home with someone every holiday?"

"Whenever possible," he replied.

Her brow knit. "I thought so. Douglas described your life with no small amount of envy;
merry and carefree, he called it. I think he was
quite envious."

Tristan snorted. "From the comfort of his own
home and family! I would have happily traded
places with him."

"But you had a home," she said slowly. "With
your aunt and uncle. Even if it was dark and cold,
it was still . . . well, it was still home, wasn't it?"

Tristan's mouth twisted. "If by home, you mean
a place where I was tolerated during any school
holiday when I couldn't wrest an invitation else-
where, then yes, I did."

"Tolerated!"

"Reluctantly," he added. "If I hadn't been the
heir—which was a circumstance of immense
regret to my aunt and uncle—I'm sure it would
have been a great relief to everyone not to have
me about at all."

"That's horrible!" She sounded appalled. "Surely that's not true!"

"No, it's quite true. Still is, I daresay, if anyone asks Aunt Mary." Tristan wondered why he was even telling her this. He folded his arms and leaned against the mantel. "Perhaps you can sympathize . . ."

She shook her head, not rising to his teasing tone. "You can be very provoking at times, but even then . . . Why did you have to wrest invitations to visit? Douglas said you were the most popular boy in school."

Had he been? Tristan would have bet money he wasn't well liked at all. He was admired, which was a far different thing. "My dear Miss Bennet. Allow me to explain something about boys. An intelligent, hardworking boy may be popular, with a wide circle of friends. But a boy who instigates boundless pranks and adventures is legendary. Friends appear from thin air, begging him to come home with them. Tales of punishment at the end of the holiday only enhance his illustrious reputation." He spread his arms wide and swept a bow, like an actor after the curtain. "I was rarely invited anywhere twice, but I was invited everywhere at least once."

Her mouth dropped open. "Are you saying Douglas invited you to Helston because you promised to be outrageous?"

"Of course; what else would induce him to offer?"

"Well—why—friendship," she stammered.

"Friendship." He flicked his fingers. "How ordinary. Where's the verve in that?"

"Oh, yes; you must have verve in everything. But my mother—my mother blamed you for all the trouble." Her eyes kindled with indignation. "She ought to have blamed Douglas! He invited you solely to see what trouble the pair of you could cause!"

Tristan's mouth twisted in mingled amusement and bitterness. It was nice to hear, after almost twenty years, but it certainly didn't change anything now—although he did enjoy the sight of Joan in a fury that wasn't directed at him. "I don't fault her. No one else wanted me around, either."

Her lips parted, and her eyes filled with sorrow. Damn. He hadn't wanted to make her pity him. He cleared his throat, but she spoke before he could. "Did you throw your aunt and cousins out of this house?"

"What?" He scowled. "No. My aunt informed me two months ago she was done with this house; it was too dark, too outdated, too small to host a proper Season. She moved out the day after she told me she was leaving. I never asked her to go, to say nothing of coercing her to go."

"Then why did she ask to come back?"

Tristan's eyes narrowed. "I see she spoke to you about it." Somehow the thought that Joan had listened to Aunt Mary's bile, and believed it, rankled even more than knowing Aunt Mary was telling lies about him.

"Actually it was your cousin Alice," she replied, a faint flush staining her cheeks. "She said you had callously refused to let them return, even when your aunt begged."

He opened his mouth to defend himself, and

then closed it. "I've been a cross on her back for years," he said. "Why stop now?"

Her eyes flashed. "I didn't believe it! I only wondered why she would stop complete strangers in the millinery shop to tell them such things. Evangeline said—"

"Yes?" he prodded when she snapped her mouth closed.

She bit her lip. "Evangeline said Lady Burke is a prickly, mean-spirited woman, and that she's never liked you—that she never liked your father, either." Joan turned to take in the room once more while Tristan stared at her in amazement. "She wants to come back because the house is so much better, doesn't she?" she murmured. "Because you've made it better than she ever could have. Although I expect the greatest improvement was her departure."

For some reason a grin tugged at his mouth. "I concur."

Joan was irrationally pleased by the incredulous smile hovering on his lips. He looked so startled, and so pleased, by her words, as if she'd shocked him right out of his normal brash mien. His eyes had the same expression as when he said he could never insult her face, and instead of being unsettled by it, she found it thrilling—because she thought it was the most honest glimpse of him she'd ever had.

And now she understood why he showed himself so rarely. It made her heart hurt to picture him as a lonely little boy, made to feel unwelcome in his own family, desperate for any sort of affection or loyalty or even just companionship. For years

Douglas had spoken enviously of Tristan's freedom to do as he wished—and Joan had blithely agreed—but now she understood the other side of that freedom. He had no parents to punish him, to scold him, to restrain him . . . or to comfort him, to applaud him, to love him. Of course he'd wanted to go home with schoolmates on holiday, if his only choice was to live with a woman who openly despised him. And that was when he'd learned to say anything, and dare anything, to achieve what he wanted. Any consequences only came later.

"Enough of that topic," she said, sick of talking about the hateful Burkes. "Will you show me the rest of the house?"

"Of course." He offered his arm, and she took it, letting him lead the way into the rear parlor, a small room with diamond-cut mullioned windows and a vaulted ceiling. "The most modern of conveniences," he said, sweeping open a narrow panel set in the side of the fireplace surround.

"What is it?" With a quizzical smile, she leaned down. There were some ropes hanging inside the void, but nothing else.

Tristan went down on one knee and began tugging one rope. "It's a dumbwaiter," he said. "For coal. It can be filled in the cellar below and then retrieved as needed, with no need for servants to carry heavy scuttles on the stairs."

"How ingenious!" She bent lower, craning her neck to peer into the cavity in the wall as a metal bin finally appeared. "Did you think of it?"

He took his time replying. Joan glanced at him and realized her posture was indiscreet; his gaze had dropped to the neckline of her dress, which was right in front of his face, affording him a clear view down her bodice. All she had to do was stand up straight, but she couldn't move. She didn't want to move. There was no mocking, no teasing, no cynical amusement in his expression now. His eyes were dark with raw desire, and suddenly Joan knew exactly how Lady Constance felt when her lovers looked at her. Now she knew why Constance risked so much for her affairs; it made a woman feel reckless and bold and *eager* to have a man's attention fixed on her this way.

Slowly Tristan's gaze traveled up her throat, as bold as a physical touch, and her skin seemed to grow taut. She remembered the feel of her own fingers caressing that same path. A soft sigh rasped between her lips at the thought of his fingers doing the same. Evangeline had vanished into another room, and only the distant sounds of hammering reminded her they were not utterly alone.

"Yes," he murmured. "It was my idea." Deliberately, openly, he looked back down at her bosom, which prickled and warmed under his intense regard. "I have many, many ideas."

"A—a coal dumbwaiter is brilliant." She had to grope for an intelligent thought.

"Do you really think so?" With one finger he traced the gold lacing that edged her neckline. "It's not even my favorite idea."

Joan knew she must be on the verge of fainting. It was the only explanation for why she felt unsteady on her feet, as if she might lose her balance at any moment. Everything seemed to recede except him, still on his knee before her. His finger brushed the skin of her shoulder, and she shivered. His green eyes were unguarded for once, and he raised his chin as if he meant to lean forward, just a little bit, and kiss her . . .

A loud crash echoed behind her. "Oh, bloody—beg pardon, m'lord."

Joan jerked upright. Two workmen had come in from the dining room. One was stooping to pick up the hammer he'd dropped and the other was ducking his head uncomfortably.

Tristan got to his feet. "No trouble. We'll go upstairs so you can work." He offered her his arm again and they went back through the hall to the stairs. "If you're impressed by a coal dumbwaiter, we may need smelling salts when you see the upstairs."

She smiled, her heart still pounding. "I can't wait."

Chapter 21

❧

They met Evangeline in the hall and went up the stairs, still unfinished but lit by a beautiful skylight above. Her aunt paused to exclaim over the beauty of it and the way it allowed natural light into all floors, but Joan marveled at how much care Tristan was taking. The house wasn't merely being restored, it was being almost rebuilt. He was eradicating what had made him unhappy and making the house his own, right down to the floorboards and mechanisms. She had seen and heard of modern improvements, but never seen so many collected in one place. She trailed her fingertips along the oak banister, trying not to wonder if he pictured his modern, welcoming house filled with a wife and family.

They went through all the rooms. Evangeline joined them as they went up to see where the greatest damage had been, where the air was thick with fresh sawdust and the limey smell of plaster. Tristan pointed out the improved bell system, which ran all the way into the servants' quarters. He showed them the addition being built out at the back of the house to allow for water closets on every floor. He demonstrated the water pumps in the servants' closet upstairs, enabling water to be drawn easily and quickly for the bedrooms. He showed them the main drawing room overlooking the Square, where the floor was being relaid in an intricate parquet pattern because the old boards had been burned by loose coals and warped by the flood.

"I have rarely been filled with such envy for a house," Evangeline told Tristan as she watched the workmen fitting floorboards together. "I shall shamelessly copy this design in my own house."

"I give full credit to Mr. Davies." Tristan motioned to one of the workmen, who looked up and doffed his cap.

"Indeed! Mr. Davies, how long will it take to cover this whole floor?"

Tristan drew her away as Evangeline questioned the workers. "You must help me choose the furnishings," he said.

Joan laughed as he led the way to the master bedchamber. "I've no idea! You must have some preferences of your own."

"I do," he assured her. "Mechanical improvements, and things I prefer changed. Servants' quarters where the servants can stand upright, for instance. But the finer points—draperies and carpets and such—elude me."

"Anyone can choose those," she tried to say, but Tristan shook his head.

"You're wrong. Anyone can, but not everyone can choose them well, to make a house warm and welcoming. I care for that more than for creating a grand palace for entertaining."

Joan didn't know what to say. He was looking at her in such an intense, direct way . . .

"This is the master's bedchamber," she said. "Your bedroom."

"There's no bed in here yet."

She wet her lips. "But there will be."

"Yes," he agreed. "In a few weeks. What should I see when I wake?"

Me, she thought on a sudden burst of longing. Oh, help. She was falling in love with him, and picturing him in his bed, forging a home out of this once dark and gloomy house, was not helping her peace of mind.

"Er . . . deep blue," she said softly. Blue was her favorite color. "With patterned bed hangings."

"What sort of pattern? Chinoiserie?"

"No." She tried not to think of it as her room, or her bed. "Something natural, as if to bring a bit of the garden indoors."

His eyes lit with a slow smile. "Excellent suggestion. Thanks to you I shall have the whole house finished in half the time."

She gave a startled little laugh. "That still seems a long time from now."

"Don't underestimate my determination. I want it done sooner." He paused. "I often get what I want." Joan waited, at once hopeful and anxious, but he turned away. "This room was almost untouched by the water. Only the windows needed repair. I expect it will be painted within a week—blue, thanks to you."

She let out her breath. "When will you take up residence?"

"Soon. Very soon." He crossed the room to a door in the far corner. "I have something else to show you. This is the most impressive room."

Joan followed him, feeling very impressed already. And this room was no different. It was small but bright, painted a brilliant yellow with a row of casement windows running almost the length of the back wall. But they were high, so high she could just see out of them while standing. And right beneath them . . .

"What do you think?" Tristan asked.

"Is this a room for—for bathing?" Joan eyed the tub. It was rather large.

"Of course."

"A whole room for bathing," she repeated. "Why?" It wasn't unheard of for country houses to have rooms for bathing, or even whole bathing houses. But that was in the country, where houses had plenty of space to expand and rooms to spare. This was a London town house, and not an exceptionally large one at that.

"Because of this." With a flourish he opened the doors of a large cupboard in the corner.

Joan stared at the mass of metal within. "What is it?"

"It's a water heating system. This tank fills with water from a collection device on the roof." He rapped his knuckles against it, and it gave a resounding glug. "It's quite ingenious; rainwater fills it with just enough for a full bath, and then the rest runs down into the main cistern in the courtyard. When you light a fire in the stove beneath it, the water is heated, all at once. Then you open this valve"—he turned the lever mounted on the wall as he spoke—"and heated water flows into the bath." And right before her eyes, water streamed from the mouth of a lion's head mounted on the wall just above the tub.

"Is the water really warm?" Joan stripped off her glove and put her fingers in the water still pouring out the lion's mouth. It felt cold to her.

"It has to be heated first. See, there's a specially built stove here." He opened the grate beneath the water tank. "In half an hour, this entire tank of water can be heated. And if you work this agitator, it can take even less time," he added, grabbing a handle near the top of the tank. "It stirs the water so it heats evenly. That was my idea."

"Your idea!" she exclaimed. "You designed this?"

He laughed. "No, just the agitator." He turned the valve, and the water running from the lion's mouth slowed and stopped. As they watched, the water drained out a hole in the bottom of the tub. "Far superior to carrying buckets up and down from the kitchen. This apparatus only requires one servant, to stoke the fire and work the agitator, and takes less time. And then the water drains out into the sewer at the end, saving more labor."

"Yes, I see what you mean." She looked around the room with considerably more respect. It was an extravagance to be sure, but a very appealing one. Joan quite liked the idea of bathing in a tub of toasty hot water; Janet frowned on such things, saying brisk water was best for young people.

And Tristan was extremely proud of this room; he opened other cupboards to display shelves for linens and toweling and soap. "The chimney from the stove rises right behind the linen cupboard, enabling it to warm the towels. A warm towel after a bath on a cold March day is just the thing."

"I can imagine," she said longingly.

"I hear a man over in Ludgate has invented a new shower-bath, to enable one to bathe standing up, with water pouring down like a waterfall," he went on. "I hope to get one."

"Standing up!" She laughed. "You could stand in your tub and have your man pour the water over you."

He grinned. "What would be the appeal of that?"

"If there is nothing mechanical about it, it cannot be appealing?" She wrinkled her nose. "I'm quite content to have a servant pour the water, thank you."

He didn't say anything. His exuberant grin slowly faded even as his attention seemed to sharpen. Joan found herself caught by his gaze, and suddenly remembered how very alone they were. The house was quiet around them; the workmen must be taking a rest.

She wet her lips. "What are you thinking?" She meant to break the tension, but instead her voice came out low and husky.

He put his hand on the edge of the tub. "I was thinking what you would look like, bathing in this room. How your skin would glisten when wet. How your hands would glide over your body as you washed. How flushed you would be from the steam."

Oh sweet heavens. It was just the sort of thing that would happen to Lady Constance. Joan's heart leapt and raced. She was being seduced.

Not even Tristan could say such things—he was picturing her in his bath!—and not know what it would sound like.

She gripped her hands together to hide their sudden trembling. "That's very forward."

"To picture it? Or to say it?"

Neither one of them had moved, but the room seemed to be shrinking by the moment. "To say it, of course." What should she do? Joan desperately wanted him to kiss her; she had wanted him to kiss her downstairs, too. There was no point in denying that any longer, but the problem was, she didn't know how to be seduced. Lady Constance would do the right thing, but she had no idea how to proceed. "I've long since admitted defeat on controlling what anyone else thinks."

One corner of his mouth turned up. "I'm the one who admits defeat. You have controlled my thoughts almost from the moment we met on your brother's doorstep." She gave him a wary look. That might not be such a good thing, given what had passed between them then . . . but the focused desire in his face stopped her from saying anything. "I wanted to strip you out of your horrible frock that day, and I thought about kissing you as a way of winning our argument. I even thought of reading you some prurient poetry in that bookseller's shop, just to see you blush."

She gasped. "You did not!"

"You know I did," he replied. "And it would have been worth being slapped because my God, Joan, you blush so beautifully."

"I do not!" She knew her face must be as red as a brick right now.

"Stop it," he said in a low voice. "Stop pointing out every flaw you imagine. You are not too tall. You are not too plump. You blush like a bowl of ripe strawberries under a mound of whipped cream, and it makes my mouth water to think of tasting you."

Her heart thudded so hard at the thought of his mouth on her skin, Joan began to fear she'd have an apoplexy. "If you thought so highly of me, why did you behave so provokingly?"

"Because that's the way I behave," he said without a hint of apology. "I'm not much of a gentleman. And my thoughts of you are decidedly not high-minded."

"What are they?" she whispered.

Instead of answering he walked across the room. His footsteps seemed to echo the thump of her pulse. Joan retreated a step only to find herself backed against the wall. She raised her eyes to his, and saw no trace of mockery or deviltry or amusement. He loomed over her, every fiber of his being obviously intent upon her—and her own body was no less attuned to his.

"Are you going to kiss me again?" she asked, unconsciously tilting forward, raising her face to his.

"Would you let me?" He touched the tip of her chin, then slowly ran his finger along her jaw until his hand curved around the back of her neck.

She wet her lips. Breathing seemed to grow more difficult. "You know I would."

"Would you welcome it?" His voice dropped into a sensual murmur. His fingers pressed ever so lightly on the back of her neck, drawing her to him.

Joan placed one palm, then the other, against his chest. He was so warm and solid. She could feel the steady beat of his heart, almost as quick as her own. "Yes."

His head dipped, his lips brushing hers. "Why?"

She let her eyes fall closed, tipping her head back even more. "Because I want you to."

Another kiss, this one lingering only a little longer than the first elusive contact. "Why?"

Her fingers closed around the lapels of his jacket. "Why do you want to kiss me?" She stretched up on her toes, trying to close the distance between them.

He cupped his other hand around her jaw, brushing his lips over her eyelids. Then that hand stroked down her nape, over her shoulder, and down her spine before closing firmly over her bottom. With surprising strength he pulled her hips against his. Joan's eyes flew wide open as she felt him, full and hard, against her. Thanks to *50 Ways to Sin*, there was no doubt what part of him was pressed so insistently against her lower belly.

"Because I want you, Joan Bennet," his voice rasped in her ear. His breath was hot on her cheek. "Desperately." As if to drive home the point, he moved, pressing her flat against the wall, and tilted his hips, causing that hard ridge to slide roughly over her woman's mound.

A strange shiver rippled through her, making her limbs tremble and her stomach knot. "Oh my," she said faintly.

"I want to kiss you until you forget your own name," he went on in a ruthless whisper. "I want to touch you until you cry out in bliss. I want to see you flush that gorgeous shade of rose from head to toe while I bring you to climax after climax. I want to do things to you that would make you blush just to hear them." He flexed his hips again, even more slowly this time. "I want you to know that you've bewitched me, and I'm going mad from wanting to see you—to talk to you—even to argue with you."

"I'm not arguing now," she said, her voice high and breathless.

"Good," he breathed, and then his mouth was on hers, dark and hot and insistent. His lips pulled at hers, teasing and nipping. Joan clung to his jacket, wanting to feel him wrapped around her. When he lifted his head, she swayed, sucking in a deep breath to stop her head from spinning.

"Oh my," she managed to gasp. "You've won your shilling . . ."

"Damn the bloody shilling," he growled. "Open your mouth when I kiss you."

"Why?" she asked, and he took advantage. His mouth met hers again, his tongue flicking between her lips. Joan started and his fingers tightened, just a fraction, on her nape, his thumb stroking the line of her jaw, tipping her head to a better angle for his possession. His tongue swept into her mouth and she moaned helplessly. Now she clung to him to keep her feet; his right hand, still cupped around her bottom, began urging her against him in a slow, primal rhythm. Her spine softened, and her hips tilted into his when he tugged. Tristan growled again, his tongue surging deeper into her mouth. Joan's hands crept up his chest until they were around his neck. She felt him tense, as if he meant to pull away, and she held on tighter with an inarticulate mew, sucking lightly on his tongue before he could break the kiss.

He shuddered hard in her arms. His grip grew stronger, lifting her onto her toes. Her blood seemed to be roaring through her veins like a stream in spring flood. It was terrifying and recklessly exhilarating, and she never wanted it to end.

Abruptly Tristan froze. Joan squirmed against him, and he pulled his lips away from hers, making a silent "shh," gesture when she blinked dazedly at him.

"Joan?" called Evangeline. "Lord Burke?" There was an edge of command to her voice. Her footsteps echoed in the other room, coming nearer. "Where have you gone?"

Joan swallowed. They were screened by the door, but only for a moment longer. Soundlessly Tristan let her back down on her own feet, holding her a second as she swayed before taking a quiet step backward. "In here," she said, then cleared her throat to rid it of whatever made it so husky. "In here, Evangeline."

Her aunt swung the door open as she repeated it. Tristan had managed to move another step back, and he made a little bow. He had also smoothed his jacket back into place, so the only sign of their moment of frantic passion was the heightened color in his cheeks and a certain glitter in his eyes. "I was showing Miss Bennet my bathing room," he said. "It is my primary point of pride in the house."

Evangeline's sharp eyes darted between the two of them. Joan tried to look innocent, hoping desperately that her hair wasn't in a betraying mess. "It was very quiet. I didn't know where to find you."

"I was marveling at the linen cupboard," she said quickly. Fortunately Tristan had left the cupboard door open, and she gestured at it. "It's warmed by the chimney. Can you imagine, always having warm toweling on a cold day? Does that not sound like the most delicious luxury?"

"Indeed." Her aunt's gaze lingered on her. "Very impressive, Lord Burke."

He bowed his head. "Thank you, ma'am. Do you approve of the color scheme?"

"Most cheerful." Finally Evangeline turned away, and Joan fought off the urge to collapse against the wall in relief. "What do you think of it, Joan?"

"I think it's splendid," she said in perfect honesty. "A whole room for bathing! I don't think I've ever seen a finer house."

Behind her aunt's back, Tristan gave her a simmering look. Joan blushed, but gave him a small smile in return.

"When do you expect to take up residence, sir?" Evangeline asked, running her hand along the edge of the wide copper tub.

"In a month, if all goes well," he said. "As soon as the main bedchamber is painted. I've imposed on Mr. Bennet's kindness long enough."

"Excellent." Evangeline's smile seemed laden with satisfaction. "How very fortunate for you it's so near completion."

He turned and gazed directly at Joan, until she feared she would blush again, from the memory of how he'd held her and kissed her and whispered he wanted her madly. "I quite agree," he said. "Very, very fortunate."

Chapter 22

The Brentwood ball was excruciatingly dull.

Sir Paul Brentwood fancied himself something of a patron of the sciences, and his wife liked to throw extravagant balls. These two desires found common expression in what Lady Brentwood called honorarium balls, or balls thrown mainly for the purpose of demonstrating how very many famous people Sir Paul knew. Tonight the guests of honor included Sir Richard Campion, whose explorations in Africa had been partially funded by Sir Paul. Tristan had no idea what Sir Paul got in return for his investment other than obliging Campion to attend events like this, but he didn't really care. Tristan had accepted the invitation only because Joan had promised him a dance tonight.

It seemed a year had gone by since the day he kissed her in his bath chamber, instead of a mere two days. Now he couldn't set foot in his house without being sure he smelled lingering traces of her perfume. He couldn't make any decision about the fittings or furnishings without wondering what she would think of his choices. And he could think of nothing but making love to her in the large new bed that was delivered the day after her visit.

Unfortunately, she had yet to appear tonight, and he was beginning to fear they had reconsidered.

"Fancy seeing you tonight." William Spence, one of Douglas Bennet's more reprobate friends, wandered up beside him. "I didn't think you cared for gatherings such as this."

"I thought the same about you." Tristan didn't bother looking at him. He didn't like Spence, and he didn't know how Bennet put up with him. He supposed it must be a result of shared habits; Spence favored the same gaming establishments as Bennet, and was quick to lend money to a friend in need, as Bennet often was. But Spence was a petty, spiteful man, and Tristan had long suspected he was a cheat at cards, too. He'd never thought Joan's brother was the noblest personage, but the man was honorable at heart. Witness his care for his sister. Tristan couldn't imagine Spence caring one whit for any sister's amusement, but Bennet had begged him to keep Joan's spirits up—and to keep her away from Spence, now that he thought about it.

"Dunwood dragged me," said Spence idly. "A sad waste of time it's been, too. No table is playing for more than twenty guineas a hand. What brings you here?"

"Boredom." He stopped a footman passing with a tray of wineglasses.

"Boredom!" Spence chuckled. "Has London

grown that tedious? Perhaps you should carouse with us tonight."

"I'm not that bored." Tristan sipped the wine. Across the room, a gleam of chestnut caught his eye. Joan was here, walking into the room behind a diminutive lady with a full brace of feathers in her hair. He saw the bright excitement in her face, mixed with a trace of amusement as the feathers waved at her, and unconsciously he straightened his shoulders. Now he wasn't bored. The crowd shifted, the plumed lady turned aside, and his mouth went dry as he got a full look at Joan. Her gown was gold, gleaming brocade that bared her shoulders and made her seem to glow in the candlelight. She wasn't just tolerable; with her hair up and her figure expertly displayed, she was stunning.

Unfortunately, Spence noticed his reaction. "Who is she?" He craned his head to look. "What beauty has struck you dumb? No—is that—Bennet's sister?" he added incredulously. "Good God, Burke!"

There was a very good God indeed, to have put her here in that gown. Tristan said a small prayer of thanks and took a hearty gulp of his wine. He had told her to wear gold, that she would look lovely in gold, and he had been right, bloody, bloody right. In fact, it almost felt like a sign from above, that perhaps he'd been right about her all along, and it was time for him to stop resisting it.

"I almost asked her to dance the other night," remarked Spence, still watching her with amused disdain.

Tristan swallowed some more wine. "Why?"

"A wager with Ashford, of course," said Spence carelessly. "Fifty quid just to dance with the Amazon."

"Rather a lot to wager on a single dance."

"Isn't it? Especially when one thinks what Bennet would say." Spence grimaced. "The gel's not even pretty. And her frock! She's got no sense of fashion—either that or her dowry isn't what it's reputed to be. Have the Bennets fallen on hard times? I can't help but notice they all left town, except for her."

"I wouldn't know." Tristan drained his glass. Across the room Joan was smiling and enjoying herself, unaware of the malice aimed at her.

"Perhaps they left her to the scandalous countess for instruction." Spence laughed. "Can you imagine a less likely chaperone than Lady Courtesan! Yes, perhaps that's it! If she can't be someone's proper wife, she might make a fetching lightskirt."

Tristan thought about punching Spence in the face. He was sure he could hit him hard enough to knock the other man senseless. It would liven up the evening considerably, for a number of reasons. "You just said she wasn't even pretty. Now you think she'd thrive as a courtesan?"

"No, she's not pretty." Spence's gaze narrowed on him. "Although it doesn't seem to have put you off. Everyone noticed you danced with her at the Malcolm ball, and you can't take your eyes off her tonight. Bennet's sister? By God, I thought you had requirements."

Slowly Tristan turned his head, trying to pretend he hadn't been watching Joan like a man mesmerized. "Which I have never discussed with you. Nor do I intend to begin doing so."

"Ahh, I see." The other man's eyes gleamed with speculation. "You have particular information about the lady. Some . . . talent, perhaps, that she possesses, to make a man forget how tall and mannish she is."

"Mannish?" Tristan was so surprised he gave a bark of laughter. "You need a quizzing glass, Spence."

Spence frowned and turned to scrutinize Joan. Her gown tonight was far too simple for the latest style, it was true, but it did show off her figure, especially her trim waist and spectacular bosom. If one forgot about current ladies' fashion, Tristan thought she looked nothing short of alluring. It was as if she'd brought out one of the thin gowns of a decade ago, but woven of sunshine and cleaved to her curves instead of falling in a straight column. In this deceptively plain gown, anyone could see just how unlike a man she was.

"She's still too tall," muttered Spence.

He shrugged. "You're too short."

Spence's mouth thinned. "So you're declaring your intentions, are you, Burke? I assume Bennet will be pleased beyond endurance to hear that."

"Spence, you're an idiot," said Tristan bluntly. "Always have been. Bennet might not worship his sister, but he'll beat you bloody for insulting her. Go on," he said as the other man stared at him. "Ten guineas, that you wouldn't dare repeat to him half the insults you've made tonight."

Spence's gaze turned venomous. Bennet would

thrash Spence within an inch of his life, and they both knew it. "I haven't insulted—"

"Not pretty? Too tall? *Mannish*?" He snorted. "And we mustn't forget the implication that she's aiming to become a whore."

His companion flushed brick red. "I never said that . . ."

"I daresay there are some who wouldn't appreciate the imprecation on Lady Courtenay's name, either." Tristan nodded at Sir Richard Campion, who had joined the ladies across the room. If there was anyone in London with a reputation that preceded him, it was Campion. While Bennet's reputation came from his fists, however, the explorer was known for the brace of Swiss pistols he allegedly kept in his carriage or on his person at all times.

"Very well," said Spence hastily. "Very well, indeed. I see how things lie."

"Good." Tristan flashed him an ominous smile. "Don't forget it."

"No," said the other man. "I won't." He gave Tristan a long, measured look before he turned on his heel and walked away.

Tristan turned back to watching Joan. God above. She was beautiful tonight. Not just the gown, although it suited her perfectly, but because she glowed. She smiled and talked with her friends, and as he watched, she nodded and gave her hand to Campion. Tristan would have bet his last farthing that Campion's interest lay solely with Lady Courtenay, but the sight of the man holding Joan's hand and leading her into the dance set his teeth on edge because he was jealous. Insanely, desperately jealous of Campion, just for dancing with the woman he loved.

Loved.

Tristan held very still, turning the unexpected word over in his mind. He loved the impish look in her eyes when she had him in a twist. He loved the breathless joy in her face when they hovered above the city in a balloon. He loved that she wasn't shocked by his deliberate provocations, and even answered them in kind. He loved the way she listened to him and refused to accept his self-effacing answers. Everyone had believed him a wild, uncaring rogue for so long. Only she pushed him to explain himself, and confronted him on his more foolish actions.

And most of all he loved that she wanted him to kiss her. He wanted to see her in his bathing room, naked and wet. He wanted to see her in his bed, and discover how unpredictable she could be. He wanted to feel her arms around him and know she cared for him—not for his money, not for his house, not for his title, just for him. And he thought, with a little persuasion, she just might do all those things . . .

He wasn't sure if love was the proper term for his feelings. There hadn't been much love in his life. He only knew he needed Joan, craved her company, and if she were to care for him, he would probably shout aloud in triumph, as if he'd won the biggest wager in his life.

That, more than anything else, brought his thoughts into clarity. Wagering, as he had once told her, made things more interesting—more important. Lady Courtenay had warned him to consider his intentions, and tonight he realized exactly what those were. He lingered a few moments, waiting for any sort of alarm or doubt, even apprehension of being trapped, to surface. Instead all he felt was the overpowering urge to walk across the room to Joan's side. And so, with very little qualm, he gave in to it.

Joan had looked forward to the Brentwood ball for several days, but it didn't begin as a roaring success.

She thought she looked rather well—almost lovely, in fact—thanks to Mr. Salvatore's latest creation. Every time she and Evangeline had visited him, she had brought up the idea of a gold gown, and every time he'd brushed her query aside. But one day, to her surprise, he had sent her a swatch of fabric, a shimmering gold brocade with a pattern of leaves and flowers woven into it, saying he'd found it in a silk warehouse and was willing to make it up into a gown with some ivory satin if she still wanted it. Since Mr. Salvatore had never missed yet, in her opinion, Joan sent back an acceptance the same day. And when the gown arrived two days later, she'd almost gasped in joy. It was lovely; it made her hair look darker, her skin paler, and really needed no ornamentation at all. And best of all, the cut emphasized her waist, making her look slimmer.

Evangeline had lent her a pair of white satin slippers with an arched heel. Joan felt very daring wearing them, but she held her head high as she walked into the room. As her aunt had pointed out, Tristan was tall enough that she could wear raised heels and not tower over him, and he was the only man she really wanted to dance with. The kiss in his bathing room had branded itself on her mind so hotly that she'd given up pretending she didn't want his attention. She wanted him to notice her, she wanted him to be stunned by how lovely she looked, and she wanted him to kiss her again. And if it led to one of those moments all spinsters dreamt of, when a gentleman got down on one knee and confessed his undying love and asked her to marry him, she was prepared to say yes.

She didn't expect it, but that didn't mean she couldn't imagine it.

But the gown didn't make quite the difference she thought it might. Abigail looked surprised, and Penelope's eyebrows nearly went into her hairline.

"What's wrong?" she asked as soon as her aunt turned aside.

Abigail seemed mesmerized by the neckline of the gown. "It's very low cut, don't you think?"

Joan took a good look around the room. "No more than that gown, or that one." In fact, some gowns seemed designed to display the wearer's bosom. Her gown completely covered hers.

"Perhaps it appears lower than it really is because there's no lace or trim at all. It looks as simple as a chemise."

She resisted the desire to look down. "But it's not. Don't you like it?"

"It doesn't look like anyone else's dress," said Penelope.

"Everyone else's dresses don't suit me very well." Joan lifted a fold of her gleaming skirt. "If you didn't know me, how would I look to you?"

Abigail cocked her head to the side. "Sophisticated. Daring."

"Married," said Penelope. "What?" she said in response to her sister's expression. "Married to a wealthy, indulgent gentleman. Is there anything offensive about that?"

Abigail pursed her lips. "No."

"Good, for it's my goal in life." Penelope shook her head as she surveyed the gown again. "It would make me look like I was wearing a fancy dress, but it really does suit your coloring, Joan."

It was a little disappointing that they hadn't both fallen over in raptures of envy, but Joan resolved not to think of that. Wanting to wear what other women would envy had never served her well. She thought the gown was lovely, and if even just one other person did . . . for instance, perhaps Tristan . . . she would count it a success.

Abigail and Penelope excused themselves a few minutes later. Their mother, fretting over their lack of dance partners recently, had impressed her son into finding gentlemen for them to dance with, and they were now required to stand with her until the assigned partners arrived—or so Penelope described it. Abigail rolled her eyes and murmured something about her father being more upset than her mother, but they left, and Joan was once again alone with her aunt. She scanned the room as discreetly as possible, and had just caught sight of Tristan's dark head when another man made a very elegant bow in front of them.

"Good evening, Lady Courtenay, Miss Bennet," said Sir Richard Campion.

"Good evening, sir." Joan curtsied. Her aunt just dipped her head.

"You look exceptionally lovely tonight." He included both of them in his compliment, but Joan noticed that his eyes lingered a moment on Evangeline, who looked remarkable in a gown of brilliant blue.

"Did you come over here just to express the obvious?" asked Evangeline lightly. "My niece looks magnificent, and I warrant everyone recognizes it."

Joan blushed. Sir Richard smiled, his eyes crinkling. "I recognized it from the most distant corner of the room. I wonder if Miss Bennet would do me the compliment of partnering me in the next dance?"

She smiled in surprise. He was the one complimenting her. He was one of the guests of honor tonight, and gentlemen like Sir Richard Campion did not need to dance with spinsters, for any reason. And from the way her aunt looked on in approval, she was most certainly permitted.

"I would be delighted. Thank you, sir."

He led her out for the quadrille. "Are you enjoying the ball?" he asked as they took their places with the other couples.

Joan could feel the weight of the surprised glances they were drawing. "Yes. I wish my aunt would enjoy it more, though."

He paused in the act of tugging his glove for just a split second. "How so?"

She looked across the room and saw Evangeline watching them. "I think she gave up much she holds dear to play at chaperone."

He gave her a long, searching look. "Has she expressed any discontent?"

"Not a word."

The dance began and they said no more for a while. "I heard you had a great adventure the other day," remarked Sir Richard when they had a quiet moment while the other couples performed the figure.

"You must mean ballooning." She lowered her voice. "It was thrilling beyond words! But I gave my aunt quite a scare, which I regret very much."

"I daresay she was able to understand, once she'd got over any surprise." His eyes were kind.

Joan ducked her head. "Perhaps. But I had such remorse . . . would you do me a great favor, sir?"

"Of course." He took her hand and they circled the couple to their left, then their right.

"Would you ask her to dance?" Joan saw his mouth tighten. "For me. I would be so glad to see her enjoy herself."

He was quiet again for a long time. When the dance ended he led her from the floor and bowed again. "I would ask her for every dance, if she would only consent to one," he murmured. "I am not the party you need to encourage. Thank you, Miss Bennet, for a most enjoyable set."

Evangeline stepped up beside her as he walked away. "How did you find Sir Richard's dancing?"

"Very accomplished." On impulse, Joan seized her aunt's hand. "Dance with him."

Evangeline blinked. "Don't be silly, dear. I'm here as a chaperone—"

"And nothing will be amiss if you dance once."

"It would cause talk," murmured the older woman. "And he hasn't even asked me."

"Because he knows you will refuse." When her aunt merely pressed her lips together, Joan added, "Do it to please me, then. I hate to think you've given up all enjoyment for my sake."

"My dear, I would not dance with him anyway. I dare not." Evangeline steadfastly faced away from where Sir Richard had retreated to stand with their host, although his eyes veered her way more than once.

"That's rather cowardly, don't you think?" Joan caught sight of Tristan. He was winding his way through the crowd toward them, his gaze intent on her. Just the sight of his face made her heart jump and her lips curve. "Haven't you been telling me love is worth some risk?"

Her aunt glanced at her in amazement, but before she could speak, Tristan was in front of them. He bowed with a flourish. "Good evening, Lady Courtenay." His voice warmed a degree as he looked at Joan. "Miss Bennet."

"Lord Burke." Joan didn't care that everyone was staring at her anew. She couldn't keep the smile off her face as she curtsied.

"I hope you'll save the supper dance for me, Miss Bennet."

That meant he would also escort her in to supper. Joan, who had eaten most suppers at balls with her parents or with her friends, felt almost giddy. "Of course," she said, trying to sound poised and gracious instead of breathless with excitement.

He grinned, and raised one hand. "Excellent."
A servant, who must have been waiting for his
gesture, hurried forward with a tray of champagne.

When Tristan turned to take the glasses, Joan
hissed at her aunt, "Dance the supper dance with
Sir Richard. Please, Evangeline?"

Her aunt's face grew pensive as she took the
glass Tristan offered her. "Very well," she said
under her breath.

Joan exhaled, and managed to catch Sir Richard's eye. She gave him a quick, bright smile, tilting her head slightly toward Evangeline, before
accepting her own glass of champagne.

They talked lightly through the next three sets.
She had never seen Tristan so charming, so relaxed. He had a wry way of putting things that
made her smile, as long as he wasn't trying to
infuriate her. Evangeline seemed quite taken by
his manner as well, which wasn't too surprising;
she was fairly certain her aunt was doing everything possible to encourage him. And tonight of
all nights, Joan had no wish to dampen her enthusiasm. Her skin seemed to tingle every time
he looked at her, which was often. His gaze slid
over her golden gown with obvious approval.
He gazed at her with a brilliant intensity every
time she spoke. All in all, the evening seemed
to grow brighter and happier every moment. Although that might have been due in part to the
wine; every time her glass was empty, a footman
seemed to appear with another. Joan had drunk
champagne before, but she had never before felt
this same sort of thrill, as if the bubbles continued

to fizz in her veins. When she took her third glass, her aunt put up a hand. "Yes, it's my last," Joan whispered to her. "I know."

"Your pardon, Lady Courtenay," said Sir Richard, who had come up behind them. "I beg you to honor me with the supper dance."

"Oh, do!" said Joan before her aunt could speak. "As you know, I am already engaged, so you are quite free to dance yourself."

After a long pause, Evangeline gave her hand to Sir Richard. "I would be delighted, sir. I will see you in the supper room, Joan." With a quick glance of pure gratitude at Joan, Sir Richard led her off.

"Excellent work." Tristan drained his glass before taking hers as well and handing them off to the attentive footman. "At last, a moment alone."

Joan laughed, although it sounded more like a giggle. "Oh, no! I only wanted her to dance, for her own pleasure."

"I hope she enjoys it very much," he returned, taking her hand and leading her out. "I intend to as well."

"Oh? How?" She seemed to have a bit of trouble getting her feet lined up. "Curse that champagne."

"I'll steady you." His arm went around her waist, pulling her shockingly close. He grinned down at her. "Better?"

"Yes, thank you," she said breathlessly as the music began. "Much."

Joan gave herself up to the pleasure of the waltz. Her borrowed shoes seemed to have been made for dancing; she felt willowy and graceful in them, and not even a quarter inch too tall.

Her gown might look unfashionable or daring to some, but all she cared for was the avid admiration on Tristan's face.

"What are you thinking?" he asked.

She smiled dreamily. "Nothing, really. I was merely savoring the dance. You do waltz very well, my lord."

"That's something, not nothing."

"But I didn't think it until you asked, so when you asked, the correct answer was nothing."

He grinned. "Thank you. You are my most desired partner."

She blinked. "For . . . the waltz?"

"Yes," he murmured, although his jade-green eyes seemed to convey a larger answer.

Her pulse leapt. "I might say the same."

"I am very, very gratified to hear that." Without lifting his head he scanned the room. The waltz was winding down. Joan also glanced around; Evangeline and Sir Richard were on the other side of the dancing area, nearest the supper room. They seemed to be absorbed in each other, and she felt a moment's hope that Sir Richard would persuade Evangeline to marry him. She was sure he wished it, just as she was sure Evangeline wanted it, too, if she could only allow herself to say yes . . .

"Do you trust me?" Tristan murmured, his gaze still flicking from side to side.

If he hadn't been sweeping her about in the dance figure, Joan would have stopped dead. "Why?"

His lips quirked. "Is that no?"

"No," she said slowly.

"Is that yes?"

She hesitated only a moment. "Yes."

Chapter 23

Without another word he turned her around a pillar and through the servants' doorway, almost colliding with a footman as he did so. With a quick excuse to the startled servant, Tristan pulled her down the plain corridor until they reached the back stairs. Heart thumping, Joan followed him up and up the winding stair and then down a long corridor. This floor was not open for guests, and it was quiet and deserted. Tristan tried a door, and swung it open to reveal a small library or study. The walls were lined with shelves of well-worn books, and a comfortable-looking sofa, positioned in front of the fireplace, had more books stacked on one end. A pair of French windows opened onto a tiny balcony at the other end of the room, with the rooftops of London visible in the moonlight.

"What is this?" Joan turned to Tristan. "Did you know this room was here?"

"Yes." He closed the door softly behind him. "It's Sir Paul's private library. I was at school with his son Tom, and came to visit on holiday one term. We sat up here and drank his brandy one night until we were sick."

Yet another lonely holiday for him, brazening his way into a friend's home and trying to act like a man. She put her hand on his arm. "Such a bold boy you were."

"Well." He smirked. "We were nineteen, not quite babes in arms."

Joan blinked, then laughed. She laughed and laughed, even as he gathered her into his arms and pressed his face against her neck.

"Christ above, you smell good," he breathed, his lips whispering over her skin.

"Bergamot." She let her head fall to the side to better revel in his attentions. "And orange."

"I could devour you." His teeth grazed her earlobe, and she had to cling to his jacket to remain on her feet, she felt so unsteady. "Would you let me?"

Her head was already spinning—cursed champagne—but his words conjured images straight out of *50 Ways to Sin*. "How?"

"One long, slow kiss at a time." He pressed examples along her jaw. "From your head to your toe and back to your maddening, gorgeous mouth."

She was leaning against him, her head thrown back in abandon. "Maddening?"

"In all senses of the word." He brushed a light kiss on the corner of her lips. "Infuriating and beguiling enough to drive me out of my wits from desire."

She shivered. "Desire . . ."

His low laugh was harsh. "You know I want you—beyond all temperance or reason. Do you want me? Tell me, Joan, before I truly do run mad . . ."

She opened her eyes, more than a little drunk on the fervor in his words and the burning passion in his kisses. And, perhaps, just a shade, on the champagne. His face was taut with hunger, his body rigid in her arms. "I do," she said. "Now kiss me."

He kissed her. Deeply, hungrily, possessively. Joan felt a flicker of surprise—was this the sort of unwise kiss Evangeline had warned her about?—before she succumbed to the carnal promise it offered. It seemed as though she had waited her entire life for a kiss such as this. He tasted of champagne, and every stroke of his tongue against hers seemed to reinvigorate the feeling of fizzing in her blood. She clung to him, laying herself open for his conquest. There was no more resistance in her; he had won—her heart, her mind, and most definitely her body.

"I want to taste your skin." He whispered the words against her lips as his fingers played with the fastening of her gown.

"Yes," she sighed, letting him urge her back until she leaned against the pilaster. Her bodice loosened and he skimmed his fingers along the neckline, teasing it down until her breasts were only covered by her shift. His mouth followed, blazing a hot, wet trail over the highly sensitized flesh of her bosom. By the time his thumb grazed her nipple, it was already standing firm and eager. With a faint growl he yanked her corset and shift down, and sucked the rigid nub into his mouth.

Her mouth fell open in a silent cry. He sank

down on one knee, suckling her by turns roughly, and then delicately. She groped for support and ended with her hands threaded through his long hair, speechlessly urging him on as he moved to her other breast, leaving each stinging and full.

"Sweeter than strawberries," he rasped. "Richer than cream." His hands moved down, from her waist over her hips and down the backs of her legs until he reached her knee. "Spread your legs a little for me, darling. Yes, like that . . ." he crooned, urging her feet apart. "I want to drive you mad."

"You're doing a damned"—she gulped for air—"damned fine job of it already!"

He laughed quietly. "And I've hardly begun." His fingers traced feathery circles over her ankle before drifting upward.

Joan held very still, every breath rippling through her like a strong breeze through the leaves. She couldn't see anything but his face, dark and focused in the moonlight. She couldn't feel anything but his fingers stroking lightly up her shin . . . now at her knee . . . now climbing her thigh, pausing to move aside the cloth of her pantalets . . .

"By my bloody eyes," she gasped, her body arcing as he parted the damp curls and laid his thumb on a spot that seemed to burst at his touch.

"God Almighty," he said, his voice shaking. "You're so soft—so wet—" His thumb circled and rubbed, and Joan twisted in a pleasure so sharp, it was almost pain.

"Stop," she whimpered. "What is that?"

"Not yet." But his touch gentled, until she had the sensation of being coaxed along, guided. She held still for a while, until some primal feeling made her hips rock and sway of their own accord. The shudders of pleasure built anew. He pulled her closer with a wordless murmur, kissing her breast again. Joan sighed and melted against him, letting him drown her apprehensions in the wicked stroke of his fingers between her legs and in the delicious attention he lavished on her bared bosom.

"By all the gods, I want to make love to you." He kissed her again. She cupped her hands around his jaw and held him to her, marveling at the sheen of perspiration on his face.

"What do you mean?"

She could feel his pulse hammering under her palms. Tristan gazed deep into her eyes, his own gaze feverishly bright, as he slowly probed and then inserted his finger inside her body.

"I want to lodge myself here," he whispered. His finger withdrew and then slid back in. Joan could hardly breathe. "Again and again." He repeated his earlier action, sliding higher and deeper than before. His thumb rolled over that locus of nerves, and her knees almost gave out. "Until you scream my name in the pinnacle of pleasure and I expire inside you." Again he penetrated her, but this time a little harder, and his thumb pressed in time with the stroke.

The blood roared through her veins. Her body shook. She should say no, but . . . She was in love with him. No matter how many times she told herself he wasn't the sort of man a girl like her married, she loved him. No matter what her mother thought of him, she wanted him. She had pictured him making love to her as wantonly as Lady Constance's lovers did to her, and now it was happening. And just as she had dreamed, he was looking at her as though she was the most beautiful, desirable woman in the world. For the first time in her life she felt the thrill of being wanted—madly and passionately—and if it made her wicked to revel in that, then she was glad to be wicked.

"Yes," she whispered. "Yes, Tristan."

He went very still, except for the heaving of his chest. "What?"

She nodded, even though the action almost made her lose her balance. "Yes. I want you."

He quaked. She felt it. Then he slipped his hand out from between her legs. She was shocked at how bereft she felt by that, but he wrapped his arms around her and lifted her off her feet, carrying her to the sofa, where he leaned her back against a pile of cushions and dropped to his knees between her parted legs.

"You need to see how desperately I want you." He stripped off his jacket and unbuttoned his trousers.

Joan gaped as he shoved down his trousers and smallclothes and bared his male member to her gaze. It looked enormous, jutting fiercely from his body. It was too dim to tell much detail, but it was darker than the skin of his face, and as she stared in fascination, it twitched and surged upward all on its own.

"It stands at attention, insistent and distracting, whenever you come near me." He folded his shirt out of the way and reached for her hand. "It knows no reason, no caution, no restraint, only that you make it rise, hard and furious, every time you simper at me or deliver a stinging set-down or cling to my arm because you fear the balloon is about to crash." He laid her fingers on his member, and Joan's eyes widened even more. It was hot and smooth, thick and long and so very hard.

"It was like this in the balloon?"

"Not quite so frantic, but ready at a moment's notice." He exhaled, moving his hips so that her hand glided along his length. "You know it was like this in my bathing room."

She managed a nod. Yes, she'd felt it, although she'd had no real idea how much larger it would look.

Slowly he drew up her skirts. "And if I make love to you, it will fit here." He touched her again, sliding his finger as high inside her as it would go. Joan shuddered, spreading her knees wider without conscious thought and flexing her spine to bear down on that invading finger. Dear heaven—if it felt this good with just his finger inside her, how much better would it be when he thrust his prick inside her? Every prurient story and poem she had ever read in the secrecy of her bed ran through her mind in a jumble. Stories of satisfaction and pleasure so extreme, both man and woman barely survived it. Stories of men driven joyfully mad from thrusting themselves inside their lovers. Of women delighting in every penetration until they screamed and almost died away in bliss when their lovers gave them a climax, something so amazing there weren't enough adjectives to adequately describe it. And so far, everything seemed to indicate the stories were true. She did feel a throbbing ache inside her. She wanted him to make love to her, over and over again until she fell senseless with pleasure.

"Yes," she breathed. "Show me."

"God, darling, yes." His finger withdrew, and then he pressed two fingers inside her, pushing harder. Joan felt a tightness, a slight burning, and she squirmed, but the discomfort faded as he stroked her again, gently working his fingers in and out of her. "I want to make it easier for you," he whispered, dipping his head once more to her breasts.

She gave herself up to him, reveling in every touch of his mouth on her skin. She clutched his head to her breast, rocking her hips to meet every stroke of his fingers.

"Just like that," he muttered. "Yes—wait—now—" He reared back, yanking her hips so that she slid down among the cushions until her hips were almost off the sofa. Panting, he took himself once more in his hand before setting the blunt knob against her throbbing opening where his fingers had just been. "Push," he rasped.

She arched her back a little, letting her weight slip toward him. At the same moment he pushed forward, and he slipped inside her, stretching her. He met her gaze as if seeking reassurance. "Again," he said in the same dark, velvet tone.

Joan pressed down at the same moment he bore forward. The pressure between her legs grew keener, less pleasurable. "Tristan?" she said uncertainly.

"I know." He laid his hand on her belly and

thumbed aside the curls covering the place where his body met hers. "Let me help . . . just feel . . ." He spoke soothingly but there was a raw undercurrent to his voice.

She lay still a moment, concentrating on every swirl and stroke of his thumb. The heat in her veins increased again, until she gave a sigh and pushed her hips, only to realize he had been slowly pressing deeper as she whirled away. Tristan seemed mesmerized by it; his long hair had come loose and hung over his face as he stared at the junction of their bodies, but Joan could almost feel the heat of his gaze, so she looked, too. It was shocking, and somehow arousing, to see his hand against the pale skin of her thighs, his fingers parting the curls between her legs, his flesh sliding one thick, hard inch at a time inside her . . .

"Almost . . ." His voice was strained and guttural. His touch grew a little rougher, making her jolt and gasp as new bolts of excitement shot through her. As she flung her head back and drew up her legs beside his hips, he surged forward, driving himself fully inside her.

Joan trembled. She felt so full, so stretched, it seemed she would split apart if either of them moved. Tristan seemed to be under some similar perception; for a long moment he just gripped her hip with one hand, his other hand tense on her mound, and let his head hang down as he struggled to breathe.

Finally he lifted his glittering eyes to meet hers. "Now you're mine," he whispered. "My gorgeous, lovely Joan."

Still holding her, he began to move, rocking

back and forth, in and out, slowly and gently at first, but growing more urgent. The sense that she would be torn asunder disappeared; now she didn't want him to leave her, and hooked her legs around his hips to urge him back, ever harder and deeper. He teased her with his fingers and nipped at her breast with his teeth until she writhed frantically beneath him.

"I want," she gasped. "I want—I need—" Something was building inside her, something frightening and vital and so, so close . . .

"God!" He closed his mouth around her nipple and suckled hard. His hips surged against her relentlessly, driving his hardness deeper, retreating, then filling her again. His fingers encircled that aching kernel of sensation and pinched it so firmly she thought she would go blind from it, and then something inside her broke, finally releasing the tension in a crescendo of waves that seemed to pull every muscle in her body tight. And as the taut urgency drained away, Tristan let his weight fall forward, gripping her to him with a harsh groan as he bore down on her and she felt him swell even larger inside her.

"That—that was a climax, wasn't it?" she whispered a moment later, her arms locked around him.

He gave a huff. "Not just any climax. God in heaven, I thought I would fall unconscious."

She stretched in instinctive female satisfaction, liking the way he caught his breath and pressed his hips against hers, as if he was as reluctant to part from her as she was from him. "So it's not always that way when you make love to a woman?"

"It has never, in all my life, nor even in my imagination, been like that before." He kissed her, long and slow, as if they had all the time in the world. "And it was only your first time."

She blushed. "Will we do that again, then?"

"Repeatedly. Until I learn every last thing that makes you wild." He grinned, the lazy, relaxed grin that burrowed straight into her heart. "But not tonight."

"Oh. Oh!" Her mouth dropped open in alarm as she abruptly recalled where they were. "We could be discovered at any moment!"

He shrugged. "Unlikely. But we should return before anyone misses you." With one last kiss he pushed himself away and got to his feet. Joan sighed as their bodies separated, but then giggled at the sight of Tristan with his trousers around his knees and his shirt hanging loose.

"Idle wench," he said in amusement. "Here." He pulled up his trousers and buttoned them, then pulled a handkerchief from his waistcoat pocket and gently pressed it between her legs. "Does it hurt?"

She shook her head. His face eased, and he ran his palm once, just lightly, over her woman's place—what *50 Ways to Sin* called her quim—before he helped her up.

"It's much more enjoyable to unfasten your dress," he murmured as he redid her buttons after she tugged her corset and shift back into place.

"I suppose that must be one's penance for being wicked during a ball." She smoothed her skirts, hoping they weren't horribly wrinkled in back. He laughed quietly, adjusting his own clothing, and she turned to the mirror over the fireplace to repair her hair. Thank goodness Polly had put it in a simple knot tonight; she would have been betrayed at once if she'd had to contend with braids and ringlets.

"Were we wicked?" He put his arms around her as she fixed the last pin. "Are you racked with guilt?"

Joan blushed. "No. At least—well, probably not as much as I should be."

He regarded her seriously in the mirror. "How much would that be?"

The blush crept down her throat. "I suppose that depends on what comes next."

This was the moment. He had remained by her side for all to see, all evening long. He had declared himself mad for her. He had called her gorgeous and bewitching and darling. He had made love to her and said it had been incomparable. Now was his opportunity to fall on his knees and swear his heart was hers, to beg for her hand in marriage, to begin a life of devoted happiness and contentment.

"Joan! Joan!" Evangeline's frantic voice broke the pregnant pause. Before she or Tristan could speak, there was a furious rattling of the knob, and a moment later the door flew open and her aunt almost fell into the room, with Sir Richard close on her heels.

"Oh my," cried Evangeline, clutching one hand to her heart as she spied them, still in each other's arms. "Oh my God—Richard—!"

"What the devil are you doing?" that gentleman asked Tristan in an ominous tone.

Tristan looked down at her. Joan looked up at him. "What does it look like?" he asked.

He didn't say anything else, though the whole room seemed to be waiting for something. Joan began to feel a prickle of unease. Had she misinterpreted . . . ? Or misheard . . . ? Surely if he loved her, he could still confess it . . .

"Joan—Joan, come with me right now." Evangeline sounded on the brink of tears. "We have to go."

Tristan released her at once. "Good night, darling." He caught up her hand and brushed a lingering kiss on her knuckles. "I will see you later," he added softly.

"Good night," she replied with a tremulous smile. She wasn't wrong about him. She didn't—couldn't—believe that. It would come out right. She was sure of it.

It had to. Didn't it?

Evangeline seized her wrist and towed her down the hall, swiping at her eyes once or twice. Joan glanced behind her, but didn't see either Sir Richard or Tristan following. In the hall her aunt sent a footman off to fetch the carriage, snapping at him to hurry. Another servant rushed to bring their cloaks, and Evangeline almost shoved Joan out the door.

"I hope," she said when they were alone in the carriage, "that my fears are unfounded. I hope my trust has not been abused. I hope—" Her voice broke. "I hope I shall have nothing dreadful to confess to your parents."

Joan was grateful for the darkness that hid her face. "I'm sure you don't."

"When I suggested you let him kiss you, I never meant you should walk away from a ball, where dozens of people might notice your absence and his! I never meant you should be indiscreet—a kiss could be given in a moment of privacy, behind a garden hedge or around a corner. You should not have stolen away to the loneliest part of the house where everyone will draw the worst conclusions!" This time there was a definite sob in her aunt's anguished cry.

She began to feel very guilty. As much as she longed to, there was no real defense available to her. She couldn't protest that nothing had happened, because it most certainly had. She couldn't wave aside the notice of gossips and busybodies, because she knew quite well it was almost guaranteed. Not only were she and Tristan both taller than average, her gown had drawn attention. She knew people had been remarking his presence at her side, although she'd never really regretted that fact the way she did right now. It was inevitable that someone would whisper about it, and then it would be all over London. The notorious Lord Burke seduced the daughter of the very proper Lady Bennet! The first frisson of panic went up her spine as the realization crashed over her that her mother would hear of this.

"I'm very, very sorry," she told her aunt. "I didn't think . . . well, not clearly enough. He didn't really tell me we were sneaking off, he just took my hand, and then . . ." She blinked, her own eyes growing wet. "But I wanted to go with him. He—he did kiss me, Evangeline—"

Her aunt made a sound like a strangled sob.

"And it was lovely," Joan added longingly. "I love him. And I think he loves me."

"Did he say so?" Evangeline leaned forward anxiously. "If he declared himself, my dear, this will all end well. Your father will allow it, if your heart is engaged. Your mother will see the wisdom of the match; it's a very good one for both parties. Tell me he proposed marriage, or made any promise at all, and I shall stop haranguing you at once."

"Not—not precisely marriage, no," she said in a small voice.

Evangeline sat back and put her hands over her face. "Then I needn't waste time worrying over whether Richard will shoot him. If Richard doesn't, I most assuredly will."

"Oh, no!" she gasped. "Why would you?"

"Joan." Her aunt's voice sharpened. "You are not that naive."

"But I want to marry him," she protested.

"I should bloody well hope so! You may have no other choice."

"I could say I felt unwell and went to the retiring room alone . . ." Joan offered, more for her aunt's sake than her own.

"I looked for you there," snapped her aunt. "Another young lady stepped on her flounce and tore it off; there were several people helping calm her and mend it. They will know you weren't there."

"Perhaps I found a quiet room to sit and recover from a headache . . ."

"More than one person remarked Lord Burke's absence. How will you explain that coincidence, after the attention he paid you? It looked to everyone as though he was declaring his intentions, and then both of you disappeared. And you, sly minx! Encouraging me to dance with Sir Richard so I would be distracted!"

"No!" Joan protested at once. "That is not why. I'd no idea Tristan and I would . . . I only wanted you to dance and enjoy yourself."

Evangeline sighed. "In the end, that matters naught. My dear, you are caught. Take it from one who has made the same mistake and searched in vain for a way out."

Joan bit her lip as the carriage turned into South Audley Street. "What will you tell my parents?"

Her aunt said nothing. She had the front facing seat, and her gaze was fixed out the window. In the lamplight her face was pale, but she seemed suddenly turned to stone.

"Evangeline?" Joan leaned forward and touched her aunt's arm. "Are you ill?"

"Not yet," said the other woman in a strained voice. "Your parents are home."

Chapter 24

The frisson of panic bloomed into full-scale alarm. It was one thing to contemplate her mother hearing about tonight, and a very different thing to be faced with the consequences right this minute. "Now?"

"It looks as though they've just arrived." Evangeline's face and voice had settled into a chill calm.

The carriage stopped. Joan scrambled to look out the window. A large travel coach stood in the street, with servants handing down trunks and boxes. Her home was ablaze with light, and the front door was wide open to admit the servants with those trunks and boxes. "Oh, help," she whispered.

Evangeline seized her wrist in an iron grip. "Say nothing," she commanded. "I will speak to them." She didn't let go until Joan gave a nod. Then she took a deep breath and gathered her skirt as the footman swung open the door. "My goodness," she cried in apparent delight as she stepped out of the carriage. "Have Sir George and Lady Bennet returned, Smythe?"

The butler bowed to her from his place near the door. "Indeed, my lady."

"How timely!" A wide smile fixed on her face, Evangeline turned to look at Joan as she, too, stepped down. "Joan dear, your parents have returned!" she called. "Your mother must be restored to health. I must say, it doesn't seem at all a pity now that I felt tired and made you leave the ball early, does it?"

Joan shook her head, too tense to speak. Evangeline was trying to save her, but she knew all too well it would only be a matter of time before her mother heard about tonight. Trying to mimic her aunt's pleased demeanor, she followed Evangeline into the house.

Papa appeared as the servants were carrying away their cloaks. Evangeline saw him first. "George, you should have sent word that you were returning tonight!" She rushed toward him to clasp his hands. "I'm so sorry we were away; if I'd known, we would have stayed home to welcome you."

Papa kissed her cheek, but his gaze never wavered from Joan. "We came in a hurry, Evangeline; forgive me."

"Welcome home, Papa." Joan hurried forward to embrace him. "Is everything all right? Why were you in a hurry?"

He peered closely at her, a thin line creasing his forehead. "Are you well, poppet?"

She wet her lips and tried to smile. "Perfectly. Why?"

"Is there anything you would like to tell me?" he pressed, in a low, meaningful tone that made her heart almost stop. He knew. How could he know? It happened only an hour ago! Papa hadn't even been at the ball! How on earth could he know?

"Not really, no," she squeaked. "Why do you ask?"

His shoulders seemed to fall. His jaw set. "Are you certain, Joan?"

Somehow he knew, and no plausible lie was ready on her tongue. She just stared at her father, wide-eyed.

"Joan." Everyone turned. Mother stood in the dining room doorway. She looked thinner, with a thick shawl around her shoulders, and she leaned on a cane, but otherwise she looked the same. "What have you been up to?"

Panic rendered her mute. She looked to her aunt in desperation, but Evangeline was already sweeping across the hall. "Marion! How well you look. Come, let us go into the drawing room. Standing so near the open door cannot be good for any of us."

"Yes, my dear, let us retire to the drawing room." Papa went and offered Mother his arm. Mother's gaze didn't waver from Joan, but she didn't say another word until they reached the drawing room and Papa closed the doors.

"How was your journey back to London?" Evangeline kept up her determined cheer, pretending not to notice the tension among the rest of them.

"Whatever has been going on here?" Mother asked Joan, ignoring Evangeline's question.

She swallowed. She'd had a moment to calm

herself and think rationally. There was no possible way Papa could have heard about this evening. Whatever had brought them back to London
in a hurry had happened days ago. It was possible
someone had heard about the ballooning trip, but
Joan thought it far more likely that Tristan's presence in South Audley Street was sufficient. Someone would have noticed his visits and written to
her mother. "We were at the Brentwood ball this
evening. Evangeline felt a trifle unwell, so we returned home early—happily, as it turns out. I'd
no idea you were coming back to town so soon,
Mother."

"We decided rather quickly." Her mother's eyes
grew wide as she looked down. "Good heavens,
what are you wearing?"

She spread her palms against the cool silk of
her skirt. "A new gown. Do you like it?"

"I took her to my dressmaker," said Evangeline
quickly, shooting Joan an encouraging glance.
"It's not the most conventional gown, but I think
it looks beautiful on her."

"Can we discuss the gown later?" asked Papa.

"George, she went out in society like this!"
Mother sounded aghast. "In conjunction with the
other news—" She broke off. "What was wrong
with your other gowns?"

"I wanted to try something new. And . . . I
didn't think the other gowns were as flattering."

Dismay flashed across her mother's face. "They
were perfectly fashionable!"

"Again, I must take the blame," Evangeline tried
again. "I noticed a—a certain similarity between
Joan's figure and mine, and since I look absolutely

wretched in the current fashions, I thought she might like to try something else as well. I encouraged her—in fact, it was my gift to her, so you aren't out of pocket for it, George."

"Hang the bill," said Papa testily.

"But it's so plain!" said Mother at the same time, still staring at the gown in shock. "My daughter—out in that chemise!"

"I think it's lovely," murmured Joan.

"Now, Marion, ten years ago she would have worn sheer white muslin over a single petticoat. In our youth, she would have worn painted silk with all manner of birds on it. And in our mother's day, it would have been heavy brocade." Evangeline's voice was growing strained. "This is a lovely silk, and—"

Mother looked up. "Evangeline, she's an unmarried young lady. She ought not to dress like this."

"But a simple design suits her. She hasn't got your figure, Marion—she's got mine! Ladies like us can't wear the ruffles and trimmings you can," Evangeline went on, almost pleadingly. "I only wanted her to wear something becoming."

Mother's lips parted in affront. "And the fashions I helped her select weren't becoming—is that what you're saying? At least I have the sense not to dress her in something that a loose woman might wear."

The silence was painful. Joan wanted to sink through the floor, her fingers clenched on the folds of her glorious gold dress, the new dress that suited her and made her feel pretty—even beautiful, if Tristan could be believed. It made her ill to

hear her mother's words, though; not because she
thought she looked like a loose woman, but because she knew she was one. She had been wanton
and loose and she had loved every minute of it.

"Joan does not look like a loose woman," said
her father firmly, breaking the overpowering
tension in the room. "She looks lovely, although
far more sophisticated than I'm accustomed to
seeing." He gave her a nod. "That color suits you."

Her cheeks warmed. "Thank you, Papa."

"And I did not race back to London to argue
over fashion." He directed a stern look on his sister
and his wife before turning back to Joan. "Do you
know why we've come home so suddenly?"

She had been throttling her brain in pursuit of
that very answer. "I suppose someone wrote to
you," she began, "saying I'd been misbehaving."
This seemed the best plan. It involved some pain,
but her chances were better with Papa in the room
than they were with Mother alone.

"Go on," said her father, confirming her suspi-
cion.

She drew a long, shaky breath and turned to
her mother. "I owe you an apology. I broke my
promise to you. I—I did dance with Lord Burke
again."

"Oh, Joan," exclaimed Mother in disappointed
tones. "You gave me your word—"

"Marion," said her husband. "Let her speak."

"I danced with him because he asked me
when no one else did, and I—I wanted to dance,
Mother," she confessed—honestly, as it turned
out. "And he asked me, at first, because Douglas
bade him do it; he told me that himself, and I

trust Douglas will admit to it. Douglas thought he was doing a kind thing by asking Lord Burke to call on me and dance with me," she went on, her voice growing stronger. She had done wrong, of course, but her brother had played a part in instigating the trouble—as usual—and she wasn't about to shoulder the entire blame herself. "Since both he and Papa would be away from town, he didn't want me to go into a decline worrying about Mother. I gather Lord Burke is the most respectable of his friends, so he asked it as a favor."

"And was that the extent of Lord Burke's attentions?"

"No," she said, hoping her face wasn't growing pinker with each word. "He came to tea and took me driving once, and he showed me and Evangeline his house."

Her father's gaze moved to her mother. But now her mother was staring in shock at Evangeline—Evangeline, who had been both very good and very bad for Joan these last few weeks. It made her stomach knot even though she didn't know what to say. Defend her aunt and lie? Admit all that Evangeline had allowed her to do and suffer severe consequences? She couldn't repay her aunt by turning her mother's anger on her. After all, Evangeline might be at fault for not keeping closer watch on her, but any sins were solely Joan's own. She couldn't even blame Tristan for seducing her. If she had behaved as her mother's daughter ought, none of this would have happened.

"Did Joan not tell you we disapproved of the gentleman?" Mother sounded as though she was choosing every word with care.

Evangeline was pale but composed. "I saw no harm in it. He's a very eligible match—"

"He is wild," Mother cut in. "He's a notorious rake. His gambling habits are infamous. He's not on speaking terms with his own family, and when he does appear in society, he usually leaves a scandal in his wake. There is more to eligibility than a charming smile."

"He's also titled, wealthy, and young enough to grow into a good husband, with the right encouragement," argued Evangeline. "He's not irretrievably wicked."

"Well," said Mother quietly, "you've been wrong about that before."

The remaining color drained from Evangeline's face. She didn't say a word.

"I wanted to dance with him, Mother." Joan quaked at the look her mother gave her, but she forged on. "I've come to admire Lord Burke a great deal. I danced again with him tonight."

Mother closed her eyes. "Oh, my dear. Tell me it was only because you wanted to dance. Tell me you only admire his dancing. Tell me—" She seemed to waver, as if she would fall, and Papa was at her side in a moment.

"Dearest, you must go upstairs and let Janet tend you. I will talk to Joan."

"George, please," she whispered, trying to shake off his arm.

"I will carry you up the stairs if I must," he told her. "Joan, ring for Janet."

Joan did as she was told, and when her mother's maid came to the door, Lady Bennet went. Her eyes filled with worry as she looked at Joan, but she left without a word.

"George, I'm entirely to blame," said Evangeline as soon as the door closed. "Whatever happened that displeased Marion, it was my fault—"

Papa held up one hand. "I'm not looking to cast blame. Don't berate yourself. May I speak with Joan alone now?"

Evangeline bowed her head. Silently she went out the door, closing it behind her.

Papa turned to Joan and leveled a weary gaze on her. "This is a fine mess, poppet."

"I didn't mean to do it."

"I know. Come sit with me." He led the way to the sofa and sat down. Joan perched on the other end of the sofa, feeling much less brave now that she would have to explain things to her father. "Why did you dance with the one man your mother told you to avoid?"

She clasped her hands on her lap and studied them. Evangeline had said Papa would give his blessing if he knew Joan really loved Tristan. This might be her best chance to set her father straight, since it was clear Mother's disapproval was as strong as ever. "Because I wanted to dance with him, and go driving with him, and go ballooning."

Her father frowned. "Ballooning?"

She nodded even as her cheeks grew warm. So they hadn't heard about that. At least it wouldn't be hanging over her head now. "It was thrilling, Papa. I've rarely enjoyed myself so much. He can be very charming and engaging when he wishes to be. And—and he's very handsome, too."

"Hmph." His brow was still lowered. "And he took you to see his house?"

"Yes, and Evangeline, too," Joan replied. "Lord Burke is rebuilding the house, since the roof gave way and several rooms were flooded, and he's incorporated a number of wonderful inventions. He's got a whole room just for bathing, Papa, with a water collection system and a special stove to heat the bathwater. I've never seen anything so perfectly designed for one's comfort in a London house! He's put pipes inside the walls and floor to heat the house even when the fires are out. And there's a dumbwaiter for coal, so the servants can't drop it on the stairs. Isn't that the cleverest thing you've ever heard of?"

"Indeed. How very modern." Papa was still watching her closely, but there was a more contemplative look in his eyes. "And this is why he's staying in your brother's house?"

"Yes, because his house isn't finished. He said he hadn't decided what color to paint the walls, and he asked my opinion about the draperies and carpets because there are none."

"Hmm."

He was taking this rather well. Perhaps Evangeline had been right. "Why does Mother dislike him so?" she asked, encouraged by his tempered response. "I remember he and Douglas got up to loads of trouble when they were boys, but that was a very long time ago."

He sighed, but with a hint of a guilty grin. "I suppose I'm to blame for that. When I was Douglas's age, I ran with a wild crowd. They were capital mates for a young man in search of trouble, but your mother found them reprehensible. I think she was correct, too, so don't scowl at me, miss," he added. "Not until I left that behind did I realize how right she was. I think she views young Burke as a similarly bad influence on Douglas, and needless to say, he's the last sort of man she would want her only daughter to marry."

"But you changed, even though you were one of that wild crowd."

"I did. And it was largely thanks to your mother."

Joan thought of what Evangeline had said: Papa changed in order to win Mother's heart. "Mightn't Lord Burke be able to do the same? He's far from the worst of Douglas's friends."

"High praise," her father muttered.

"By that measure, she must think Douglas is wildly unsuitable as well, and yet she was actively conspiring to see him marry Felicity Drummond a month ago."

"She hopes the right lady will be able to settle his unruly urges and inspire him to become more respectable as a husband."

She pursed her lips. "Couldn't one say the same of Lord Burke?" She longed to suggest that she could be the lady who coaxed him to abandon some of his worst habits and behave a bit more respectably, but that unanswered question from Sir Paul Brentwood's private library clouded her heart; what did Tristan want to come next? She would have sworn he meant to say more, but he hadn't.

"Perhaps," her father allowed. "But Mother worries more for Douglas's refinement than she does for Burke's—and she's not eager to risk your happiness on the chance of him reforming. A little excitement—or even a lot—right now isn't worth a lifetime of despair."

"No, Papa," she murmured.

"Well." He got to his feet. "You should go to bed. We'll sort this out in the morning."

"How?"

He looked at her somberly. "I don't know, my dear."

Chapter 25

After a sleepless night, Joan dragged herself out of bed. When she rang the bell, Janet came instead of Polly, gimlet-eyed and thin-lipped, as if she disapproved as much as Lady Bennet did of Joan's failings.

But if Janet's appearance was meant to encourage a return to better habits as well, it failed spectacularly. When Janet brought cold water to wash in, Joan sent her back to get warm water. Ever since Tristan had shown her his bathing room, she had asked Polly to bring warm water in the morning, and she wasn't about to go back to splashing herself with frigid water first thing in the morning. When Janet asked what she wished to wear, Joan deliberately ignored the pink-striped dress the abigail suggested, and chose the bright blue dress she had worn when Tristan took her and Evangeline on the tour of his home. Janet shook her head but she buttoned up the dress without a word. In fact, she said little of anything until Joan stopped her from plaiting her hair into a braided coronet.

"Just smooth it back into a knot, not too tightly," she directed.

Her mother's abigail put her hands on her hips. "And what's got into you, Miss Bennet? I've fixed your hair this way a hundred times."

"I know. But I had a chance to try things differently while you were away, and I like it better looser."

"It's not the fashion," Janet protested. "It's so plain!"

"I think plain suits me." She took a deep breath. "In dresses and in hair. If I were a slim, dainty girl, ringlets and ruffles would look lovely on me, but I'm not, and they don't. Every time we pulled my corset as tight as it would go, to minimize my figure, I only felt short of breath. My hair might as well have been a wig, covered in pomade to make it hold the curls. This way I feel much better, and I believe I look better, too."

Janet was taken aback by this speech, but slowly a look of faint respect came over her face. "You're finding your own style, then. There's not many ladies who have the will to defy current fashions, miss."

Joan faced herself in the mirror. She had tried every fashionable thing, and never been pleased with how she looked. Now, for the first time she thought she looked attractive. "I do."

"Just like your mother," murmured Janet, sweeping Joan's long hair back and twisting it into a knot. "The Bennet ladies know what they want, and won't be deterred from it."

That statement sank into her mind like a balm. As Janet pinned up her hair—a much quicker job, now that it didn't require several braids and the curling tongs—she thought maybe it was more true than she had expected. She had worn what her mother suggested, but that was before she'd discovered what would be most flattering to her. She had wanted to look lovely in those other dresses, but when they didn't, she didn't have much idea why not or what else to try. As much as she wished to be dainty and petite, there was no escaping the fact that she wasn't . . . and Tristan liked her as she was. Now that she knew simplicity suited her, she was determined not to wear the puffs and lace and ruffles that had made her look ridiculous before. That determination *was* very like her mother, she belatedly realized; the main difference was that Mother looked beautiful in the latest fashions, so there was no conflict for her. Joan would have to be braver, or pray for a radical change in fashion, but either way she intended to keep to her new style.

Emboldened, she went in search of her mother. She wasn't ready to make a complete confession, but she felt far more confident about her choices, both in fashion and in conduct. Until she had some sign otherwise, she chose to believe that Tristan had honorable intentions.

To her surprise, Evangeline was with her mother. Mother was settled on a chaise near the window, a warm throw over her legs. The table beside her was spread with breakfast for two. After last night Joan would have sworn they wouldn't be on speaking terms, but things appeared quite civil between them now. Evangeline rose from her chair opposite Mother as Joan hesitated in the doorway.

"Good morning," her aunt said brightly. "Come in, have some tea with us."

Joan crossed the room and pulled up another chair. "How are you this morning, Mother?"

"Happy to be home. It was a long drive from Bath."

Joan darted a glance at Evangeline, but her aunt was busy preparing a cup of tea. "I'm glad you're back," she murmured.

Her mother gave her a wry look. "Are you, indeed?"

She nodded. "I missed you. And I'm enormously relieved to see you so well."

"We all are, Marion," added Evangeline as she offered Joan a plate of muffins.

Mother smiled. "Thank you both." She hesitated, then reached for Joan's hand. "My dear, I owe you an apology. I was wrong to criticize your gown last night. I was very . . . startled by it, and spoke rashly. It did not make you look like a loose woman, and I regret ever saying that."

"Oh," she said, taken aback. "I—I understand." Evangeline beamed at her. "I think it suits me, Mother. I wish I could wear lace and flounces and be fashionable," she said with real yearning. "But those trimmings just make me look like a giantess."

"Of course they don't," her mother replied. "But you should wear what fits your taste, and you're certainly old enough to choose that for yourself. Your father—and your aunt—were thoroughly correct about that, and I was wrong."

"Oh," said Joan again, too shocked to say anything else.

"And about Lord Burke . . ." Mother paused.

Joan braced herself. "I should have offered you a chance to explain. I would like to hear what happened."

She took a deep breath. "Douglas asked him to call on me while you were away. He came to tea . . ." She hesitated, looking to her aunt for guidance, but Evangeline merely nodded. "He asked me to go driving, and he sent me flowers. And he asked me to dance last night." She wasn't about to admit the last sinfully wonderful thing she had done with Tristan to anyone on God's earth.

Lady Bennet closed her eyes and heaved a deep sigh. "Are you in love with him?"

Her face burned. "Perhaps," she murmured. "I think so. Yes."

Mother faced her again. "Has he given you any sign he intends to propose marriage?"

What to say? Both her aunt and her mother were watching her intently. Her throat felt dry. "No," she whispered. "Not specifically."

Mother seemed to wilt. "Dearest," she began. "My darling girl. I've always wanted you to be happy, with a family of your own and a husband who respects and adores you. Lord Burke . . ." She shook her head helplessly.

"He hasn't given any sign he doesn't intend to propose, either," Joan pointed out.

"Well, that's a little harder to judge, isn't it?" Mother asked dryly. "I don't want you to be swayed by a handsome face and rakish air. I know how alluring a dangerous man can seem. You wouldn't be the first to be foolish over a man, but I want—desperately—to spare you an unhappy end. Many a woman has thought herself in love, only to discover she was the only party who felt so deeply. I don't want to see you led down the path to heartbreak or ruin."

She gaped at her mother. "Not the first—? You don't mean *you*—?"

"She means me," said Evangeline quietly. "And if anyone wants to spare you that unhappiness more than your mother does, I do."

Joan snapped her mouth closed.

"You asked me once if I loved my husbands, and the truth is, I was miserable in both my marriages." Evangeline was pale but her voice was even. "I first married when I was young—barely more than a girl, really—to Lord Cunningham. He was old enough to be my father; in fact, he had been at university with my father. I was impulsive, even headstrong as a girl, and my father believed I needed a firm hand. Needless to say, the marriage was a dismal failure, and the best that could be said was that it was mercifully short. Cunningham had a weak heart, and the strain of reining me in must have been too much for him."

"I'd no idea," said Joan softly.

Her aunt's smile was forced. "It's not something I remember fondly. But there I was, a young widow, determined to enjoy my life a little at last. I embarked on an affair with the Earl of Courtenay within weeks of Cunningham's death. I felt I deserved a little pleasure, and . . ." Her voice faltered. "I was reckless and indiscreet. My father discovered us and demanded a marriage. I tried to argue that I was a widow and had the freedom to do as I chose, but my father was an old-fashioned man, and he cared nothing for my opinion. He challenged Courtenay to a duel if there were no wedding, and so we were wed within a fortnight. I persuaded myself it meant Courtenay loved me, but I soon realized it meant he didn't want to face my father. Courtenay had a fondness for young women, and having a wife didn't dampen his enthusiasm for seducing them. He lingered too long in the bed of a pretty young bride a few years after we married, and her husband shot him on the spot." She sighed. "So you see, it's really dismal luck for me to marry."

"Courtenay was a snake," said Mother with fervor. "He was handsome and charming but full of ill intent. He deserved to be shot, in my opinion, and you were well rid of him."

Evangeline turned to her gratefully. "Thank you, Marion. I ought to have listened to your advice about him." The two women shared a glance before turning back to Joan.

"I don't want to frighten you, dear, but I— we"—Mother corrected herself with a nod at Evangeline—"want you to understand how a woman can be lured into wickedness and not realize what she's fallen into until it's too late."

It took her a moment to reply. Her heart ached for Evangeline. No wonder she held Sir Richard at bay. Of course, Joan didn't think Sir Richard was like either of Evangeline's first two husbands, but what a terrible blow . . . "I don't believe Lord Burke is a hard-hearted rake," she said. "He's not the most respectable person, but Papa was also once a rake, and he changed. Evangeline told me he did, Mother—for you."

"Your father was never as scandalous as Lord Burke," Mother replied. "He kept some bad company, but he was decent at heart. He never would have trifled with me. His father was strict and raised him to be an honorable man. Lord Burke, on the other hand, has run wild his whole life, unmoderated by any family influence."

"But his parents died when he was only a small child!"

Lady Bennet held up her hands calmingly at Joan's protest. "I don't blame him for it, my dear. I am only stating a fact: Lord Burke has been allowed to do whatever he wished since he was a boy, and it's apparent in his behavior today."

"He was allowed to run wild because he was all alone," Joan said. "With no one to comfort him or guide him. Who would not run wild, if forced to live with his dour aunt, Lady Burke? Yes, she disowned him, although she did manage to live in his house, on his charity, for almost ten years. And that meant Tris—Lord Burke has had to be responsible for himself from a young age. He had no father to control his spending, no mother to gentle his manners. I think he's turned out at least as well as Douglas, who had every advantage you named."

Mother's lips tightened at the mention of Douglas. "I shall never forgive him if he's blinded you to his true nature."

Joan looked at her aunt. "I don't believe he has." Silently she begged her aunt to agree with her.

"I do believe the young man is honorable, Marion," said Evangeline. "I never would have received him if I'd had the slightest uncertainty."

Mother sighed. "If he shows signs of becoming more respectable, I shall give him the benefit of the doubt. Your father made a great many changes to his behavior *before* I received him," she admonished Joan. "If Lord Burke can do the same, I will be very pleased to see it."

A servant came in with a tray of letters. Evangeline got to her feet as Mother sorted through the post. "I must begin packing."

"You're leaving?" Joan followed her aunt toward the door.

"Yes!" Evangeline smiled and clasped her hand. "I miss my Louis, and now that your parents are home, you've no more need of me."

Of course she'd known her aunt would leave when Mother and Papa returned home, but Joan was more dismayed than she'd expected to be. She had come to like Evangeline a great deal in the last month. "I'll miss you," she said, sounding a little forlorn even to her own ears.

"I'm not saying farewell forever! I regret not having made a greater effort to know you and your brother, and I want to remedy that."

Joan pressed her hands. "Please do come to call. I will always be glad to see you."

Evangeline smiled—gratefully, Joan thought—and embraced her. "Gladly! Thank you, my dear. You are welcome to visit me at any time. Louis would be wild with joy to see you again. He never forgets a kind person with bacon."

"I must remember to bring bacon with me, to shamelessly win his heart." She grinned.

"You have already won his eternal devotion,"

replied her aunt dryly. "All it takes is a single rasher. Dogs' affections are so easily won."

"Unlike men's." She sighed. "What should I do?"

Evangeline glanced at Lady Bennet, who was reading a letter, before she, too, lowered her voice to a whisper. "What does your heart tell you to do?"

"It would be easier to answer if I knew what *his* heart felt."

"Wouldn't it?" Evangeline put her hands on Joan's shoulders. "I did my best to explain everything to your parents. I sincerely believe Lord Burke meant—means—to treat you honorably. I have known many rakes and rogues in my day, and he doesn't fit their mold. Only if one believed him devoid of human feeling and sensibility could his actions be explained in a dishonorable way. It would be extremely foolish of him to think he could abuse your reputation and walk away unscathed. For one thing, you have a father and a brother who show no signs of sitting idly by and letting you be ruined."

"But wouldn't it be awful for Papa to force him to marry me if he doesn't wish to?" Joan frowned at the thought.

"Why? You love him. He obviously finds you attractive and intriguing. I assure you, there are worse beginnings for a marriage."

"But I want to be loved," she whispered in longing.

"Don't abandon hope of it yet!" Her aunt gave her a wry smile. "Perhaps he already loves you; I wouldn't be surprised at all if he did. Men don't always blurt it out, you know. And some of them take a fearfully long time to acknowledge it is love they feel."

That made some sense. Papa admitted he loved Mother, but there was no reason to hide it, after thirty years of marriage. Douglas, though, would deny the truth until it slapped him in the face. Joan expected her brother would fight the emotion every inch of the way, but she also expected he would love his wife simply because he was very like their father in most other ways. Tristan was every bit as stubborn as Douglas, but he hadn't been raised with the example of loving parents. Of course it might take him longer to admit his feelings—presuming he did, in fact, love her as Evangeline said.

"Thank you, Evangeline," she said fervently. "For coming to chaperone me, for taking me to Mr. Salvatore, for lending me your white shoes, and—and for everything else."

Her aunt smiled, some of the usual light reappearing in her eyes. "It has been very much my pleasure, Joan."

A sharp exclamation from the other side of the room made them both look up. Lady Bennet had one hand clapped to her bosom, and her face was white. The letter in her hand trembled. Slowly she raised stricken eyes to them.

"You lied to me."

Joan froze. She didn't dare look at her aunt, since it wasn't clear which of them her mother meant. "What?"

Lady Bennet held up her letter. Joan said a silent curse on her mother's many prolific correspondents. "You disappeared from the Brentwood ball with Lord Burke last night and weren't seen again."

"I made her come home," Evangeline said quickly, but with a faint note of alarm in her voice. "I felt a headache—"

"And you were remarked searching the house for Joan!" Mother's eyes flashed. "Where did you go, young lady?"

She thought wildly. "Just out for a breath of fresh air . . ."

Her mother slashed one hand through the air in patent disbelief. "And you couldn't go with one of the Weston girls? Or with your aunt? Or with a maid?"

"They . . . ah . . . they weren't nearby . . ."

Lady Bennet shook her head, looking amazed and furious at the same time. "Lord Burke's absence at the same time was also noticed—in fact, the last anyone saw of either of you was when you were waltzing with him, indecently close!" She threw off the shawl covering her legs and rose to her feet. "Can you tell me that nothing improper happened last night? Nothing I would find objectionable? Can you swear it, Joan?"

A quick glance at her aunt told her Evangeline couldn't help her anymore. She was doomed. She hadn't expected to escape unscathed, but another few days, perhaps, would have allowed her some time to discover what Tristan intended. Evangeline had said everything would be cured by a marriage proposal . . . but now it was too late.

Mother's jaw tightened at her prolonged, guilty, silence. "He means to be honorable and reform his ways," she said acidly, throwing Joan's own words back at her. "When is this transformation to begin? It certainly won't come in time to save you from a storm of gossip! Did you not think this worthy of mention when you were defending his motives and upbringing, and casting all your actions in a virtuous light?"

She shifted miserably. "Not really, no."

"Well, I hope you do now. Your father will have to see to him—and I pray it doesn't lead to bloodshed." Her mother's voice broke as she stared at Joan in bitter disappointment. "Oh, Joan, what have you done?"

Chapter 26

⎯⎯⎯◠◯◯◠⎯⎯⎯

A great many things became clear to Tristan the morning after the Brentwood ball.

First, he had to get his house finished. For the first time he was a little sorry he'd drawn up such a long list of improvements. They were all worth the cost, in his opinion, but they had added tremendously to the time it would take to have the house ready, and that was now a problem. He went to Hanover Square early in the morning and walked through the house, finding fault everywhere. There needed to be more plasterers. More painters. The woodwork in the dining room simply had to be replaced. The plumbing was done and the roof was once more solid, but the heating system wasn't operational. The kitchens were still firmly rooted in the early part of the eighteenth century, and the large modern stove hadn't even been delivered. He took the master builder through the house with him and told the man to hire as many extra workmen as he needed and press hard to get the main rooms, at the very least, ready for occupancy within a fortnight.

Second, he needed to recall his servants. Since moving to Bennet's house, he'd given his valet a holiday and sent his man of business, Williams, out to Hampshire to see to things at Wildwood. His family estate should be in fine shape by now, and Tristan finally had need of the man again. He dashed off notes to each of them, summoning them back to Hanover Square, with an addendum to Williams to hire a full house staff when he reached London.

Third, he needed to see his solicitor. Mr. Tompkins raised his eyebrows when he heard Tristan's instruction, but he merely bowed his head. "What are the particulars, my lord?" he asked, reaching for his pen.

"I've no idea." Tristan grinned at the man's expression. "Just leave those parts blank for now, will you?"

"As you wish, sir, but it is customary to agree on the terms before writing the contract. In the event you and the gentleman cannot agree—"

"We'll reach an agreement," Tristan assured him. "Even if it costs me a fortune. Just begin drawing it up."

Because, fourth, he needed to go to Bath. This was the most important part of his plan, and he wanted to think it through. He went to the boxing saloon again and took a few turns sparring with other members, working out in his mind how best to approach the issue. It would be a delicate negotiation; his own behavior was not above reproach, after all, and to make matters worse, he would probably face some stiff opposition. For the first time in weeks he wished Bennet was in London, and then he promptly discarded that idea. Bennet might well be outraged, rather than helpful. Sometimes it was better to act without asking permission—not that Douglas Bennet had any authority in this anyway, but Tristan wouldn't have liked having to hit his friend.

Not until he returned to Bennet's house and was soaking in a cool bath did he allow himself to contemplate the pleasurable part of his plan: telling Joan. Should he make a grand gesture? Should he be quiet and discreet about it? He spent some time imagining her manner of response to his proposal, and then all the ways he would make love to her once she was his. God Almighty, every wicked thought he'd ever had about her had been right. She was sweet and hot, wet and tight, delicious and unpredictable . . . and she wanted him. Women had wanted him before, but not the way she did. And even more important, he had never wanted any other woman the way he wanted her. He wanted to make love to her in his bed. On his desk. In the comfortable old leather chair he'd carted around with him for over twenty years now, the one that had been his father's. He wanted to feel the soft leather at his back while she straddled him and rode him and made him laugh while the blood almost scalded his veins. He contemplated that last fantasy for several minutes, wondering how she would react when he told her about it. And the beautiful thing was, he really didn't know. He liked that about Joan; unlike other women, she constantly surprised him. Sometimes it was to his immense satisfaction—when she told him she wanted him to make love to her, for one—and sometimes less so, but Tristan loved few things like he loved a challenge. Persuading her to try something a bit more erotic would probably drive him out of his mind with anticipation.

The prospect made him impatient to be off. He dressed quickly and began packing. It would take two days to reach Bath, and two days to return. He hoped his request would be met with a quick acceptance, but if not, he would have to stay an extra day for persuasion. Wanting to begin with the very best impression he could salvage, he had Murdoch brush his best coats as he sorted through his shirts, tossing a couple aside for frayed collars or stained cuffs. By the time Murdoch was done with the coats, Tristan realized he was out of shaving soap and needed new stockings, so he sent the servant out to get them before the shops closed.

And no sooner had Murdoch departed than someone knocked on the door, the clang of the knocker echoing through Bennet's house. Tristan cursed under his breath; it had better not be Aunt Mary, come to ask for more money or even worse, his house. He was in such a fine mood and really had no patience for her pinched, angry demeanor now. But then the knocker sounded again, very like the time Joan had nearly banged down the door when she came to roust Bennet out of bed, and instead barged her way right into his life and his heart. Grinning at the memory of her shocked expression when he'd opened the door wearing nothing but a pair of breeches, he went downstairs and swept open the door with a flourish. "What?"

To his astonishment, Sir George Bennet stood on the step, as grim as a thundercloud. "Good," he said. "You're still here."

Tristan straightened his shoulders and stood a little taller. "Yes, sir. Won't you come in?"

The baronet walked into the narrow hall and peeled off his gloves. "I expect you can guess why I'm here."

There were three possible explanations. One: Joan had told her parents what happened between them at the Brentwood ball, and Sir George was here to demand satisfaction. Based on what he'd seen and heard from Joan, this didn't seem likely. Two: Lady Courtenay had decided to intervene and summoned the elder Bennets back to London so Sir George could demand satisfaction. From the way Sir Richard Campion had ordered him to keep his mouth shut and his trousers buttoned after Lady Courtenay dragged her niece out of the Brentwood house, this also didn't seem likely. Or three: someone else, some busybody with an overactive tongue, had tattled on him for . . . something . . . and Sir George was here to demand satisfaction.

Either way, Tristan decided to give him satisfaction. "No, sir, to be perfectly honest, but I am nonetheless pleased to see you."

The baronet gave him a sharp look. "I trust we won't have any trouble, then." He turned and walked into the small parlor, his heels ringing on the bare floor.

Tristan followed. This was both good and bad; good, in that it appeared he wouldn't have to argue for Joan's hand, but bad, in that he already seemed to be in his future father-in-law's bad graces. That shouldn't be too great a surprise, but this time he had truly meant to do things properly. "I was packing just now in anticipation of leaving for Bath tomorrow," he said, still hoping to redirect the conversation in a more positive way. "I have a proposition of some delicacy to put to you."

The older man turned. His every word was clipped with frost. "And was this proposition formed before or after rumors swept London that you ruined my daughter at the Brentwood ball?"

To his disgust Tristan felt his face heat like a naughty boy's. "I never heard any such rumors . . ."

"That's because you aren't a middle-aged matron with a fiendish interest in other people's whereabouts during each and every ball of the Season." Sir George glared at him. "Care to tell me if it's true?"

He hadn't felt this cornered since he broke part of Aunt Mary's new tea service with an errant cricket ball. Every persuasive word he'd planned so carefully vanished right out of his brain. "I'd rather not."

The baronet started to speak, then closed his mouth. He paced in a circuit of the room, his fists on his hips. "My wife would be pleased if I returned home with your severed head on a pike," he growled. "And it begins to hold some appeal for me as well."

Bloody hell. "I want to marry your daughter," he blurted.

"That was Lady Bennet's second, far less preferred, suggestion." Sir George folded his arms. "I ought to beat some sense into you before I let you have my girl."

That last bit sounded promising. "If you wish," said Tristan cautiously. "Provided that is another way of saying yes to my proposal."

The older man snorted. "You always did have ballocks of brass." He sighed and dropped into one of the mismatched chairs, then waved his hand at another. "Tell me what the bloody blazes brought this about."

Still wary, Tristan sat, remaining bolt upright in the chair. "Where should I begin?"

"What did my son ask you do to?"

That, at least, was innocent enough. Tristan relaxed a little, grateful for an easy answer. "He asked me to look in on Miss Bennet while you and Lady Bennet were away from town."

"And dance with her?"

"Yes." Tristan remembered that with clarity.

"Anything else?" The baronet fixed a piercing gaze on him. Unfortunately, he had the same keen look on his face that Joan sometimes got, which threw Tristan off his stride a bit.

"Er . . . take tea with her, and see that she had a bit of amusement from time to time," he said, trying not to think of the last thing he'd done with Joan, which Douglas Bennet had most certainly not had in mind.

"That all sounds perfectly innocent. How, pray, did things progress from taking tea and the occasional dance to the vivid stories of scandalous behavior that burned my ears today?"

Oh Lord. Tristan racked his brain; when had things changed? He wasn't even sure he knew. In the beginning she had been a spitting Fury, and he'd been mainly intent on besting her. But then he noticed her mouth, and her bosom, and the way her eyes glinted with gold sparkles when she delivered a stinging set-down, and before long all he'd thought about had been her: laughing, teasing, somber, breathless with desire. When had he stopped telling himself she was trouble? "I believe the tipping point was when I persuaded her to go ballooning with me." The baronet's eyebrows lowered, but Tristan forged on. "I help fund the man responsible for the balloon at His Majesty's coronation festivities, Mr. Charles Green. Miss Bennet made a passing mention of how dull and commonplace it is to drive around a park like everyone else, so I conceived the idea of a balloon trip. I hoped it would amuse her, or at least divert her mind from worries over her mother's health. Ten men held the ropes at all times," he added quickly. "We never left London and were able to descend at a moment's notice."

"Hmmph. Joan enjoyed this?"

He pictured her face as they rose into the crisp morning air. "She did," he said softly. "Her eyes grew bright and she exclaimed with such delight when we were high enough to see from St. Paul's to Greenwich. I had to persuade her to chance it, and worried that she would never let me forget it, but she felt the thrill and excitement as keenly as I did, once we were aloft. It was the first time we spoke without arguing, and I—" He stopped abruptly. "I think she and I would deal well together as husband and wife. Will you bless my suit?"

The baronet leaned back in his chair, stretching out his legs and resting his chin in one hand. "You have no sisters, do you, Burke?"

"No, sir."

"And your mother died years ago, I believe."

"Yes, sir."

His visitor's face grew a shade more compassionate. "I always thought you were dealt a poor hand in life. Your uncle was a good man, if utterly without humor, but your aunt . . . I felt sorry for any boy growing up under her hand."

"I avoided it as much as possible," Tristan agreed.

"Yes, I gathered," said the baronet dryly. "Your visit to Helston was the stuff of legend."

His ears burned. "Er . . . yes. I offer my most sincere apologies for that."

"No, no." Sir George waved this away. "I knew exactly what was going on. My son thought you were the most capital fellow in Britain, and within two days I understood why. A boy with no parents and no fixed home would have no boundaries, no qualms about braving any adventure, no fear whatsoever of a parent's reprimand." He hesitated, his gaze growing stern for a moment. "I trust you've outgrown most of that."

"I will never endanger your daughter," said Tristan quickly. "Never."

"It would be much worse if you bored her." The baronet nodded at his surprised look. "I've had thirty years of marriage and over twenty years of raising a daughter, and I tell you without equivocation that a bored woman is the greatest danger in the world to a man's peace. Women need occupation. They also need affection and respect and attention and at least two new bonnets a year, but above all they need something important to occupy their days."

"So I should find something for her to do?" Tristan frowned.

Sir George snorted. "God forbid you tell her what to do! No, you need to allow her some freedom to find her own pursuit. My mother was devoted to her gardens, my wife to her children and her fashions. I hope my daughter will have children someday to devote herself to, but either way, I advise you, as one man to another, to use the words 'forbid' and 'prohibit' very lightly. The Bennet women are known for their wills of iron, and woe to the man who thinks to bend that will to his liking. It's much more likely to snap back in his face and leave a deep dent in his skull."

"Thank you for the warning," Tristan said, adding under his breath, "although you might have told me sooner."

The baronet's eyes gleamed. "She's already demonstrated that, has she? Well, my Joan is a clever girl, quick-witted and determined. But she's got a kind, loving heart, and if she's bestowed it on you, there's very little for me to say." He lifted one shoulder. "I did mention that one doesn't easily deny a Bennet lady, didn't I?"

"So we are in agreement?"

"We are." The baronet put out his hand, and Tristan clasped it. "I'll have my attorney call upon yours to draw up a marriage contract."

"Good!" He grinned, his heart thumping hard in delight. "I'm sure we'll reach a fair settlement."

"I intend to take full advantage of you, my boy. This is not the way I wanted to see my daughter married."

Tristan grinned. "You can try." The baronet cocked one brow, and Tristan wiped the grin away. "No, sir. I am very sorry for any upset my actions may have caused your family."

"Soon to be your family," his visitor pointed out.

He'd thought of that, but even Lady Bennet at her most severe couldn't be worse than Aunt Mary, and he had high hopes that both Joan's parents would soften toward him once he proved himself a good husband. "Yes, sir."

Sir George chuckled. "I'd hate to regret this," he said, giving Tristan an appraising glance. "I've no doubt you could beat me to a cinder, but I'm still a crack shot."

"Ah—right. I understand perfectly."

"Good. Make my daughter happy." He clapped Tristan's shoulder, at last breaking into a genial smile. "It would be very upsetting to all if I had to inflict a flesh wound or two by way of reminder."

"Er . . . yes, sir."

The baronet surveyed the room. "Joan tells me you've filled your Hanover Square house with innovation. Will you show me?"

For the second time, Tristan blinked in surprise. "You want to see the house?"

"Of course." Sir George got to his feet. "I knew we would end up here, you know. As soon as my daughter grew eloquent about water closets and coal dumbwaiters, I knew she'd given you her approval, and it was only a matter of time before we had this talk." He cocked his head. "And, I understand, you even consulted her about the paint and the carpets."

"She has excellent taste," he muttered.

"Like her mother before her." The baronet pulled out his watch and checked it, then tucked it back into his waistcoat. "Let's go, young man. I expect this is the last peaceful morning either of us will have until after the wedding."

Chapter 27

The wedding day began promisingly—but perhaps it only seemed that way to Joan because it meant an end to the week of horror.

A shocking number of people, it turned out, had noticed Joan's disappearance with Tristan at the Brentwood ball. There was little doubt that only Lady Bennet's personal friendships with the more avid gossipmongers had prevented a storm of scandal. The wedding announcement that appeared in the newspapers the day after Papa called on Tristan also probably helped. And although Mother had decided the wedding would be held soon, she refused to let it appear hasty or ramshackle. To that end, Joan was kept busy from morning until night, writing invitations, planning the menu, ordering items for her trousseau, and receiving all the well-wishers who appeared in the drawing room, ostensibly to offer congratulations but really, in Joan's opinion, prying for scandalous details.

Douglas arrived back in London the day before the wedding. Joan braced herself, but her brother must have got over any astonishment on the journey back to town. He murmured his congratulations and kissed her cheek, and didn't say a word about how she came to marry his friend. She wondered who had warned him away from the subject, her father or Tristan himself.

Tristan was permitted to call once. Lady Bennet sat beside Joan on the sofa, a stern gaze fixed on him, and only withdrew for a few minutes to allow him the pretense of proposing. Tristan eyed the door, left partially open behind her, and cleared his throat.

"I didn't want things to happen this way."

She had longed to talk to him, and now didn't know quite what to say. She imagined her mother overhearing every word. "How did you want them to happen?"

His green eyes were no longer bright and mischievous, but somber. "I had hoped to speak to you before everything was settled."

"Well, now you have your chance," she said with a faltering smile.

"Right." He glanced at the door again. "Will you do me the honor of becoming my wife?"

As a declaration, it was a bit wanting. She had hoped for more, or at least for the usual easiness between them. Was he pleased about this? Did he want to marry her, scandal notwithstanding? They both already knew the answer to his question. "Yes," she murmured, trying not to be let down.

For a moment his usual grin flashed at her. "Good," he whispered. "Then I can do this." He caught her wrist and pulled her forward to kiss her. It was heart-stopping and urgent and over in a moment. Joan fell back on the sofa, gasping for air when he released her. "The rest will have to wait for later," he added in the same sensual murmur.

"I trust you've made your proposal," said Lady Bennet, almost at the same moment. She stood in the open door, and Joan desperately hoped her mother hadn't seen any part of the kiss.

Tristan bowed. "Yes, ma'am, and happily Miss Bennet has accepted. Shall we fix a date?"

"Friday next," she replied.

"Very good. Until then." With one more bow, he was gone, and Joan was left to wonder whether the scorching kiss or the dispassionate proposal had reflected his true feelings.

But finally the day arrived. Abigail Weston arrived before Joan had even risen from her bed. Abigail would be standing up with her, and was permitted to help her get dressed.

"Are you happy?" was the first question that burst from Abigail's lips. They hadn't had a moment since the Brentwood ball to speak without witnesses.

"Of course. I'm getting married, aren't I?" She got out of bed and put on her wrapper. Her dress—the beautiful gold silk dress that had started all the trouble—lay over a chair, pressed and ready for the wedding. She hoped today ended on a happier note than the last time she'd worn it.

"I know." Abigail closed the door. "And so I brought you something. Pen and I ransacked the house, and even got Olivia to help us. We felt you needed something to inspire you, now that you'll be able to do more than just read about lovemaking." She opened her prayer book and pulled out six issues of *50 Ways to Sin*. "None of them are new, but we thought you should have them," she whispered.

Joan barely had time to shove them into her own prayer book before Polly came in with the warm water for her to wash. "Thank you," she mouthed at her friend, who nodded gravely, as though Joan was embarking on some dark and dangerous mission, fraught with peril, from which she might not return alive.

To be honest, at moments that seemed an apt description. Did Tristan love her? He wanted to kiss her and make love to her, and he was willing to marry her, but did he feel anything more tender? If only Mother had allowed them more time together. Joan had great hopes for her marriage, but she also had some fear.

In remarkably short order, she was bathed and dressed, her hair arranged and a veil of fine lace arranged over it. She stared at herself in the mirror as Abigail fastened a string of pearls around her neck and Polly fluffed the folds of her skirt. Papa knocked on the door just as they finished.

"Are you ready?" His eyes softened as she nodded. "You look beautiful," he murmured, kissing her cheek as Abigail and Polly slipped from the room. "Burke had better appreciate his good fortune."

"Do you think he does, Papa?"

He smiled at her anxious question. "If I didn't think he would, I'd have just shot him and been done with it."

She hoped that was enough. "Then I am ready to go."

The day passed in a blur. Joan concentrated so hard on not missing her cue during the ceremony, she barely registered anything else. The feel of a ring on her finger felt so foreign, she could hardly stop staring at it. The congratulations of the guests melded into one long stream of chatter. She didn't have a moment alone, not with her friends, not with Tristan, not even with her parents.

By evening, her nerves had resurfaced. After a long day receiving guests and smiling until her face hurt, she finally had a moment of peace. Polly, her newly promoted lady's maid, helped her into her nightdress and left her alone in the large bedroom of Tristan's house in Hanover Square, with nothing to distract her from her unanswered questions.

The bedchamber walls were painted blue, as she had suggested, and the bed hangings had a pattern of vines and leaves. It made her heart swell to think that he had remembered everything she said that day, when she had first allowed herself to acknowledge that she was falling in love with him. She peeked into the bathing room, remembering how he had kissed her in there. And how he would be at liberty to do it again, all the time. No more frantic stolen kisses; he was her husband, not only permitted but practically required to kiss her—among many other things.

The thought of other things made her heart

skip a beat. Her mother had given her some rather basic advice on consummating her marriage, but Joan suddenly remembered Abigail's gift. It might not be the most virtuous source of guidance, but it promised far more pleasure than her mother's brief instructions.

She found her prayer book and took out the copies of *50 Ways to Sin*, blushing to think they'd been there while she stood in the church. Tristan would probably roar with laughter if he knew— presuming he had any idea what the stories were. With a start she realized she'd never read the issue he gave her the day they went ballooning. She'd already scoured the older issues, but she might have missed something. Lady Constance always ended up limp with satisfaction, so sated she could hardly rise from bed. And even more, she pleasured her lovers just as thoroughly. That was the part Joan wanted to study.

She got into bed and read it once, then again, ending with her eyes wide and her mouth open. Oh heavens. Was it really possible for a man to pleasure a woman by putting his mouth *there*? And Constance did the same to him! Joan read that page again in disbelief, but Constance seemed to relish her role, on her knees ministering to him until she felt lightheaded. Her lover, Lord Masterly, certainly enjoyed her efforts.

The door opened. "Good evening," said Tristan, coming into the room wearing a familiar dark green dressing gown.

She started and hastily stuffed the pamphlet under her pillow. "Good evening!"

He sat on the bed and slid his arm around her

waist, pulling her across the bed until her back was against his chest. "Were you bored waiting for me?" he murmured, his lips brushing the nape of her neck.

"No," she said quickly.

"No? That's not what a new husband wants to hear." He eased her down into the mattress, stretching out behind her. "What were you reading that distracted you?"

"Mmm?" It was hard to think when he was unfastening her nightdress, undoing the little ribbon ties down the front with shocking speed. Just the touch of his fingers on her bare skin was enough to scatter all rational thought. He cupped her breast, his thumb stroking her nipple. She arched her back, pressing into his hand. That felt wonderful; it sent shivers down her limbs. Perhaps she didn't need any special technique. Now that she thought about it, in *50 Ways to Sin* the man always guided Constance, and Tristan, of all men, seemed to know what he was doing.

Her husband rolled her over onto her back and pressed his lips to her neck, nibbling his way down. His hand remained on her breast, teasing her flesh until she writhed under him, helping him remove her nightdress. He made a low growling sound deep in his throat and rolled fully on top of her, just as naked as she was. "Now, what was it?" he murmured, still brushing little kisses over her jaw.

"What?" She had no idea what he was talking about. Her main concern was freeing her foot from the twisted bedsheets so she could wrap her legs around him. She could feel him, thick and hard, against her thigh. Oh goodness, this was very promising. All her worries and anxiety melted away as he kissed her.

"What were you looking at so secretively?" Joan blinked at him, and he returned a rather devilish grin. "This is the first day of our marriage. What caught your attention so thoroughly on your wedding night, and why did you try to hide it from me?"

"Oh!" Her face burned as she realized what he meant. "*That*. It was nothing, truly."

"Nothing?" He pushed his hand beneath her pillow, ignoring her frantic struggles to get out from under him. "But there's something here . . ."

"I was just trying to pass the time," she cried, mortified. "It's nothing important!"

"No, no, this is an important husband's duty," he replied, managing to get the pamphlet out even though she had pressed her head down hard against the pillow. "I should know what distracts my wife so completely that she forgets I'm coming to make love to her."

"Oh, ah, I'm ready for that," she exclaimed, giving her hips a little wiggle. She'd much rather make love with him than . . . well, than do much else, but especially more than have him read her contraband pamphlet. He flexed his spine in response to her shimmy, but otherwise remained focused on that wretched story.

"*Fifty Ways to Sin*?" He frowned at the title. "This is that ladies' story you wanted me to get for you."

"Yes, that's it." Joan nodded, grasping at the excuse. "It's, ah, for ladies. I was just checking it for any bits of advice, you know, about married life . . ." Her voice faded away as he opened to the first page.

"Married life!" His eyes gleamed. "Then I should read it, too, being newly married."

"Oh—well—no, I think it's just for ladies . . ."

"All the more reason for me to read it. Don't you want me to know what's expected of me?" He caught her hand when she reached for the pamphlet, kissed her knuckles, and began reading.

For several minutes he just read, propped on his elbows above her. She began to feel horribly self-conscious, and devoted herself to studying the plasterwork on the ceiling, over Tristan's shoulder. Just her luck, to find herself married to, and in bed with, a devilishly handsome man, and now he would think her a complete widgeon because she failed to hide that silly pamphlet well enough.

"Who wrote this?" He turned another page and read on, his expression a curious mixture of fascination and disbelief.

"No one knows. It's the most closely held secret in London."

"No wonder." He gave her an appraising look. "You think this is a comic guide to married life?"

Joan bit her lip, staring fiercely at the plaster rose right above her. "I could hardly tell you what it really was, could I? Besides, the more I think about it, the more I think it's just a lot of piffle."

"Piffle?" He glanced down at her with that lazy grin that always made her wonder what wicked thoughts were going through his mind. "It's not piffle if you read it, my dear. I merely want to be . . . educated in your tastes." He went back to the pamphlet and turned the page. "Good God. No wonder your mother didn't want you to have this." Her husband looked at her with . . . was it approval? "You're a wicked wench at heart, aren't you?" he growled, swooping down to kiss her hard on the mouth.

Joan cleared her throat. "Well, it's not really proper for unmarried ladies to read things like that . . ."

He laughed. "I understand why!"

"But absolutely everyone is talking of it," she protested. "How viciously unfair it is for everyone to simply decide that unmarried ladies shouldn't see it. Nobody cared when *you* bought it, as an unmarried gentleman, but I would have been in such trouble if I'd been caught with it."

"How fortunate you are now a married lady, and subject only to me."

Her eyes narrowed. "And if you think you're going to prohibit me from reading what I like, you shall have a very hard and combative marriage, Lord Burke."

"On the contrary." He tossed the pamphlet onto the floor and lowered himself over her again. "I look forward to corrupting you in oh . . . " He kissed her jaw. "So . . ." He kissed her neck. "Many . . ." He kissed the base of her throat, where her pulse beat hardest. "Many more ways," he finished before lowering his lips to her breast.

"Good," she sighed, plowing her fingers into his long hair.

"So tell me," he murmured, flicking his tongue across her nipple, "did you picture me as Lord

Masterly? And yourself as Lady Constance?"

"How dare you ask such a thing!" she gasped, trying not to laugh. "If you had read carefully, you would know that Lord Masterly is the very model of a gentleman! He would never . . ." He had sucked her nipple between his teeth, and Joan was quickly losing the thread of her thought. "He would never be rude," she finished weakly, arching her back to offer her other breast for the same attention.

"Oh, no. Our noble gentleman only put the lady on a chair, spread her legs, and brought her to climax with his mouth. Very proper of him— at least for Lady Constance, I imagine, from the ardor with which she returned the favor."

She was blushing again even as she moved beneath him like a wanton. "How—how does a man do that?" she whispered. "Is it even possible?"

Tristan lifted his head, looking faintly surprised. "You think it's not?"

"I just don't know," she admitted. "It sounds . . . alarming."

"Alarming!" His eyebrows shot up.

Her face must be purple by now. "Oh, never mind! I can't imagine any decent lady tolerating it. I suspect that it's just another incredible thing the author created. An author can make up anything and make it sound appealing, can't she?"

He grinned wickedly. "It sounds appealing to you, does it?"

"It doesn't seem likely to matter, since you don't know how it's done, either," she retorted, wishing he would go away. Either that or quit talking and make love to her like a normal husband would.

He stopped laughing. "Now there is your second mistake this evening, my dear. Haven't I warned you about issuing challenges?" He pushed himself up and jumped off the bed. "Stay there," he said in a deep, stern voice, holding up one hand as she struggled to sit up. "As your lord and master, I command it."

"Lord and master!" Just to show him, she flung herself out of bed. "Lord and master, perhaps, but not of me. And how dare you accuse me of not one but two mistakes. Perhaps my real mistake was made this morning."

He picked up his dressing gown and leveled a dangerously glinting gaze at her. "Joan," he said evenly, "get back on the bed."

"Why?" She retreated a step, eyeing the garment in his hand.

"Not doing so would be your third mistake of the day." He pulled the sash from the dressing gown and wrapped it around his hand, then waved her backward. "On the bed, please."

"What does the sash have to do with it?" She was beginning to feel aroused again. Tristan clearly was; he walked toward her, unashamedly naked, and she stared at his erection. She had seen it before—even touched it before—and yet it looked larger now.

"It's to prevent any hindrances." He cocked his head. "Do you want me to show you what made Lady Constance melt in rapture?"

"You must be quite the crudest man in all of England," she said, but she sat on the edge of the bed.

Tristan just shook his head and tied one end of

the cloth around her wrist, then wound it through the carving on the headboard. He caught her other arm and bound her other wrist, pushing her back against the pillows, her arms held wide by the sash.

Her heart was thumping furiously, half in nerves, half in anticipation. She tugged at the sash, but he had left little slack. "Why do you have to do that?"

"Because you don't follow instructions well." He slid down the length of her body, insinuating himself between her legs. He paused and moved his hips forward as his cock stroked against that private part of her, and Joan moaned, trying in vain to meet his thrust appropriately. But he only laughed under his breath and slid down some more until his gleaming eyes were level with her breasts. "This takes a little time to do well," he murmured. "I shan't be hurried along."

Joan blushed. "I don't know what you mean!"

"I know." He stroked both hands down the insides of her thighs and gently but firmly spread her legs further apart. He gazed with rapt attention at her nether parts, causing her to blush almost painfully red.

"I—I think I've changed my mind," she said in a rush. The nymphs in the painting on the opposite wall seemed to be watching in horror. A servant could walk in at any moment to find her naked and bound to the headboard with his head between her legs. Someone in the house across the square might look through the windows and see what he was doing through the gap in the drapes.

"Too late," he whispered, and lowered his head.

She jumped at the first touch of his mouth, soft and wet and very warm. "Stop," she cried in a desperate whisper. "Stop—oh—oh—oh my goodness, what are you doing?"

"I shall tie a handkerchief over your mouth if you ask me to stop even once more." He peered up at her, his dark hair rumpled very rakishly. "You can say anything else, though."

"Tristan," she gasped, and then she could hardly speak at all, as he probed with his tongue, first gently, then more firmly, licking and stroking until she was almost sobbing. She twisted and arched, pulling so hard at her bonds that the headboard creaked, but he held her hips firmly in place and wedged his shoulders under her thighs and relentlessly teased her with his tongue and lips. He was right—it took longer—but sweet blessed heavens, it led to the same tension, the same restless ache, the same feeling of the earth dropping out from under her as her body finally couldn't take it anymore and gave in to the long, hard pull of his mouth.

She was still gasping and trembling with the aftershocks when he hauled himself up and sheathed himself inside her with one swift stroke. Joan cried out at the intrusion, and he paused.

"Are you hurt?"

She could only shake her head. She felt utterly raw and defenseless, her arms bound and her legs spread as he pressed ever deeper into her.

"Good." He inhaled, his breath rough and ragged. "I'm so hard with wanting you, I might explode if you told me to stop."

"Don't stop," she managed to choke out before he surged forward again.

"Don't worry." He braced his hands beside her shoulders. His dark hair fell over his brow, not quite hiding the harsh set of his features as he rode her with driving thrusts that made her writhe, first from the assault on her still-throbbing flesh, then in more harmony as his passion stoked her own, raising that razor-sharp tension within her until she could hardly breathe. It didn't seem possible to experience such ecstasy so soon again, but her body appeared ready and eager, leaping to ever-higher pitches of arousal until she felt it beating through her muscles, and she arched her back with a low keening cry of release. Tristan growled, and she curled her legs around his hips to hold him inside her as the waves of climax rolled on and on. He said a very bad word under his breath and held himself deep within her, his hips jerking in short, sharp thrusts until he, too, shook and shouted with release.

Joan forced her eyes open and looked up at her husband. His face was drawn into a fierce expression, but it gradually softened until his eyes opened. He gave her a lazy, heavy-lidded grin.

"I trust you believe it's possible now." He eased away from her and flopped heavily onto his back. With one hand he groped above him, and a moment later pulled loose the knot that had held her hand bound.

She lay where she was. Not only was it too much effort to move, she had no real desire to. She couldn't even think of a smart reply to his comment. But slowly her brain began to work again.

Absently she reached up and freed her other hand.

This seemed like a propitious moment. He was lying next to her, no doubt feeling the same bubbling contentment that hummed through her own veins. If he were to ask her right now, she would throw her arms around him and declare herself hopelessly, helplessly lost in love. That would be ideal. She even found that she was holding her breath in anticipation of that glorious moment.

But as the silence stretched on, she had to breathe again, and acknowledge that he was lying very still beside her—almost as if he were asleep. In fact, when she stole a peek at him, his eyes were closed and he looked very peaceful. Blissfully happy, but in a sleeping sort of way.

She couldn't wait any longer. She had waited patiently, hoping he would confess any sort of feeling, but finally she just wanted to know. "Tristan," she began. "I want to ask you something."

"The answer is yes," he mumbled. "Whatever you want, darling."

"No, not like that. A serious question."

He didn't say anything for a very long minute. "Must we be serious? It seems silly to begin now . . ."

"Will you give me an honest answer?" She didn't laugh, refusing to let him wiggle away so easily. "That's all I want, whatever the answer is."

"I won't lie to you," he said slowly.

Joan stole a glance at him and saw he was awake now, his eyes open but staring fixedly at the ceiling. There was a tense set to his jaw that made her think he was girding himself to deliver bad news. Her heart seemed to shrink. Oh, help. He knew what she was going to ask, and he dreaded it. For a wild second a stupid, inconsequential question hovered on her tongue, but she took a deep breath and screwed up her courage.

"I only want to know what you feel right now. Of course one's thoughts and feelings can change with time, and as we are married and will be for years and years to come, naturally I expect there will be some change in how you feel—"

"What is your question?" he interrupted.

She hoped she wasn't ruining her marriage before it was even one day old. "I wondered if you think it possible that you might someday come to truly care for me."

He said nothing. From the corner of her eye, she saw his face knit in a frown, and then he lurched over, propping himself up on one elbow so quickly she flinched. "What?"

Joan bit her lip at the incredulity in his tone, and shrugged even as she avoided meeting his gaze. "Well, I know my father made you marry me—"

"He did not," growled her husband.

"But we have had some—some pleasant times together, even before that," she went on, blushing furiously.

"Pleasant!" He looked at her as if he couldn't believe his ears.

"I just wanted to know if you might ever want me for more than making love!" she exclaimed. Tristan gazed at her as if she'd grown another head, and Joan's nerve broke. She scrambled out of bed. "Oh, never mind! I was foolish to ask—I might have known you wouldn't listen rationally and give a dignified answer—"

"You want me to give a dignified answer when you ask if I like anything about you besides planting my cock inside you?"

"There's no need to be crude!" Joan grabbed her nightgown and began trying to put it on, but the whole thing had been twisted and pulled into a knot; the sleeves seemed to have tied themselves together. She rammed her arms into the garment, determined to rip right through the fabric if she had to.

"No. Right. I apologize." He scrubbed one hand over his face. "Come here."

"No, thank you. I'll just send Polly for some tea, and find a good book to read."

"Don't ring that bell," he warned as she reached for the rope. "Not until I give you my answer."

Her fingers hovered over the bell. "Well, what is it?" she said, refusing to look at him.

The ropes creaked as he got out of bed. "The answer is no, I do not *think* I might *someday* come to care for you." He repeated her emphasis on certain words. "I am quite certain how I feel about you, and how I expect to continue feeling about you for the next fifty years. My question is, why do you want to know? And what on earth gave you the idea your father compelled me to marry you?"

"He did! My mother told me he would—she was half afraid he would end up challenging you to a duel, if you refused!"

All expression fell away from his face. "She still despises me that much?"

Her lips parted as she realized how awful her words must have sounded. "No! That is, I don't think she's terribly fond of you yet, but she was so worried about Papa—he used to be quite as reckless and devil-may-care as you are, and she worried he would lose his temper if you didn't agree."

Her husband sighed. His shoulders slumped a little, and he turned away from her, pulling on his own dressing gown. He sat on the edge of the bed and looked a little beaten. "Did you think I would refuse, after I made love to you at the Brentwood ball?"

"Well . . ." He gave her a sideways look, not his usual cocky look but a wary one. She cleared her throat. "No. I didn't. I told Mother she was being silly."

He gave a nod.

"I also told her I was as much to blame for any scandal as you were," Joan added quietly. "You never took advantage of me—at least, not when I didn't want you to do so. I didn't want her to think any worse of you than she thought of me, because the fault was equal."

"Oh?" He tilted his head back. "Even that first time I kissed you, at the Malcolm ball?"

"I hardly invited that," she said carefully. "But, once you began, I didn't make much of an effort to fight you off . . ."

"Did you want to?"

She hesitated. "No."

His face eased a fraction. "I didn't think so. I don't kiss unwilling women, you know."

"So," Joan said when he didn't say more, "is this all because I was willing?"

He considered it a moment. "Partly." Joan's eyes popped wide open in shock. "I never would have made love to you at the Brentwoods' ball if you hadn't been willing," he added in the same off-hand manner. "But you were willing, and I took that to mean you . . . felt something for me—at least enough to risk your mother's anger. Whatever else you may think of me, I hope you don't view me as an immoral cad with no sense of a woman's reputation and dignity."

"Not at all," she protested.

He nodded. "Good. Because, to answer your question, I knew that night—before I lured you away to ruination and debauchery, mind—that I wanted to marry you. The next day I went to my solicitor and told him to begin preparing a marriage contract. I even meant to do the thing right and call on your father properly in Bath, but he anticipated me by returning to London. So you—and your mother—may rest assured, he was never in any danger when he came to see me about your hand in marriage."

Joan gaped at him. "Then he didn't have to argue with you about it?"

"He gave me a very stern lecture," said Tristan. "I expect the sort of thing a man might give his son, before his son weds, about being a respectable husband and how to deal with a woman's moods and vagaries." He grinned slightly at her scowl. "He might also have mentioned that he's a crack shot, and wouldn't hesitate to inflict a few flesh wounds on a son-in-law who bruised his daughter's heart. But otherwise, no threats were exchanged." He cocked his head and eyed her. "And you never answered my question: why do you want to know?"

Again she hesitated. "It's good for a lady to know where she stands with her husband."

"And for a man to know where he stands with his wife," he replied. "Did your father come to see me because of, or in spite of, your wishes?"

"I wasn't much consulted," she tried to say, but he shook his head.

"Were you willing this morning, Joan?"

It was the thread of yearning in his voice that undid her. Whatever his answer, whatever the depth of his feeling for her, he cared about this—about her. He wanted to know she wanted to be his wife. It was her moment to be brave and bare her heart, and she could only hope he would do the same.

"Yes," she said in a low voice. "Perfectly. You must know I was."

"Because your parents insisted," he said.

"No."

"Because I made love to you and took your virginity."

She blushed. "No."

His jaw tensed. "Because of my fortune."

"No."

"Because we suit each other so well in bed."

"You would know I was lying if I said that didn't influence my feelings," she said, blushing harder than ever. "But no—it seems clear that a lady can find pleasure with more than one man, so I didn't suppose our—our—"

"Desperate hunger for each other," he supplied.

"Yes, that—I didn't think that alone meant we were meant for each other," she finished, striving to maintain her poise even as his words made her heart skip a beat.

"Ah," he said. "You were wrong. This sort of passion does not come along all the time."

"That may be, but I married you because I fell in love with you," she cried in exasperation. "Why are you making this so difficult?"

Tristan stared at her as if dumbfounded. Joan closed her mouth and concentrated on straightening the lace on her cuff. "I certainly didn't mean to, but I did," she added more calmly. "And I would like to know if you think you might ever come to care for me in some similar way."

He got up and crossed the room to her. Joan squinted at her cuff, unwilling to face him just yet.

"No," he said. "I don't think so."

She flinched. "Never?"

"I am quite sure that I am already in love with you," he said. "Although if you intended to present an argument about why I should be, I shall listen with rapt attention."

"You'd better!" She clapped a hand over her mouth, wide-eyed. "What did you say?"

"What did *you* say?" he returned.

Joan blinked at him. "I married you because I love you."

His mouth quirked. "As did I. I just didn't know . . ."

"What?" she asked cautiously.

"I didn't know it would matter to you." He shrugged. "I haven't got much experience in being loved."

Her heart was in danger of bursting. "Why did you think it wouldn't matter to me?" she asked softly.

His gaze drifted away, and he made a face. "It doesn't seem to occur to many women. They see the Burke fortune and picture themselves in silk and diamonds."

"Well." She smiled tremulously. "I have learnt never to picture myself in anything until Mr. Salvatore tells me to." His mouth softened. Encouraged, she went on. "I don't have much experience being in love, either. I was too tall or too impertinent for the gentlemen of London, and they would rather talk to me about soup than ask me to dance. I had begun to resign myself to a life of spinsterhood, or perhaps to luring an older gentleman with poor eyesight."

Tristan reached up and touched her cheek. "You are the perfect height," he said. "And any man who could think you're not beautiful when you wear that gold gown is blind."

Joan caught his hand and pressed his fingers flat between her palms. "It matters to me that you love me." Saying the words aloud brought a smile to her face, a smile that seemed to grow wider every minute. "Do you really? You didn't just say it to spare my feelings?"

"When do I ever do anything just to spare someone's feelings?" He snaked one arm around her waist and pulled her against him, hard. "I love you halfway to madness, Lady Burke," he murmured, his lips brushing hers.

Joan put her arms around his neck and unabashedly stretched up, straining to meet his kiss. "Then kiss me."

He paused, his green eyes brilliant under his eyelids. "Say it once more. I like the sound of it."

"I love you," she said, barely getting the last

word out before his mouth descended on hers, hungry and wanting and full of joy, somehow. Joan kissed him back with all the enthusiasm in her heart. "I love you," she said again when he finally lifted his head. "Desperately. You shall never be in want of it again. And your love will always matter to me, so you'd better tell me at least once a week that you still love me, too."

"If this is the encouragement I'm to receive, I think I might muster up the words more than once a week." He was looking down with approval, and Joan realized her unfastened nightgown had fallen open; her bare breasts were against his chest.

She stepped back, out of his arms. "Is that the only thing you love about me?"

"I adore every inch of you," he said at once. "Every infuriating, challenging, bewitching, intriguing, beautiful bit of you."

"I like that!" she exclaimed. "Say it again!"

He laughed, until she threw off her nightgown again. "Ah . . ." His eyes grew dark and hot. "I can't remember it all. Suffice it to say: I love you, my darling Joan."

"That's all I need to know."

And it was.

At Avon Books, we know your passion for romance—once you finish one of our novels, you find yourself wanting more.

May we tempt you with . . .

- **Excerpts** from our upcoming releases.

- Entertaining **extras**, including authors' personal photo albums and book lists.

- Behind-the-scenes **scoop** on your favorite characters and series.

- **Sweepstakes** for the chance to win free books, romantic getaways, and other fun prizes.

- Writing **tips** from our authors and editors.

- **Blog** with our authors and find out why they love to write romance.

- **Exclusive content** that's not contained within the pages of our novels.

Join us at
www.avonbooks.com

AVON

An Imprint of HarperCollins*Publishers*
www.avonromance.com

Available wherever books are sold or please call 1-800-331-3761 to order.